Edgar & Ellen®

GRAPHIC Novelty

A COMICS COLLECTION

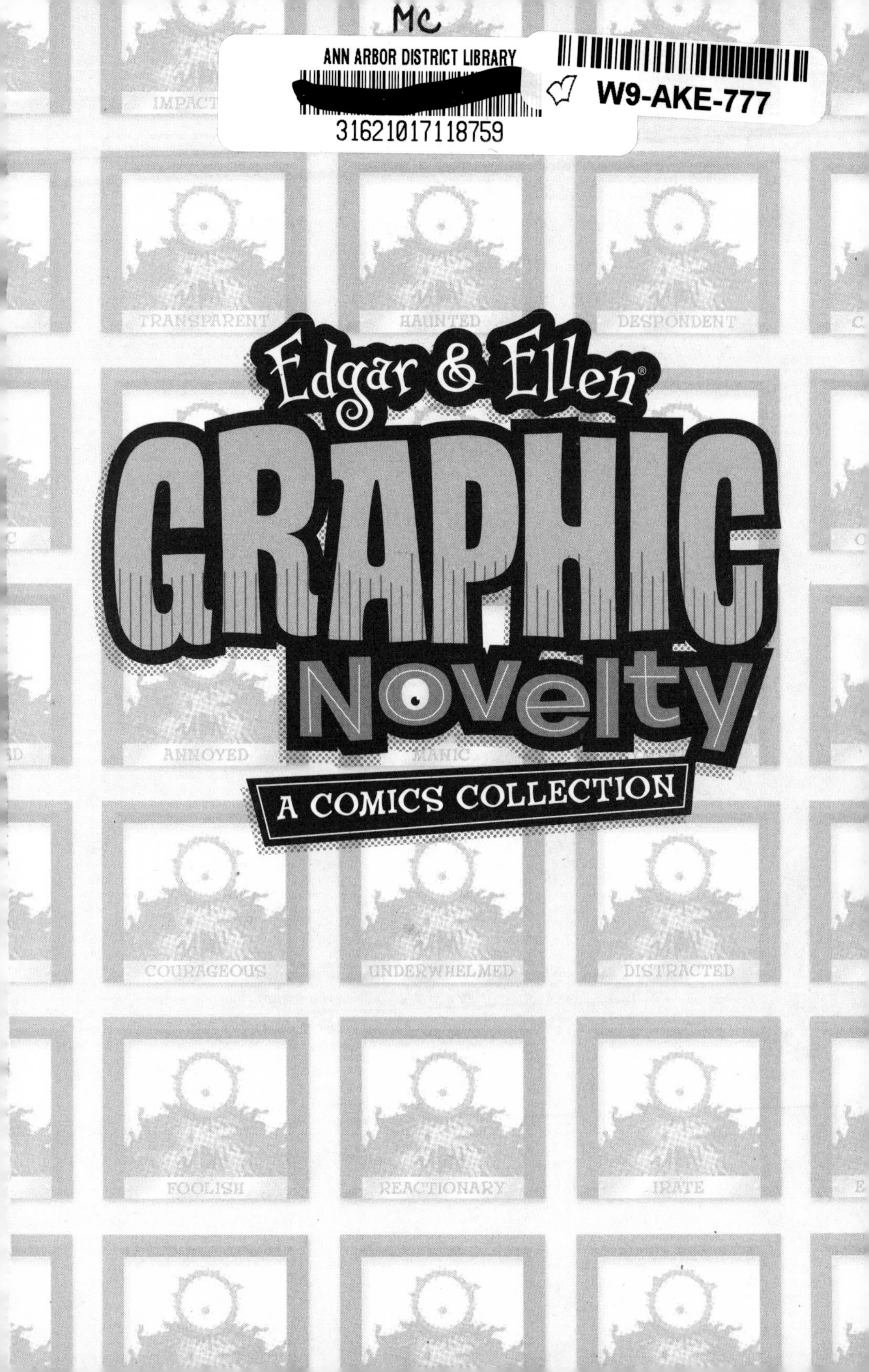
TRANSPARENT
HAUNTED
DESPONDENT
ANNOYED
MANIC
COURAGEOUS
UNDERWHELMED
DISTRACTED
FOOLISH
REACTIONARY
IRATE

IF EVER IN YOUR LIFE YOU ARE FACED WITH A CHOICE,

A DIFFICULT DECISION, A QUANDARY,

ASK YOURSELF "WHAT WOULD EDGAR AND ELLEN DO?"

AND DO EXACTLY THE CONTRARY.

Edgar & Ellen® GRAPHIC Novelty

A COMICS COLLECTION

edited by
CHARLES OGDEN

art directed by
RICK CARTON

ALADDIN PAPERBACKS
New York   London   Toronto   Sydney

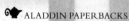 ALADDIN PAPERBACKS
An imprint of Simon & Schuster Children's Publishing Division
1230 Avenue of the Americas, New York, NY 10020
Copyright © 2009 by Star Farm Productions, LLC
All rights reserved, including the right of reproduction in whole or in part in any form.
ALADDIN PAPERBACKS and related logo are registered trademarks of Simon & Schuster, Inc.

Designed by Star Farm Productions, LLC
Manufactured in the United States of America
First Aladdin Paperbacks edition March 2009
10 9 8 7 6 5 4 3 2 1
Library of Congress Control Number 2008941788
ISBN-13: 978-1-4169-5004-2
ISBN-10: 1-4169-5004-4

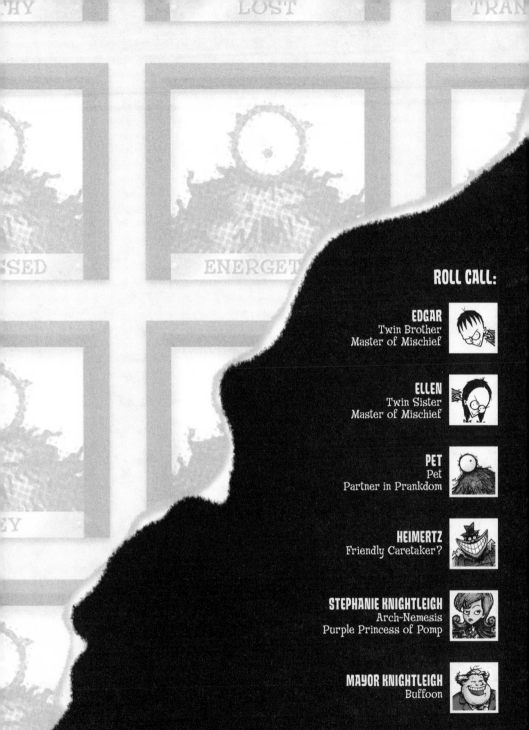

ROLL CALL:

EDGAR
Twin Brother
Master of Mischief

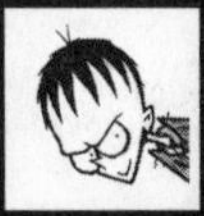

ELLEN
Twin Sister
Master of Mischief

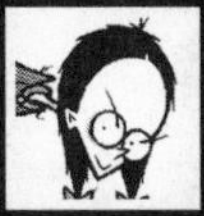

PET
Pet
Partner in Prankdom

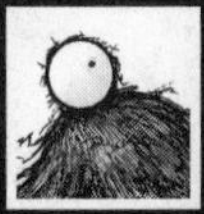

HEIMERTZ
Friendly Caretaker?

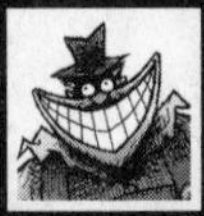

STEPHANIE KNIGHTLEIGH
Arch-Nemesis
Purple Princess of Pomp

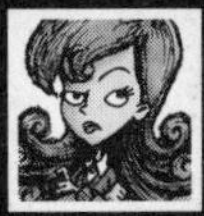

MAYOR KNIGHTLEIGH
Buffoon

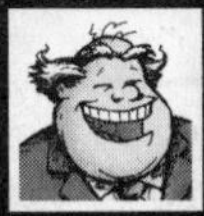

MILES KNIGHTLEIGH
Son of Buffoon

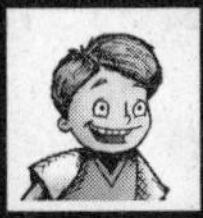

An introduction...

by Ogden
& Carton

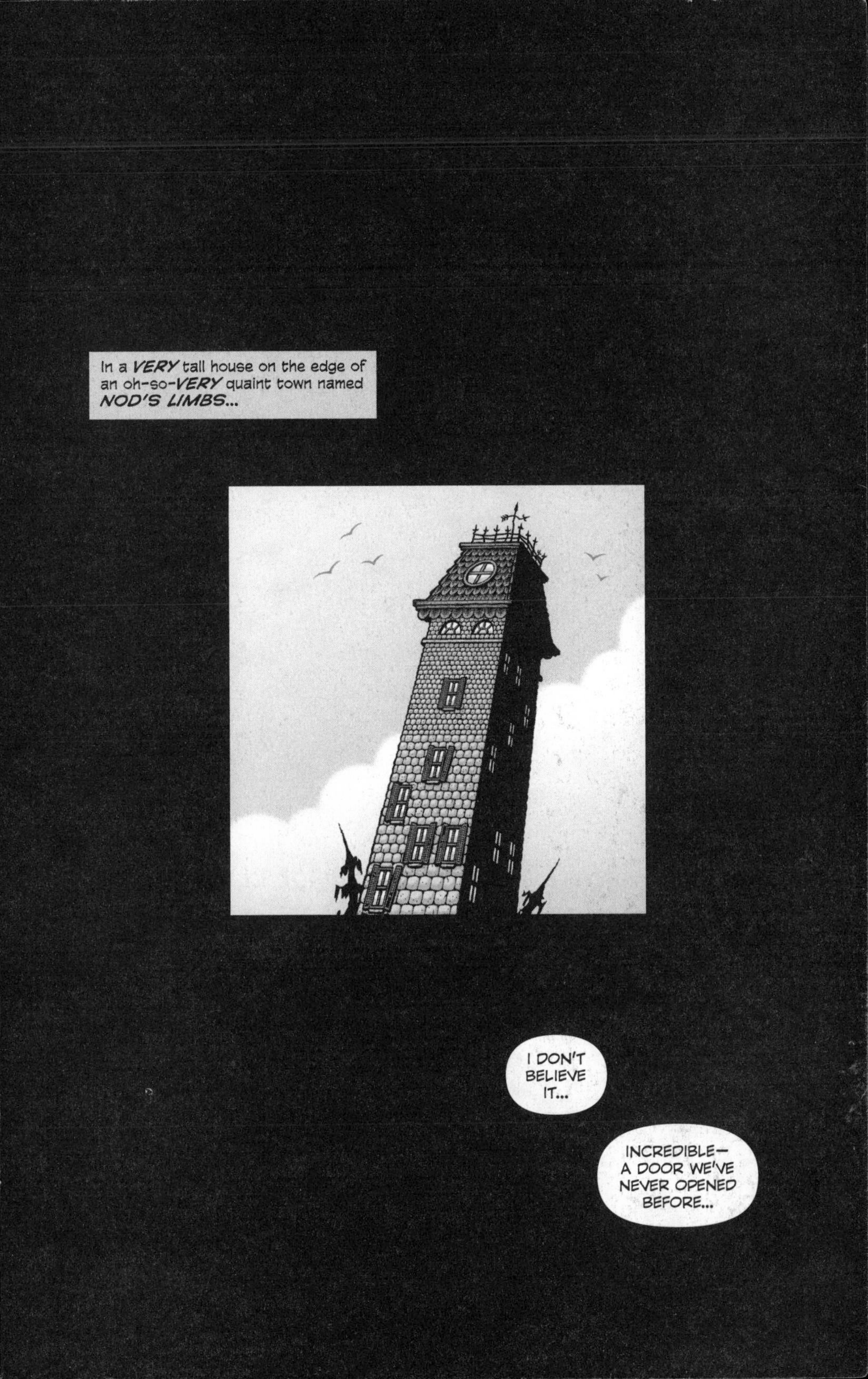
In a VERY tall house on the edge of an oh-so-VERY quaint town named NOD'S LIMBS...
I DON'T BELIEVE IT...
INCREDIBLE— A DOOR WE'VE NEVER OPENED BEFORE...

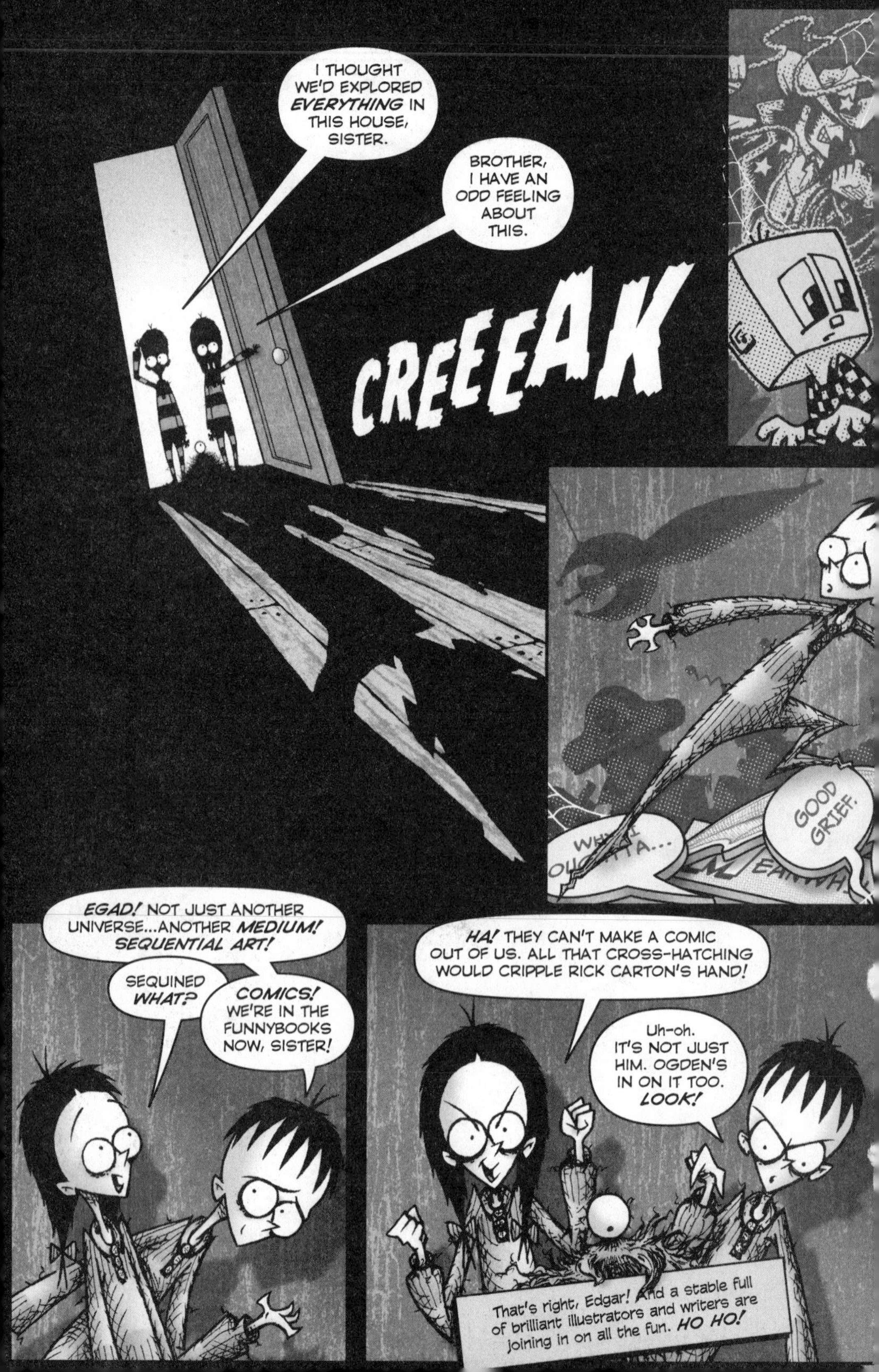
I THOUGHT WE'D EXPLORED *EVERYTHING* IN THIS HOUSE, SISTER.
BROTHER, I HAVE AN ODD FEELING ABOUT THIS.
CREEEAK
GOOD GRIEF.
EGAD! NOT JUST ANOTHER UNIVERSE...ANOTHER *MEDIUM! SEQUENTIAL ART!*
SEQUINED *WHAT?*
COMICS! WE'RE IN THE FUNNYBOOKS NOW, SISTER!
HA! THEY CAN'T MAKE A COMIC OUT OF US. ALL THAT CROSS-HATCHING WOULD CRIPPLE RICK CARTON'S HAND!
Uh-oh. IT'S NOT JUST HIM. OGDEN'S IN ON IT TOO. *LOOK!*
That's right, Edgar! And a stable full of brilliant illustrators and writers are joining in on all the fun. *HO HO!*

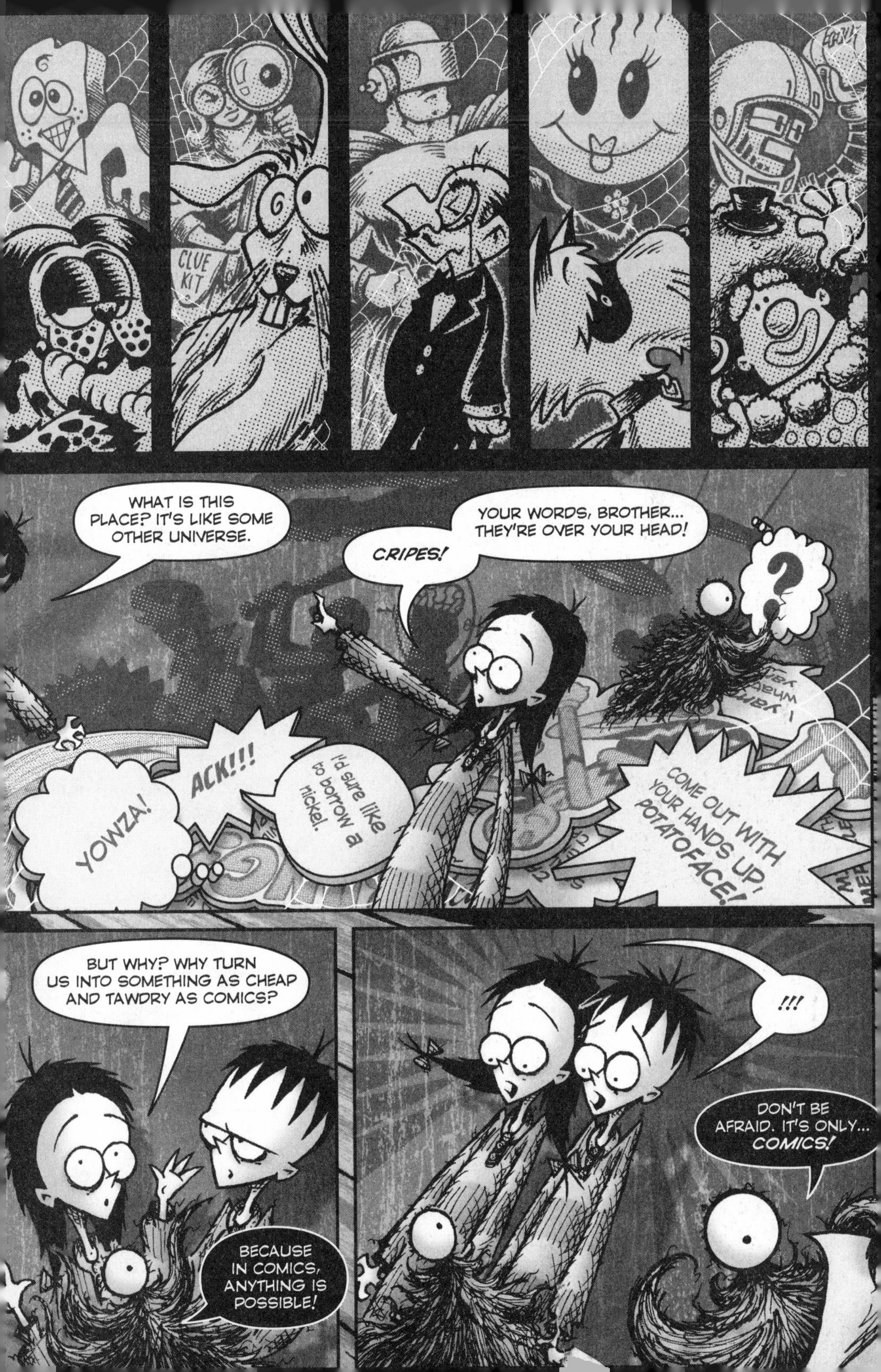
CLUE KIT
WHAT IS THIS PLACE? IT'S LIKE SOME OTHER UNIVERSE.
YOUR WORDS, BROTHER... THEY'RE OVER YOUR HEAD!
CRIPES!
?
YOWZA!
ACK!!!
I'd sure like to borrow a nickel.
COME OUT WITH YOUR HANDS UP, POTATOFACE!
BUT WHY? WHY TURN US INTO SOMETHING AS CHEAP AND TAWDRY AS COMICS?
BECAUSE IN COMICS, ANYTHING IS POSSIBLE!
!!!
DON'T BE AFRAID. IT'S ONLY... COMICS!

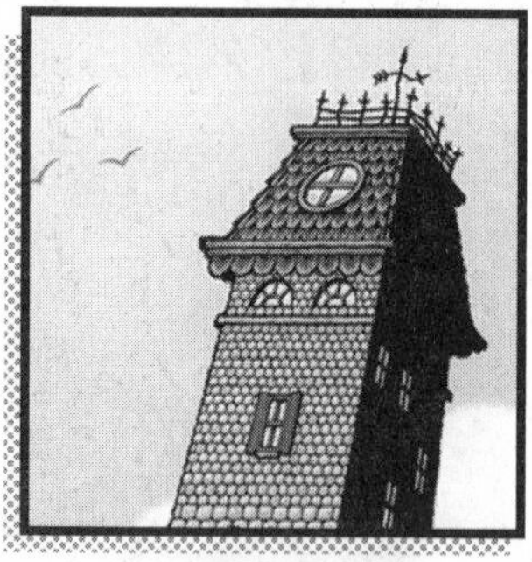

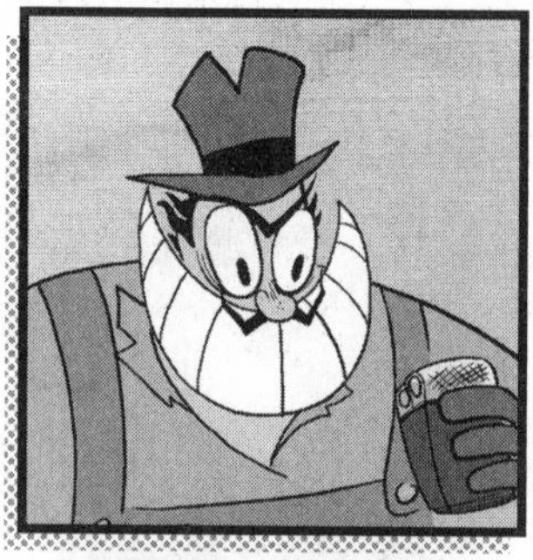

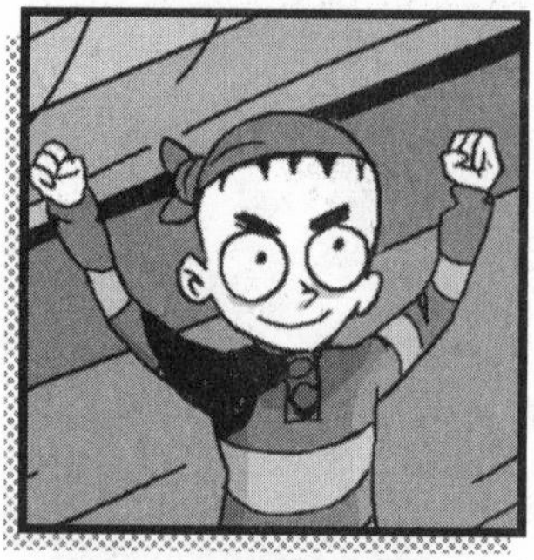

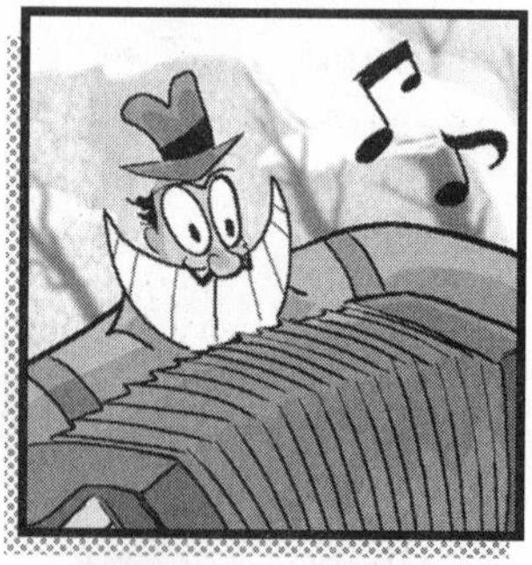

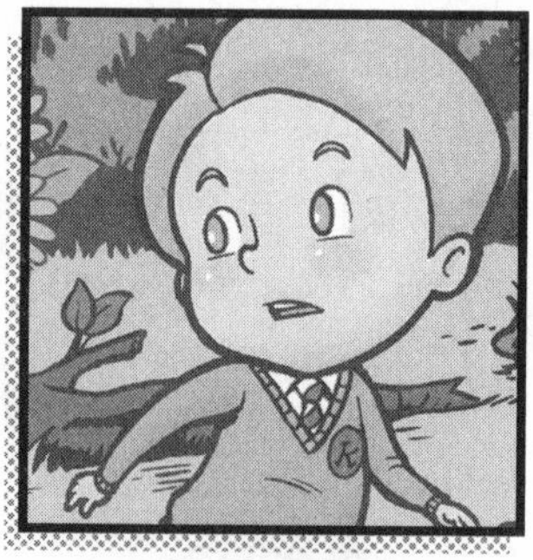

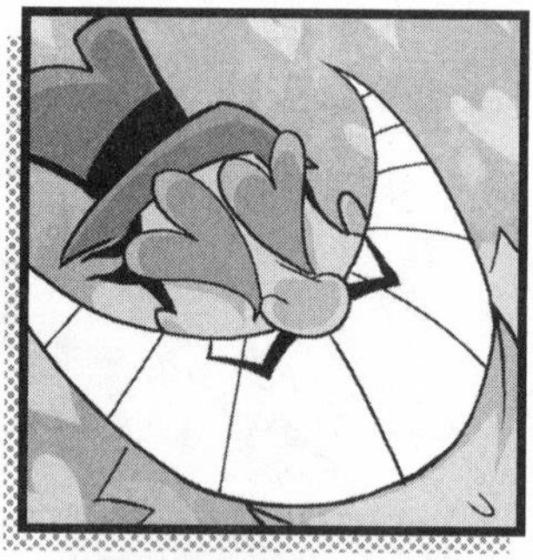

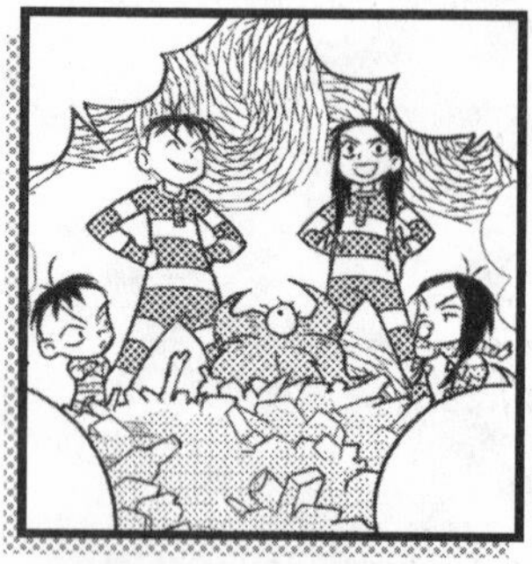

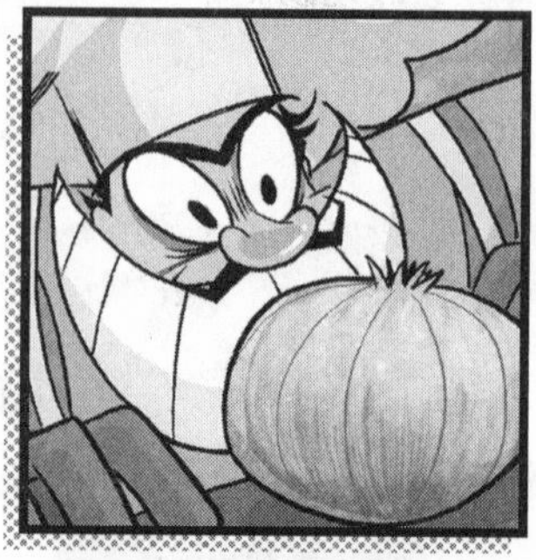

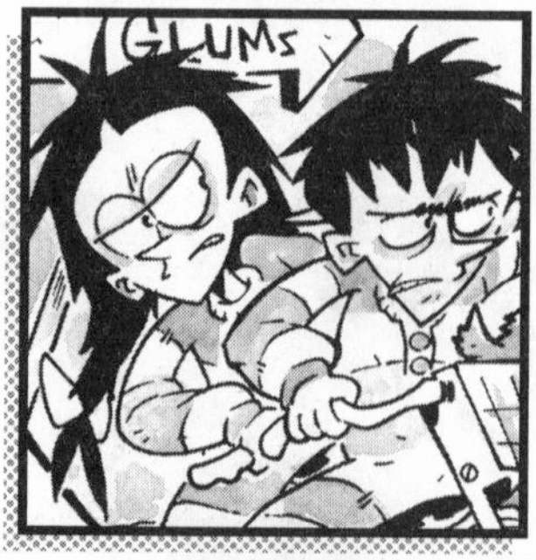
GLUMS

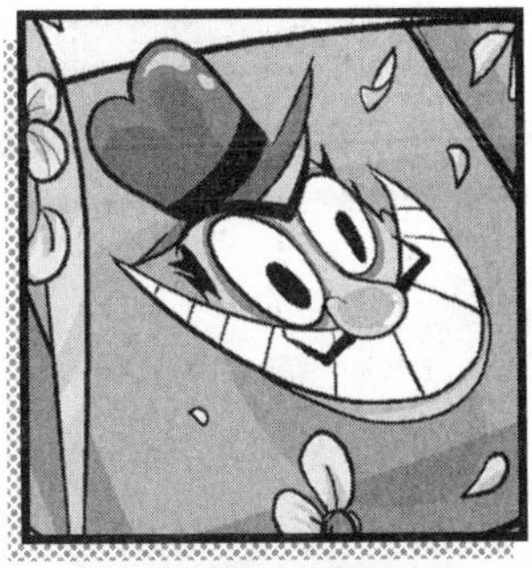

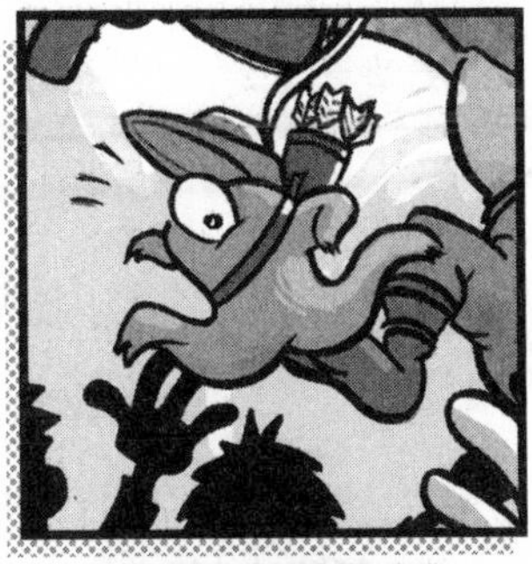

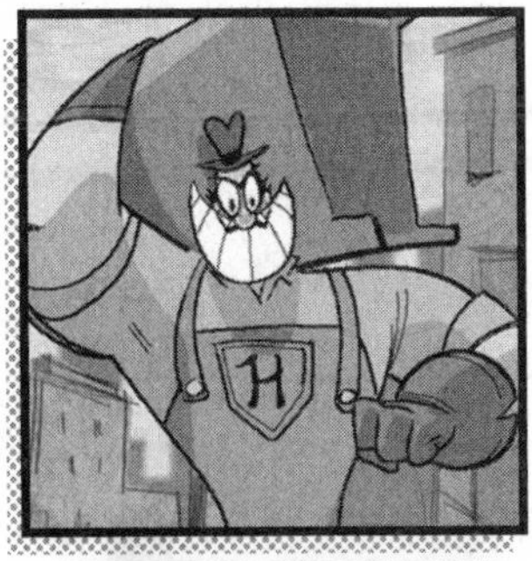

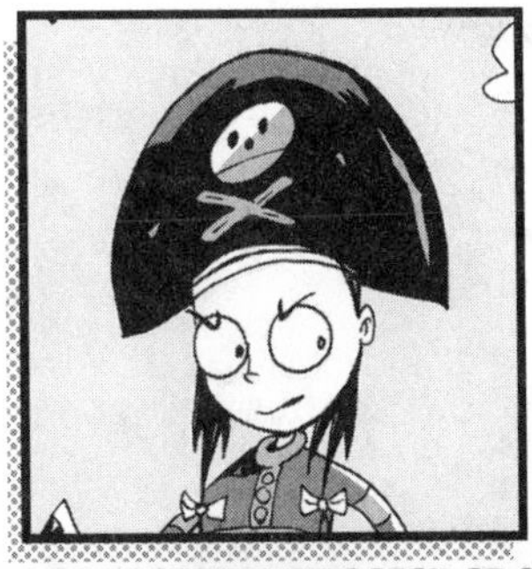

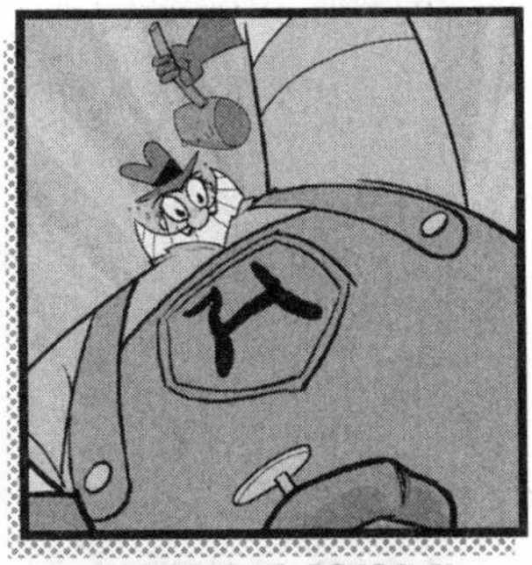

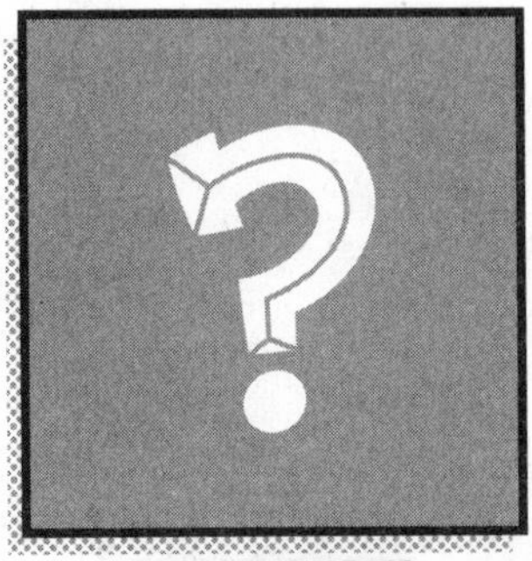

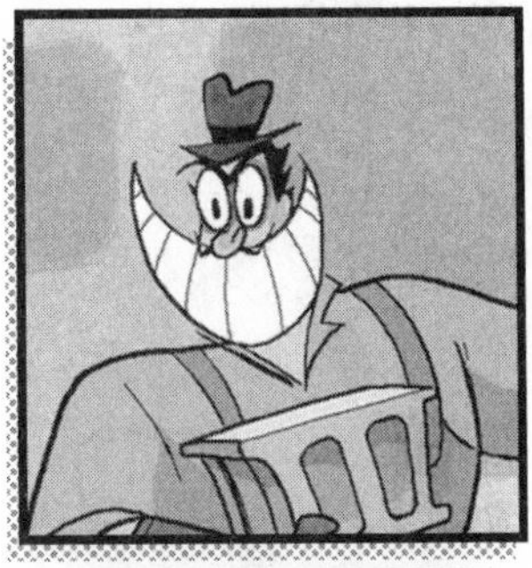

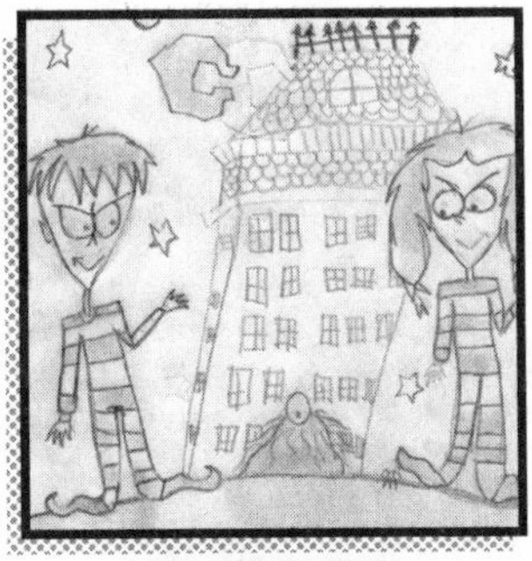

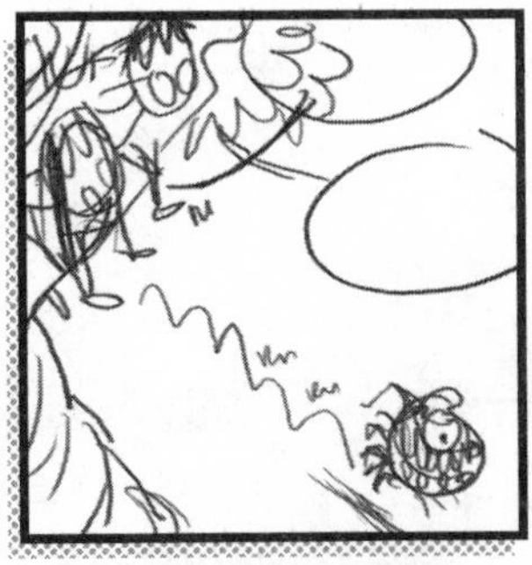

HEIMERTZ vs. ~~BIGFOOT!~~ HAIR

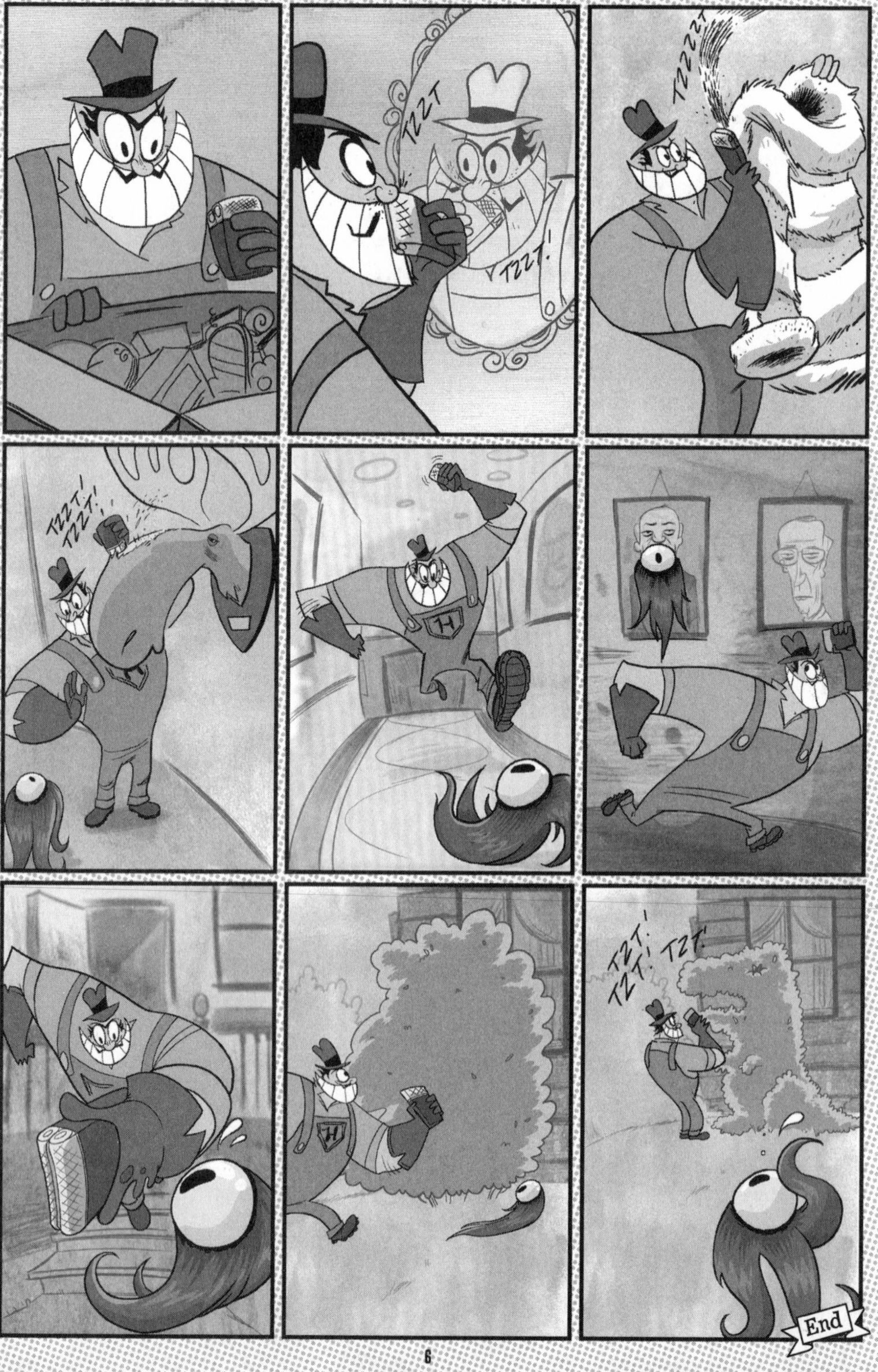
TZZT
TZZT!
TZZZZZT
TZZT!
TZZT!
TZZT!
TZZT!
TZZT
End

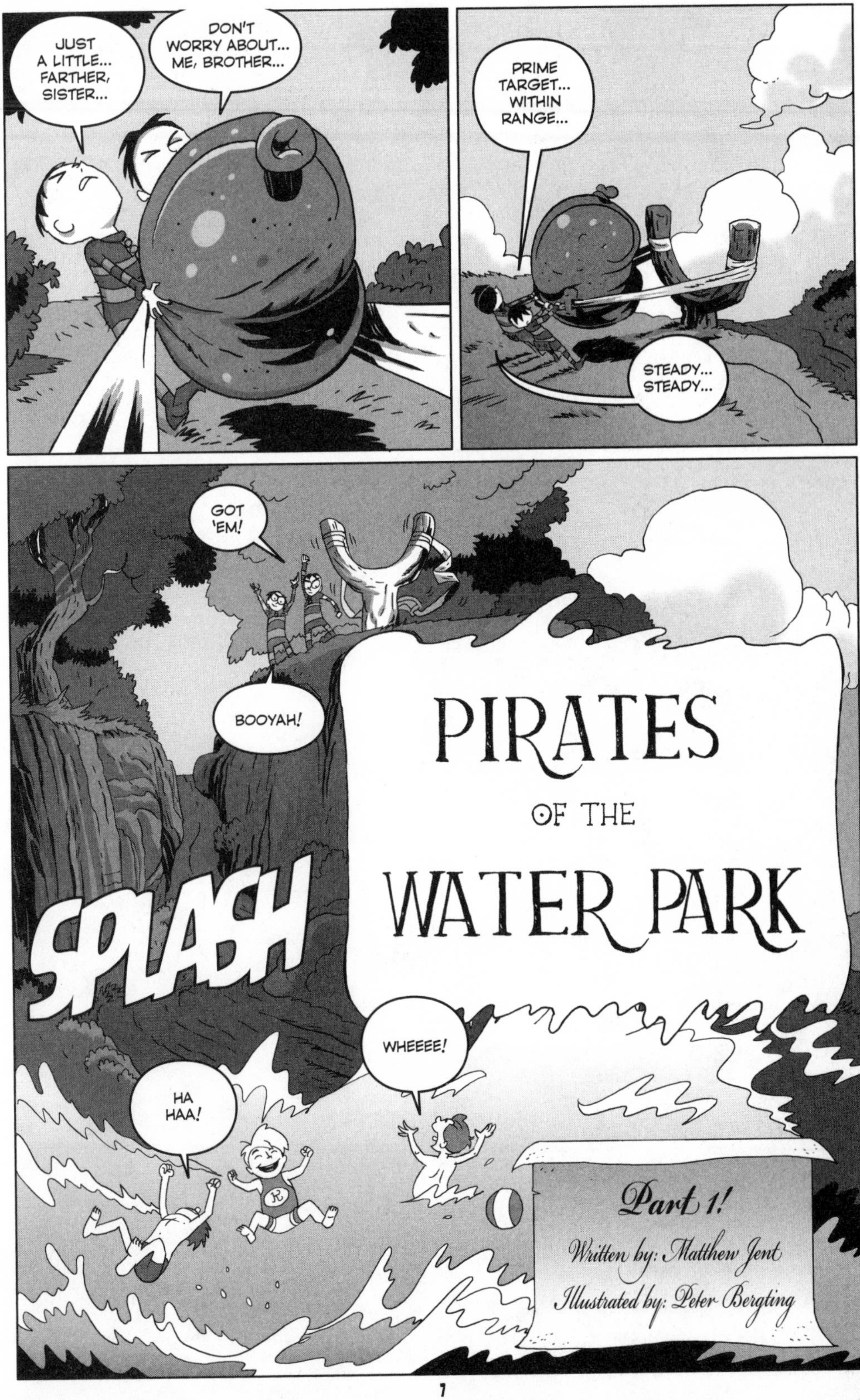
JUST A LITTLE... FARTHER, SISTER...
DON'T WORRY ABOUT... ME, BROTHER...
PRIME TARGET... WITHIN RANGE...
STEADY... STEADY...
GOT 'EM!
BOOYAH!
PIRATES OF THE WATER PARK
SPLASH
WHEEEE!
HA HAA!
Part 1!
Written by: Matthew Jent
Illustrated by: Peter Bergting

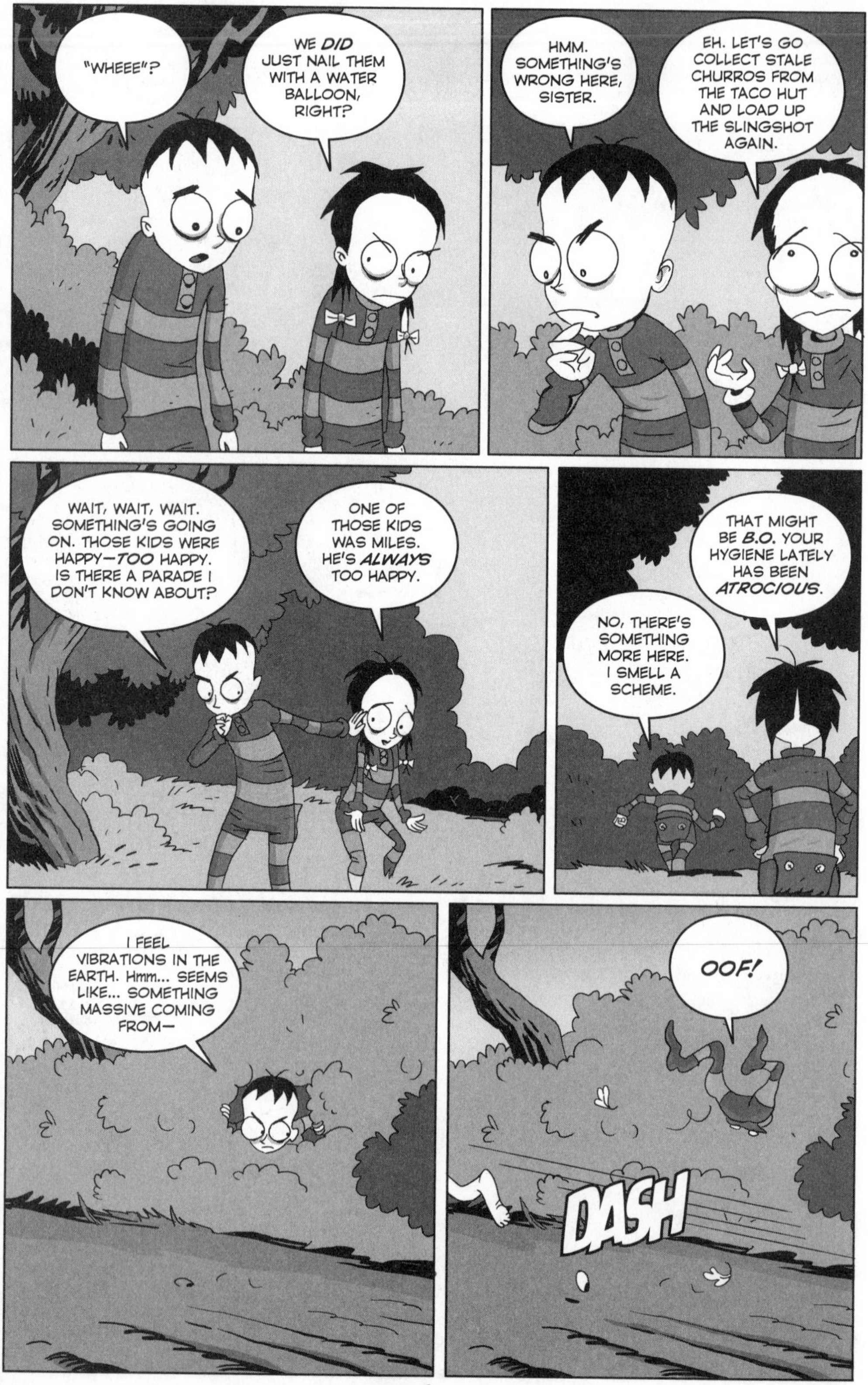
"WHEEE"?
WE DID JUST NAIL THEM WITH A WATER BALLOON, RIGHT?
HMM. SOMETHING'S WRONG HERE, SISTER.
EH. LET'S GO COLLECT STALE CHURROS FROM THE TACO HUT AND LOAD UP THE SLINGSHOT AGAIN.
WAIT, WAIT, WAIT. SOMETHING'S GOING ON. THOSE KIDS WERE HAPPY—TOO HAPPY. IS THERE A PARADE I DON'T KNOW ABOUT?
ONE OF THOSE KIDS WAS MILES. HE'S ALWAYS TOO HAPPY.
THAT MIGHT BE B.O. YOUR HYGIENE LATELY HAS BEEN ATROCIOUS.
NO, THERE'S SOMETHING MORE HERE. I SMELL A SCHEME.
I FEEL VIBRATIONS IN THE EARTH. Hmm... SEEMS LIKE... SOMETHING MASSIVE COMING FROM—
OOF!
DASH

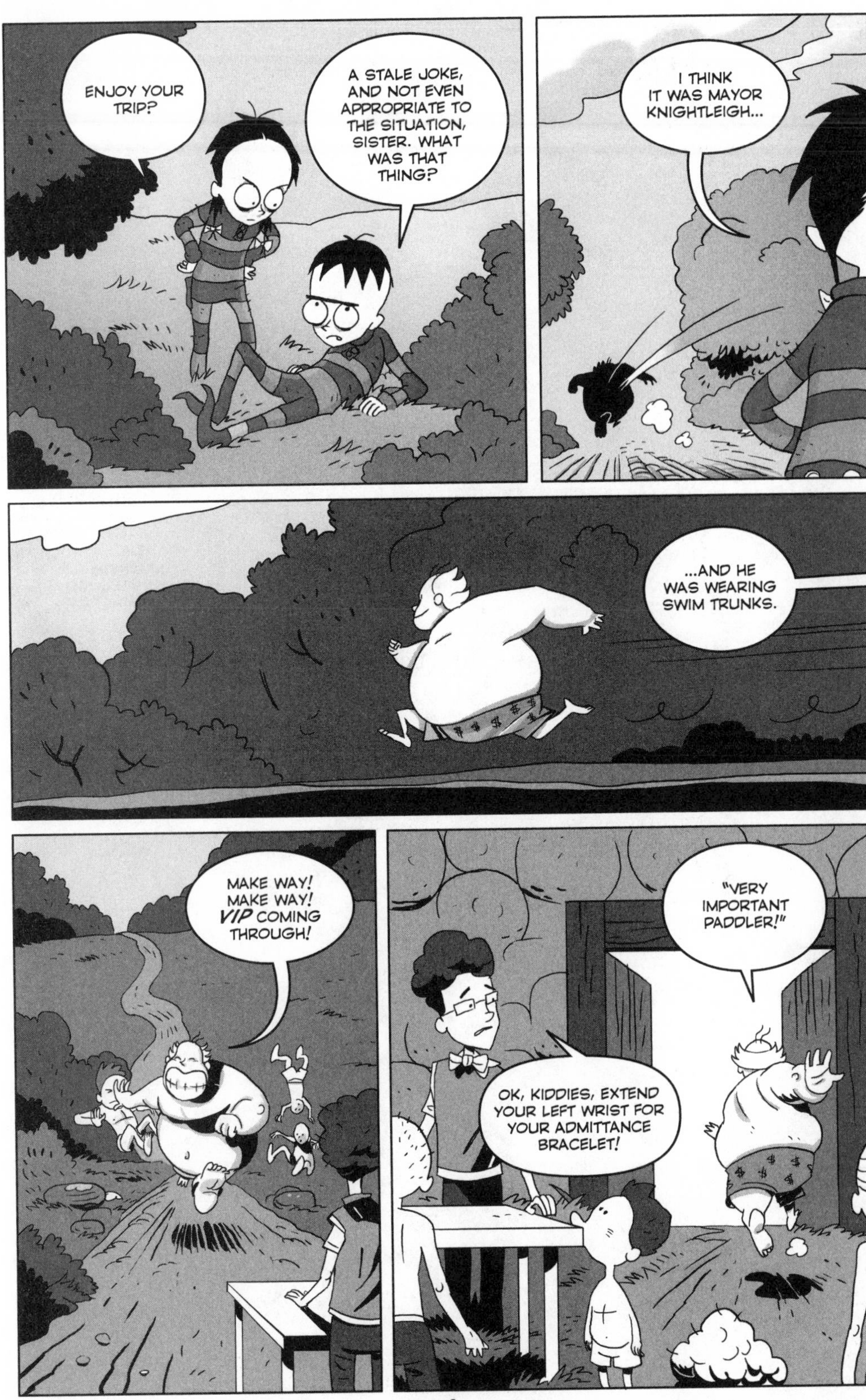
ENJOY YOUR TRIP?
A STALE JOKE, AND NOT EVEN APPROPRIATE TO THE SITUATION, SISTER. WHAT WAS THAT THING?
I THINK IT WAS MAYOR KNIGHTLEIGH...
...AND HE WAS WEARING SWIM TRUNKS.
MAKE WAY! MAKE WAY! *VIP* COMING THROUGH!
"VERY IMPORTANT PADDLER!"
OK, KIDDIES, EXTEND YOUR LEFT WRIST FOR YOUR ADMITTANCE BRACELET!

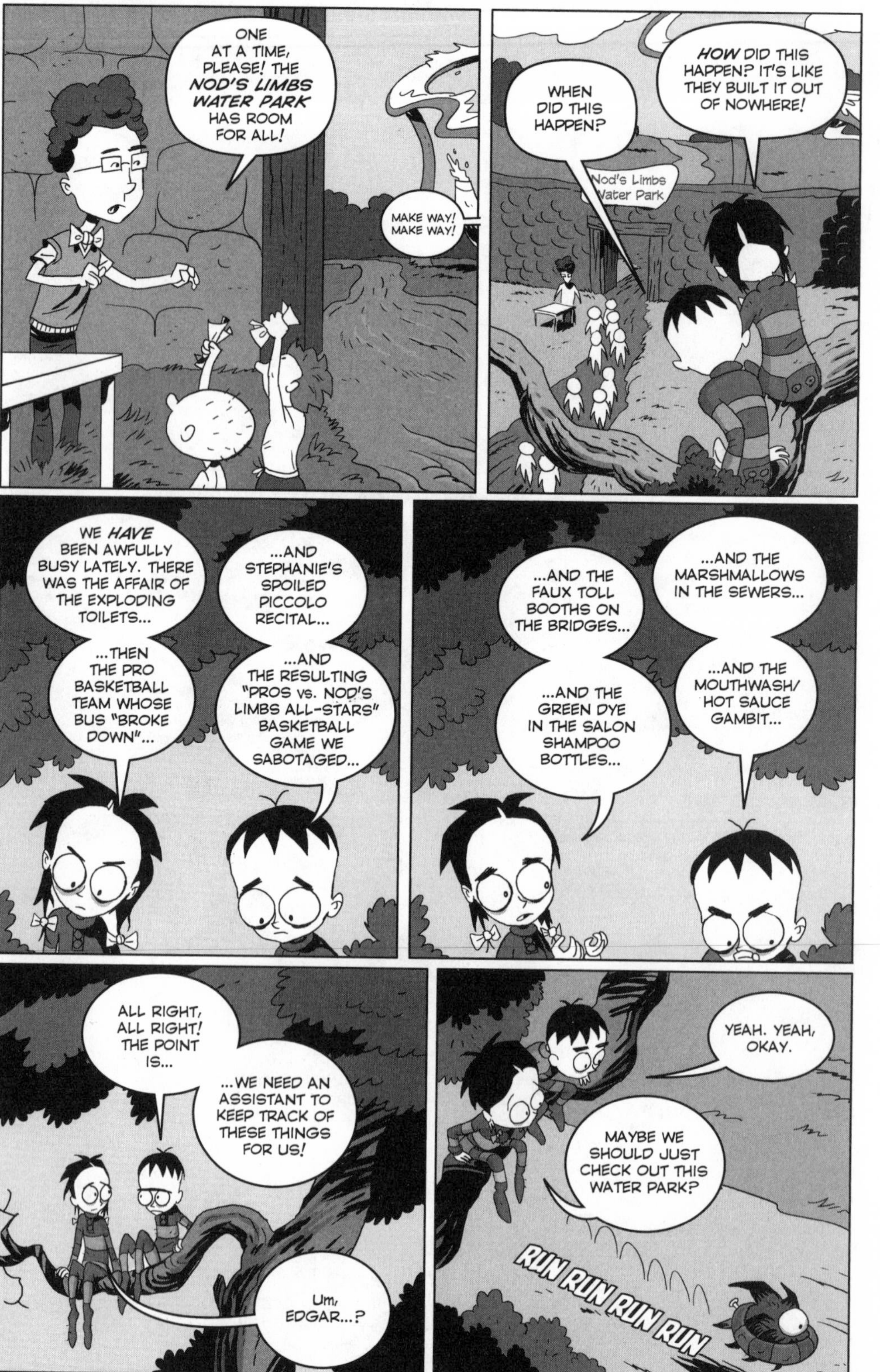

ONE AT A TIME, PLEASE! THE *NOD'S LIMBS WATER PARK* HAS ROOM FOR ALL!
MAKE WAY! MAKE WAY!
WHEN DID THIS HAPPEN?
HOW DID THIS HAPPEN? IT'S LIKE THEY BUILT IT OUT OF NOWHERE!
Nod's Limbs Water Park
WE *HAVE* BEEN AWFULLY BUSY LATELY. THERE WAS THE AFFAIR OF THE EXPLODING TOILETS...
...AND STEPHANIE'S SPOILED PICCOLO RECITAL...
...THEN THE PRO BASKETBALL TEAM WHOSE BUS "BROKE DOWN"...
...AND THE RESULTING "PROS vs. NOD'S LIMBS ALL-STARS" BASKETBALL GAME WE SABOTAGED...
...AND THE FAUX TOLL BOOTHS ON THE BRIDGES...
...AND THE MARSHMALLOWS IN THE SEWERS...
...AND THE GREEN DYE IN THE SALON SHAMPOO BOTTLES...
...AND THE MOUTHWASH/ HOT SAUCE GAMBIT...
ALL RIGHT, ALL RIGHT! THE POINT IS...
...WE NEED AN ASSISTANT TO KEEP TRACK OF THESE THINGS FOR US!
Um, EDGAR...?
YEAH. YEAH, OKAY.
MAYBE WE SHOULD JUST CHECK OUT THIS WATER PARK?
RUN RUN RUN RUN

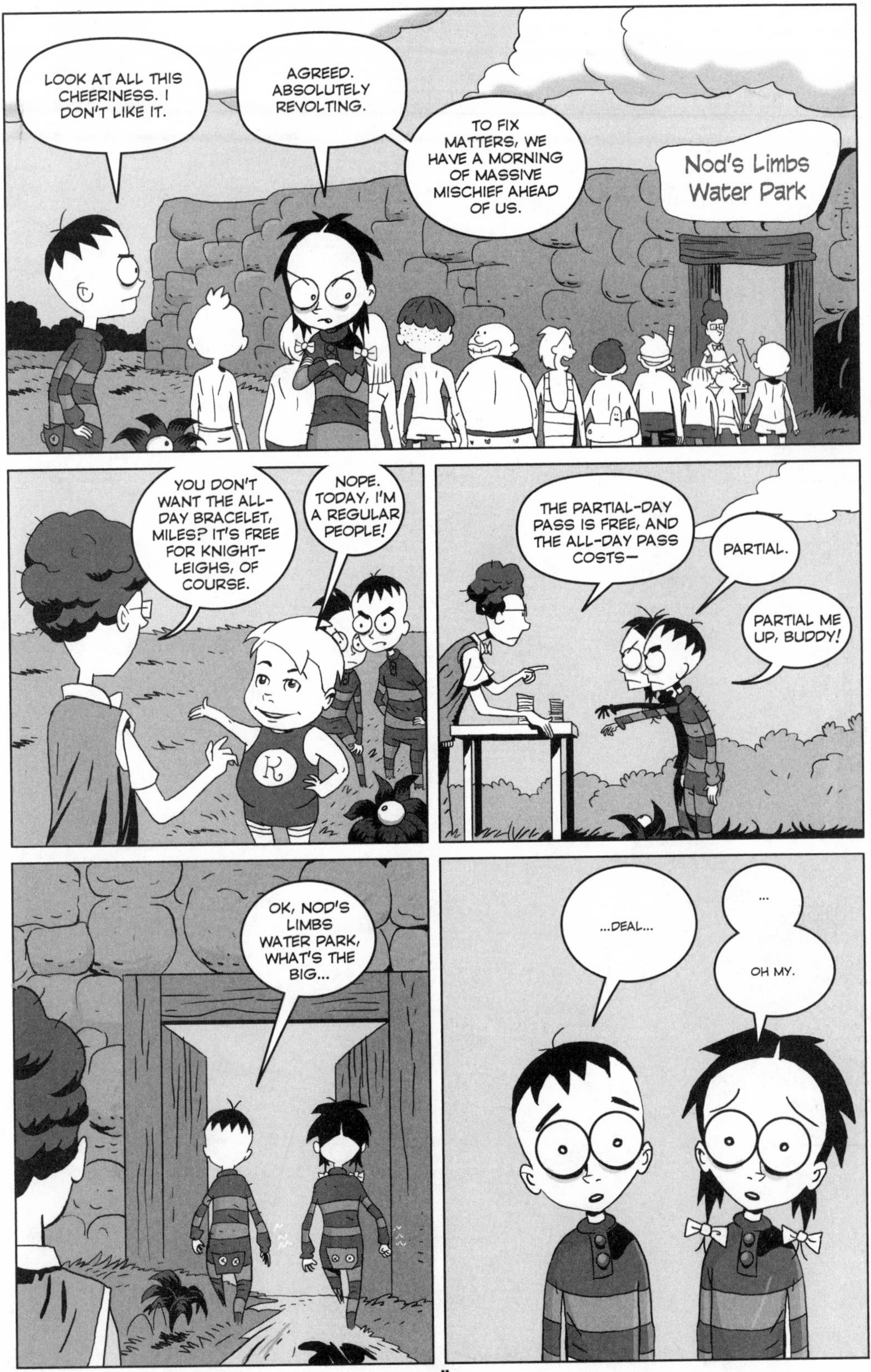
LOOK AT ALL THIS CHEERINESS. I DON'T LIKE IT.
AGREED. ABSOLUTELY REVOLTING.
TO FIX MATTERS, WE HAVE A MORNING OF MASSIVE MISCHIEF AHEAD OF US.
Nod's Limbs Water Park
YOU DON'T WANT THE ALL-DAY BRACELET, MILES? IT'S FREE FOR KNIGHT-LEIGHS, OF COURSE.
NOPE. TODAY, I'M A REGULAR PEOPLE!
THE PARTIAL-DAY PASS IS FREE, AND THE ALL-DAY PASS COSTS—
PARTIAL.
PARTIAL ME UP, BUDDY!
OK, NOD'S LIMBS WATER PARK, WHAT'S THE BIG...
...DEAL...
...
OH MY.

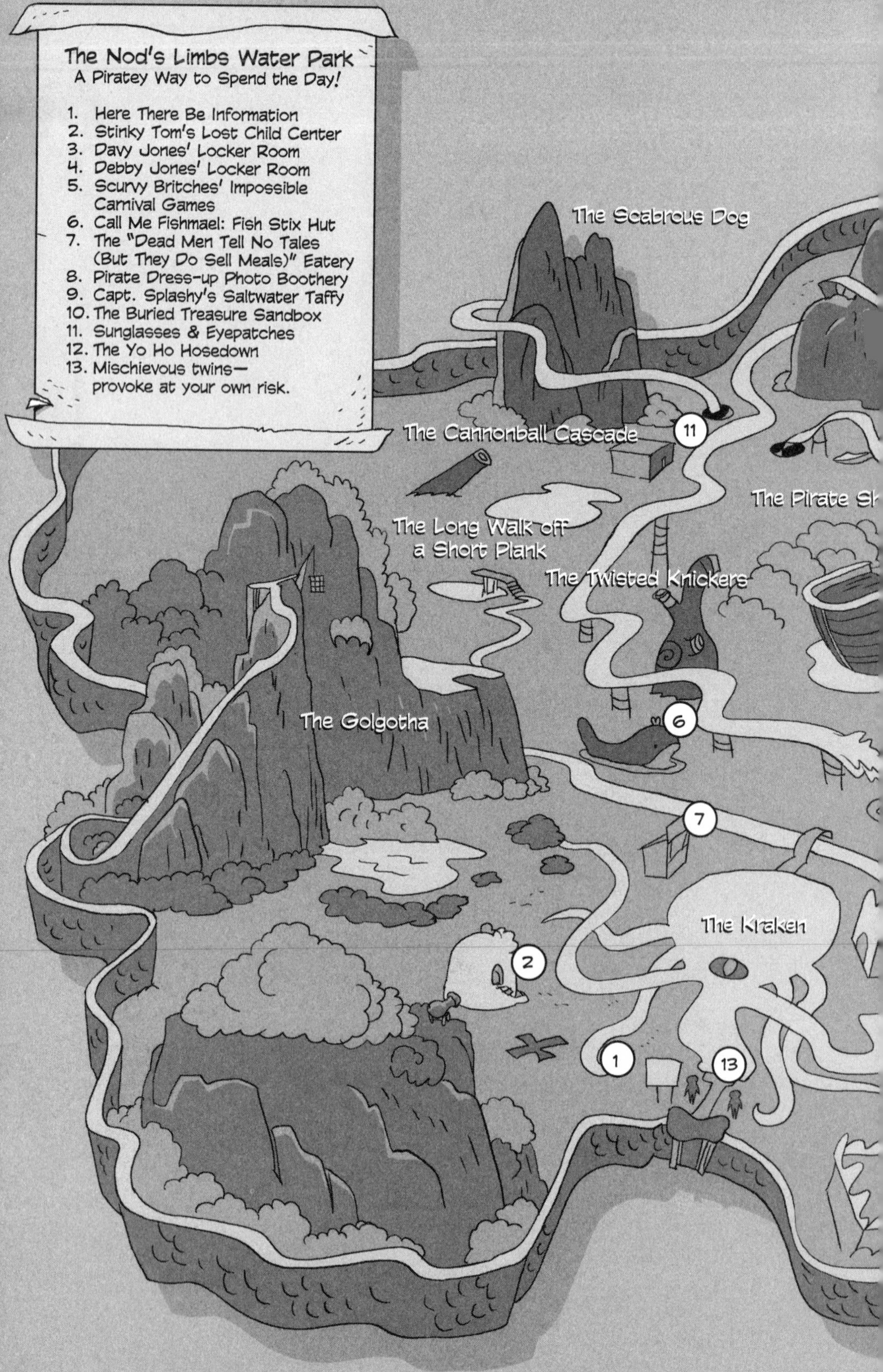
The Nod's Limbs Water Park
A Piratey Way to Spend the Day!
1. Here There Be Information
2. Stinky Tom's Lost Child Center
3. Davy Jones' Locker Room
4. Debby Jones' Locker Room
5. Scurvy Britches' Impossible Carnival Games
6. Call Me Fishmael: Fish Stix Hut
7. The "Dead Men Tell No Tales (But They Do Sell Meals)" Eatery
8. Pirate Dress-up Photo Boothery
9. Capt. Splashy's Saltwater Taffy
10. The Buried Treasure Sandbox
11. Sunglasses & Eyepatches
12. The Yo Ho Hosedown
13. Mischievous twins— provoke at your own risk.
The Scabrous Dog
The Cannonball Cascade
11
The Long Walk off a Short Plank
The Twisted Knickers
The Golgotha
6
7
The Kraken
2
1
13

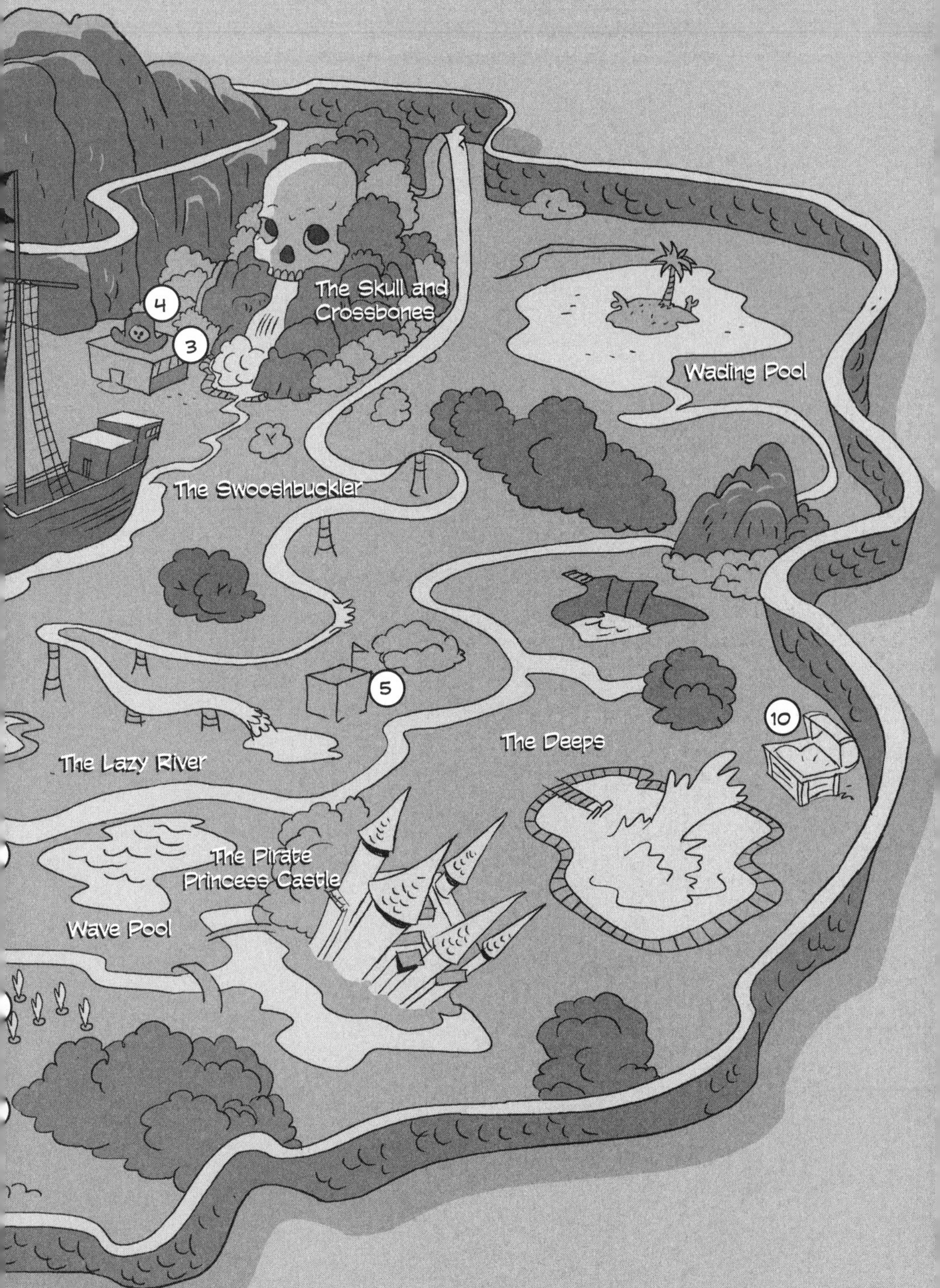
4
3
The Skull and Crossbones
Wading Pool
The Swooshbuckler
5
10
The Deeps
The Lazy River
The Pirate Princess Castle
Wave Pool

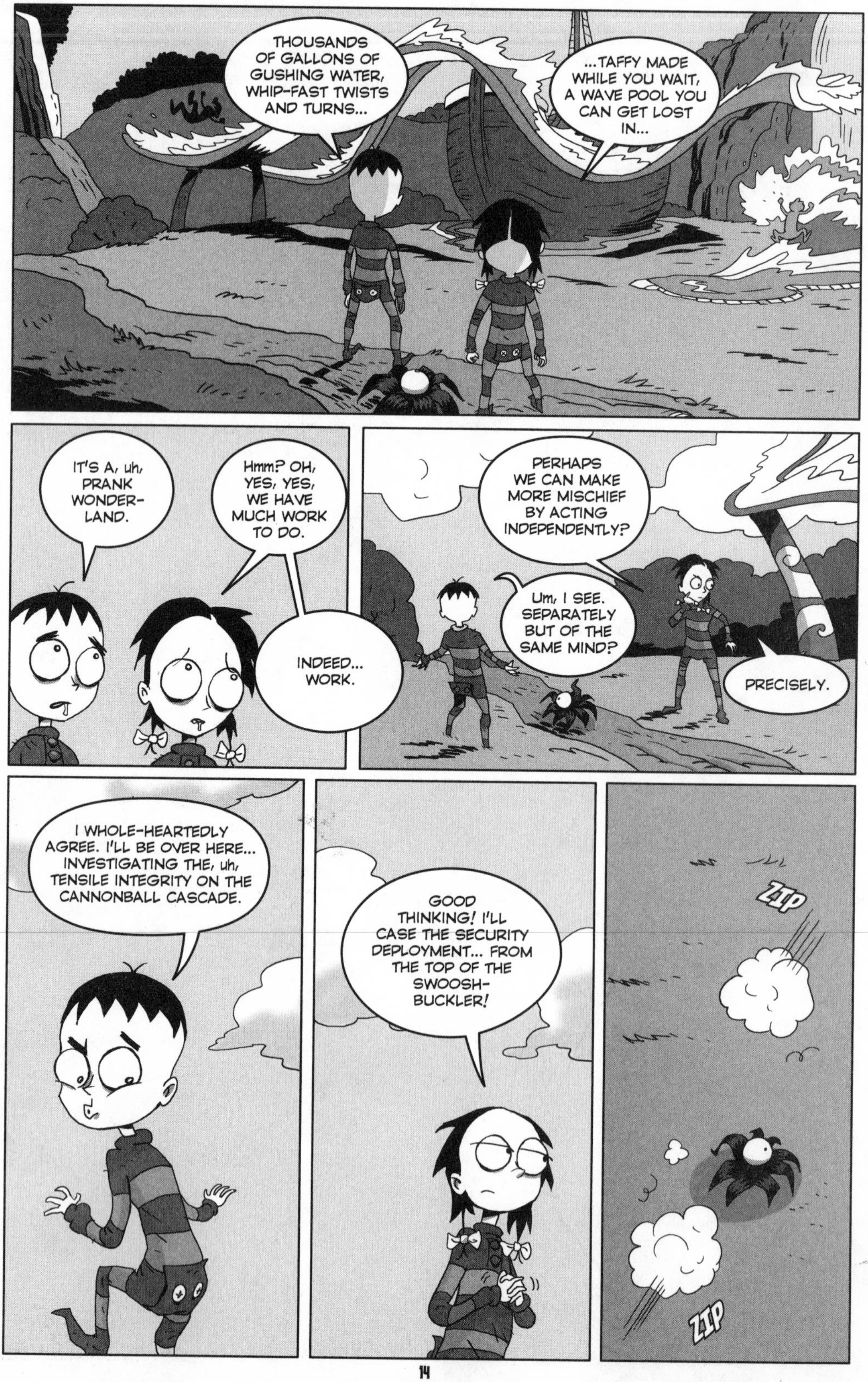
THOUSANDS OF GALLONS OF GUSHING WATER, WHIP-FAST TWISTS AND TURNS...
...TAFFY MADE WHILE YOU WAIT, A WAVE POOL YOU CAN GET LOST IN...
IT'S A, uh, PRANK WONDER-LAND.
Hmm? OH, YES, YES, WE HAVE MUCH WORK TO DO.
INDEED... WORK.
PERHAPS WE CAN MAKE MORE MISCHIEF BY ACTING INDEPENDENTLY?
Um, I SEE. SEPARATELY BUT OF THE SAME MIND?
PRECISELY.
I WHOLE-HEARTEDLY AGREE. I'LL BE OVER HERE... INVESTIGATING THE, uh, TENSILE INTEGRITY ON THE CANNONBALL CASCADE.
GOOD THINKING! I'LL CASE THE SECURITY DEPLOYMENT... FROM THE TOP OF THE SWOOSH-BUCKLER!
ZIP
ZIP

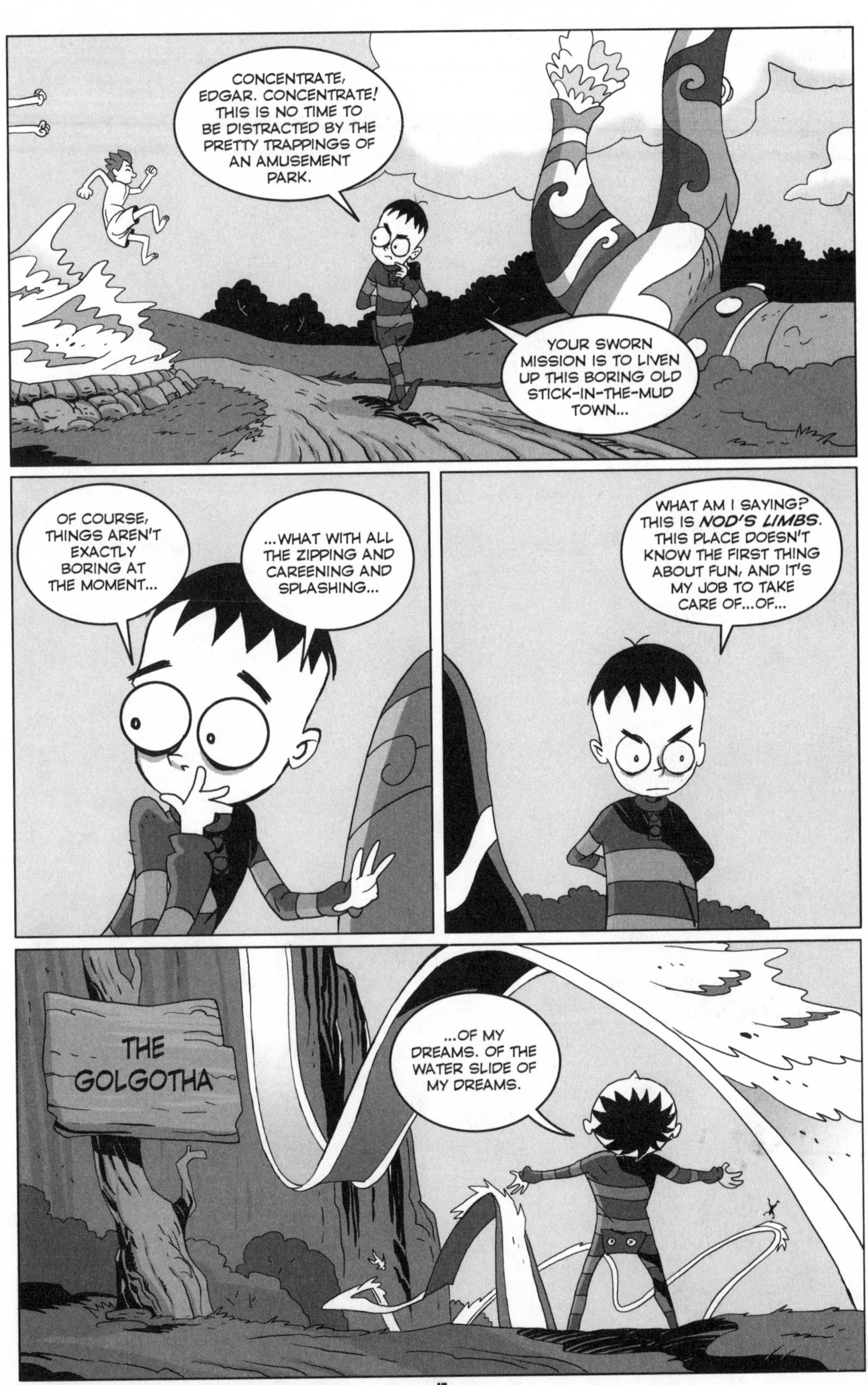
CONCENTRATE, EDGAR. CONCENTRATE! THIS IS NO TIME TO BE DISTRACTED BY THE PRETTY TRAPPINGS OF AN AMUSEMENT PARK.
YOUR SWORN MISSION IS TO LIVEN UP THIS BORING OLD STICK-IN-THE-MUD TOWN...
OF COURSE, THINGS AREN'T EXACTLY BORING AT THE MOMENT...
...WHAT WITH ALL THE ZIPPING AND CAREENING AND SPLASHING...
WHAT AM I SAYING? THIS IS NOD'S LIMBS. THIS PLACE DOESN'T KNOW THE FIRST THING ABOUT FUN, AND IT'S MY JOB TO TAKE CARE OF...OF...
THE GOLGOTHA
...OF MY DREAMS. OF THE WATER SLIDE OF MY DREAMS.

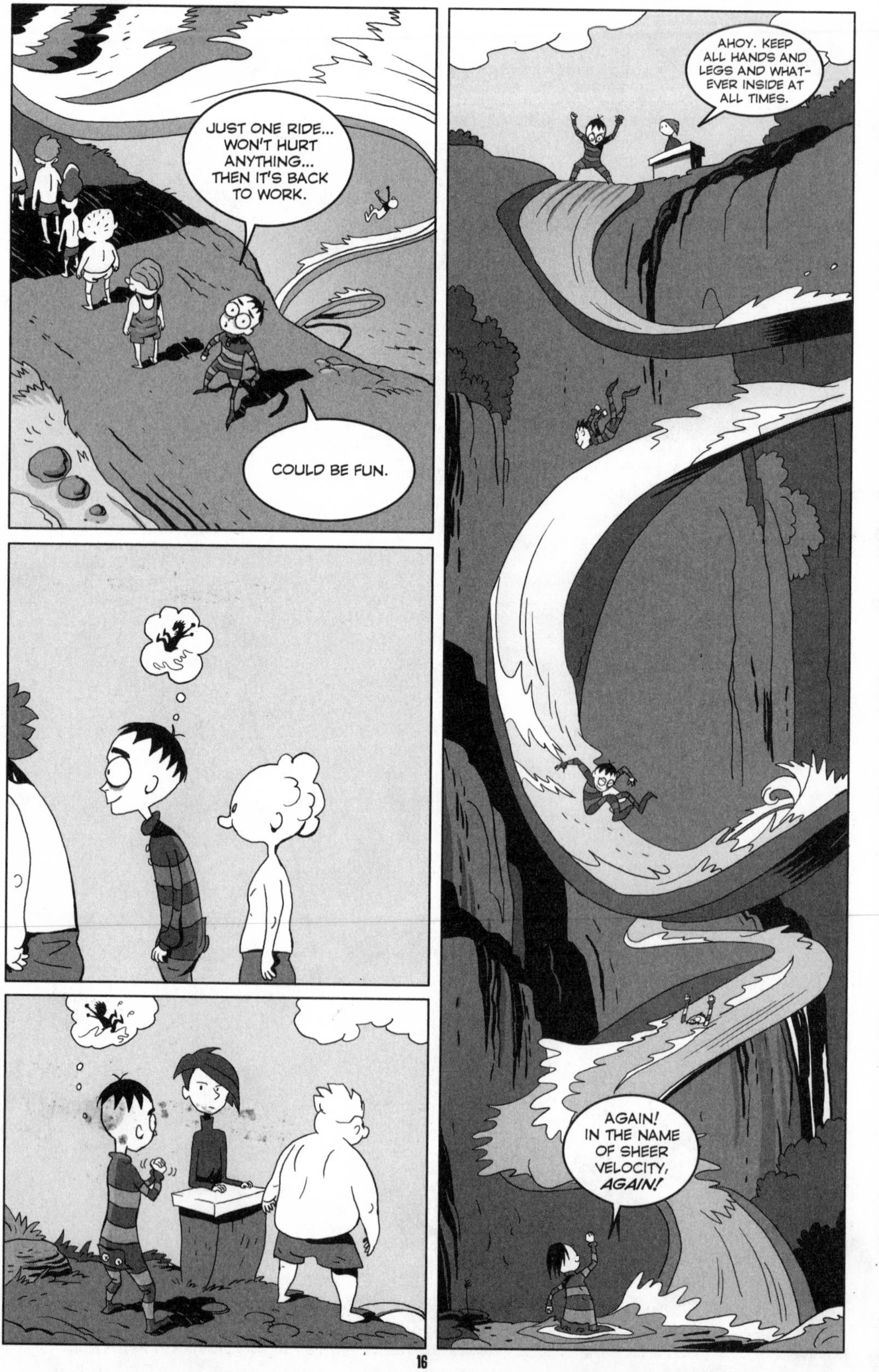
JUST ONE RIDE... WON'T HURT ANYTHING... THEN IT'S BACK TO WORK.
COULD BE FUN.
AHOY. KEEP ALL HANDS AND LEGS AND WHAT-EVER INSIDE AT ALL TIMES.
AGAIN! IN THE NAME OF SHEER VELOCITY, *AGAIN!*

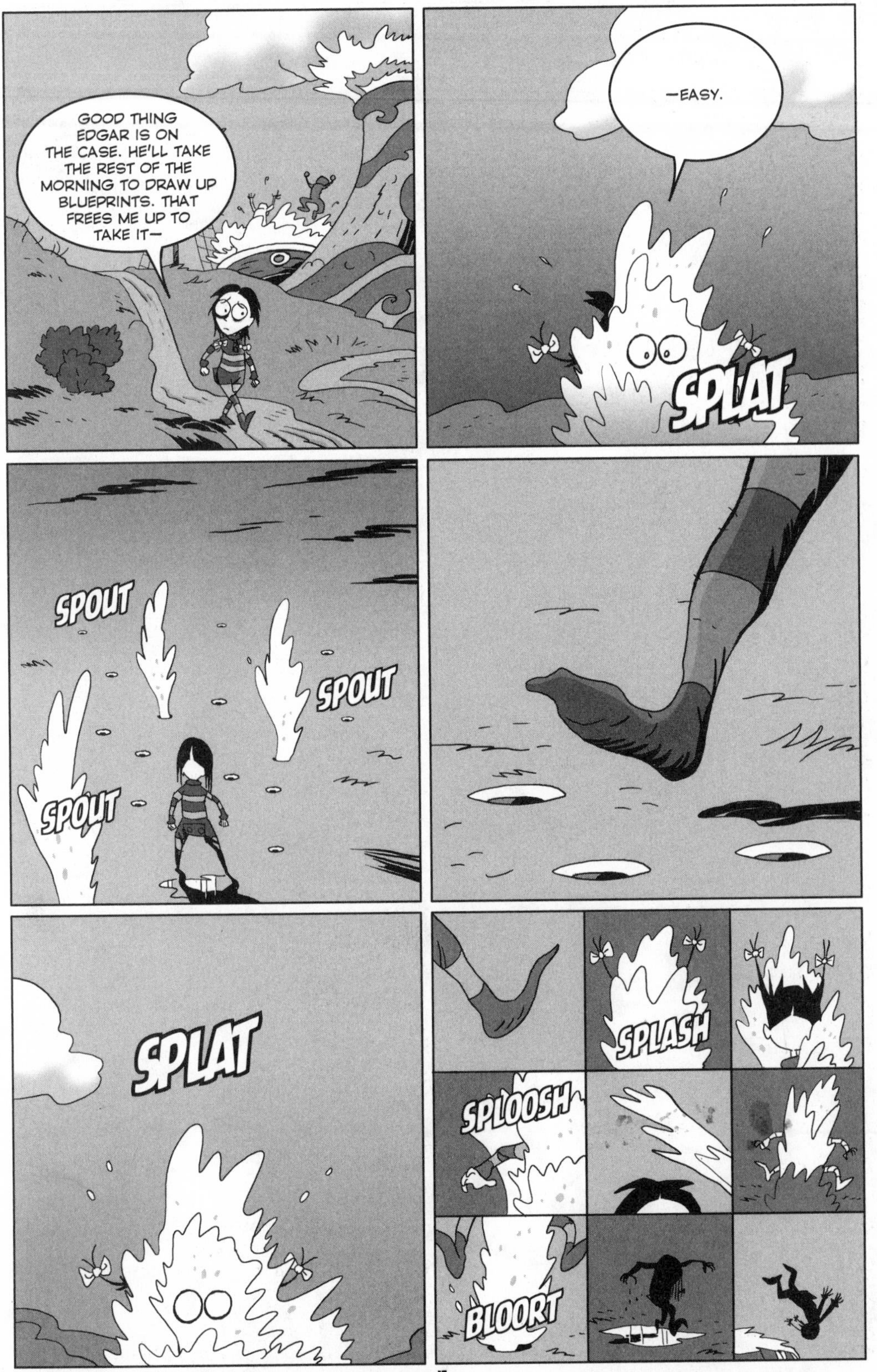
GOOD THING EDGAR IS ON THE CASE. HE'LL TAKE THE REST OF THE MORNING TO DRAW UP BLUEPRINTS. THAT FREES ME UP TO TAKE IT—
—EASY.
SPLAT
SPOUT
SPOUT
SPOUT
SPLAT
SPLASH
SPLOOSH
BLOORT

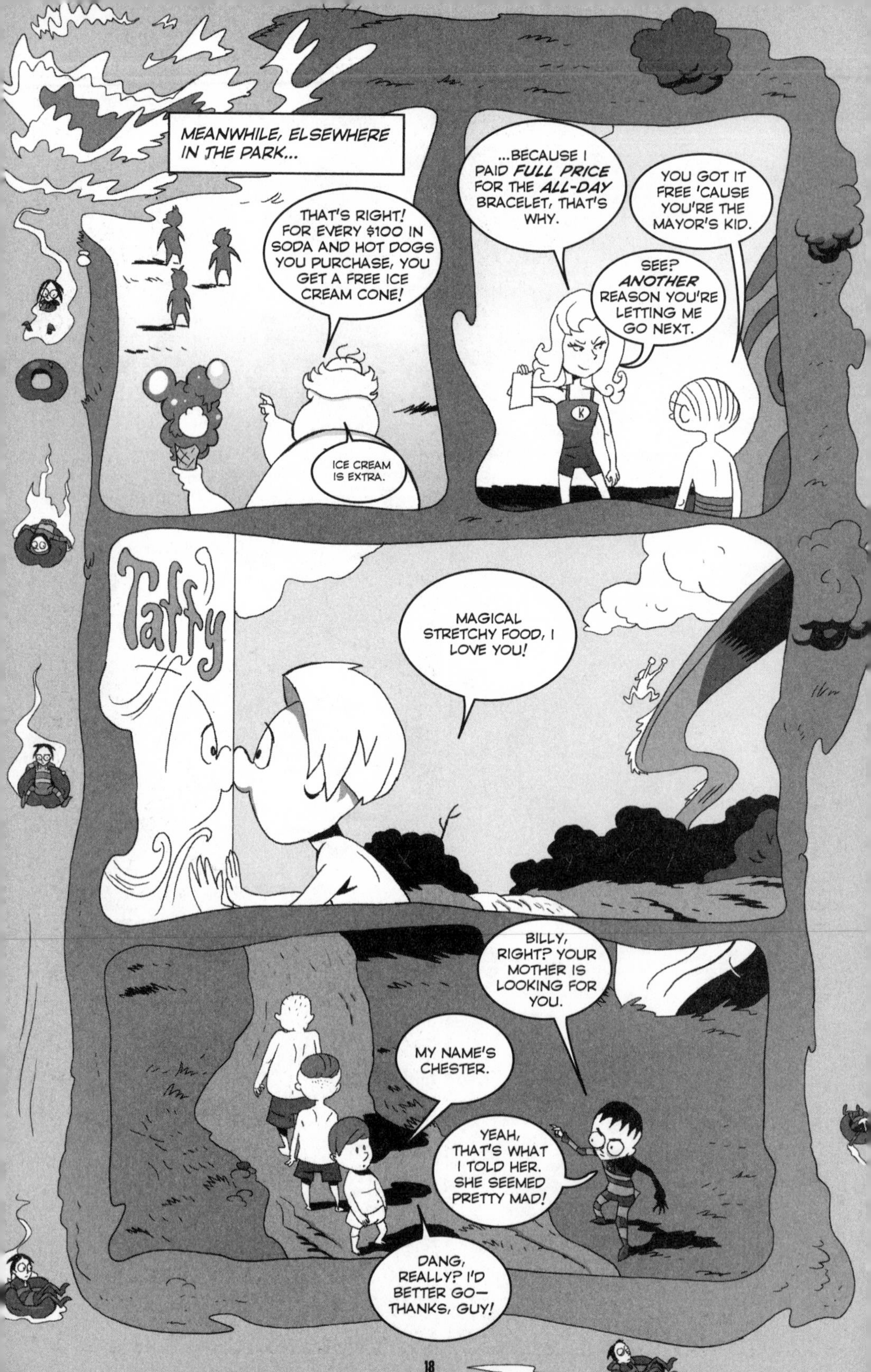
MEANWHILE, ELSEWHERE IN THE PARK...
THAT'S RIGHT! FOR EVERY $100 IN SODA AND HOT DOGS YOU PURCHASE, YOU GET A FREE ICE CREAM CONE!
ICE CREAM IS EXTRA.
...BECAUSE I PAID FULL PRICE FOR THE ALL-DAY BRACELET, THAT'S WHY.
YOU GOT IT FREE 'CAUSE YOU'RE THE MAYOR'S KID.
SEE? ANOTHER REASON YOU'RE LETTING ME GO NEXT.
Taffy
MAGICAL STRETCHY FOOD, I LOVE YOU!
BILLY, RIGHT? YOUR MOTHER IS LOOKING FOR YOU.
MY NAME'S CHESTER.
YEAH, THAT'S WHAT I TOLD HER. SHE SEEMED PRETTY MAD!
DANG, REALLY? I'D BETTER GO— THANKS, GUY!

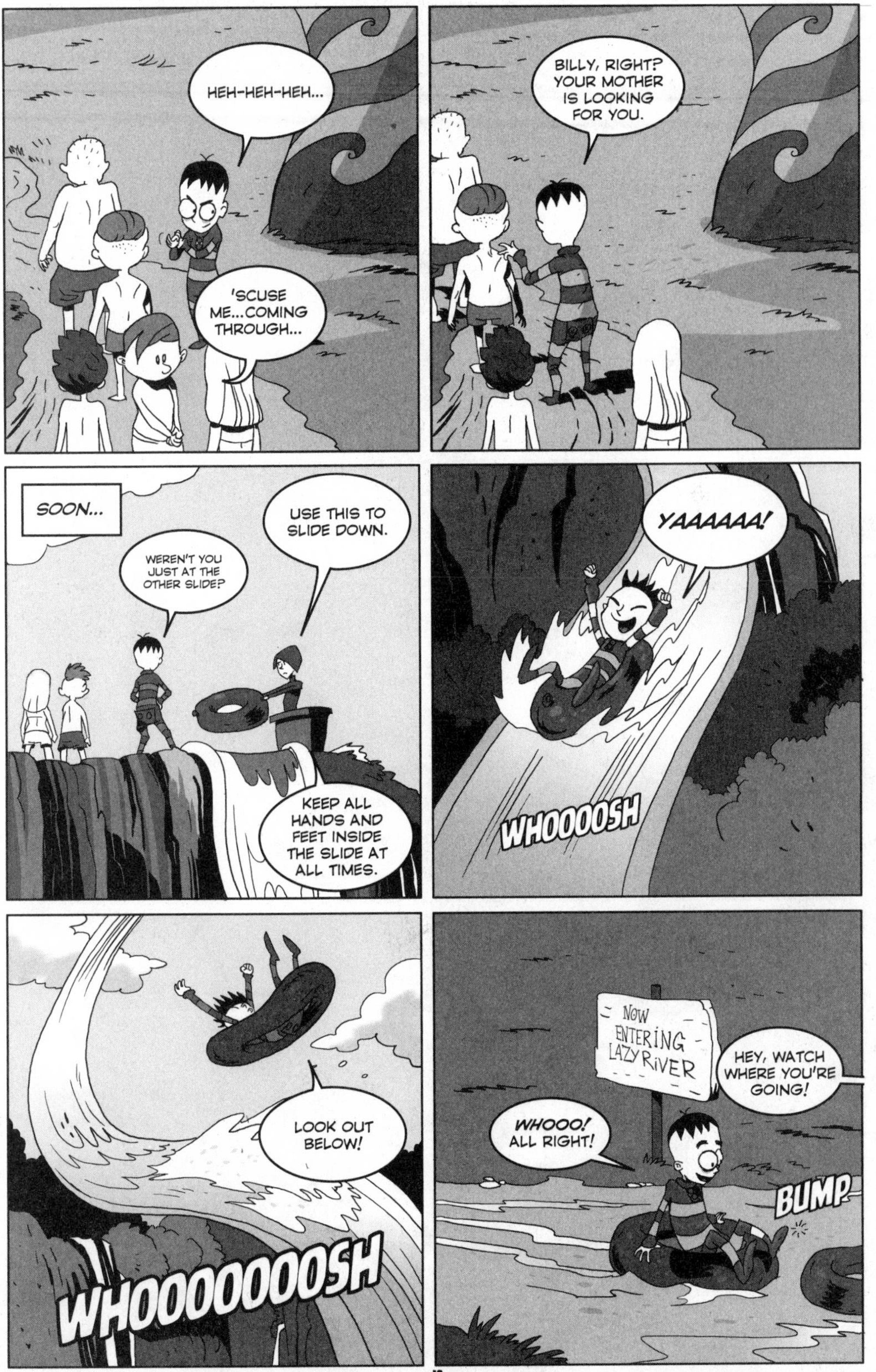
HEH-HEH-HEH...
'SCUSE ME...COMING THROUGH...
BILLY, RIGHT? YOUR MOTHER IS LOOKING FOR YOU.
SOON...
WEREN'T YOU JUST AT THE OTHER SLIDE?
USE THIS TO SLIDE DOWN.
KEEP ALL HANDS AND FEET INSIDE THE SLIDE AT ALL TIMES.
YAAAAAA!
WHOOOOSH
LOOK OUT BELOW!
WHOOOOOOOOSH
NOW ENTERING LAZY RIVER
HEY, WATCH WHERE YOU'RE GOING!
WHOOO! ALL RIGHT!
BUMP

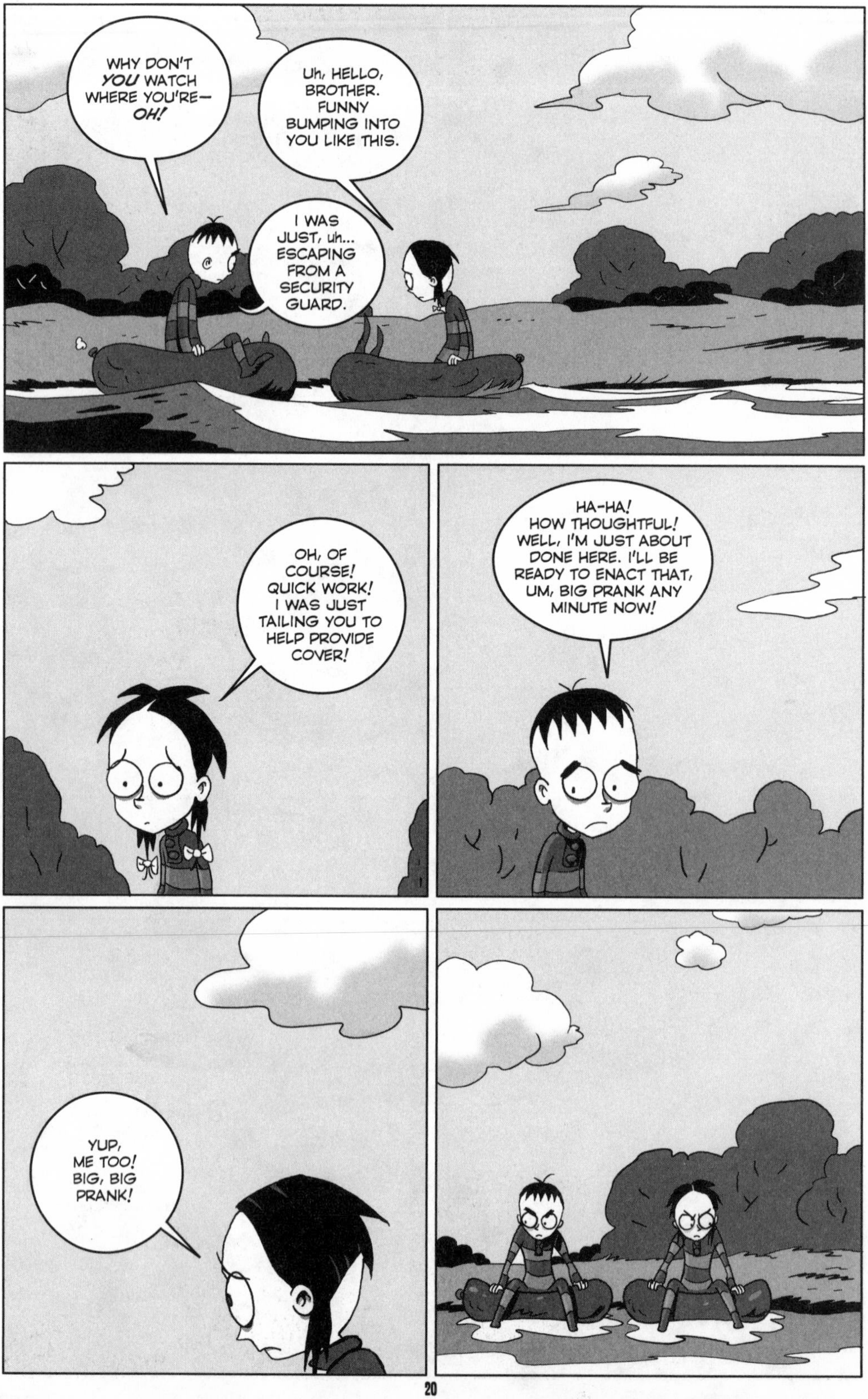
WHY DON'T *YOU* WATCH WHERE YOU'RE— *OH!*
Uh, HELLO, BROTHER. FUNNY BUMPING INTO YOU LIKE THIS.
I WAS JUST, uh... ESCAPING FROM A SECURITY GUARD.
OH, OF COURSE! QUICK WORK! I WAS JUST TAILING YOU TO HELP PROVIDE COVER!
HA-HA! HOW THOUGHTFUL! WELL, I'M JUST ABOUT DONE HERE. I'LL BE READY TO ENACT THAT, UM, BIG PRANK ANY MINUTE NOW!
YUP, ME TOO! BIG, BIG PRANK!

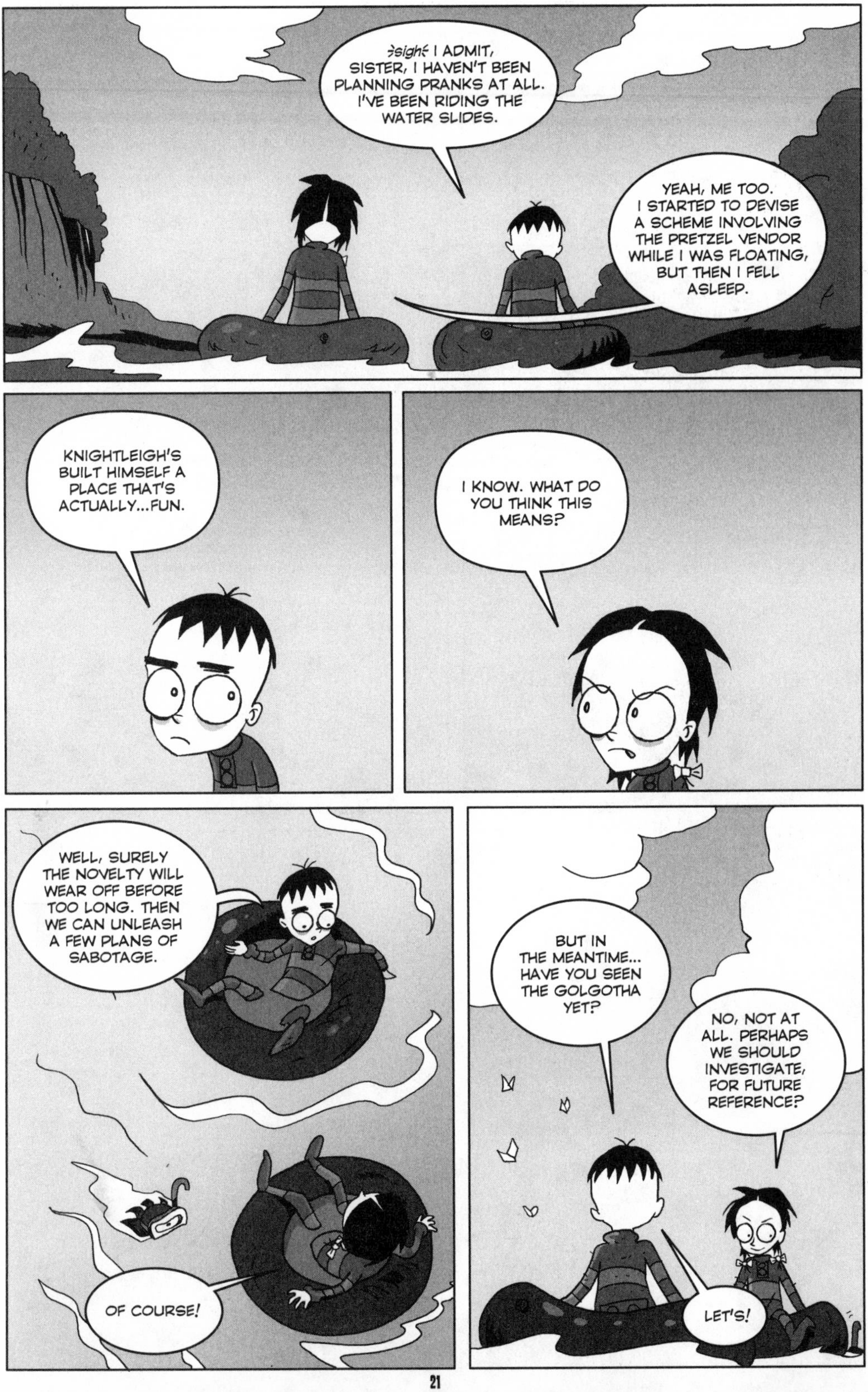

>sigh< I ADMIT, SISTER, I HAVEN'T BEEN PLANNING PRANKS AT ALL. I'VE BEEN RIDING THE WATER SLIDES.
YEAH, ME TOO. I STARTED TO DEVISE A SCHEME INVOLVING THE PRETZEL VENDOR WHILE I WAS FLOATING, BUT THEN I FELL ASLEEP.
KNIGHTLEIGH'S BUILT HIMSELF A PLACE THAT'S ACTUALLY...FUN.
I KNOW. WHAT DO YOU THINK THIS MEANS?
WELL, SURELY THE NOVELTY WILL WEAR OFF BEFORE TOO LONG. THEN WE CAN UNLEASH A FEW PLANS OF SABOTAGE.
OF COURSE!
BUT IN THE MEANTIME... HAVE YOU SEEN THE GOLGOTHA YET?
NO, NOT AT ALL. PERHAPS WE SHOULD INVESTIGATE, FOR FUTURE REFERENCE?
LET'S!

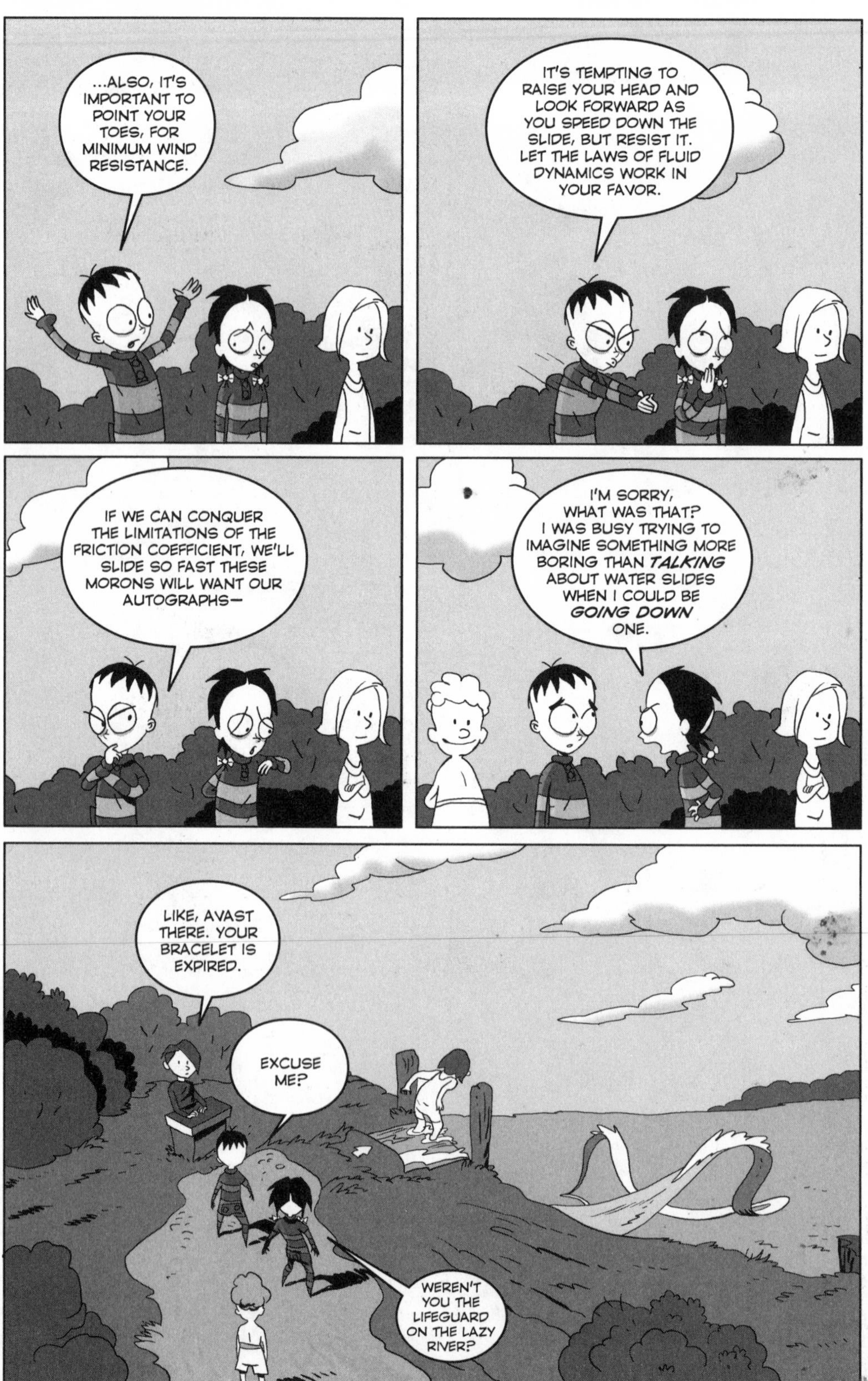
...ALSO, IT'S IMPORTANT TO POINT YOUR TOES, FOR MINIMUM WIND RESISTANCE.
IT'S TEMPTING TO RAISE YOUR HEAD AND LOOK FORWARD AS YOU SPEED DOWN THE SLIDE, BUT RESIST IT. LET THE LAWS OF FLUID DYNAMICS WORK IN YOUR FAVOR.
IF WE CAN CONQUER THE LIMITATIONS OF THE FRICTION COEFFICIENT, WE'LL SLIDE SO FAST THESE MORONS WILL WANT OUR AUTOGRAPHS—
I'M SORRY, WHAT WAS THAT? I WAS BUSY TRYING TO IMAGINE SOMETHING MORE BORING THAN *TALKING* ABOUT WATER SLIDES WHEN I COULD BE ***GOING DOWN*** ONE.
LIKE, AVAST THERE. YOUR BRACELET IS EXPIRED.
EXCUSE ME?
WEREN'T YOU THE LIFEGUARD ON THE LAZY RIVER?

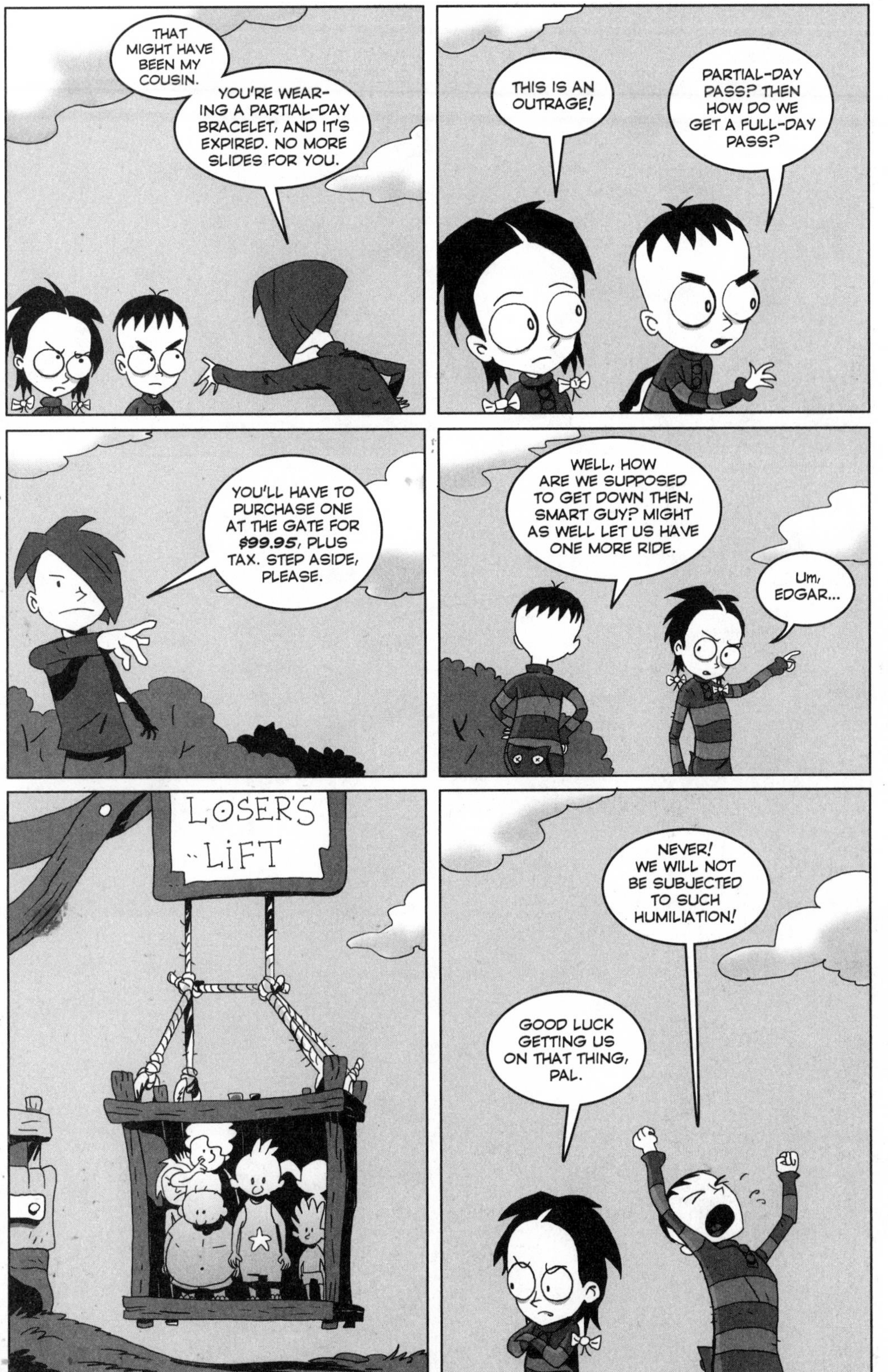
THAT MIGHT HAVE BEEN MY COUSIN.
YOU'RE WEAR-ING A PARTIAL-DAY BRACELET, AND IT'S EXPIRED. NO MORE SLIDES FOR YOU.
THIS IS AN OUTRAGE!
PARTIAL-DAY PASS? THEN HOW DO WE GET A FULL-DAY PASS?
YOU'LL HAVE TO PURCHASE ONE AT THE GATE FOR $99.95, PLUS TAX. STEP ASIDE, PLEASE.
WELL, HOW ARE WE SUPPOSED TO GET DOWN THEN, SMART GUY? MIGHT AS WELL LET US HAVE ONE MORE RIDE.
UM, EDGAR...
LOSER'S LIFT
NEVER! WE WILL NOT BE SUBJECTED TO SUCH HUMILIATION!
GOOD LUCK GETTING US ON THAT THING, PAL.

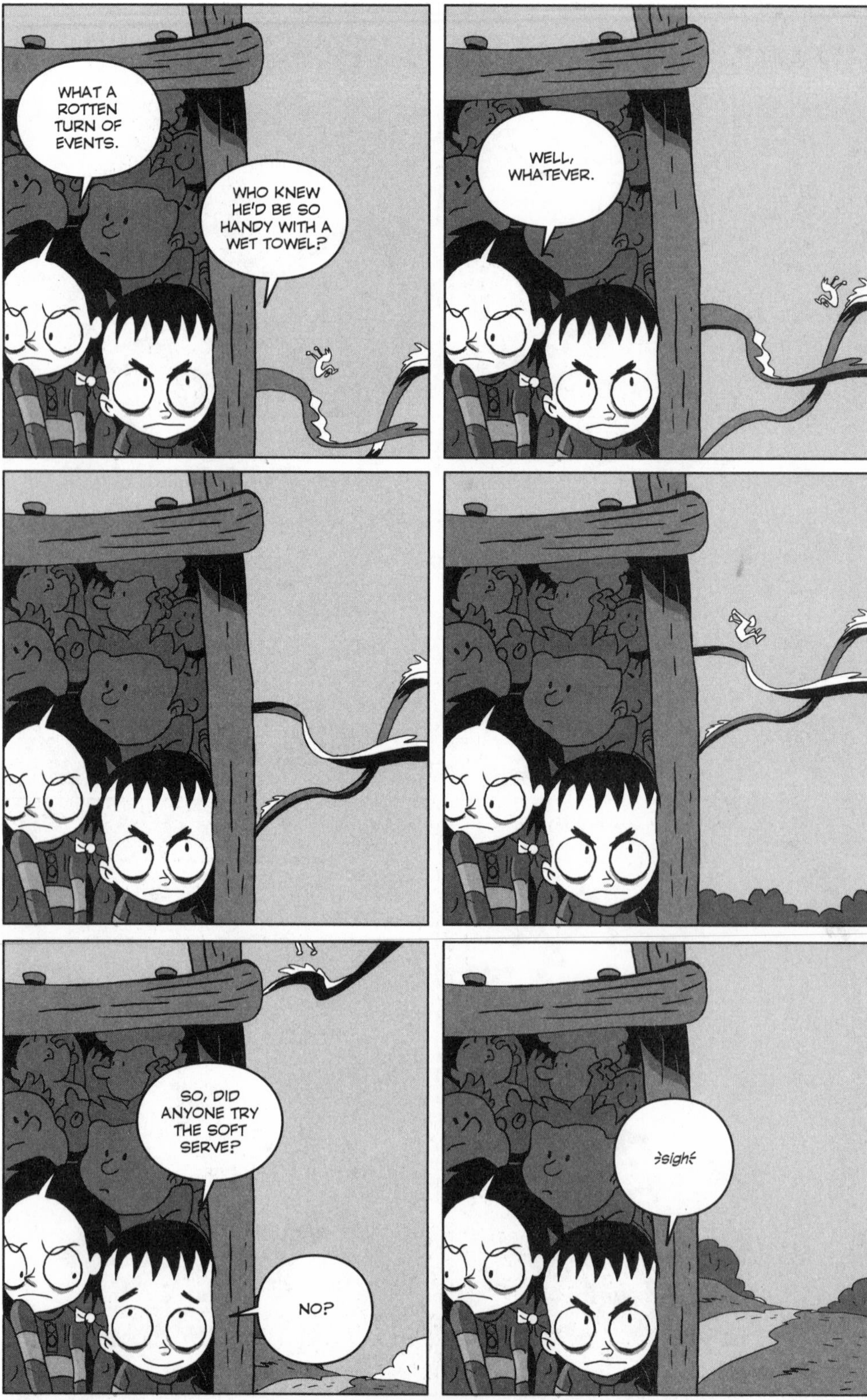
WHAT A ROTTEN TURN OF EVENTS.
WHO KNEW HE'D BE SO HANDY WITH A WET TOWEL?
WELL, WHATEVER.
SO, DID ANYONE TRY THE SOFT SERVE?
NO?
sigh

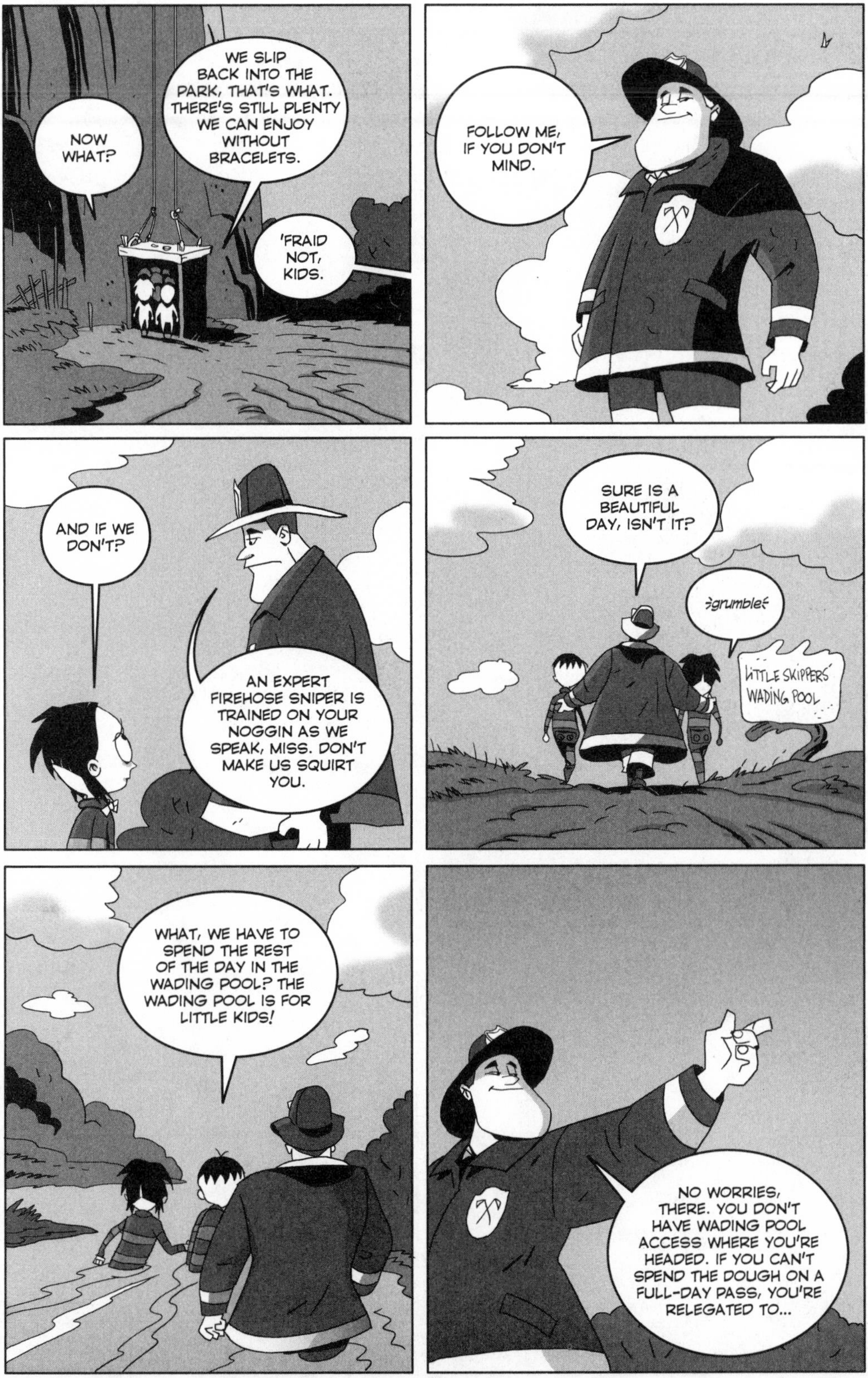
NOW WHAT?
WE SLIP BACK INTO THE PARK, THAT'S WHAT. THERE'S STILL PLENTY WE CAN ENJOY WITHOUT BRACELETS.
'FRAID NOT, KIDS.
FOLLOW ME, IF YOU DON'T MIND.
AND IF WE DON'T?
AN EXPERT FIREHOSE SNIPER IS TRAINED ON YOUR NOGGIN AS WE SPEAK, MISS. DON'T MAKE US SQUIRT YOU.
SURE IS A BEAUTIFUL DAY, ISN'T IT?
grumble
LITTLE SKIPPERS' WADING POOL
WHAT, WE HAVE TO SPEND THE REST OF THE DAY IN THE WADING POOL? THE WADING POOL IS FOR LITTLE KIDS!
NO WORRIES, THERE. YOU DON'T HAVE WADING POOL ACCESS WHERE YOU'RE HEADED. IF YOU CAN'T SPEND THE DOUGH ON A FULL-DAY PASS, YOU'RE RELEGATED TO...

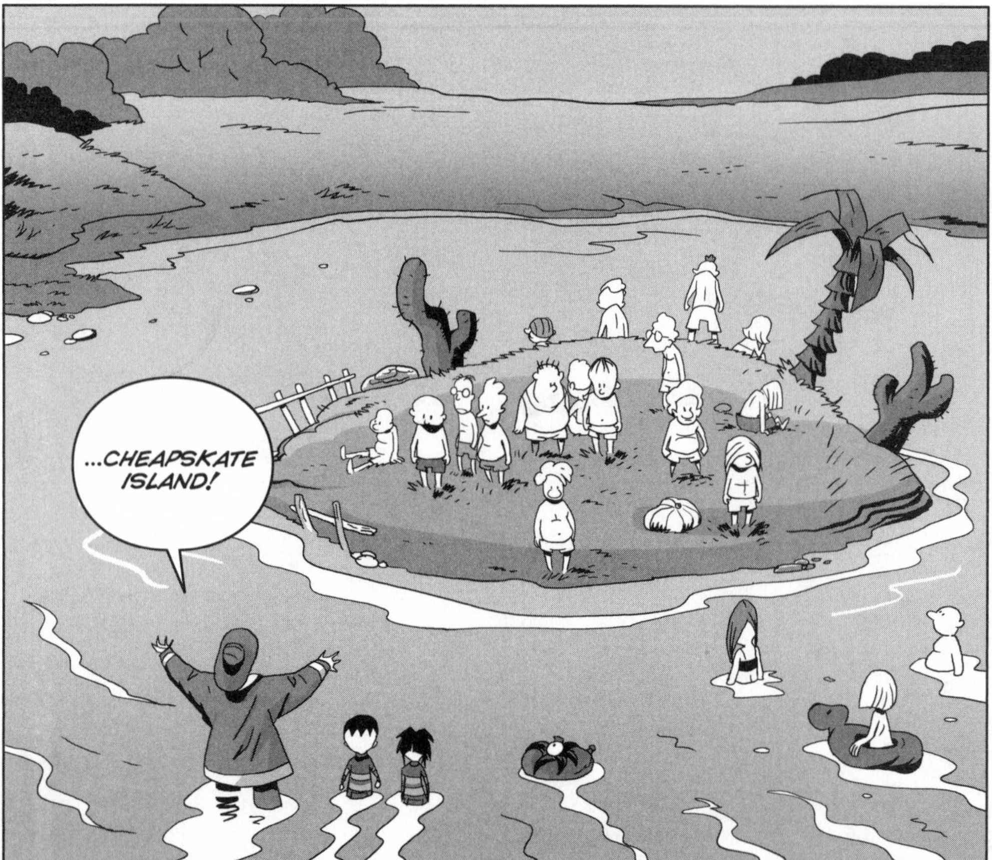
...CHEAPSKATE ISLAND!

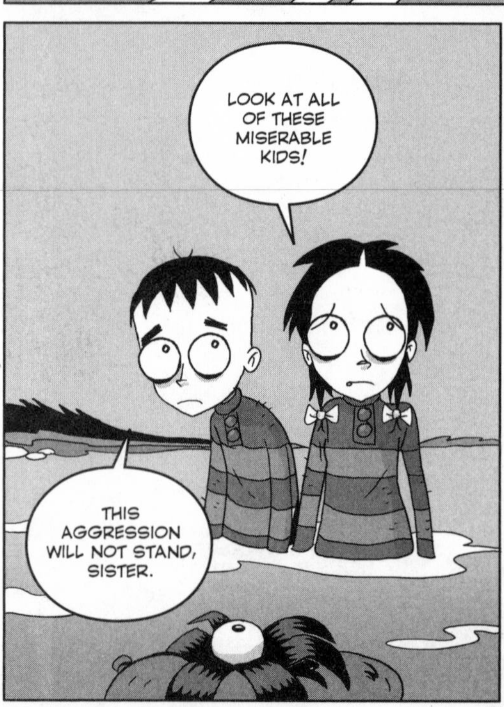
LOOK AT ALL OF THESE MISERABLE KIDS!
THIS AGGRESSION WILL NOT STAND, SISTER.

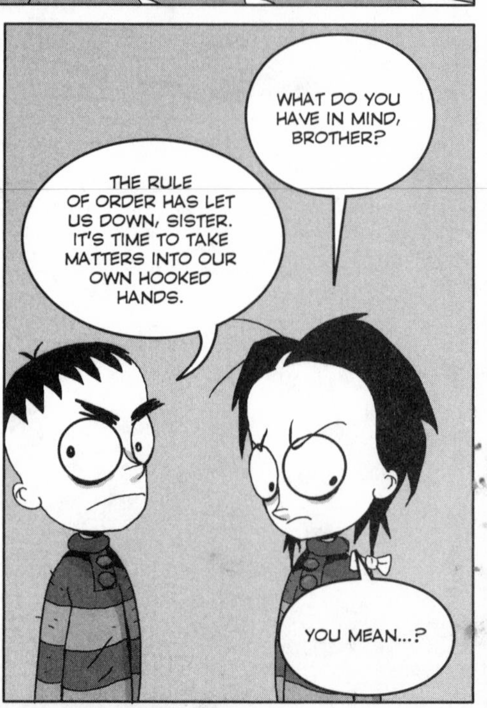
WHAT DO YOU HAVE IN MIND, BROTHER?
THE RULE OF ORDER HAS LET US DOWN, SISTER. IT'S TIME TO TAKE MATTERS INTO OUR OWN HOOKED HANDS.
YOU MEAN...?

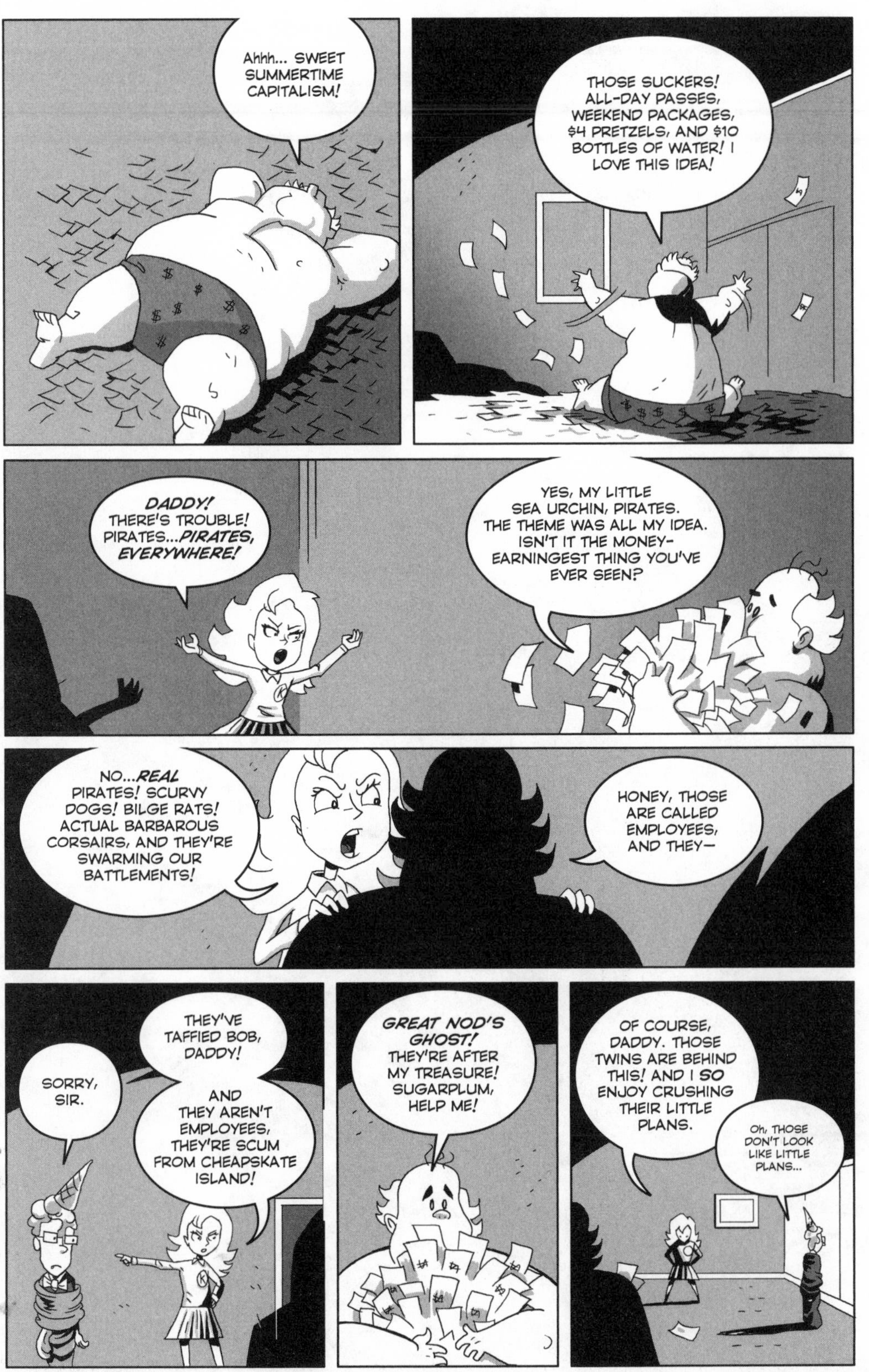

Ahhh... SWEET SUMMERTIME CAPITALISM!
THOSE SUCKERS! ALL-DAY PASSES, WEEKEND PACKAGES, $4 PRETZELS, AND $10 BOTTLES OF WATER! I LOVE THIS IDEA!
DADDY! THERE'S TROUBLE! PIRATES...PIRATES, EVERYWHERE!
YES, MY LITTLE SEA URCHIN, PIRATES. THE THEME WAS ALL MY IDEA. ISN'T IT THE MONEY-EARNINGEST THING YOU'VE EVER SEEN?
NO...REAL PIRATES! SCURVY DOGS! BILGE RATS! ACTUAL BARBAROUS CORSAIRS, AND THEY'RE SWARMING OUR BATTLEMENTS!
HONEY, THOSE ARE CALLED EMPLOYEES, AND THEY—
SORRY, SIR.
THEY'VE TAFFIED BOB, DADDY!
AND THEY AREN'T EMPLOYEES, THEY'RE SCUM FROM CHEAPSKATE ISLAND!
GREAT NOD'S GHOST! THEY'RE AFTER MY TREASURE! SUGARPLUM, HELP ME!
OF COURSE, DADDY. THOSE TWINS ARE BEHIND THIS! AND I SO ENJOY CRUSHING THEIR LITTLE PLANS.
Oh, THOSE DON'T LOOK LIKE LITTLE PLANS...

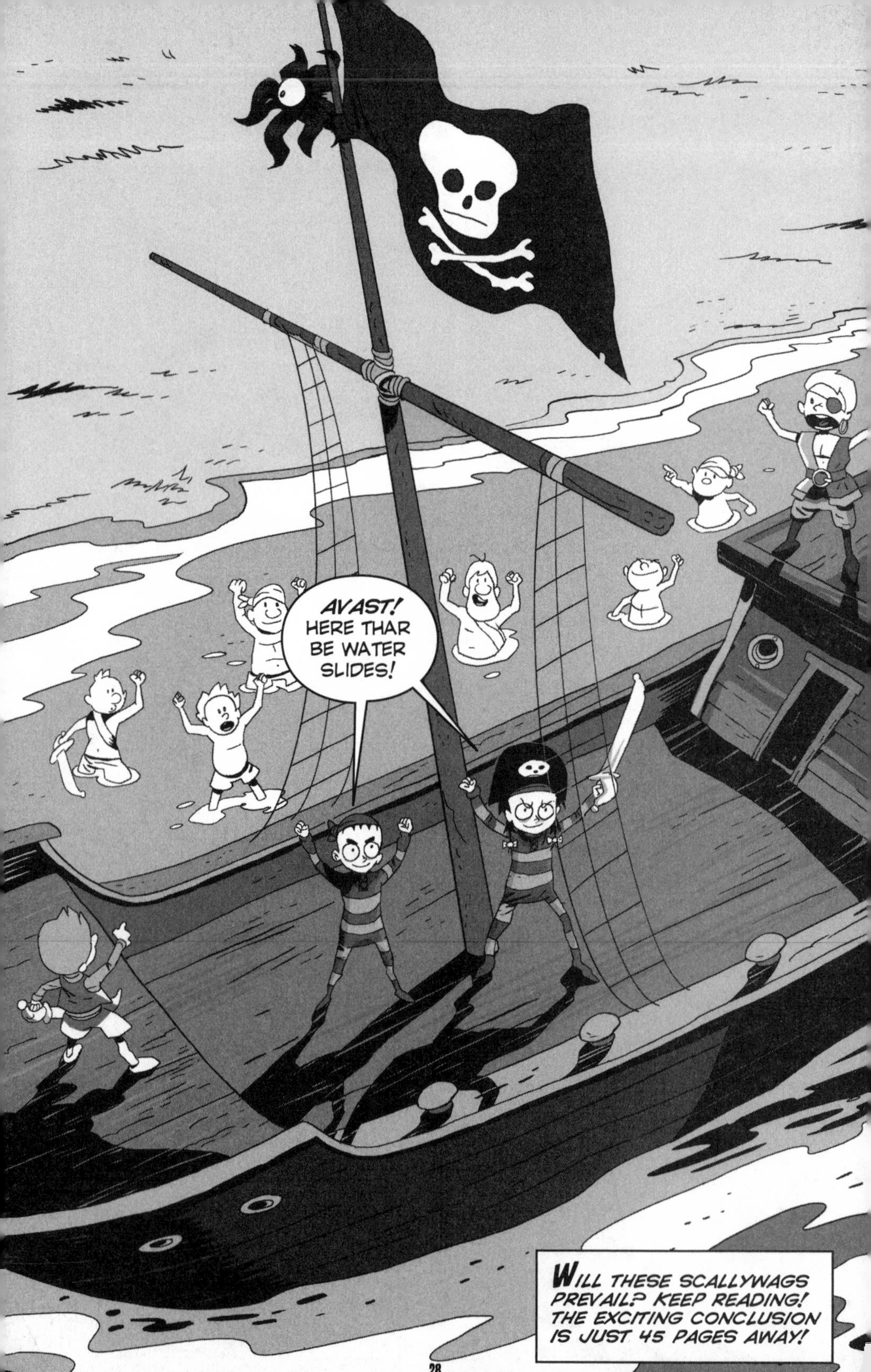
AVAST! HERE THAR BE WATER SLIDES!
WILL THESE SCALLYWAGS PREVAIL? KEEP READING! THE EXCITING CONCLUSION IS JUST 45 PAGES AWAY!

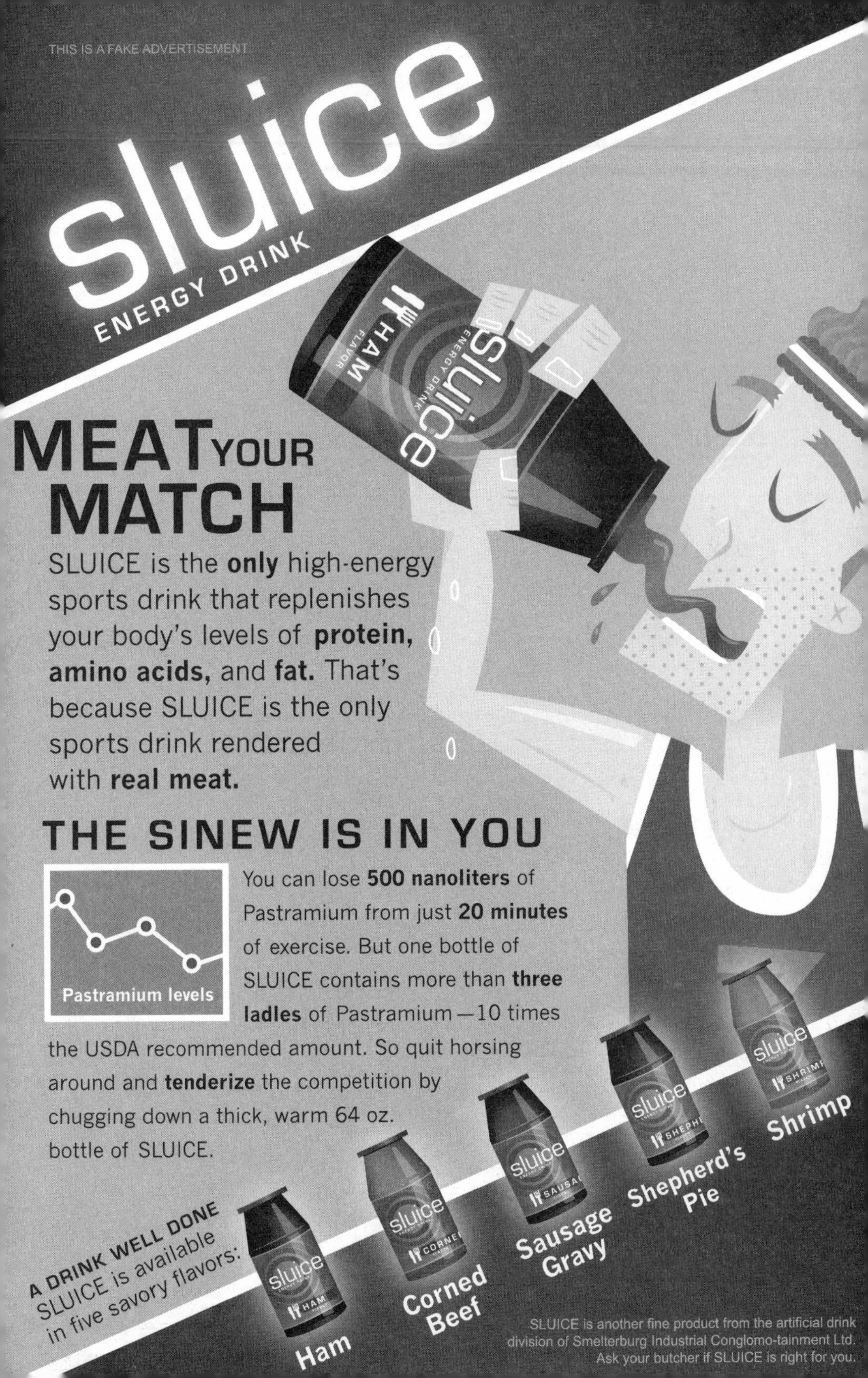

THIS IS A FAKE ADVERTISEMENT
sluice
ENERGY DRINK
sluice
ENERGY DRINK
HAM
FLAVOR
MEAT YOUR MATCH
SLUICE is the **only** high-energy sports drink that replenishes your body's levels of **protein, amino acids,** and **fat.** That's because SLUICE is the only sports drink rendered with **real meat.**
THE SINEW IS IN YOU
Pastramium levels
You can lose **500 nanoliters** of Pastramium from just **20 minutes** of exercise. But one bottle of SLUICE contains more than **three ladles** of Pastramium—10 times the USDA recommended amount. So quit horsing around and **tenderize** the competition by chugging down a thick, warm 64 oz. bottle of SLUICE.
A DRINK WELL DONE
SLUICE is available in five savory flavors:
Ham
Corned Beef
Sausage Gravy
Shepherd's Pie
Shrimp
SLUICE is another fine product from the artificial drink division of Smelterburg Industrial Conglomo-tainment Ltd.
Ask your butcher if SLUICE is right for you.

HEIMERTZ vs PIRATES! HOME REPAIR

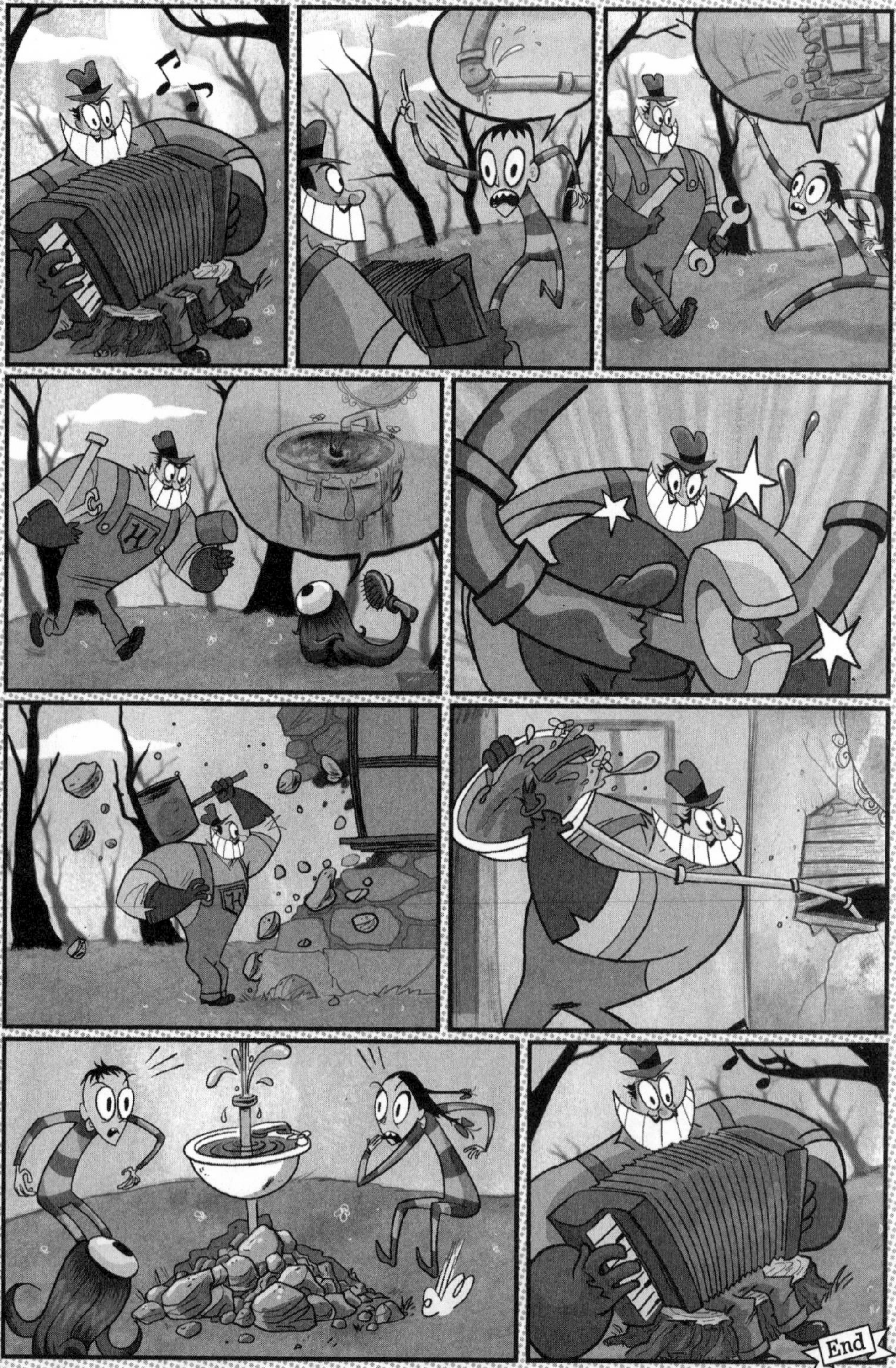
End

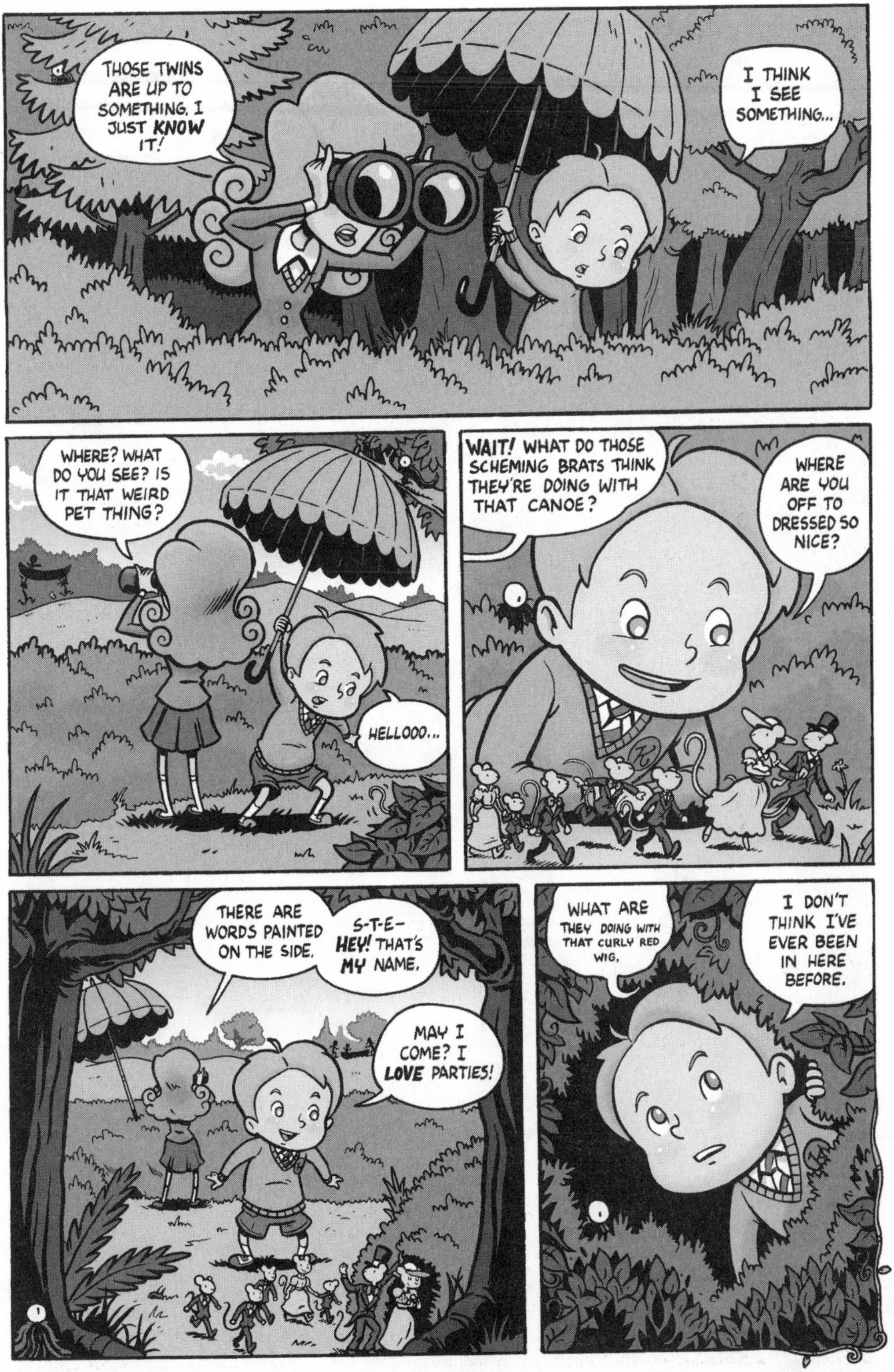
THOSE TWINS ARE UP TO SOMETHING. I JUST KNOW IT!
I THINK I SEE SOMETHING...
WHERE? WHAT DO YOU SEE? IS IT THAT WEIRD PET THING?
HELLOOO...
WAIT! WHAT DO THOSE SCHEMING BRATS THINK THEY'RE DOING WITH THAT CANOE?
WHERE ARE YOU OFF TO DRESSED SO NICE?
THERE ARE WORDS PAINTED ON THE SIDE.
S-T-E- HEY! THAT'S MY NAME.
MAY I COME? I LOVE PARTIES!
WHAT ARE THEY DOING WITH THAT CURLY RED WIG.
I DON'T THINK I'VE EVER BEEN IN HERE BEFORE.

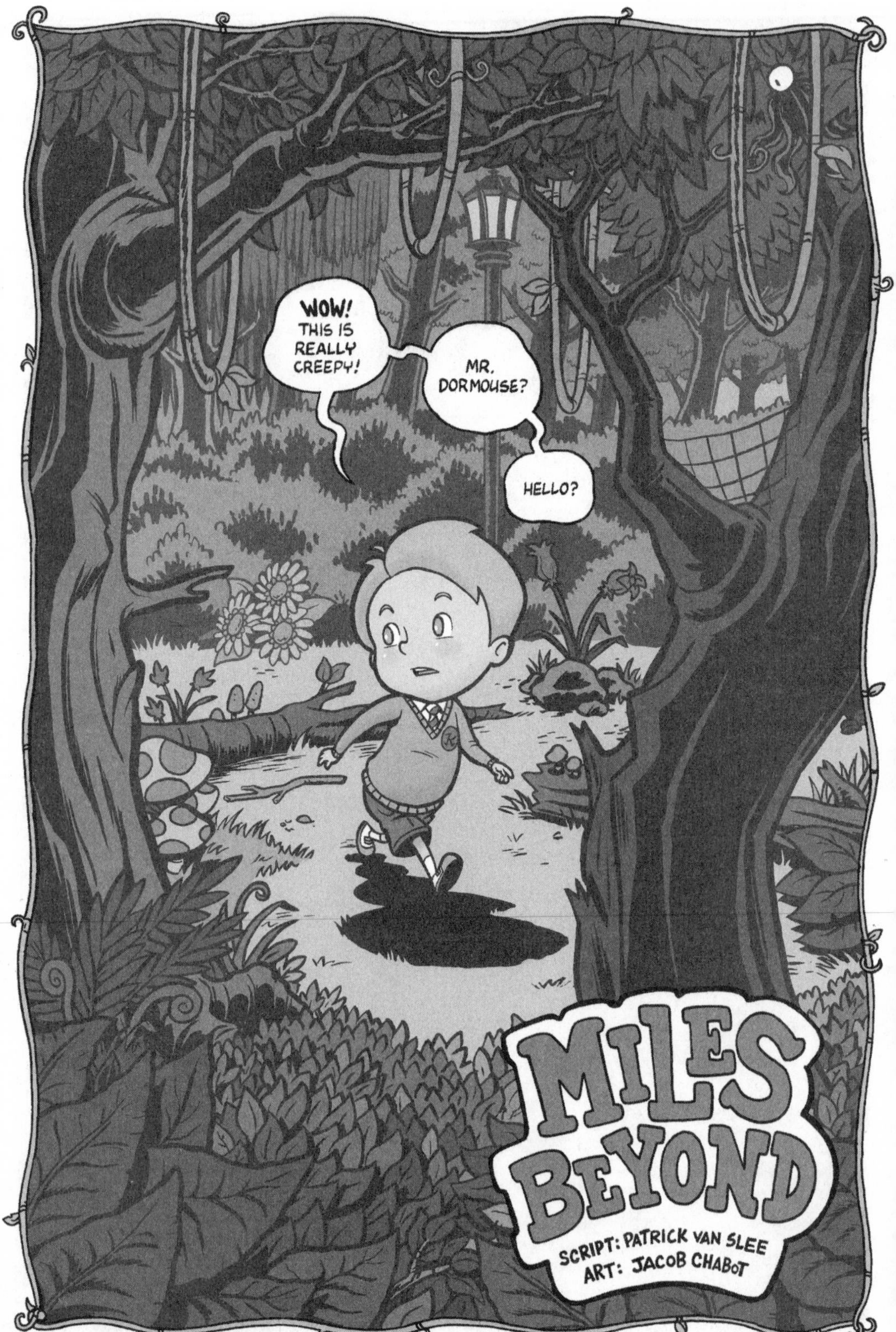
WOW! THIS IS REALLY CREEPY!
MR. DORMOUSE?
HELLO?
MILES BEYOND
SCRIPT: PATRICK VAN SLEE
ART: JACOB CHABOT

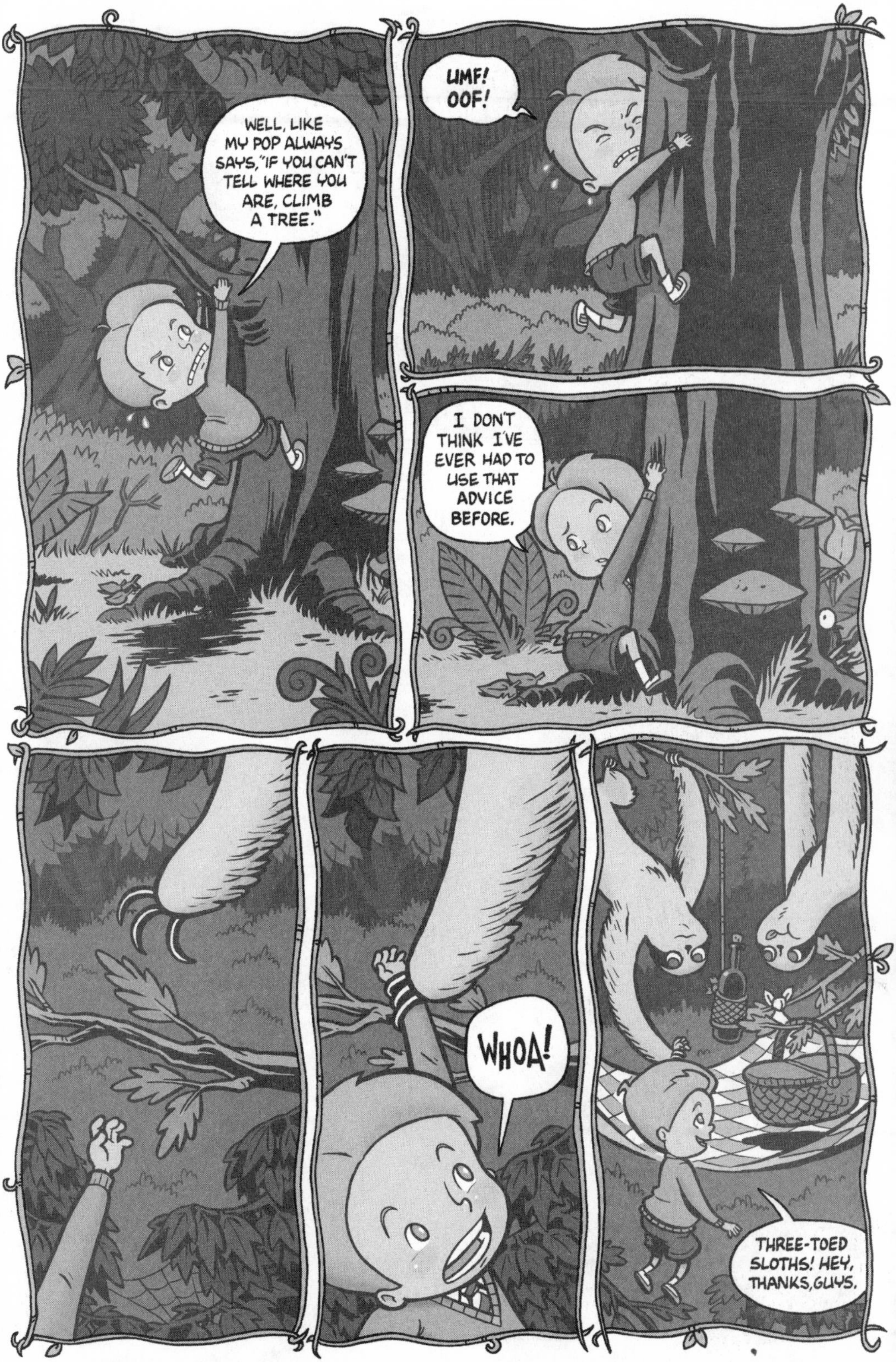
WELL, LIKE MY POP ALWAYS SAYS, "IF YOU CAN'T TELL WHERE YOU ARE, CLIMB A TREE."
UMF! OOF!
I DON'T THINK I'VE EVER HAD TO USE THAT ADVICE BEFORE.
WHOA!
THREE-TOED SLOTHS! HEY, THANKS, GUYS.

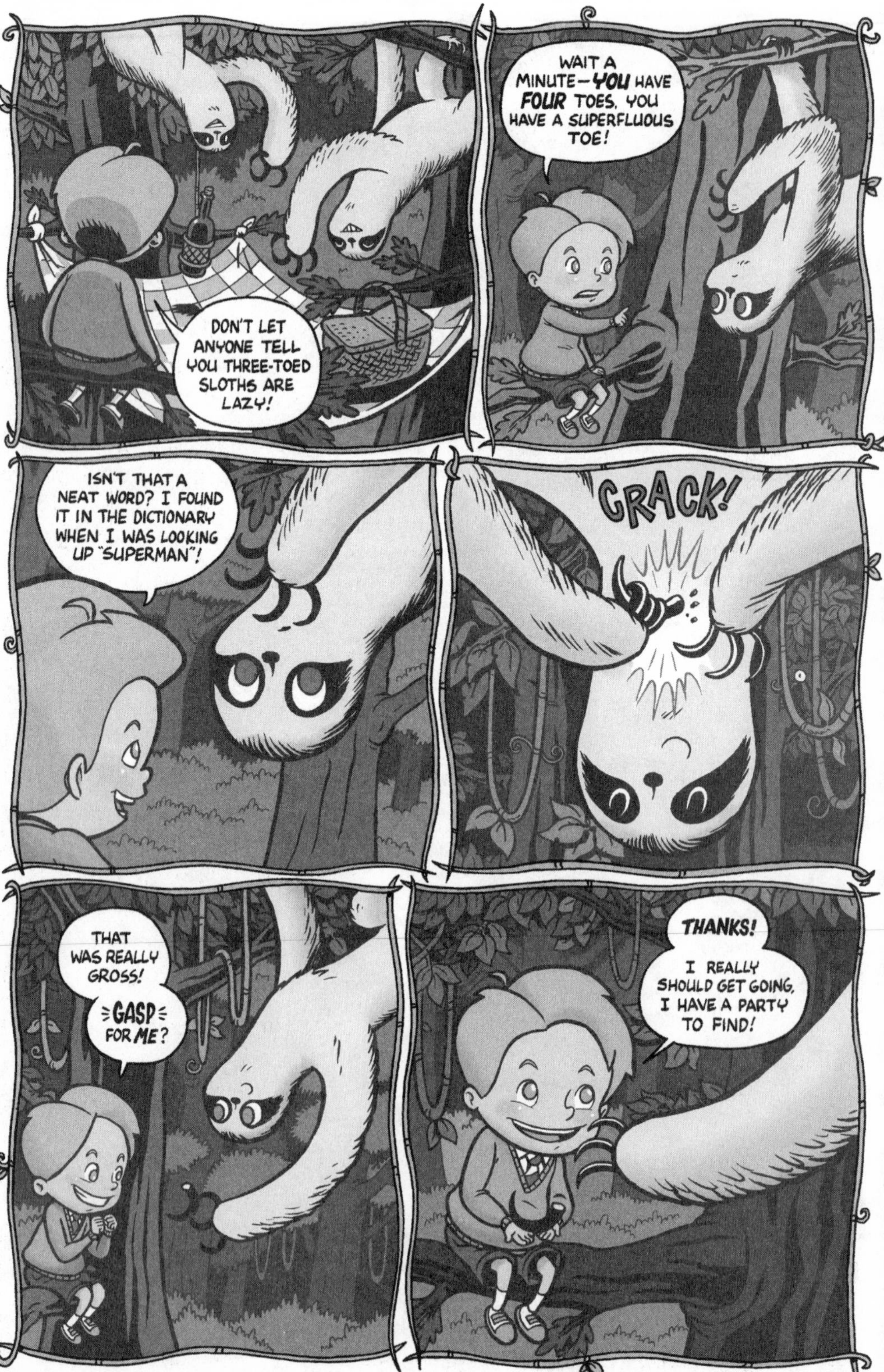
DON'T LET ANYONE TELL YOU THREE-TOED SLOTHS ARE LAZY!
WAIT A MINUTE—YOU HAVE FOUR TOES. YOU HAVE A SUPERFLUOUS TOE!
ISN'T THAT A NEAT WORD? I FOUND IT IN THE DICTIONARY WHEN I WAS LOOKING UP "SUPERMAN"!
CRACK!
THAT WAS REALLY GROSS!
GASP FOR ME?
THANKS!
I REALLY SHOULD GET GOING. I HAVE A PARTY TO FIND!

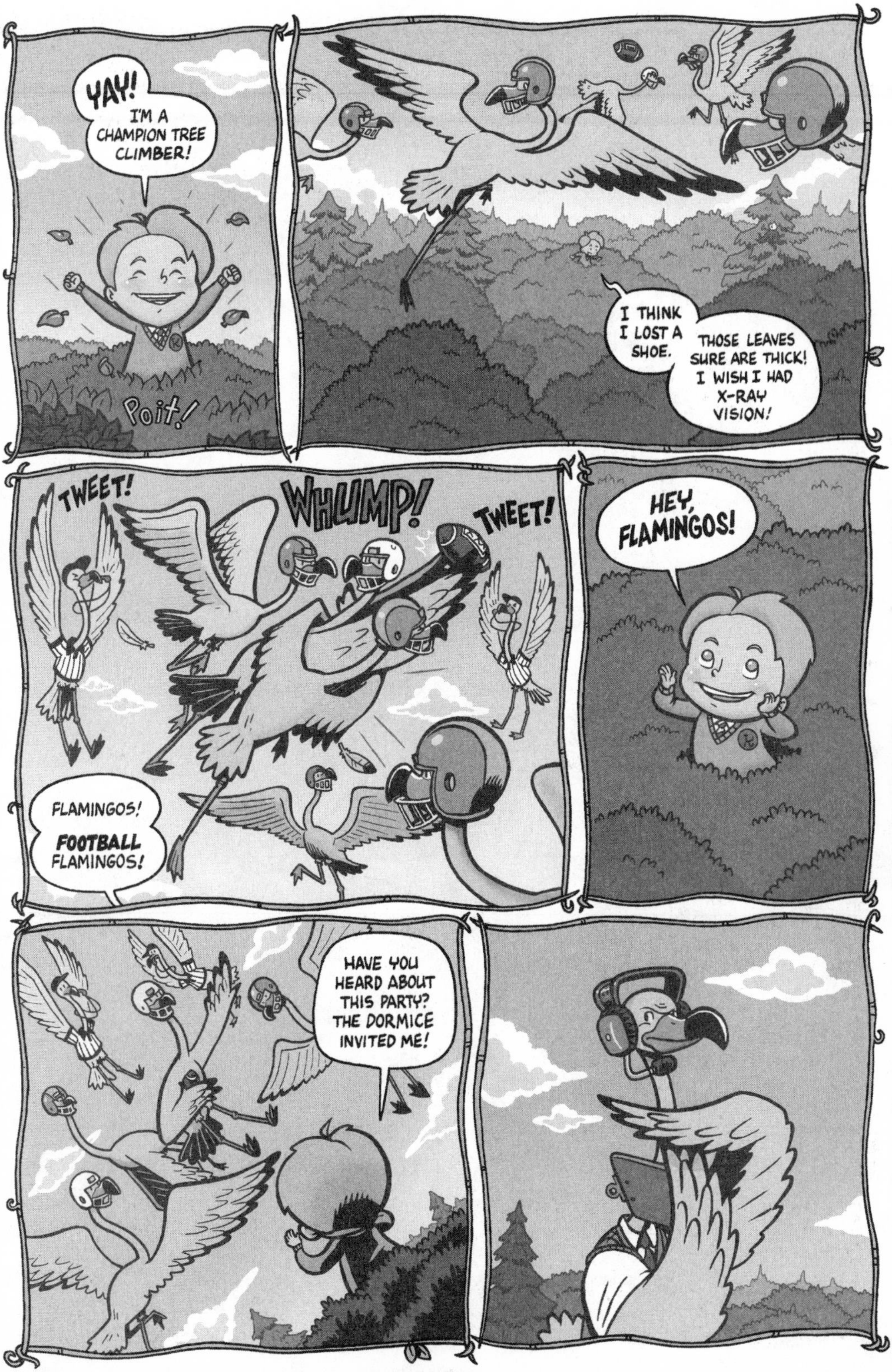
YAY!
I'M A CHAMPION TREE CLIMBER!
Poit!
I THINK I LOST A SHOE.
THOSE LEAVES SURE ARE THICK! I WISH I HAD X-RAY VISION!
TWEET!
WHUMP!
TWEET!
FLAMINGOS!
FOOTBALL FLAMINGOS!
HEY, FLAMINGOS!
HAVE YOU HEARD ABOUT THIS PARTY? THE DORMICE INVITED ME!

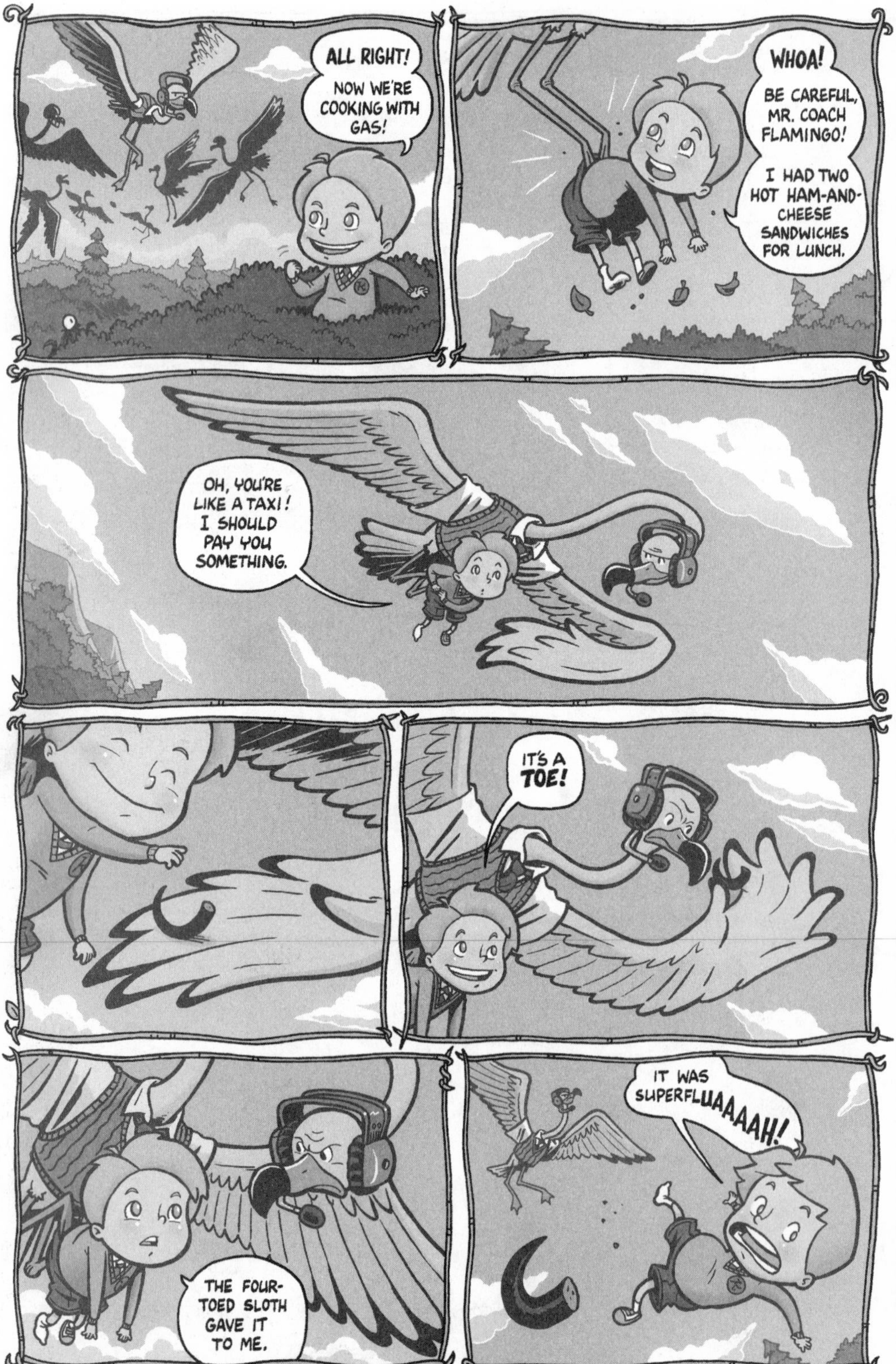
ALL RIGHT!
NOW WE'RE COOKING WITH GAS!
WHOA!
BE CAREFUL, MR. COACH FLAMINGO!
I HAD TWO HOT HAM-AND-CHEESE SANDWICHES FOR LUNCH.
OH, YOU'RE LIKE A TAXI! I SHOULD PAY YOU SOMETHING.
IT'S A TOE!
THE FOUR-TOED SLOTH GAVE IT TO ME.
IT WAS SUPERFLUAAAAH!

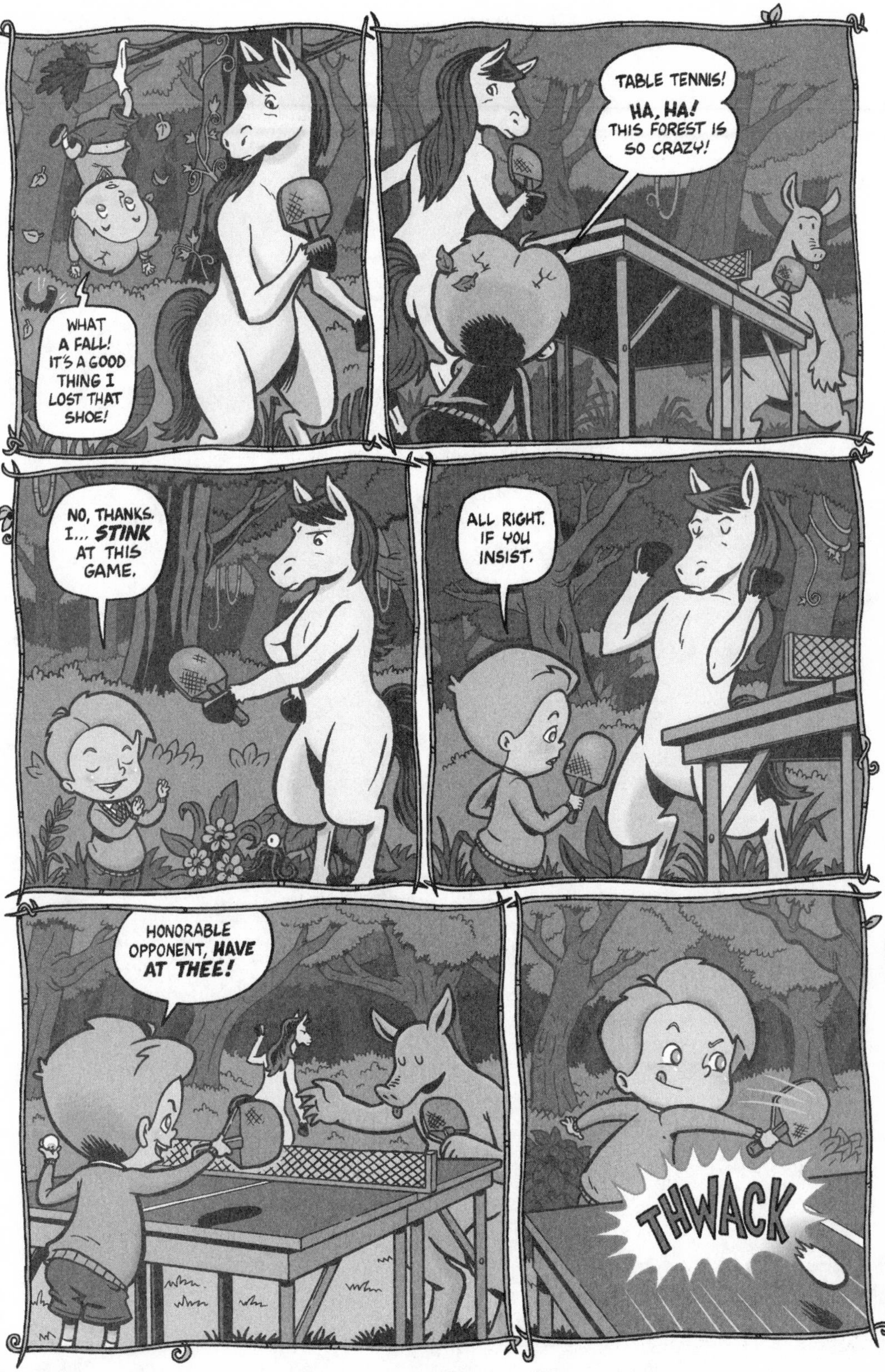
WHAT A FALL! IT'S A GOOD THING I LOST THAT SHOE!
TABLE TENNIS! HA, HA! THIS FOREST IS SO CRAZY!
NO, THANKS. I... STINK AT THIS GAME.
ALL RIGHT. IF YOU INSIST.
HONORABLE OPPONENT, HAVE AT THEE!
THWACK

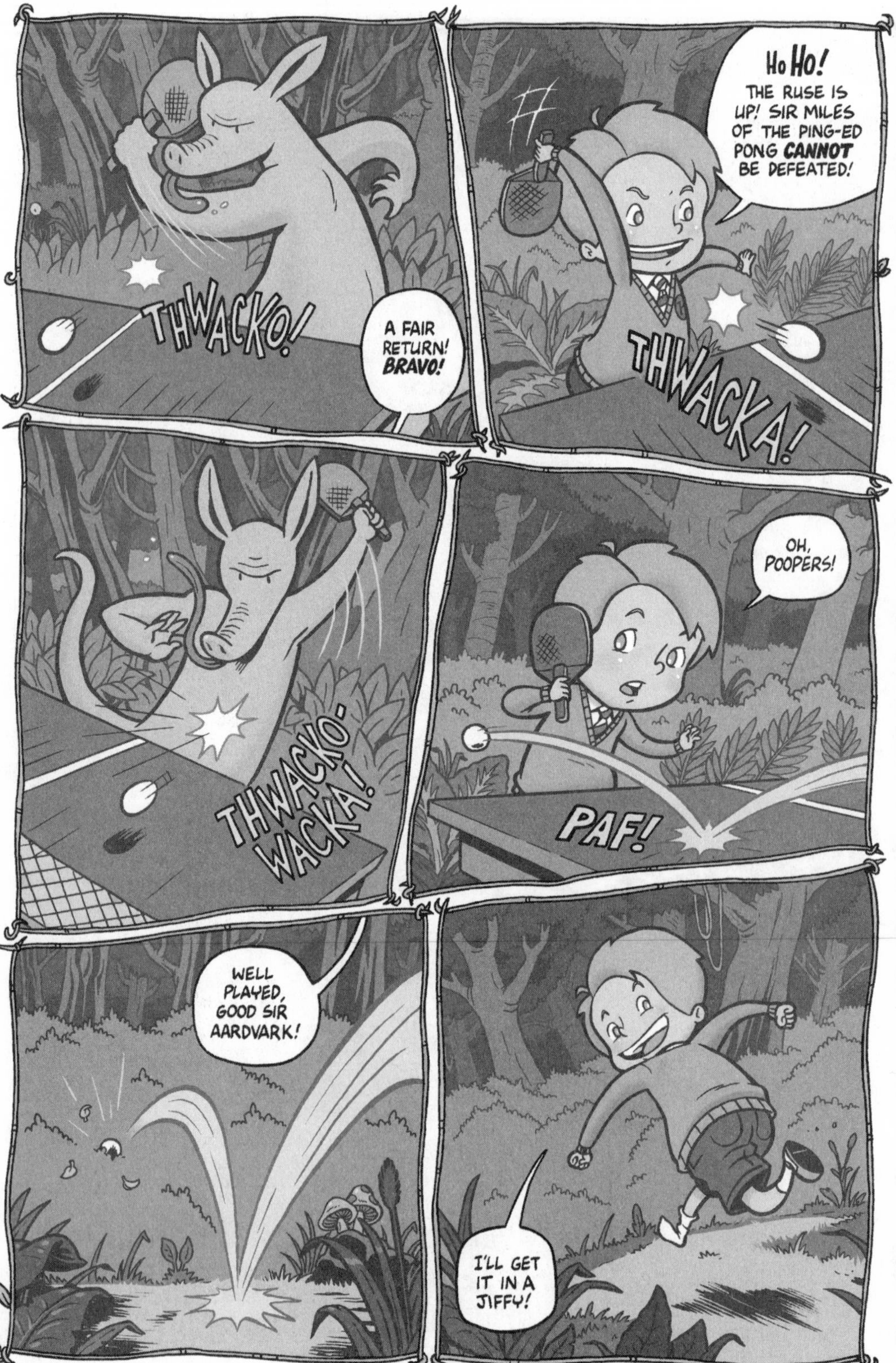
THWACKO!
A FAIR RETURN! BRAVO!
Ho Ho! THE RUSE IS UP! SIR MILES OF THE PING-ED PONG CANNOT BE DEFEATED!
THWACKA!
THWACKO-WACKA!
OH, POOPERS!
PAF!
WELL PLAYED, GOOD SIR AARDVARK!
I'LL GET IT IN A JIFFY!

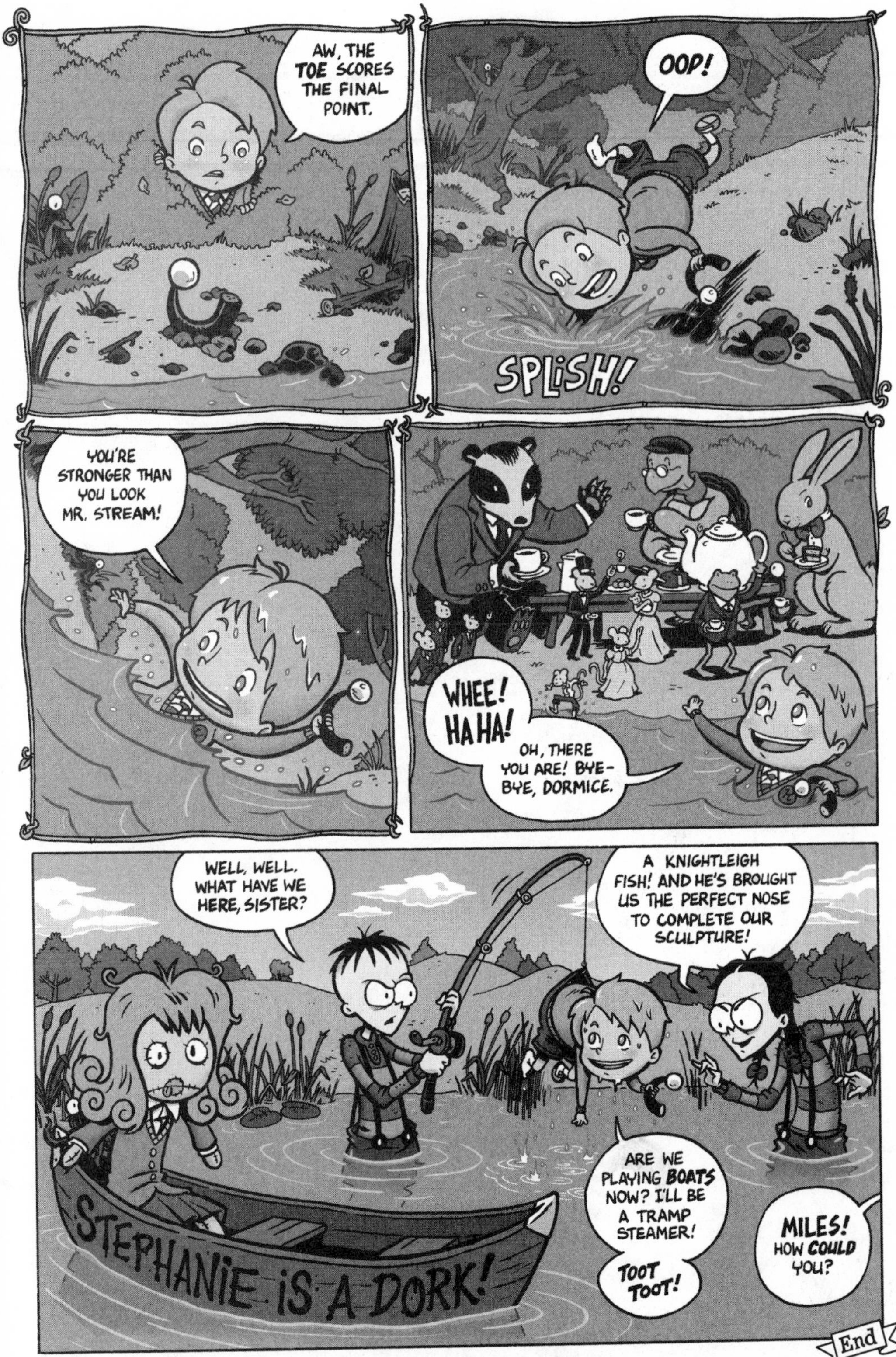
AW, THE TOE SCORES THE FINAL POINT.
OOP!
SPLISH!
YOU'RE STRONGER THAN YOU LOOK MR. STREAM!
WHEE! HAHA!
OH, THERE YOU ARE! BYE-BYE, DORMICE.
WELL, WELL. WHAT HAVE WE HERE, SISTER?
A KNIGHTLEIGH FISH! AND HE'S BROUGHT US THE PERFECT NOSE TO COMPLETE OUR SCULPTURE!
ARE WE PLAYING BOATS NOW? I'LL BE A TRAMP STEAMER!
TOOT TOOT!
MILES! HOW COULD YOU?
STEPHANIE IS A DORK!
End

HEIMERTZ vs. ~~ALIEN INVADERS!~~ LOVE

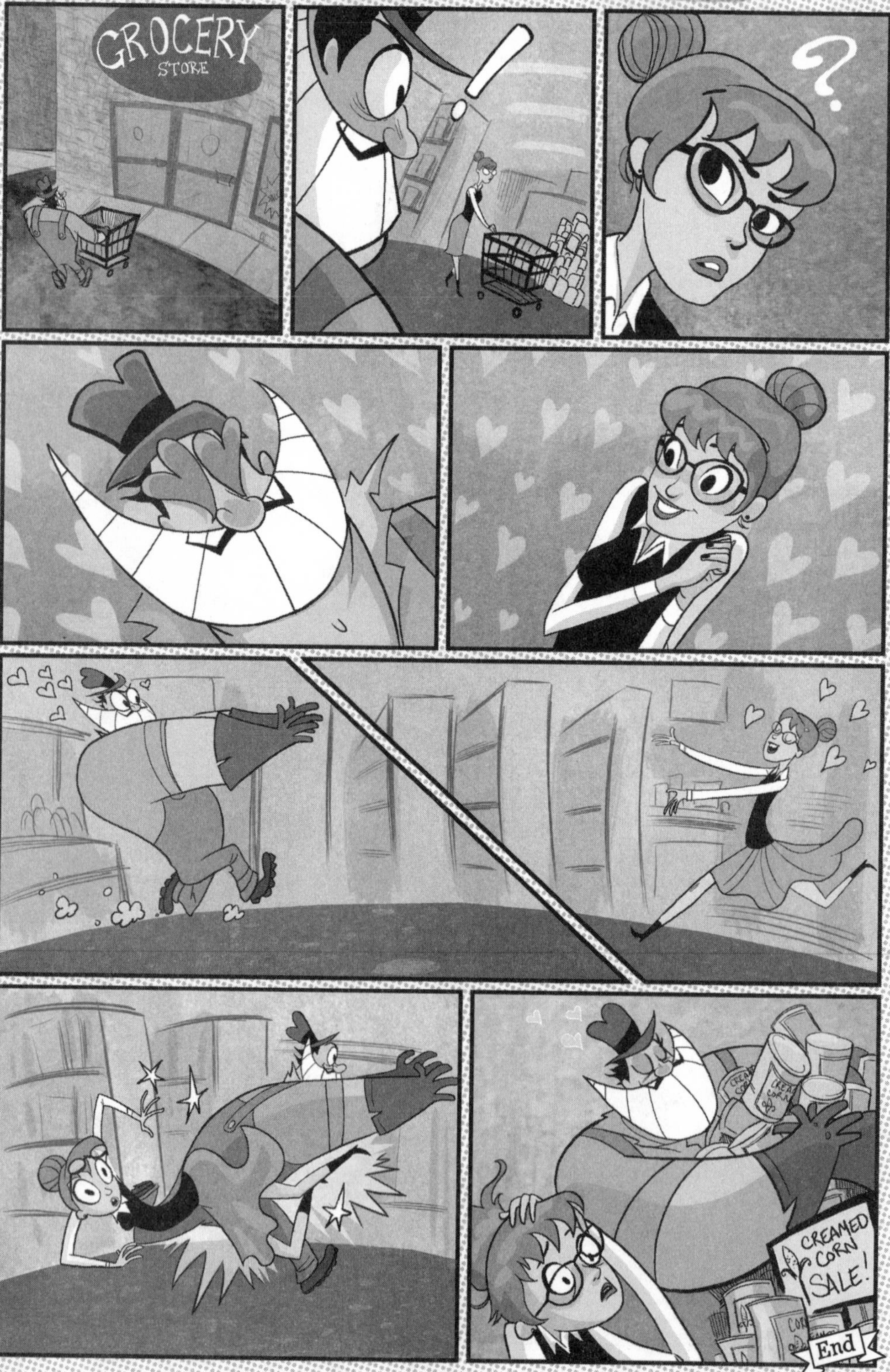
GROCERY
STORE
!
?
CREAMED CORN
CREAMED CORN SALE!
End

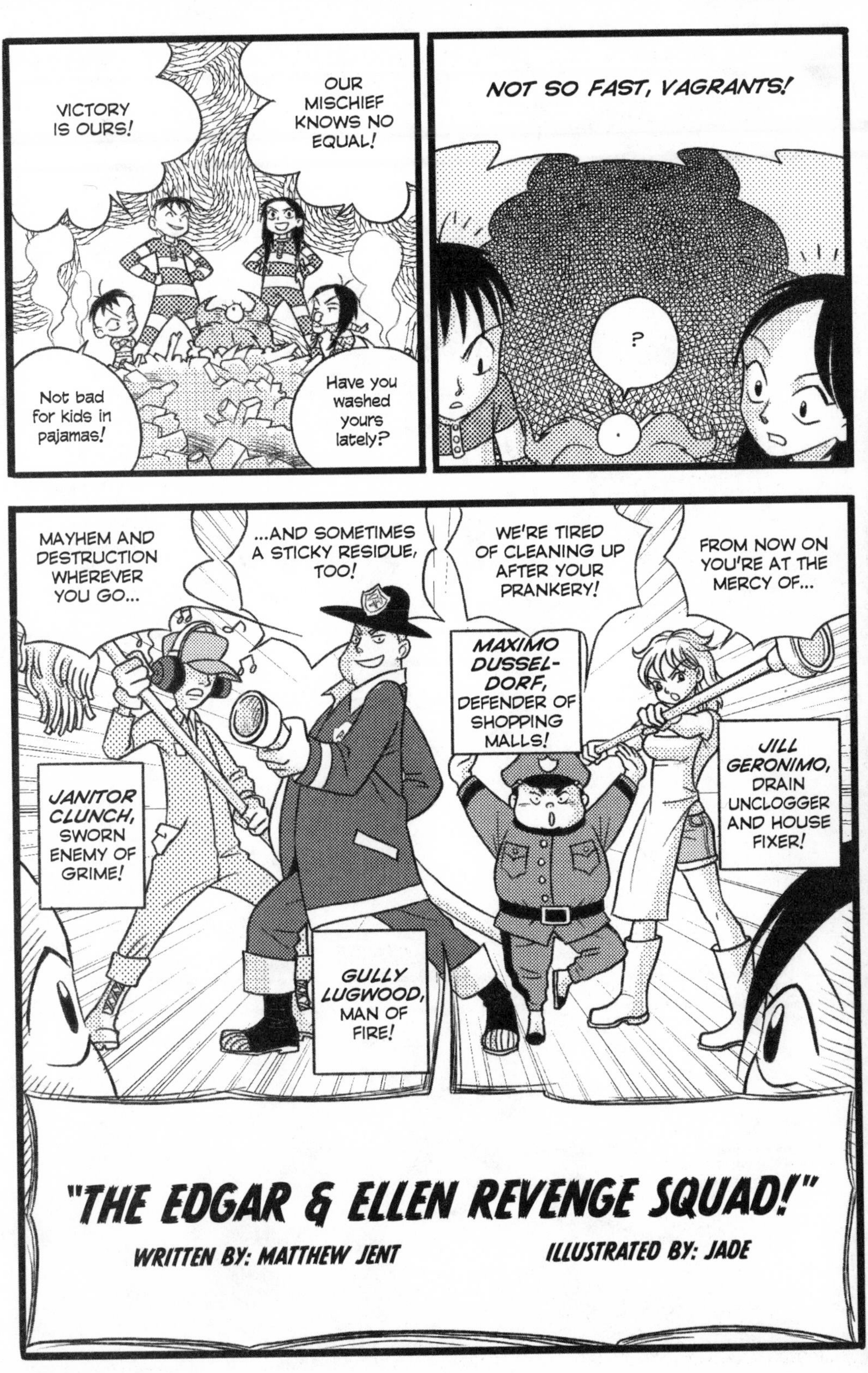
VICTORY IS OURS!
OUR MISCHIEF KNOWS NO EQUAL!
Not bad for kids in pajamas!
Have you washed yours lately?
NOT SO FAST, VAGRANTS!
?
MAYHEM AND DESTRUCTION WHEREVER YOU GO...
...AND SOMETIMES A STICKY RESIDUE, TOO!
WE'RE TIRED OF CLEANING UP AFTER YOUR PRANKERY!
FROM NOW ON YOU'RE AT THE MERCY OF...
JANITOR CLUNCH, SWORN ENEMY OF GRIME!
GULLY LUGWOOD, MAN OF FIRE!
MAXIMO DUSSEL-DORF, DEFENDER OF SHOPPING MALLS!
JILL GERONIMO, DRAIN UNCLOGGER AND HOUSE FIXER!
"THE EDGAR & ELLEN REVENGE SQUAD!"
WRITTEN BY: MATTHEW JENT
ILLUSTRATED BY: JADE

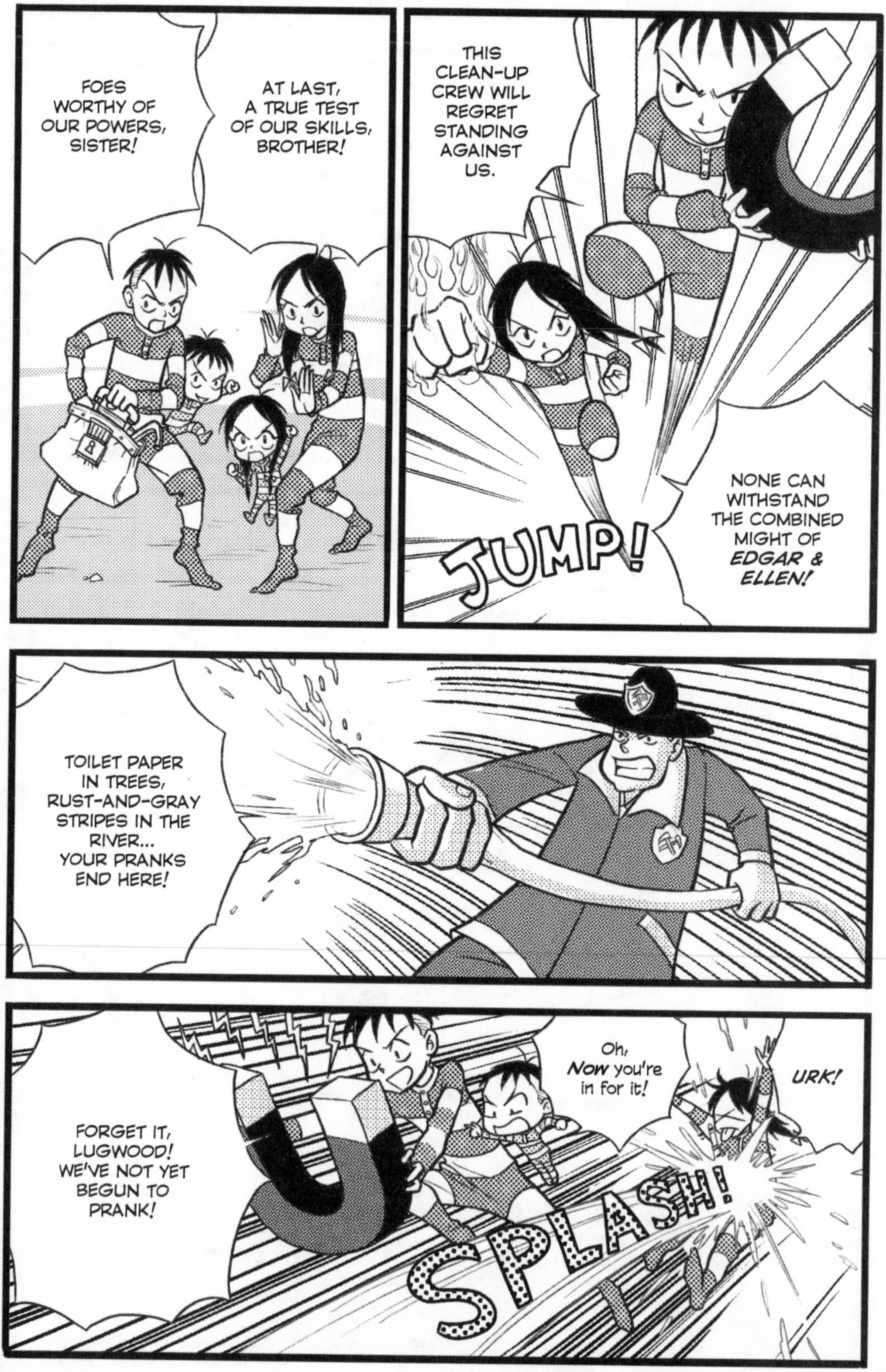
FOES WORTHY OF OUR POWERS, SISTER!
AT LAST, A TRUE TEST OF OUR SKILLS, BROTHER!
THIS CLEAN-UP CREW WILL REGRET STANDING AGAINST US.
JUMP!
NONE CAN WITHSTAND THE COMBINED MIGHT OF EDGAR & ELLEN!
TOILET PAPER IN TREES, RUST-AND-GRAY STRIPES IN THE RIVER... YOUR PRANKS END HERE!
FORGET IT, LUGWOOD! WE'VE NOT YET BEGUN TO PRANK!
Oh, Now you're in for it!
URK!
SPLASH!

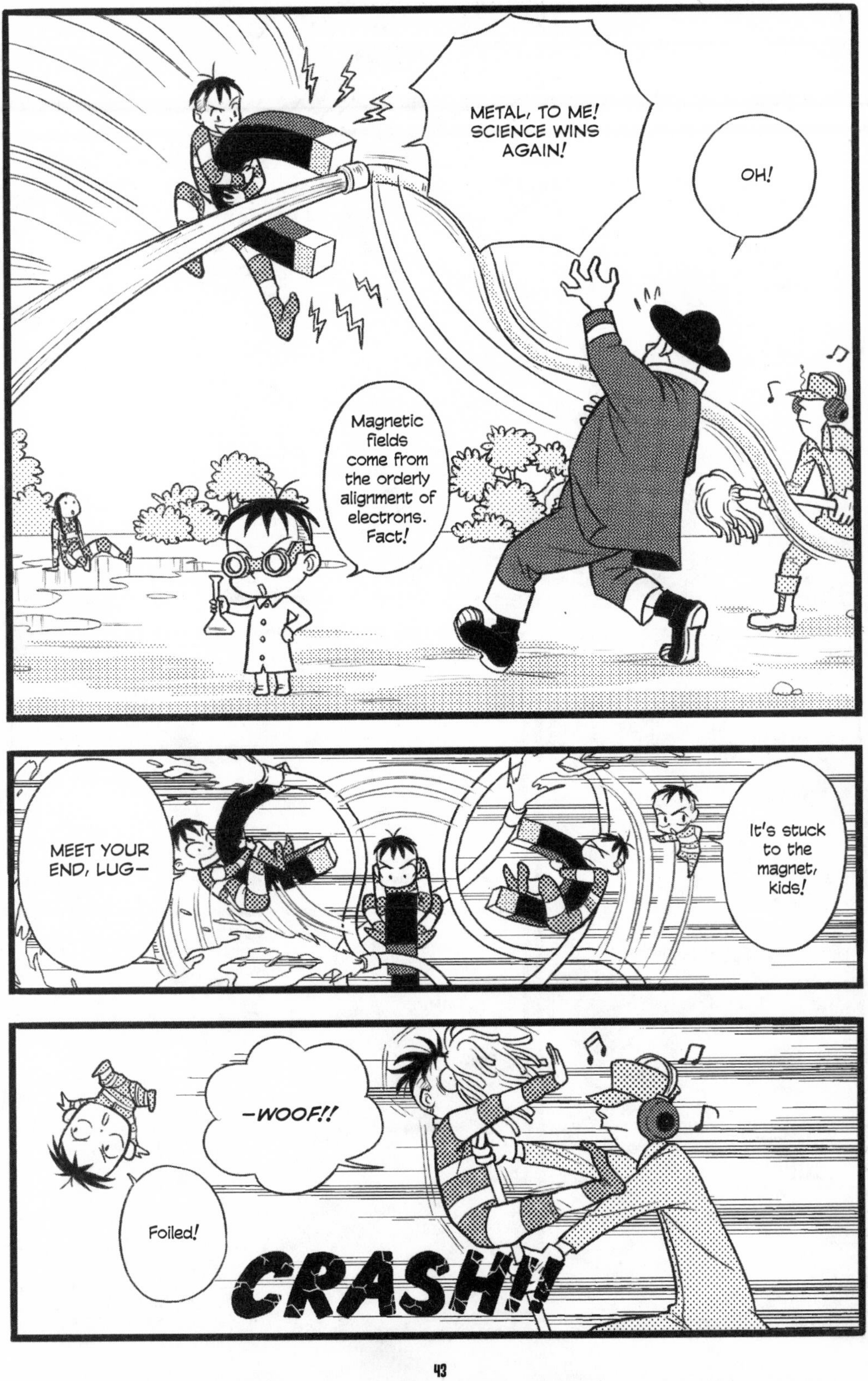
METAL, TO ME! SCIENCE WINS AGAIN!
OH!
Magnetic fields come from the orderly alignment of electrons. Fact!
MEET YOUR END, LUG—
It's stuck to the magnet, kids!
—WOOF!!
Foiled!
CRASH!!

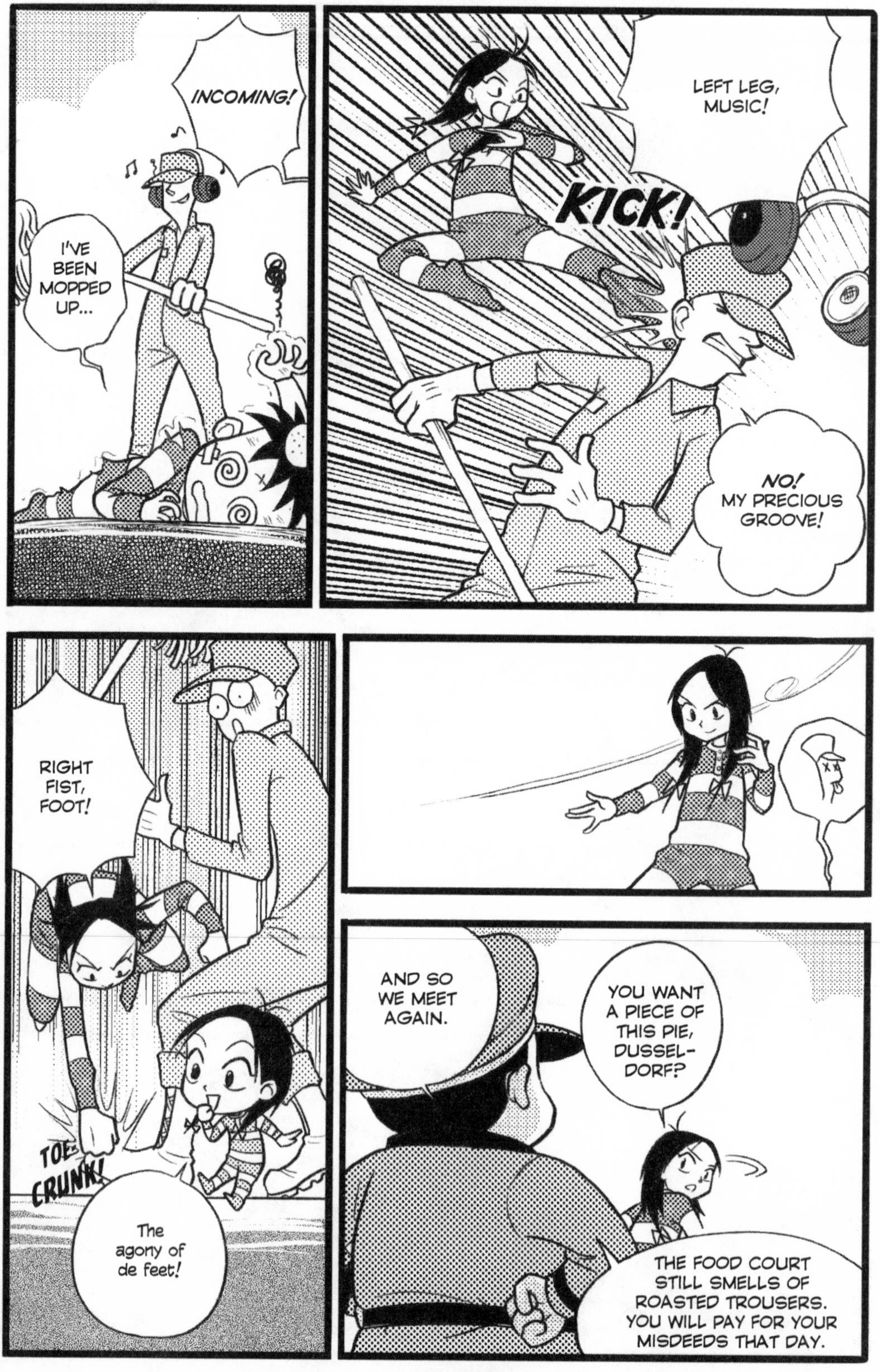
INCOMING!
I'VE BEEN MOPPED UP...
LEFT LEG, MUSIC!
KICK!
NO! MY PRECIOUS GROOVE!
RIGHT FIST, FOOT!
TOE-CRUNK!
The agony of de feet!
AND SO WE MEET AGAIN.
YOU WANT A PIECE OF THIS PIE, DUSSEL-DORF?
THE FOOD COURT STILL SMELLS OF ROASTED TROUSERS. YOU WILL PAY FOR YOUR MISDEEDS THAT DAY.

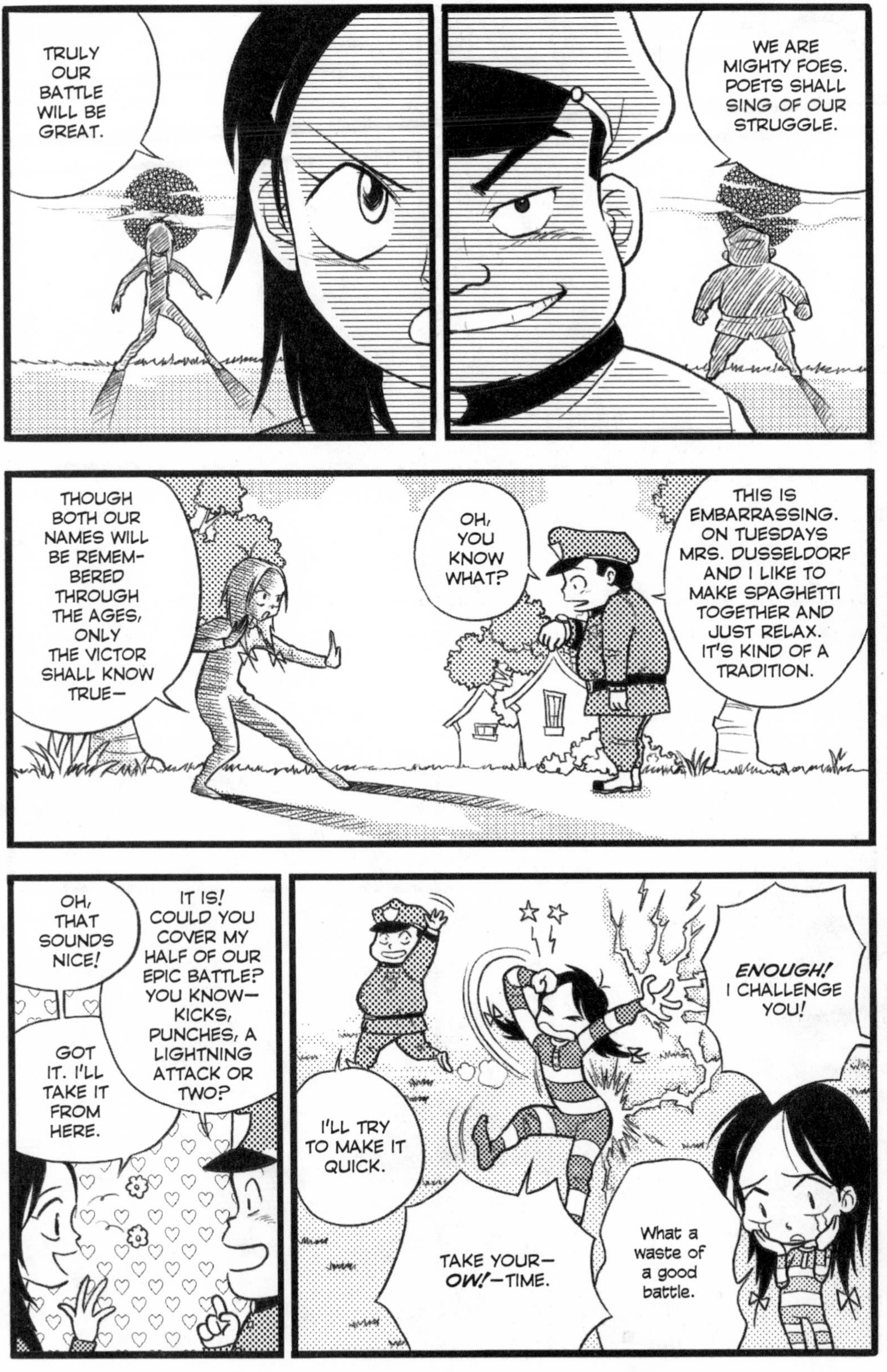
TRULY OUR BATTLE WILL BE GREAT.
WE ARE MIGHTY FOES. POETS SHALL SING OF OUR STRUGGLE.
THOUGH BOTH OUR NAMES WILL BE REMEMBERED THROUGH THE AGES, ONLY THE VICTOR SHALL KNOW TRUE—
OH, YOU KNOW WHAT?
THIS IS EMBARRASSING. ON TUESDAYS MRS. DUSSELDORF AND I LIKE TO MAKE SPAGHETTI TOGETHER AND JUST RELAX. IT'S KIND OF A TRADITION.
OH, THAT SOUNDS NICE!
IT IS! COULD YOU COVER MY HALF OF OUR EPIC BATTLE? YOU KNOW— KICKS, PUNCHES, A LIGHTNING ATTACK OR TWO?
GOT IT. I'LL TAKE IT FROM HERE.
ENOUGH! I CHALLENGE YOU!
I'LL TRY TO MAKE IT QUICK.
TAKE YOUR— OW!—TIME.
What a waste of a good battle.

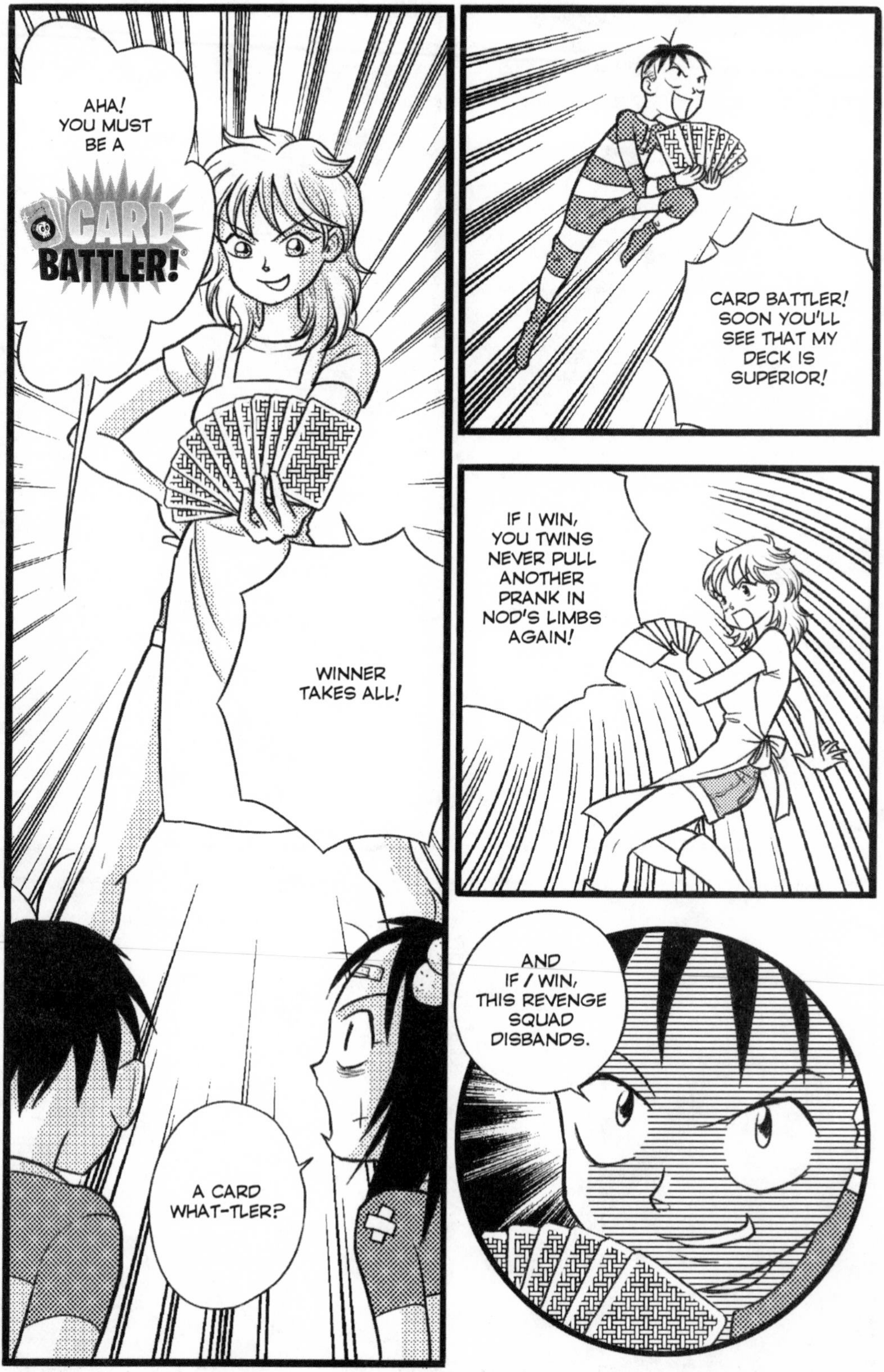
AHA! YOU MUST BE A
CARD BATTLER!
CARD BATTLER! SOON YOU'LL SEE THAT MY DECK IS SUPERIOR!
WINNER TAKES ALL!
IF I WIN, YOU TWINS NEVER PULL ANOTHER PRANK IN NOD'S LIMBS AGAIN!
A CARD WHAT-TLER?
AND IF I WIN, THIS REVENGE SQUAD DISBANDS.

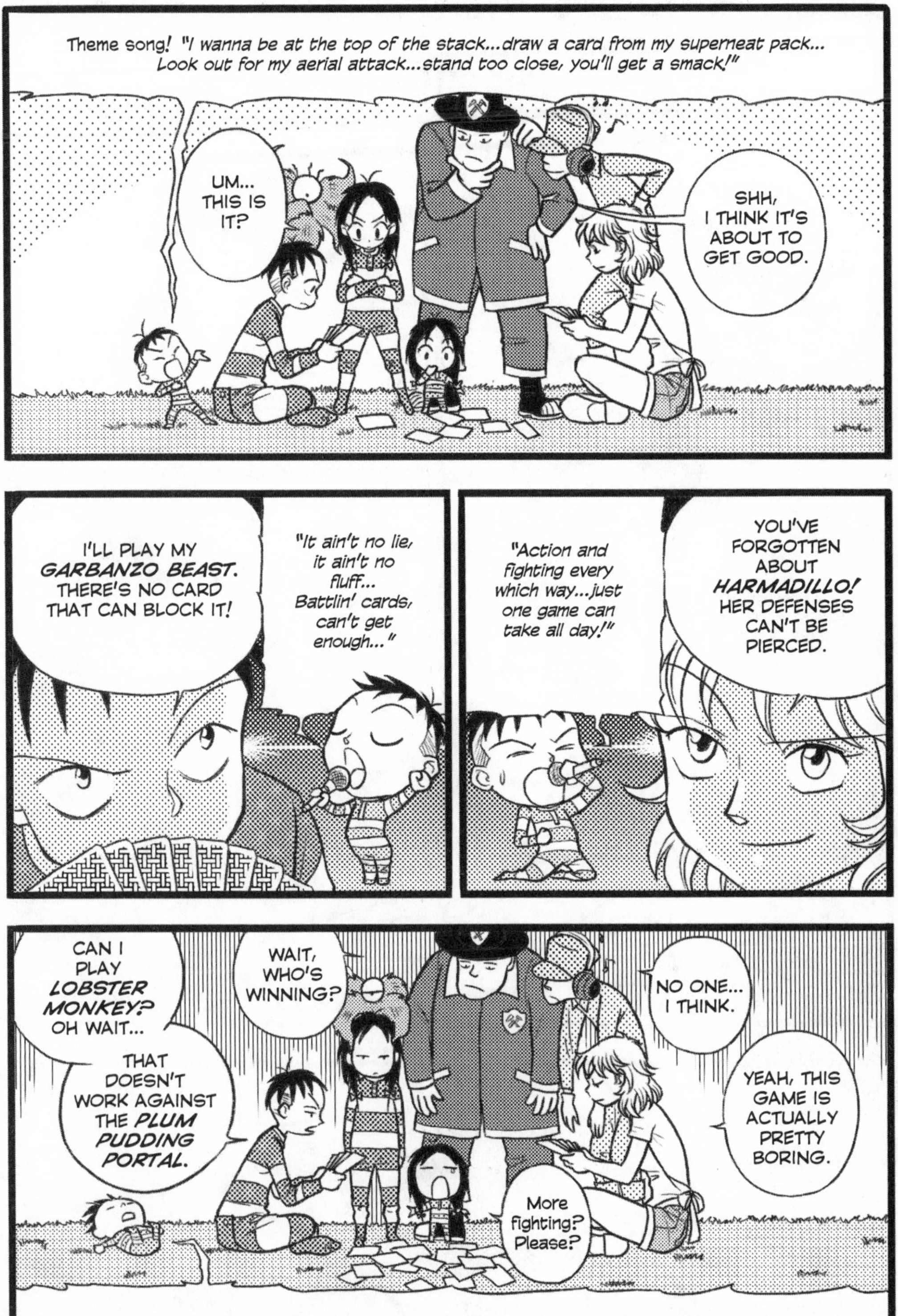
Theme song! "I wanna be at the top of the stack...draw a card from my supermeat pack... Look out for my aerial attack...stand too close, you'll get a smack!"
UM... THIS IS IT?
SHH, I THINK IT'S ABOUT TO GET GOOD.
I'LL PLAY MY *GARBANZO BEAST*. THERE'S NO CARD THAT CAN BLOCK IT!
"It ain't no lie, it ain't no fluff... Battlin' cards, can't get enough..."
"Action and fighting every which way...just one game can take all day!"
YOU'VE FORGOTTEN ABOUT *HARMADILLO!* HER DEFENSES CAN'T BE PIERCED.
CAN I PLAY *LOBSTER MONKEY?* OH WAIT...
THAT DOESN'T WORK AGAINST THE *PLUM PUDDING PORTAL*.
WAIT, WHO'S WINNING?
NO ONE... I THINK.
YEAH, THIS GAME IS ACTUALLY PRETTY BORING.
More fighting? Please?
"Card Battlers! Fight with cards!"

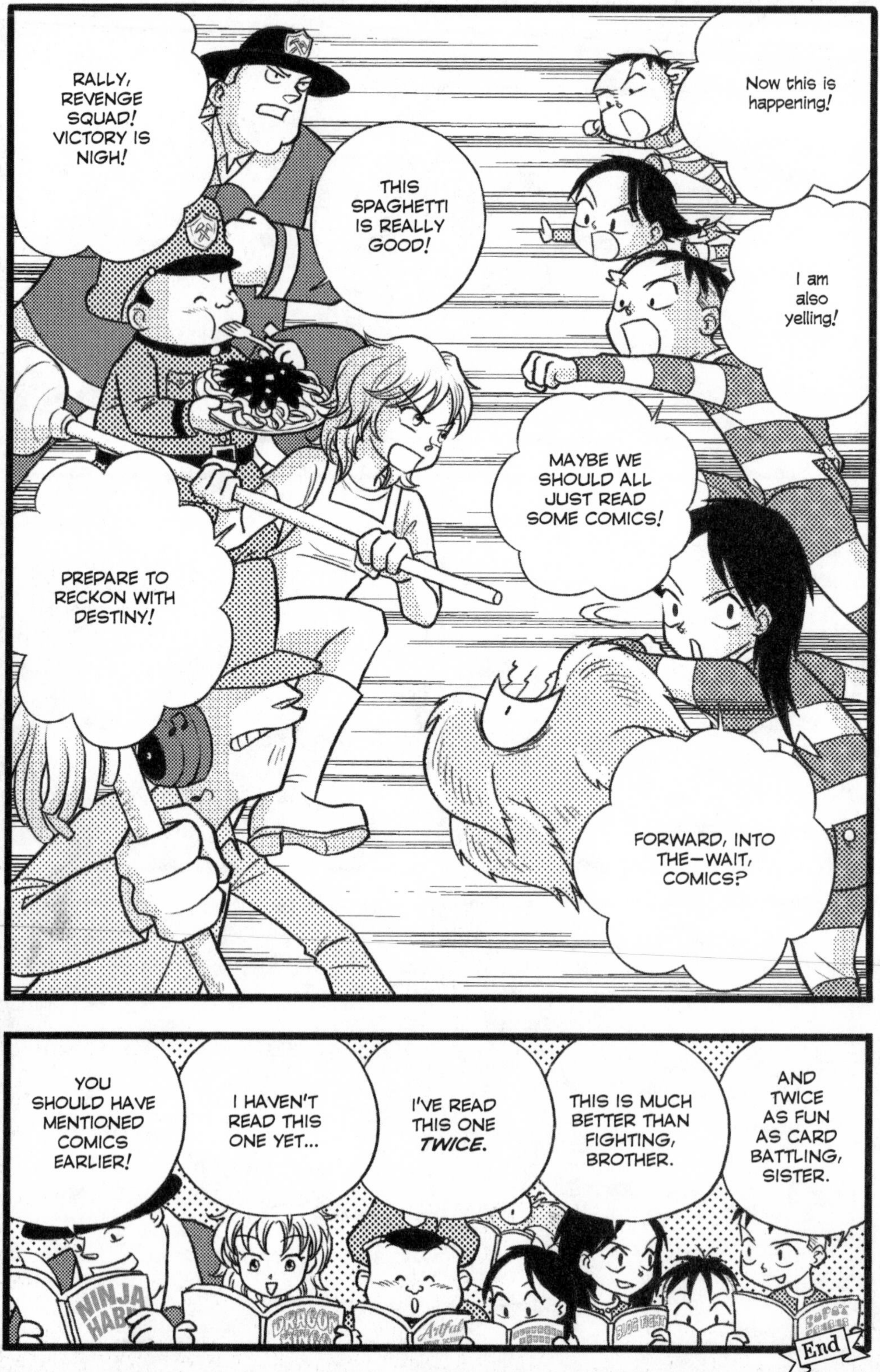

RALLY, REVENGE SQUAD! VICTORY IS NIGH!
Now this is happening!
THIS SPAGHETTI IS REALLY GOOD!
I am also yelling!
MAYBE WE SHOULD ALL JUST READ SOME COMICS!
PREPARE TO RECKON WITH DESTINY!
FORWARD, INTO THE—WAIT, COMICS?
YOU SHOULD HAVE MENTIONED COMICS EARLIER!
I HAVEN'T READ THIS ONE YET...
I'VE READ THIS ONE *TWICE*.
THIS IS MUCH BETTER THAN FIGHTING, BROTHER.
AND TWICE AS FUN AS CARD BATTLING, SISTER.
End

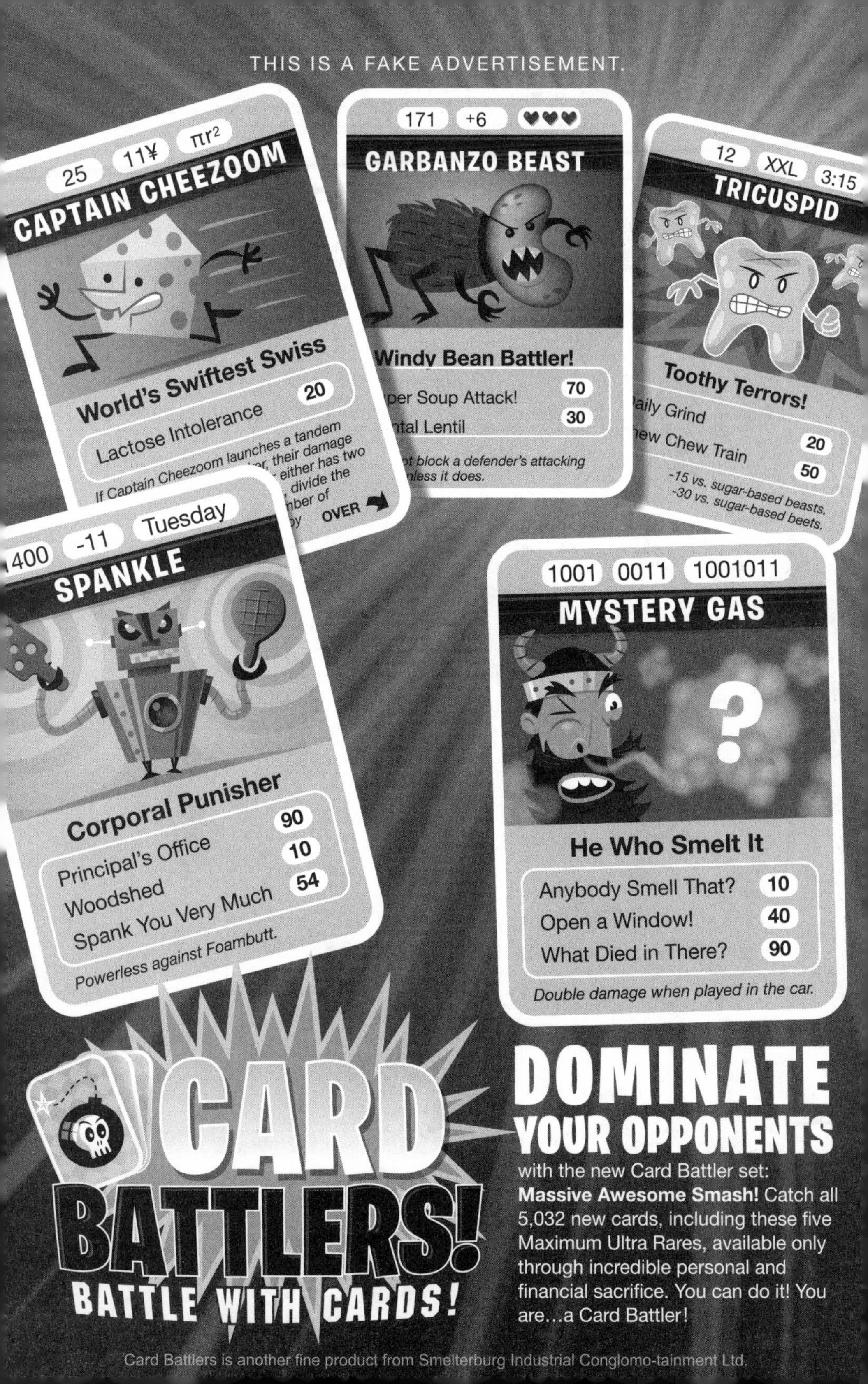

THIS IS A FAKE ADVERTISEMENT.
25 11¥ πr²
CAPTAIN CHEEZOOM
World's Swiftest Swiss
Lactose Intolerance 20
If Captain Cheezoom launches a tandem
their damage
either has two
divide the
OVER
171 +6
GARBANZO BEAST
Windy Bean Battler!
Soup Attack! 70
Lentil 30
block a defender's attacking
it does.
12 XXL 3:15
TRICUSPID
Toothy Terrors!
Grind
Chew Train 20
50
-15 vs. sugar-based beasts.
-30 vs. sugar-based beets.
400 -11 Tuesday
SPANKLE
Corporal Punisher
Principal's Office 90
Woodshed 10
Spank You Very Much 54
Powerless against Foambutt.
1001 0011 1001011
MYSTERY GAS
?
He Who Smelt It
Anybody Smell That? 10
Open a Window! 40
What Died in There? 90
Double damage when played in the car.
CARD BATTLERS!
BATTLE WITH CARDS!
DOMINATE YOUR OPPONENTS
with the new Card Battler set: Massive Awesome Smash! Catch all 5,032 new cards, including these five Maximum Ultra Rares, available only through incredible personal and financial sacrifice. You can do it! You are…a Card Battler!
Card Battlers is another fine product from Smelterburg Industrial Conglomo-tainment Ltd.

HEIMERTZ vs. the ~~HYDRA!~~ DINNER

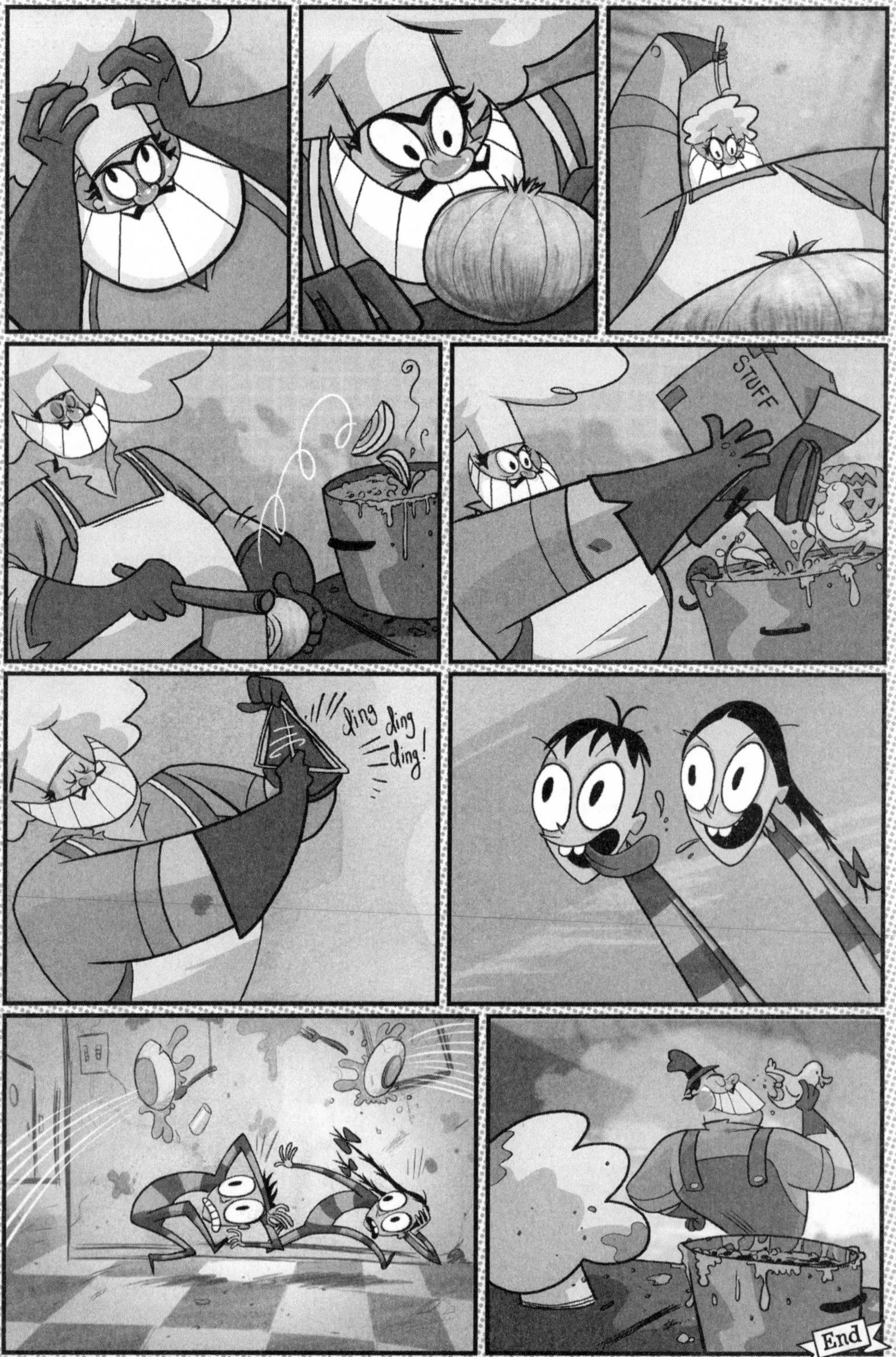
STUFF
ding ding ding!
End

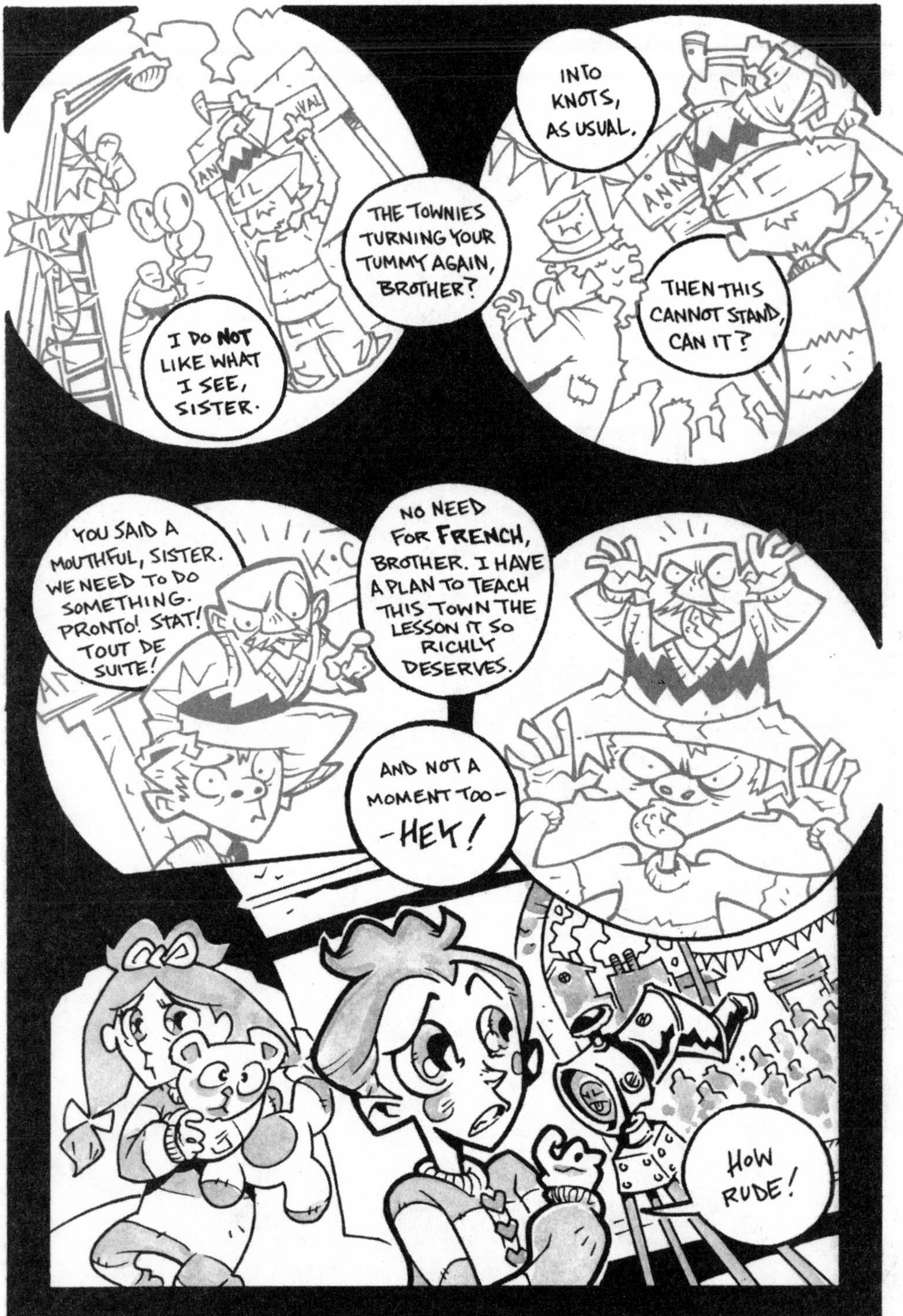
I DO NOT LIKE WHAT I SEE, SISTER.
THE TOWNIES TURNING YOUR TUMMY AGAIN, BROTHER?
INTO KNOTS, AS USUAL.
THEN THIS CANNOT STAND, CAN IT?
YOU SAID A MOUTHFUL, SISTER. WE NEED TO DO SOMETHING. PRONTO! STAT! TOUT DE SUITE!
NO NEED FOR FRENCH, BROTHER. I HAVE A PLAN TO TEACH THIS TOWN THE LESSON IT SO RICHLY DESERVES.
AND NOT A MOMENT TOO--HEY!
HOW RUDE!

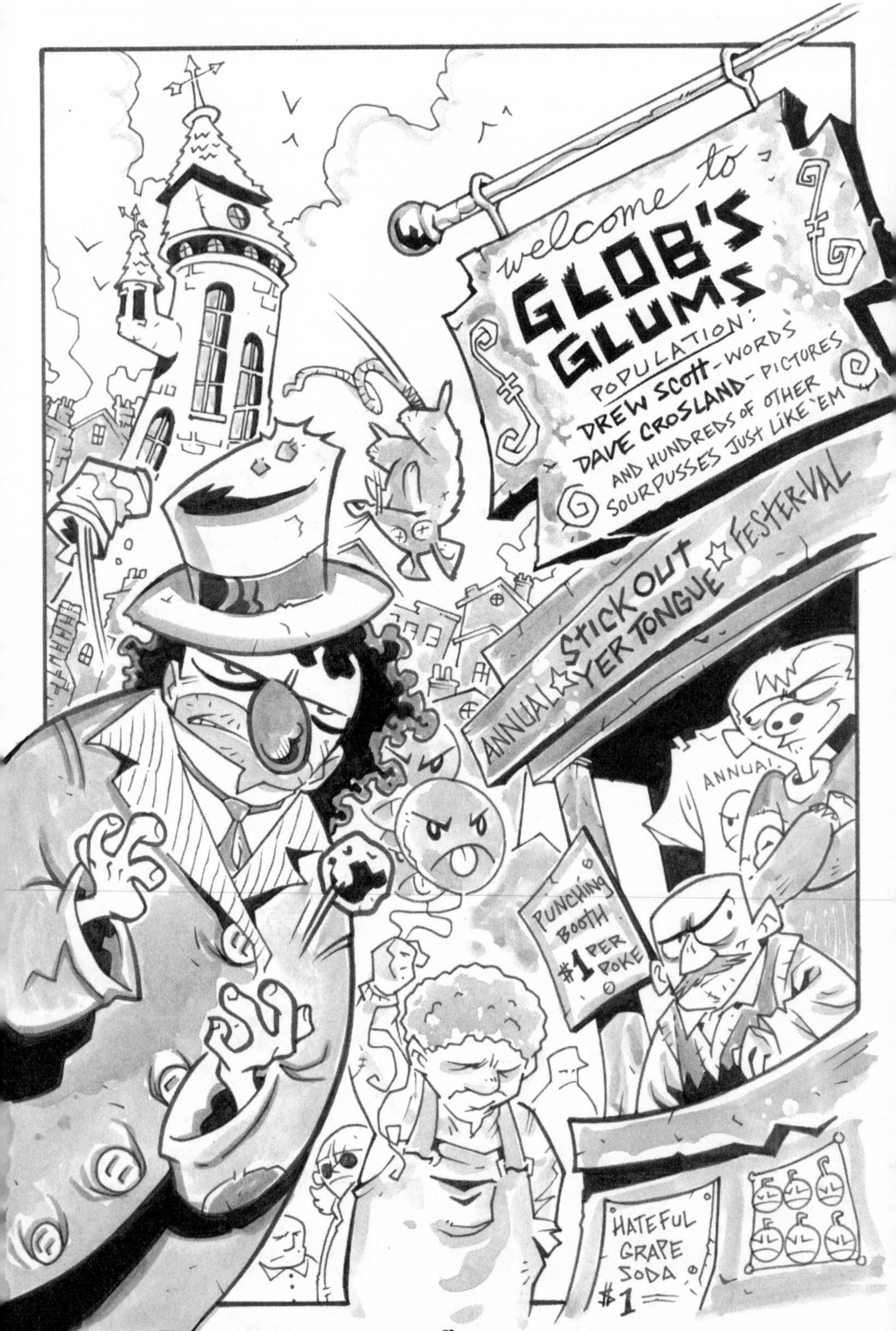

welcome to
GLOB'S GLUMS
POPULATION:
DREW SCOTT - WORDS
DAVE CROSLAND - PICTURES
AND HUNDREDS OF OTHER SOURPUSSES JUST LIKE 'EM
ANNUAL ☆ STICK OUT YER TONGUE ☆ FESTER-VAL
ANNUAL
PUNCHING BOOTH $1 PER POKE
HATEFUL GRAPE SODA $1

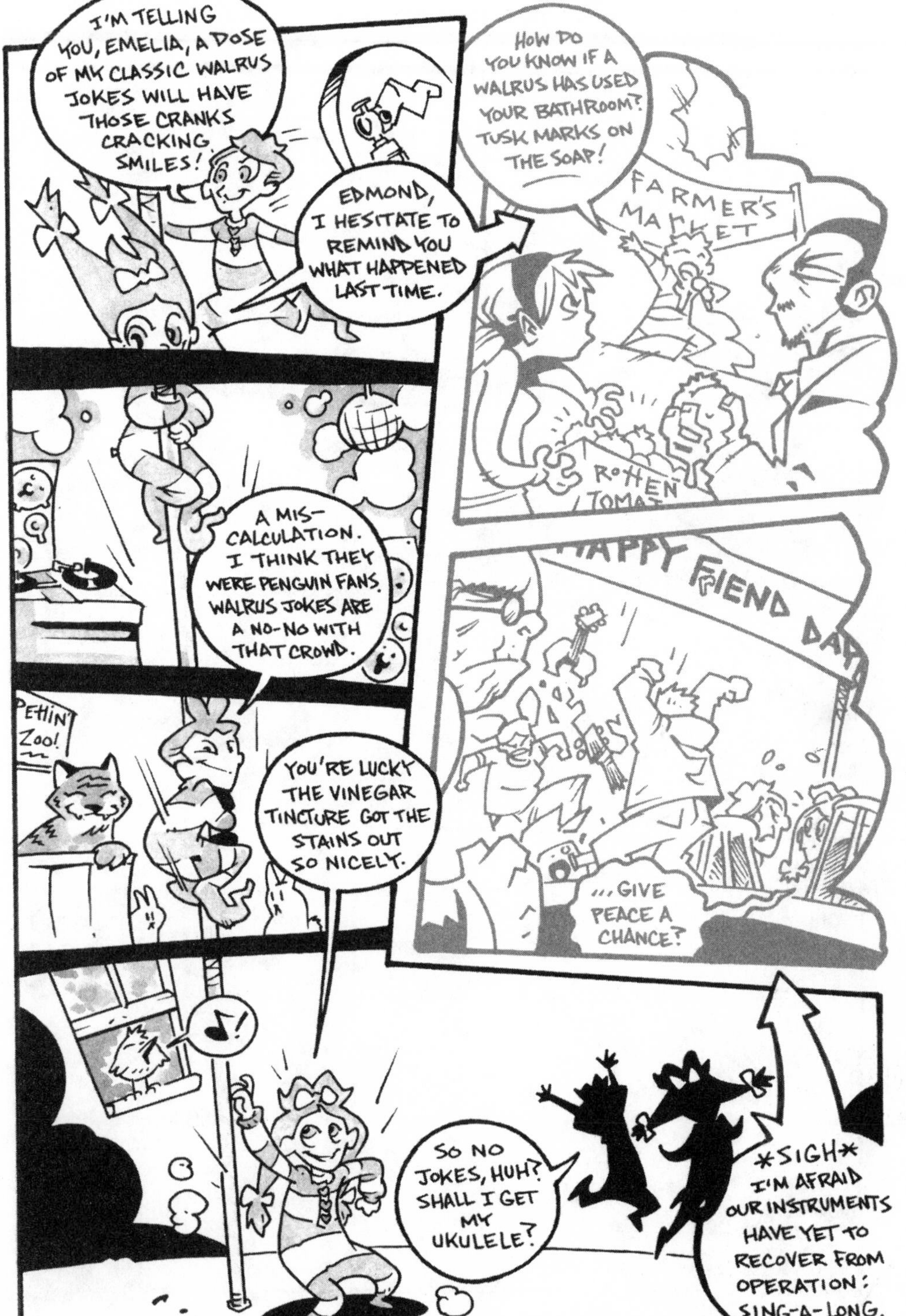

I'M TELLING YOU, EMELIA, A DOSE OF MY CLASSIC WALRUS JOKES WILL HAVE THOSE CRANKS CRACKING SMILES!
EDMOND, I HESITATE TO REMIND YOU WHAT HAPPENED LAST TIME.
HOW DO YOU KNOW IF A WALRUS HAS USED YOUR BATHROOM? TUSK MARKS ON THE SOAP!
FARMER'S MARKET
ROTTEN TOMA
A MIS-CALCULATION. I THINK THEY WERE PENGUIN FANS. WALRUS JOKES ARE A NO-NO WITH THAT CROWD.
PETTIN' ZOO!
HAPPY FIEND DA
YOU'RE LUCKY THE VINEGAR TINCTURE GOT THE STAINS OUT SO NICELY.
...GIVE PEACE A CHANCE?
SO NO JOKES, HUH? SHALL I GET MY UKULELE?
SIGH I'M AFRAID OUR INSTRUMENTS HAVE YET TO RECOVER FROM OPERATION: SING-A-LONG.

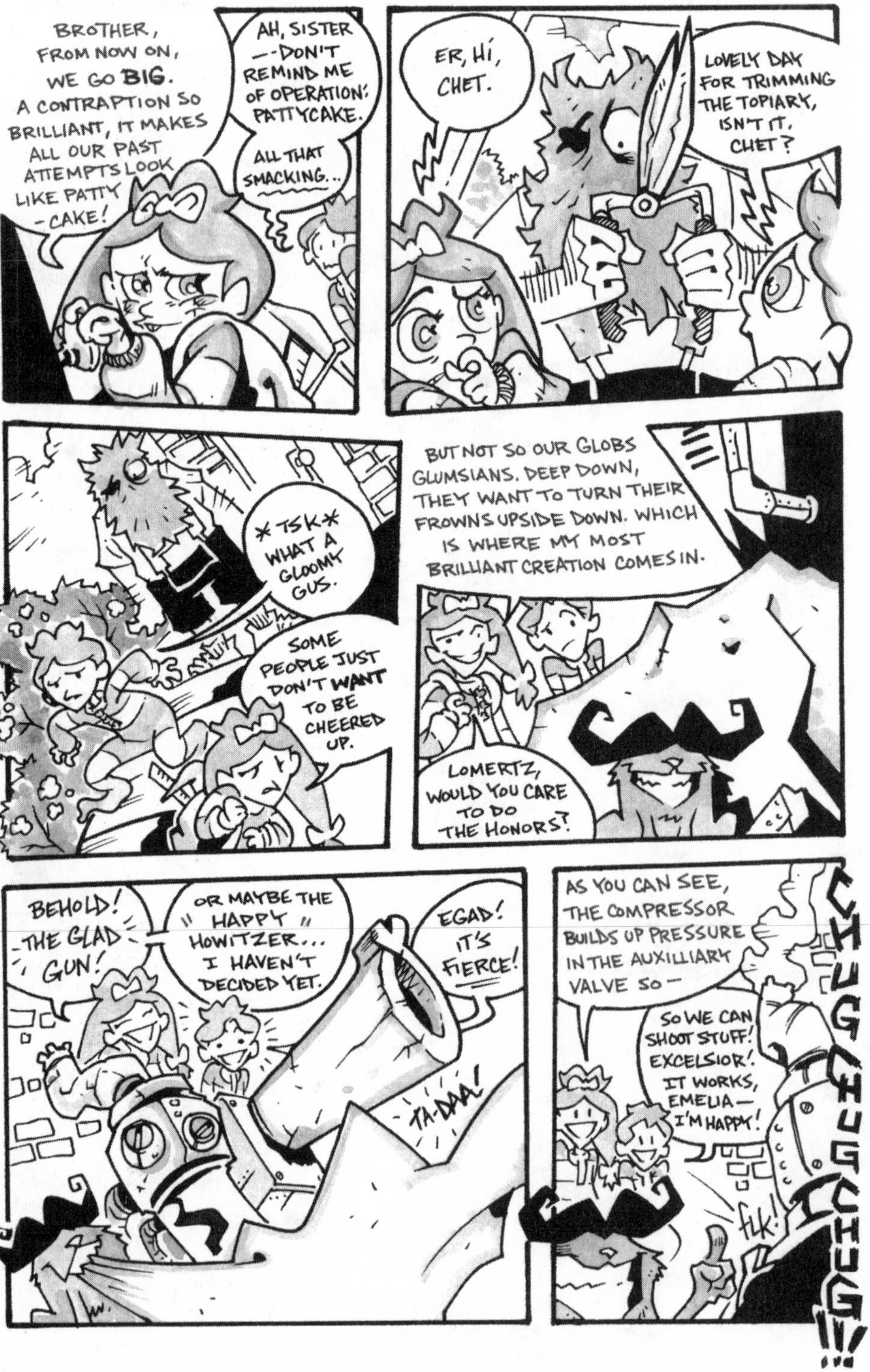
BROTHER, FROM NOW ON, WE GO BIG. A CONTRAPTION SO BRILLIANT, IT MAKES ALL OUR PAST ATTEMPTS LOOK LIKE PATTY-CAKE!
AH, SISTER--DON'T REMIND ME OF OPERATION: PATTYCAKE.
ALL THAT SMACKING...
ER, HI, CHET.
LOVELY DAY FOR TRIMMING THE TOPIARY, ISN'T IT, CHET?
TSK WHAT A GLOOMY GUS.
SOME PEOPLE JUST DON'T WANT TO BE CHEERED UP.
BUT NOT SO OUR GLOBS GLUMSIANS. DEEP DOWN, THEY WANT TO TURN THEIR FROWNS UPSIDE DOWN. WHICH IS WHERE MY MOST BRILLIANT CREATION COMES IN.
LOMERTZ, WOULD YOU CARE TO DO THE HONORS?
BEHOLD! THE GLAD GUN!
OR MAYBE THE "HAPPY HOWITZER"... I HAVEN'T DECIDED YET.
EGAD! IT'S FIERCE!
TA-DAA!
AS YOU CAN SEE, THE COMPRESSOR BUILDS UP PRESSURE IN THE AUXILLIARY VALVE SO—
SO WE CAN SHOOT STUFF! EXCELSIOR! IT WORKS, EMELIA—I'M HAPPY!
FLK!
CHUG CHUG CHUG CHUG!!!

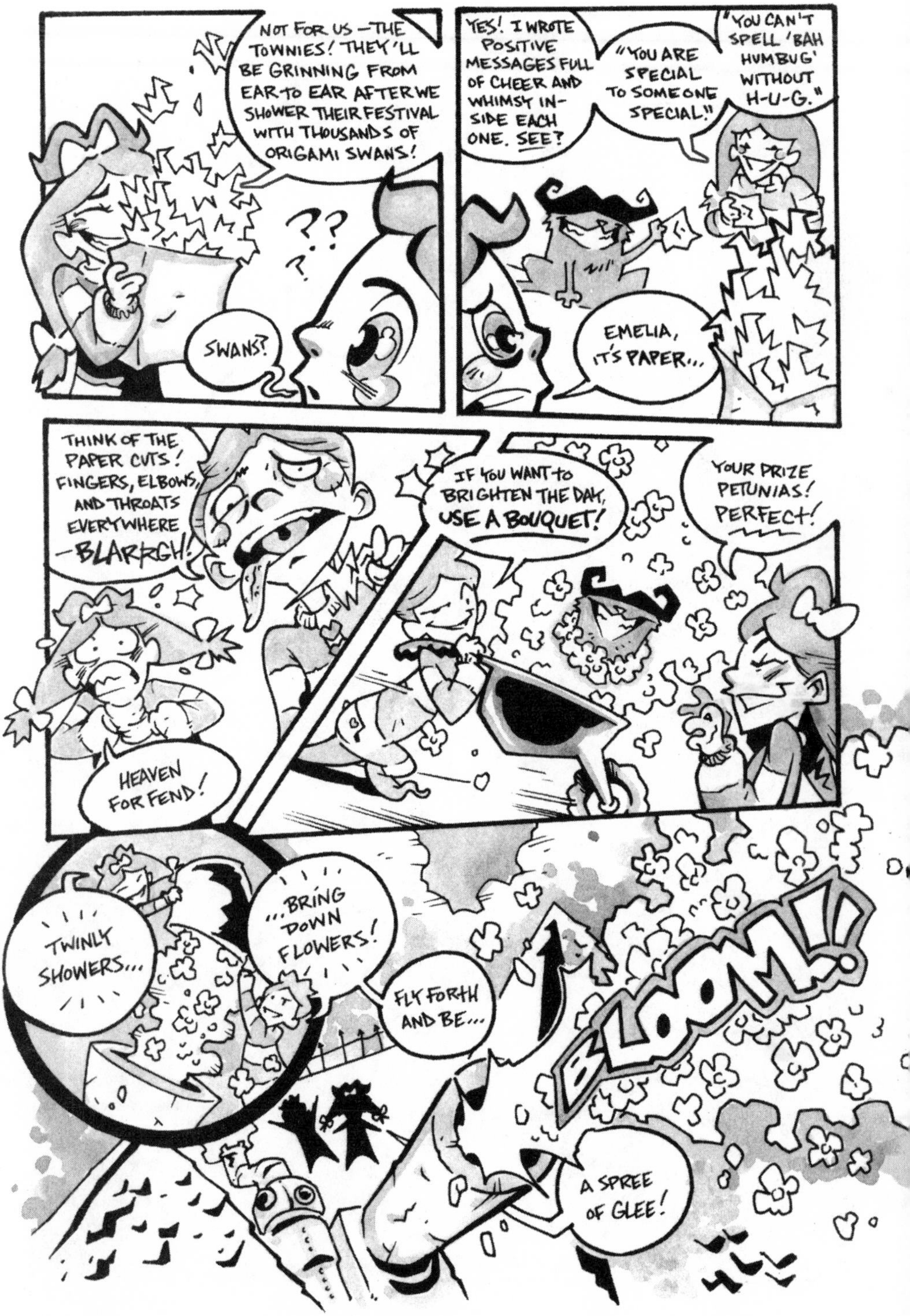
NOT FOR US —THE TOWNIES! THEY'LL BE GRINNING FROM EAR TO EAR AFTER WE SHOWER THEIR FESTIVAL WITH THOUSANDS OF ORIGAMI SWANS!
??
?
SWANS?
YES! I WROTE POSITIVE MESSAGES FULL OF CHEER AND WHIMSY INSIDE EACH ONE. SEE?
"YOU ARE SPECIAL TO SOMEONE SPECIAL!"
"YOU CAN'T SPELL 'BAH HUMBUG' WITHOUT H-U-G."
EMELIA, IT'S PAPER...
THINK OF THE PAPER CUTS! FINGERS, ELBOWS, AND THROATS EVERYWHERE —BLARRGH!
HEAVEN FORFEND!
IF YOU WANT TO BRIGHTEN THE DAY, USE A BOUQUET!
YOUR PRIZE PETUNIAS! PERFECT!
TWINLY SHOWERS...
...BRING DOWN FLOWERS!
FLY FORTH AND BE...
BLOOM!!
A SPREE OF GLEE!

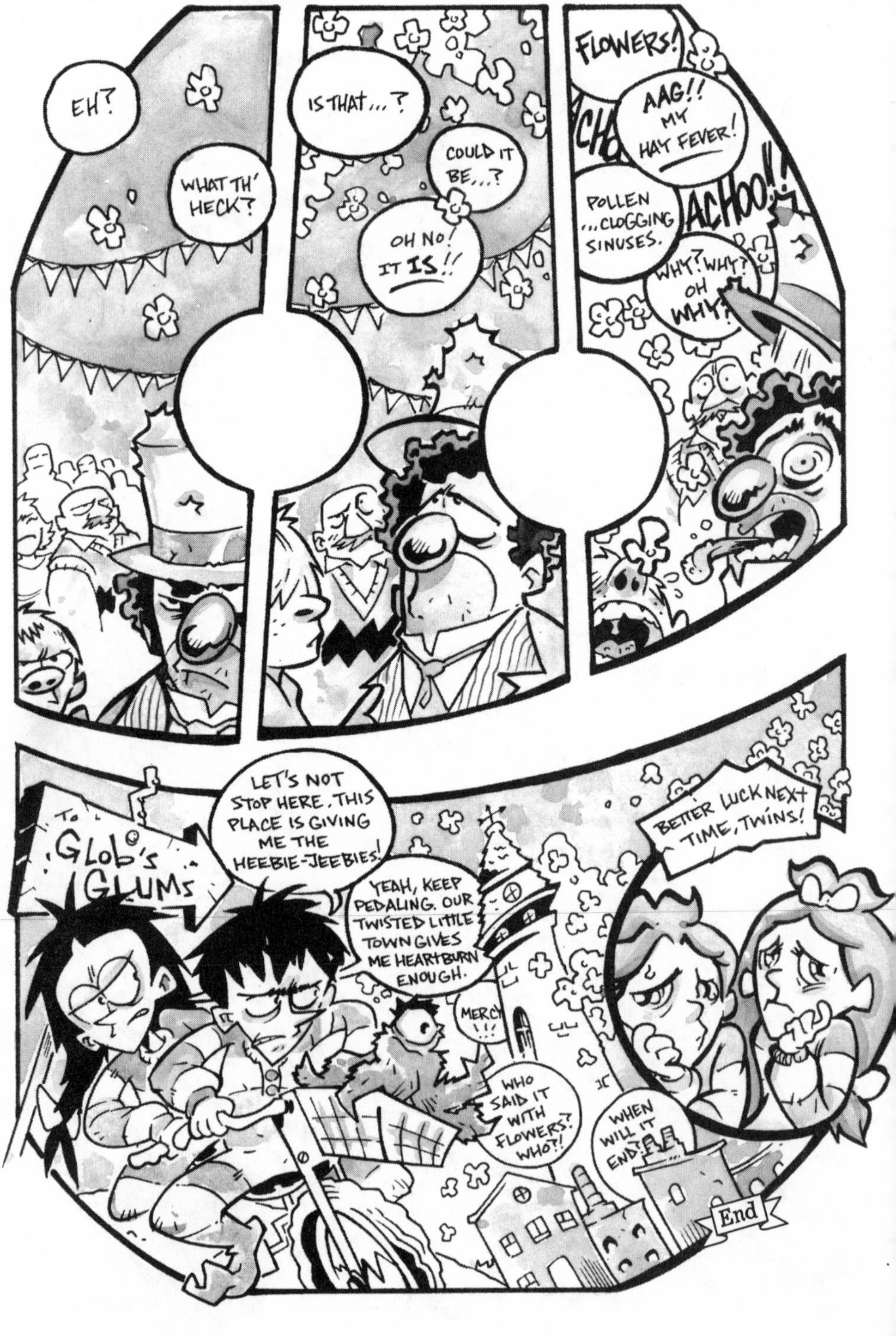
EH?
WHAT TH' HECK?
IS THAT...?
COULD IT BE...?
OH NO! IT IS!!
FLOWERS!
ACHOO!!
AAG!! MY HAY FEVER!
ACHOO!!
POLLEN ...CLOGGING SINUSES.
WHY? WHY? OH WHY?
TO GLOB'S GLUMS
LET'S NOT STOP HERE. THIS PLACE IS GIVING ME THE HEEBIE-JEEBIES!
YEAH, KEEP PEDALING. OUR TWISTED LITTLE TOWN GIVES ME HEARTBURN ENOUGH.
BETTER LUCK NEXT TIME, TWINS!
MERCY!!!
WHO SAID IT WITH FLOWERS? WHO?!
WHEN WILL IT END?
End

THIS IS A FAKE ADVERTISEMENT.

It's baby Way 2 Real

The Most Realistic Doll Ever!

With Baby Way2Real, you can have all the fun of a **real mommy!** You can feed, change, and burp Baby Way2Real until your bedtime — and beyond!

Baby Way2Real is the only doll that:

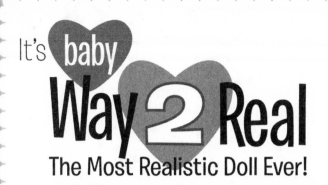

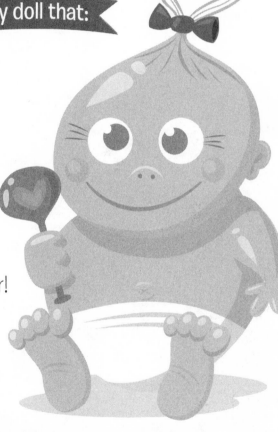

- **EATS** real food!
- **DRINKS** real milk!
- **CRIES** real tears!
- **POOS** real poo!
- **PEES** real pee!
- **BURPS** real burps!
- **BARFS** real barf!
- **DROOLS** real slobber!
- **SNOTS** real boogers!
- **PASSES** real gas!
- **GETS** real gunk in the corner of her eyes!

The Doll You Just Can't Put Down

- Performs 11 more true-to-life baby functions, and 2 secret functions you have to **unlock!**
- Emits 4 simulated odors — just like a **real baby!**
- Comes with a rattle and enough diapers to last **two days!**

Baby Way2Real is another fine product from Smelterburg Industrial Conglomo-tainment Ltd. Baby Way2Real may be allergic to peanuts or shellfish. Diapers and batteries must be changed every 2 to 3 hours. Randomly selected boxes may contain twins.

HEIMERTZ vs. ~~GODZILLA!~~ FLOWERS

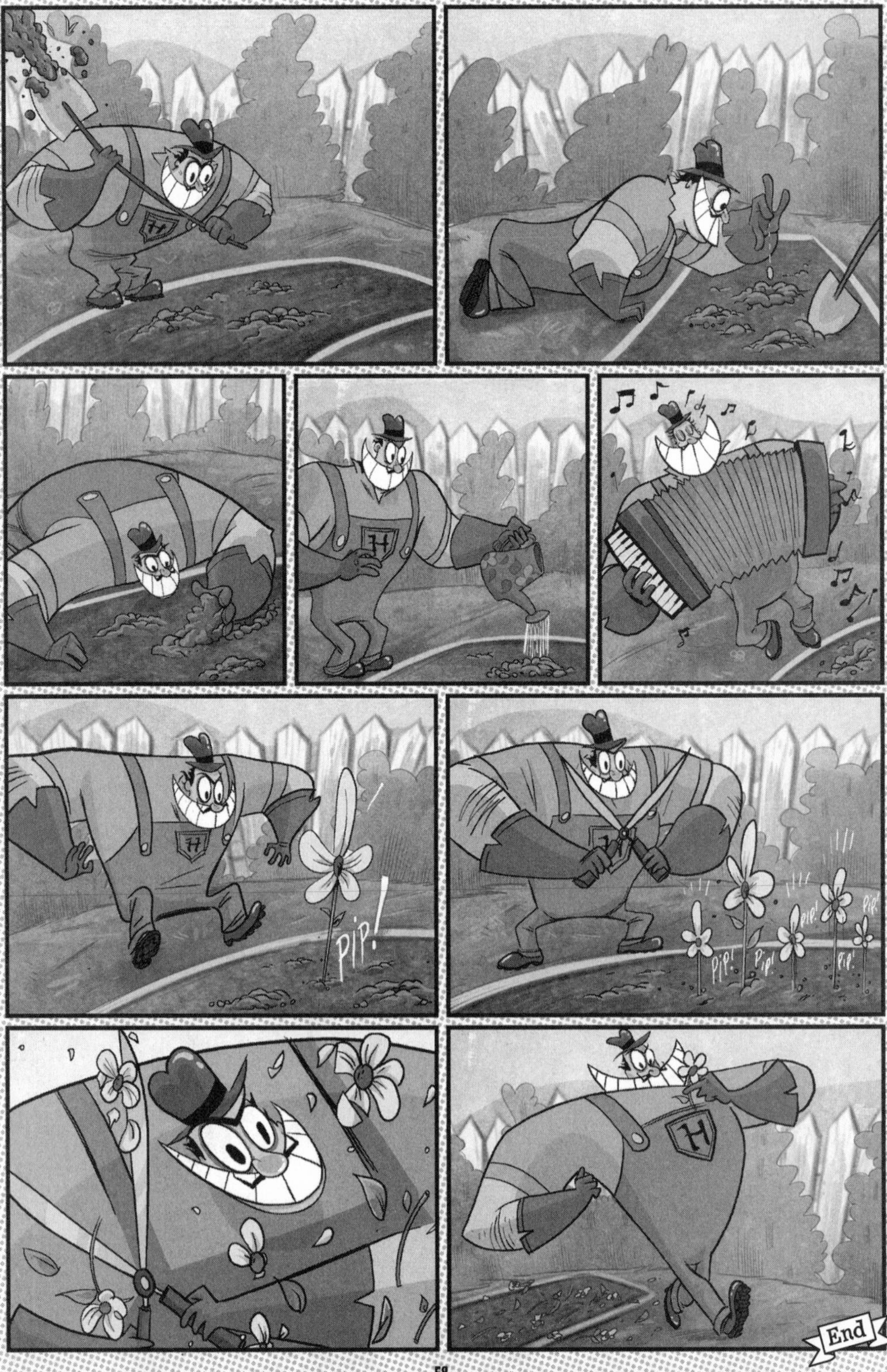

Pip!
Pip!
Pip!
Pip!
Pip!
Pip!
Pip!
End

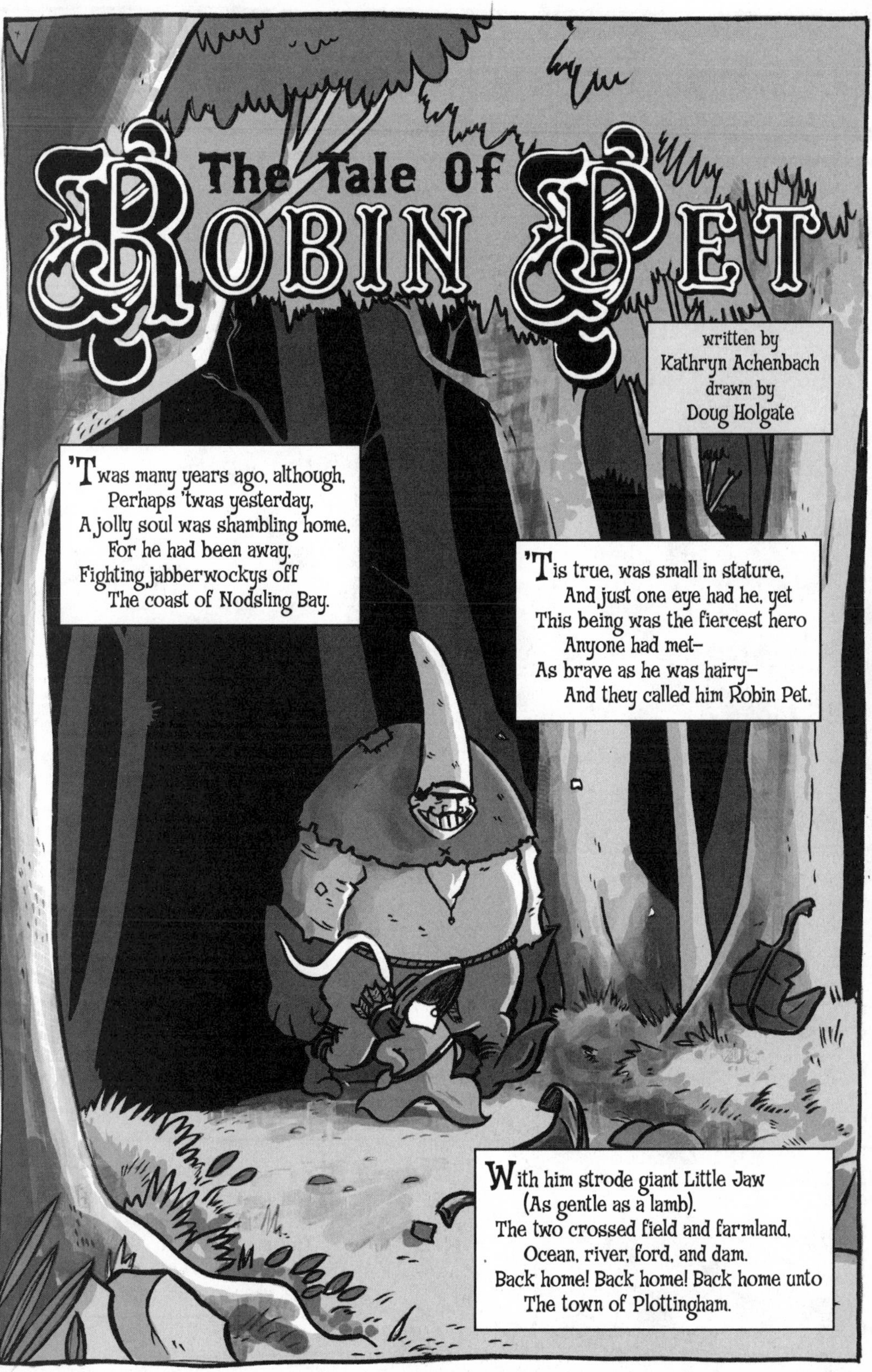
The Tale Of
ROBIN PET
written by
Kathryn Achenbach
drawn by
Doug Holgate
'Twas many years ago, although,
Perhaps 'twas yesterday,
A jolly soul was shambling home,
For he had been away,
Fighting jabberwockys off
The coast of Nodsling Bay.
'Tis true, was small in stature,
And just one eye had he, yet
This being was the fiercest hero
Anyone had met–
As brave as he was hairy–
And they called him Robin Pet.
With him strode giant Little Jaw
(As gentle as a lamb).
The two crossed field and farmland,
Ocean, river, ford, and dam.
Back home! Back home! Back home unto
The town of Plottingham.

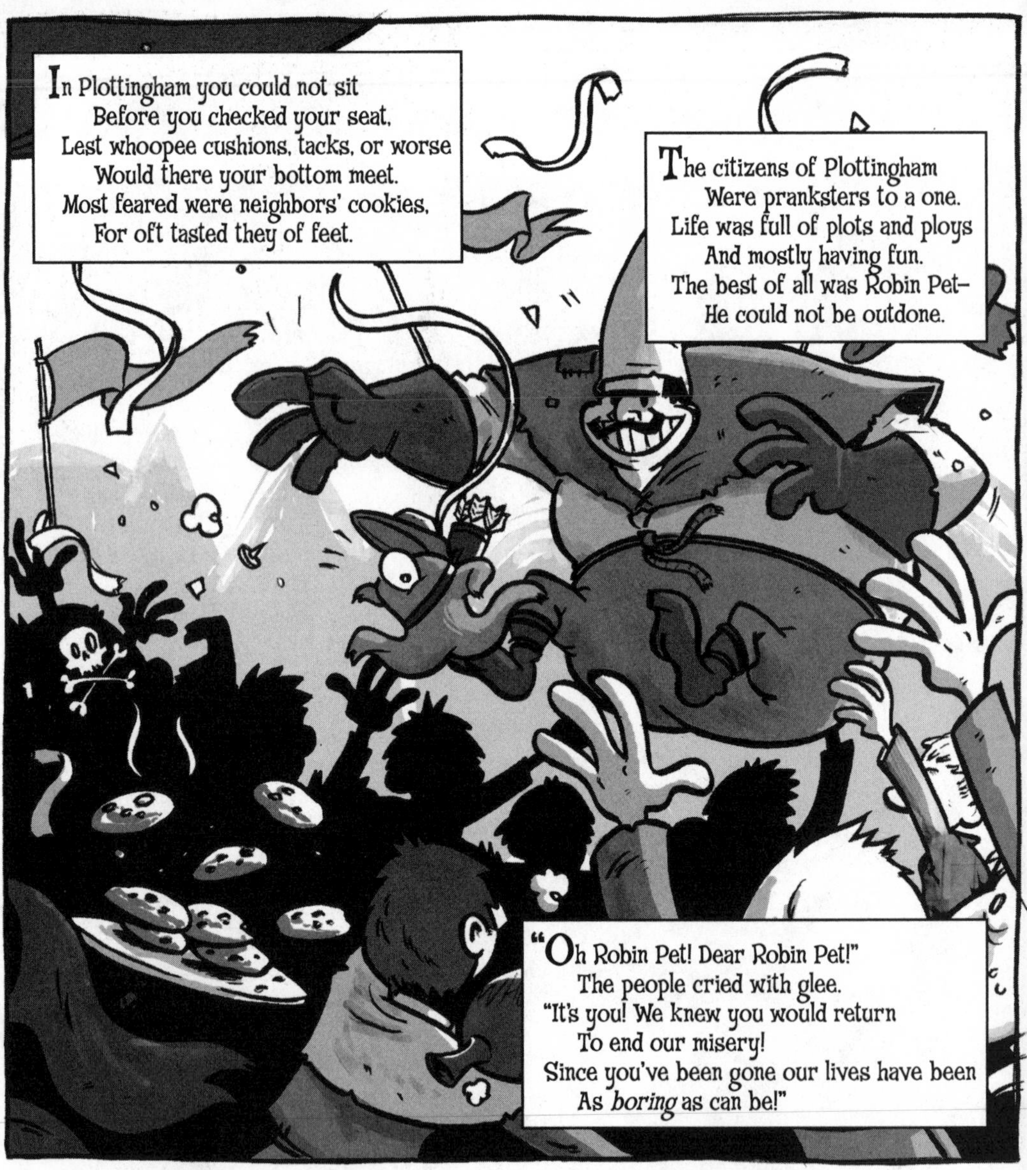
In Plottingham you could not sit
Before you checked your seat,
Lest whoopee cushions, tacks, or worse
Would there your bottom meet.
Most feared were neighbors' cookies,
For oft tasted they of feet.
The citizens of Plottingham
Were pranksters to a one.
Life was full of plots and ploys
And mostly having fun.
The best of all was Robin Pet–
He could not be outdone.
"Oh Robin Pet! Dear Robin Pet!"
The people cried with glee.
"It's you! We knew you would return
To end our misery!
Since you've been gone our lives have been
As *boring* as can be!"
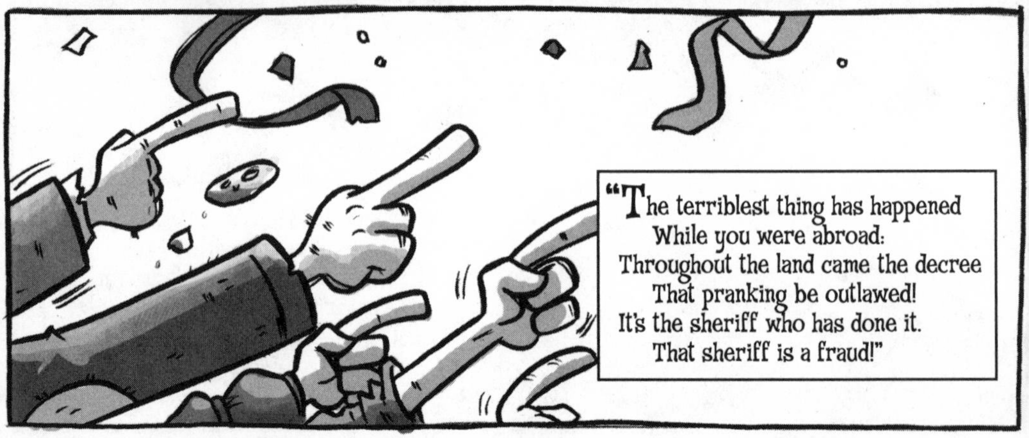
"The terriblest thing has happened
While you were abroad:
Throughout the land came the decree
That pranking be outlawed!
It's the sheriff who has done it.
That sheriff is a fraud!"

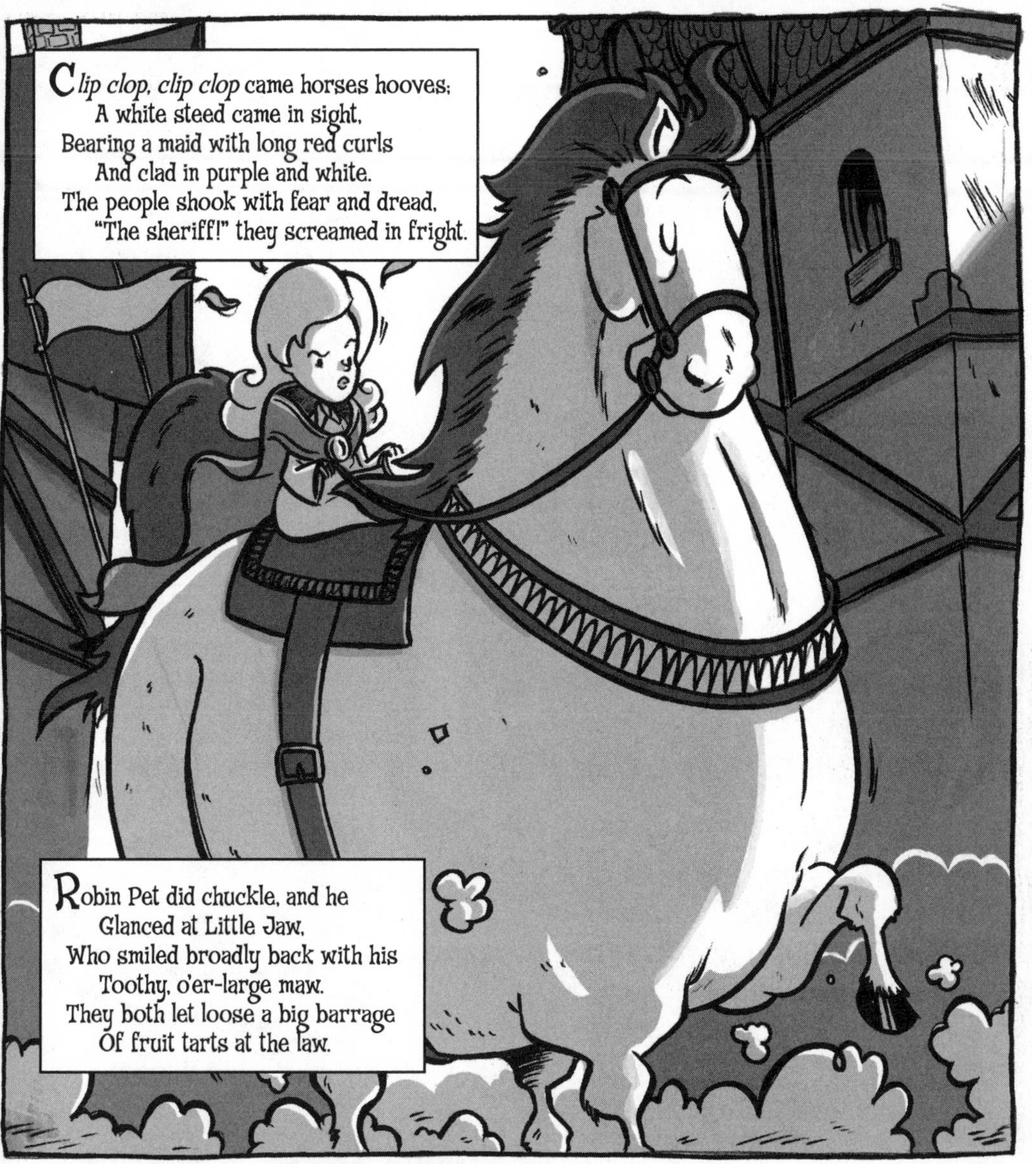
Clip clop, clip clop came horses hooves;
A white steed came in sight,
Bearing a maid with long red curls
And clad in purple and white.
The people shook with fear and dread,
"The sheriff!" they screamed in fright.
Robin Pet did chuckle, and he
Glanced at Little Jaw,
Who smiled broadly back with his
Toothy, o'er-large maw.
They both let loose a big barrage
Of fruit tarts at the law.

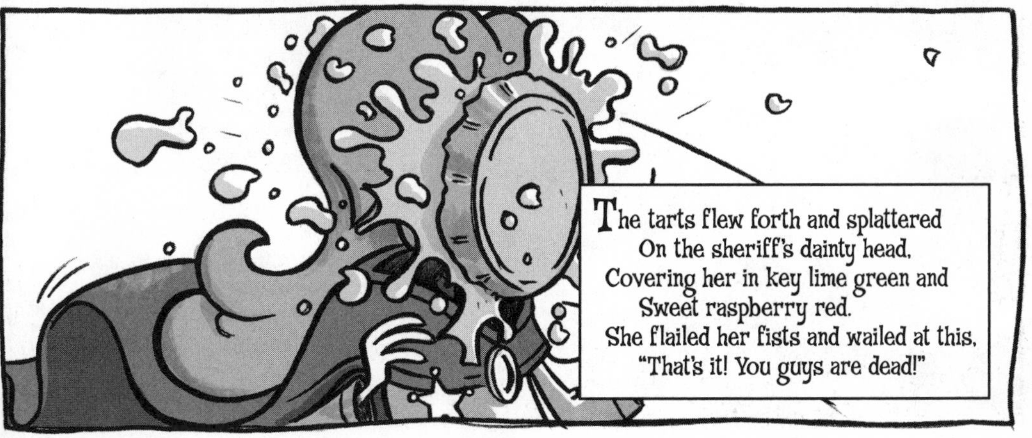
The tarts flew forth and splattered
On the sheriff's dainty head,
Covering her in key lime green and
Sweet raspberry red.
She flailed her fists and wailed at this,
"That's it! You guys are dead!"

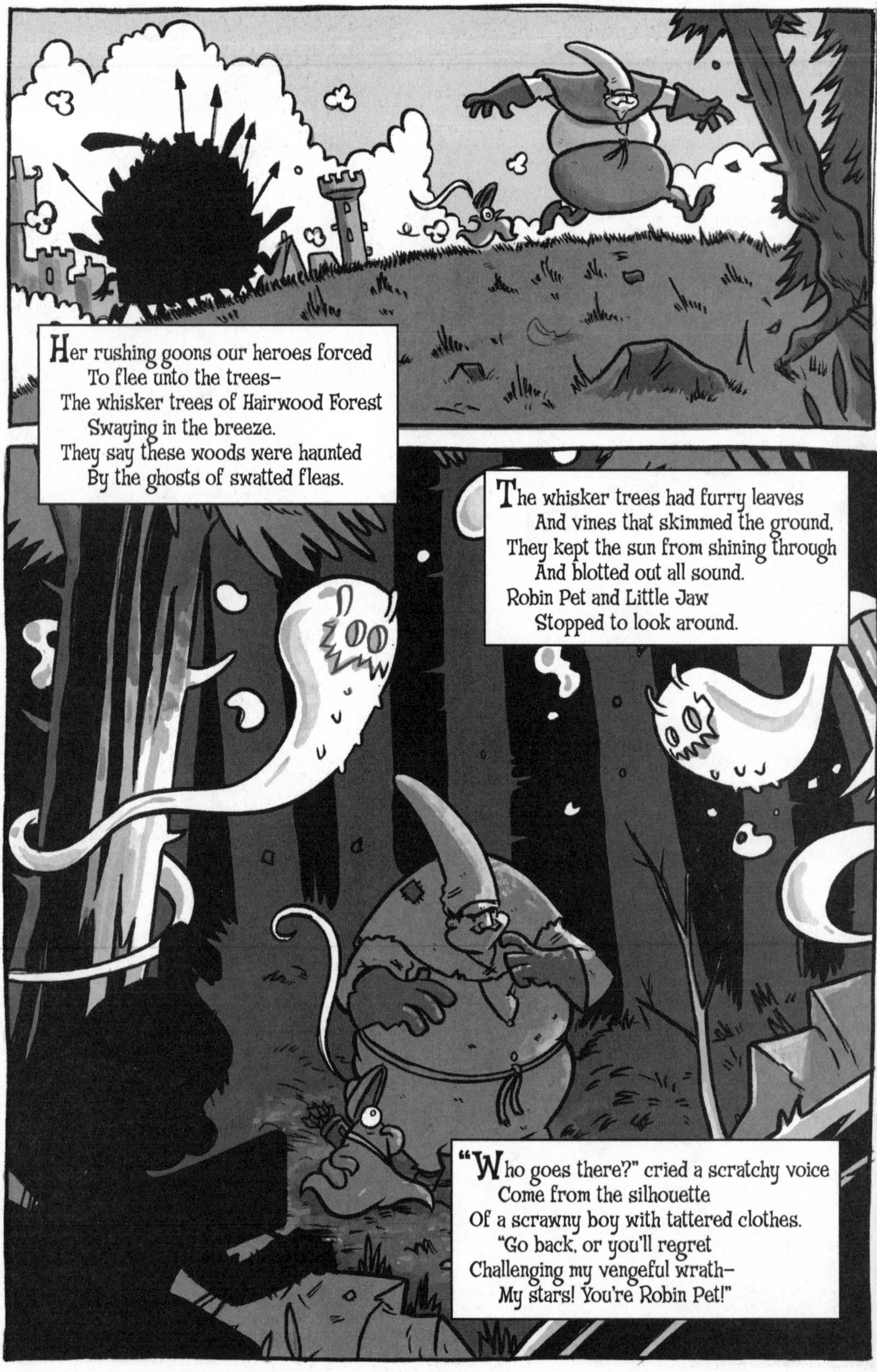
Her rushing goons our heroes forced
To flee unto the trees–
The whisker trees of Hairwood Forest
Swaying in the breeze.
They say these woods were haunted
By the ghosts of swatted fleas.
The whisker trees had furry leaves
And vines that skimmed the ground,
They kept the sun from shining through
And blotted out all sound.
Robin Pet and Little Jaw
Stopped to look around.
"Who goes there?" cried a scratchy voice
Come from the silhouette
Of a scrawny boy with tattered clothes.
"Go back, or you'll regret
Challenging my vengeful wrath–
My stars! You're Robin Pet!"

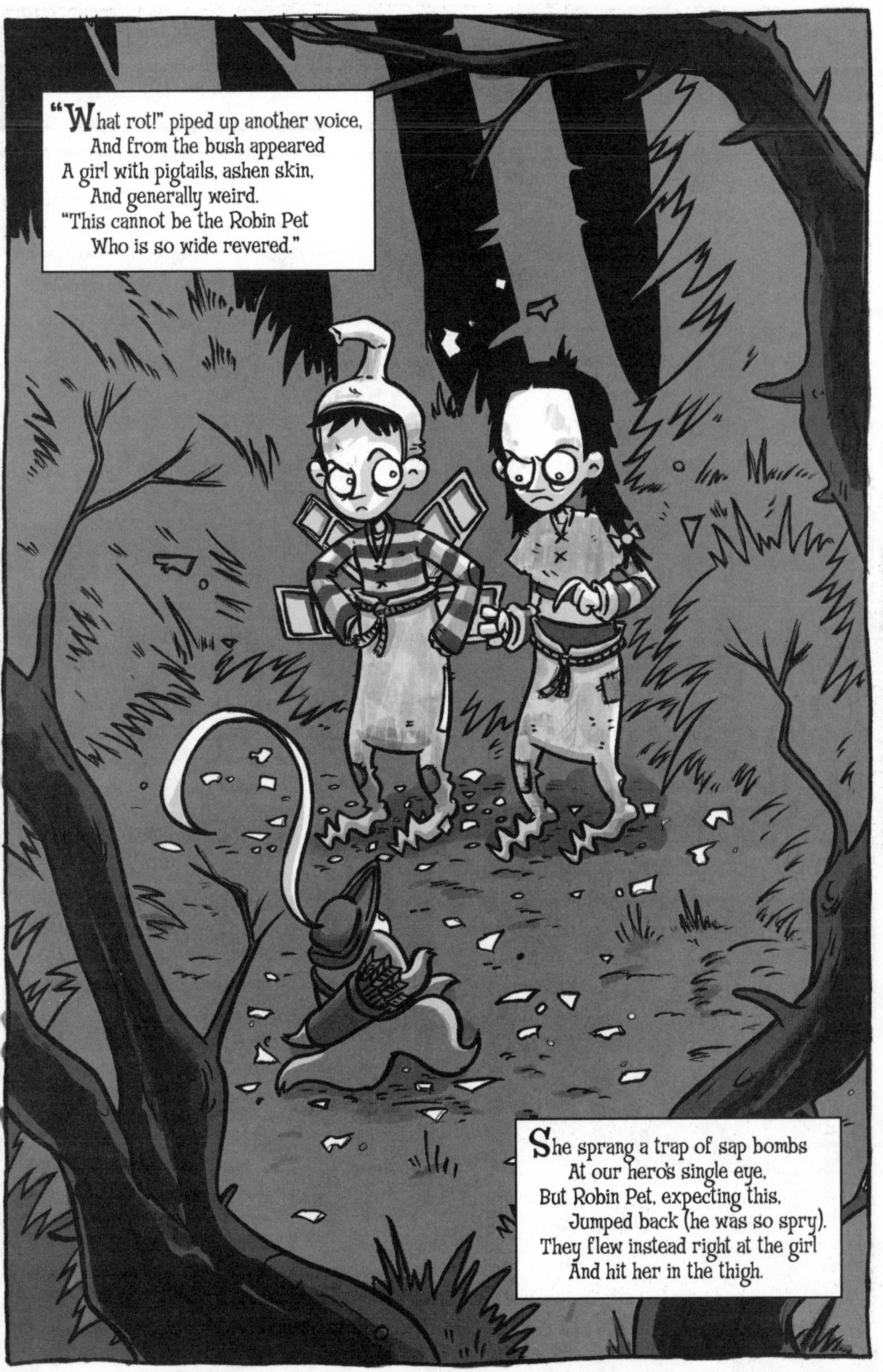
"What rot!" piped up another voice,
And from the bush appeared
A girl with pigtails, ashen skin,
And generally weird.
"This cannot be the Robin Pet
Who is so wide revered."
She sprang a trap of sap bombs
At our hero's single eye,
But Robin Pet, expecting this,
Jumped back (he was so spry).
They flew instead right at the girl
And hit her in the thigh.

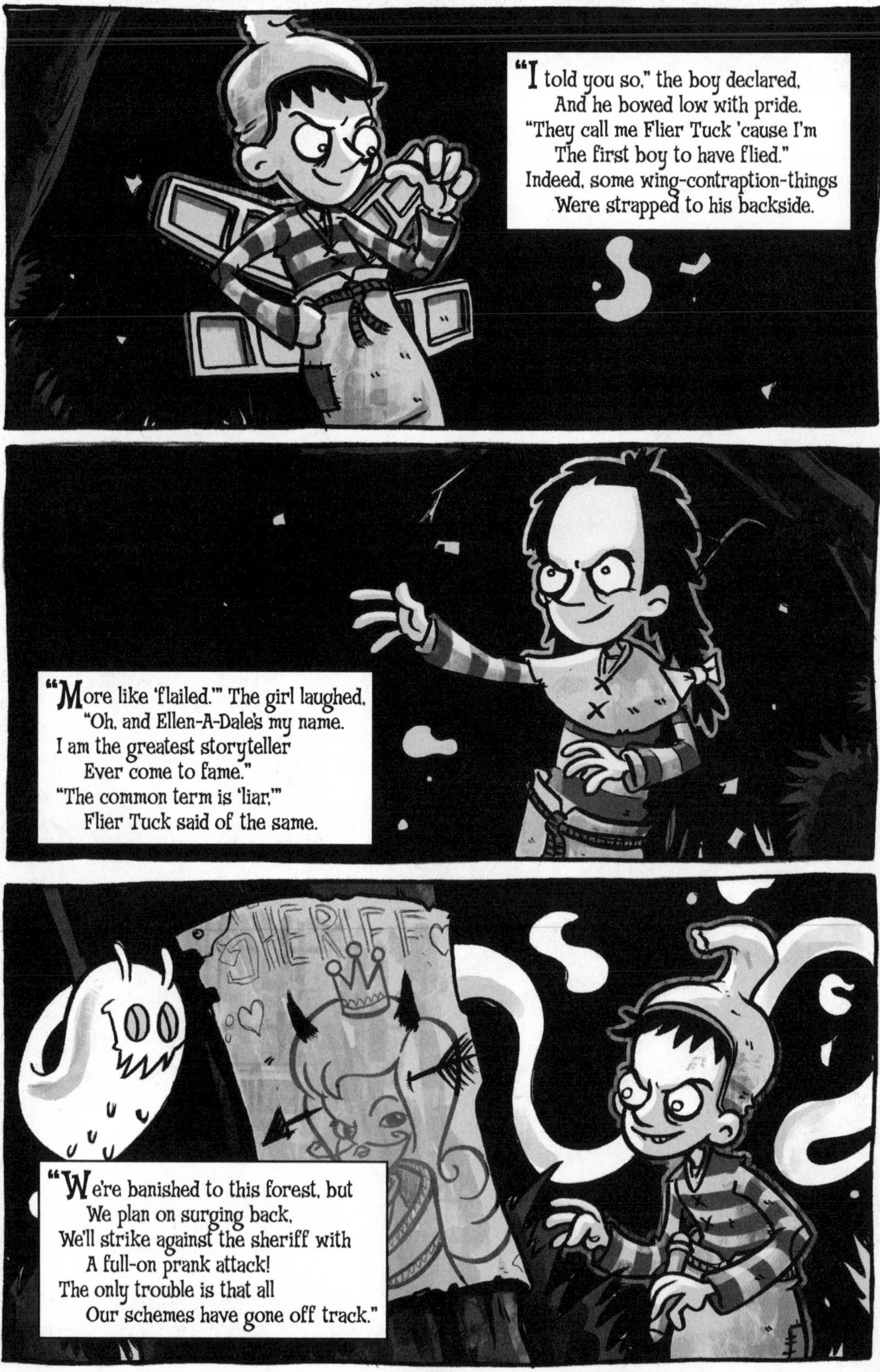
"I told you so," the boy declared,
And he bowed low with pride.
"They call me Flier Tuck 'cause I'm
The first boy to have flied."
Indeed, some wing-contraption-things
Were strapped to his backside.
"More like 'flailed.'" The girl laughed,
"Oh, and Ellen-A-Dale's my name.
I am the greatest storyteller
Ever come to fame."
"The common term is 'liar,'"
Flier Tuck said of the same.
SHERIFF
"We're banished to this forest, but
We plan on surging back,
We'll strike against the sheriff with
A full-on prank attack!
The only trouble is that all
Our schemes have gone off track."

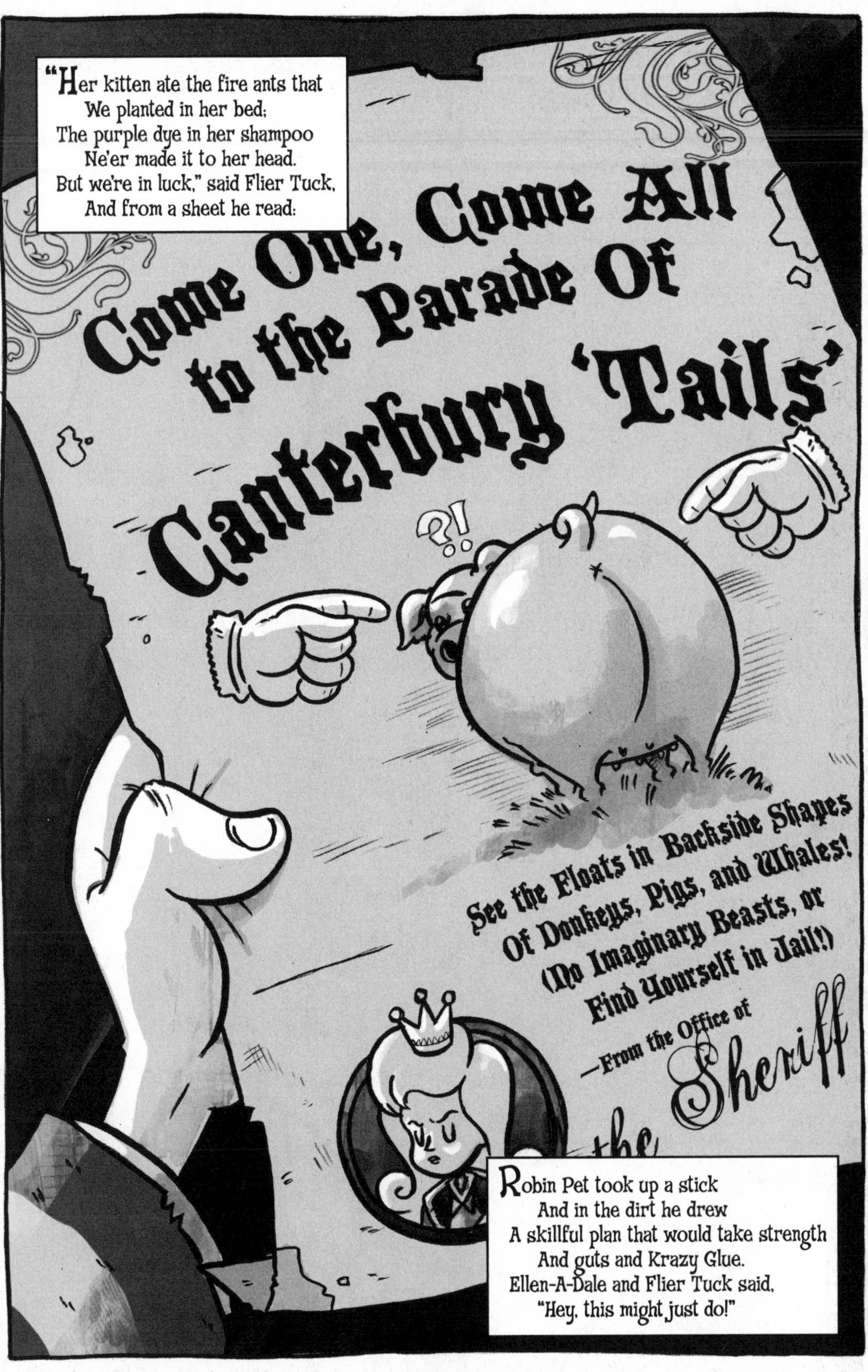
"Her kitten ate the fire ants that
We planted in her bed;
The purple dye in her shampoo
Ne'er made it to her head.
But we're in luck," said Flier Tuck,
And from a sheet he read:
Come One, Come All to the Parade Of Canterbury 'Tails'
?!
See the Floats in Backside Shapes Of Donkeys, Pigs, and Whales! (No Imaginary Beasts, or Find Yourself in Jail!)
—From the Office of the Sheriff
Robin Pet took up a stick
And in the dirt he drew
A skillful plan that would take strength
And guts and Krazy Glue.
Ellen-A-Dale and Flier Tuck said,
"Hey, this might just do!"

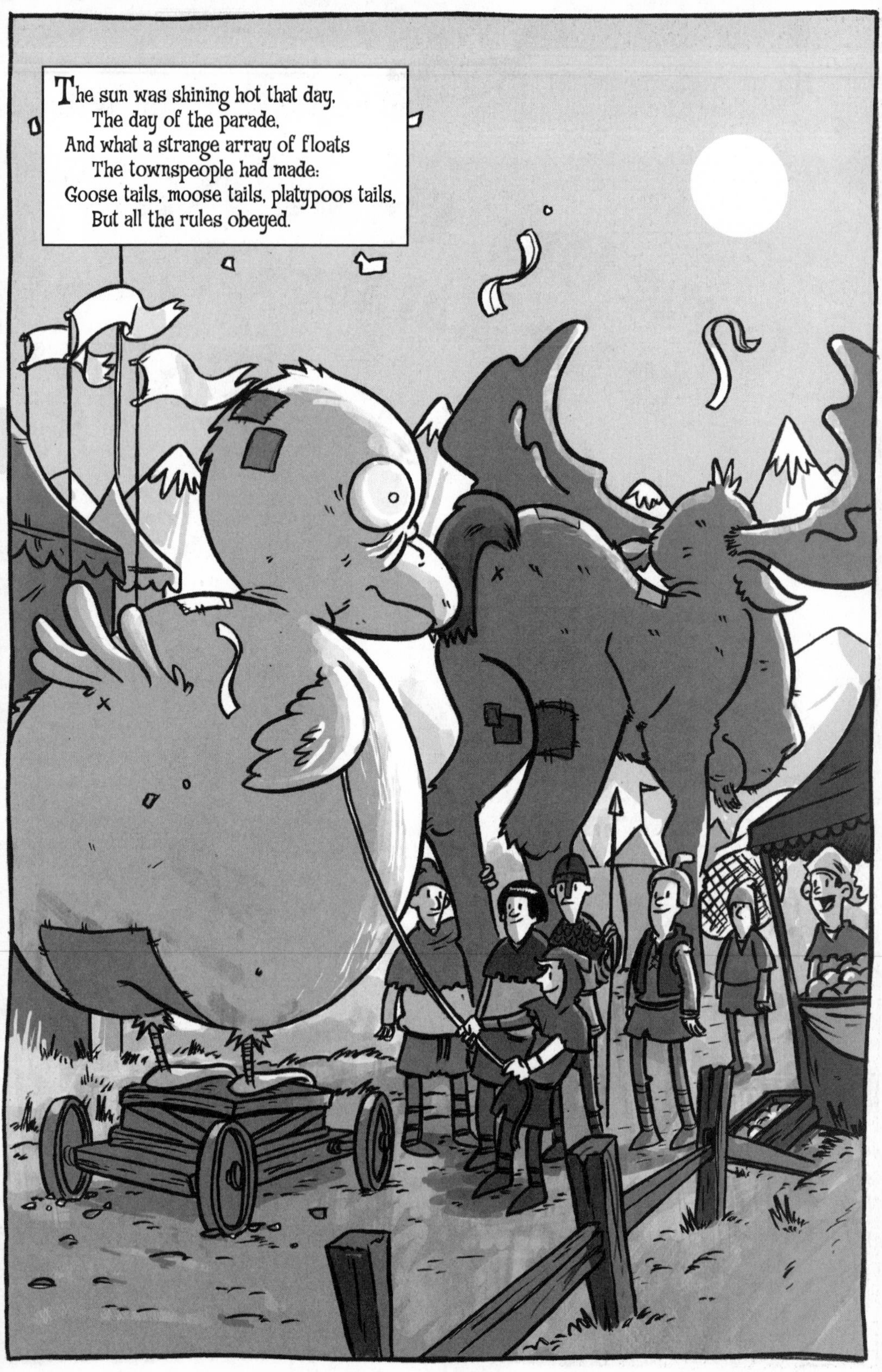
The sun was shining hot that day,
The day of the parade,
And what a strange array of floats
The townspeople had made:
Goose tails, moose tails, platypoos tails,
But all the rules obeyed.

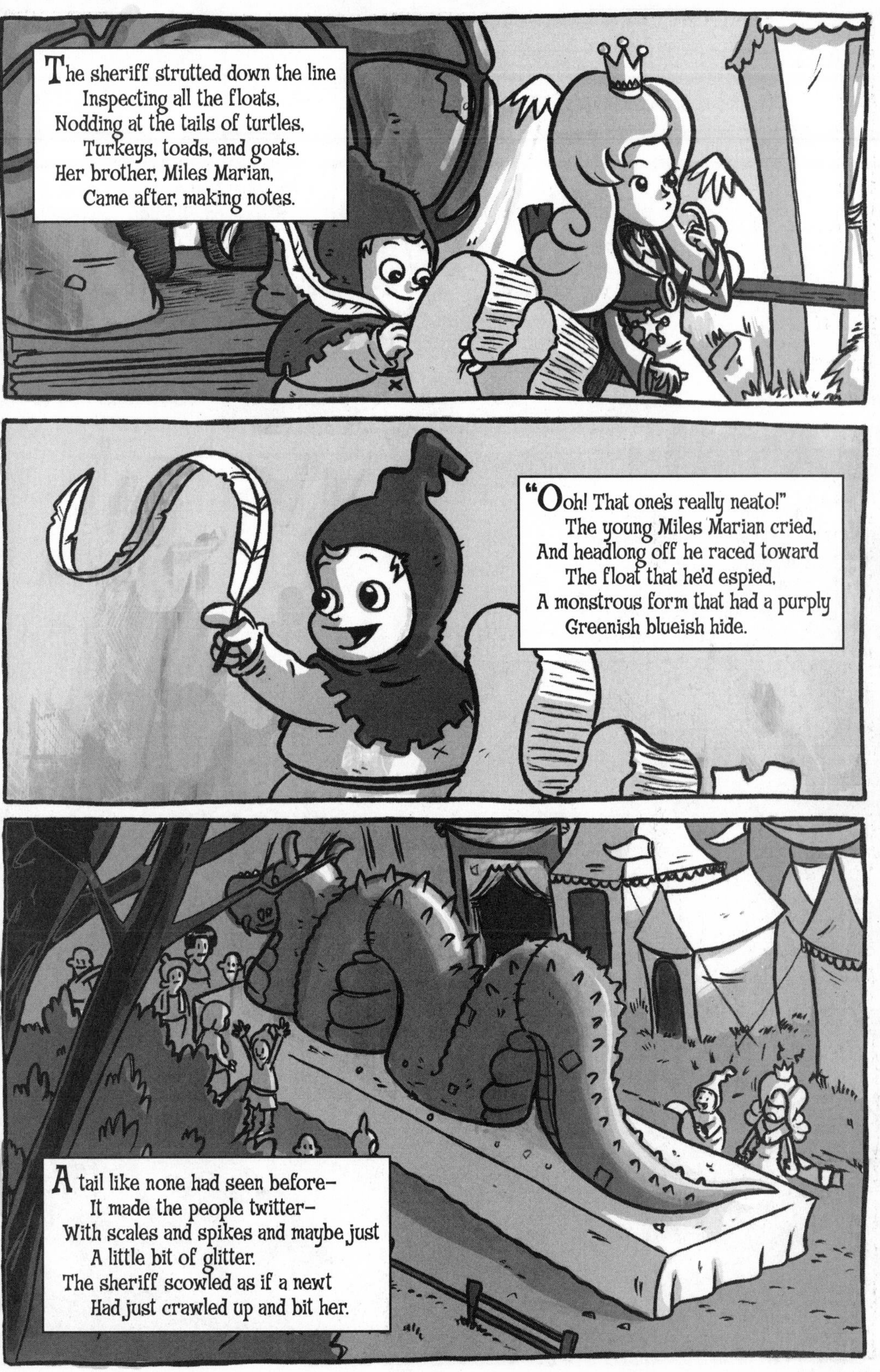
The sheriff strutted down the line
Inspecting all the floats,
Nodding at the tails of turtles,
Turkeys, toads, and goats.
Her brother, Miles Marian,
Came after, making notes.
"Ooh! That one's really neato!"
The young Miles Marian cried,
And headlong off he raced toward
The float that he'd espied,
A monstrous form that had a purply
Greenish blueish hide.
A tail like none had seen before–
It made the people twitter–
With scales and spikes and maybe just
A little bit of glitter.
The sheriff scowled as if a newt
Had just crawled up and bit her.

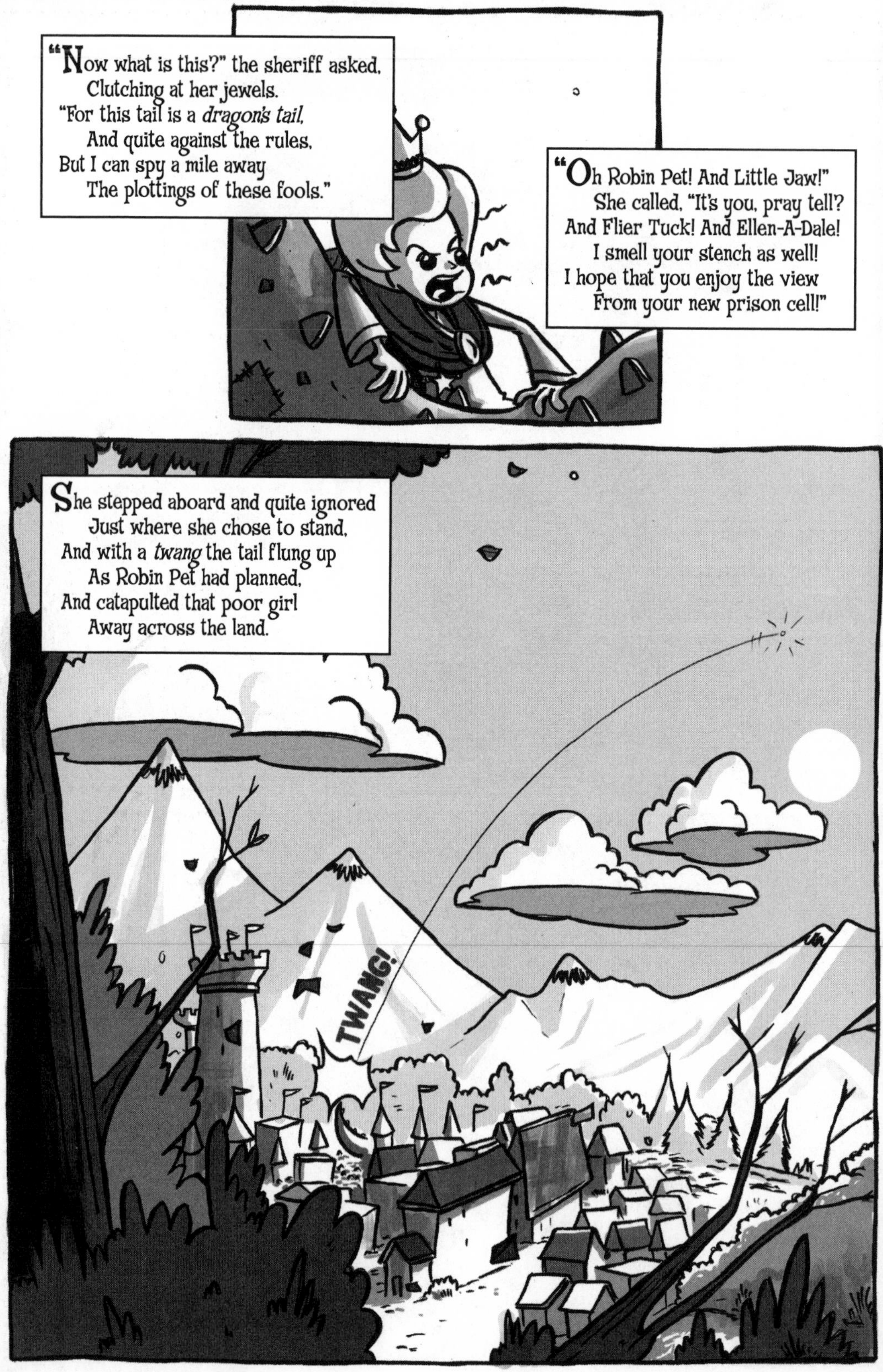
"Now what is this?" the sheriff asked,
Clutching at her jewels.
"For this tail is a *dragon's tail*,
And quite against the rules,
But I can spy a mile away
The plottings of these fools."
"Oh Robin Pet! And Little Jaw!"
She called, "It's you, pray tell?
And Flier Tuck! And Ellen-A-Dale!
I smell your stench as well!
I hope that you enjoy the view
From your new prison cell!"
She stepped aboard and quite ignored
Just where she chose to stand,
And with a *twang* the tail flung up
As Robin Pet had planned,
And catapulted that poor girl
Away across the land.
TWANG!

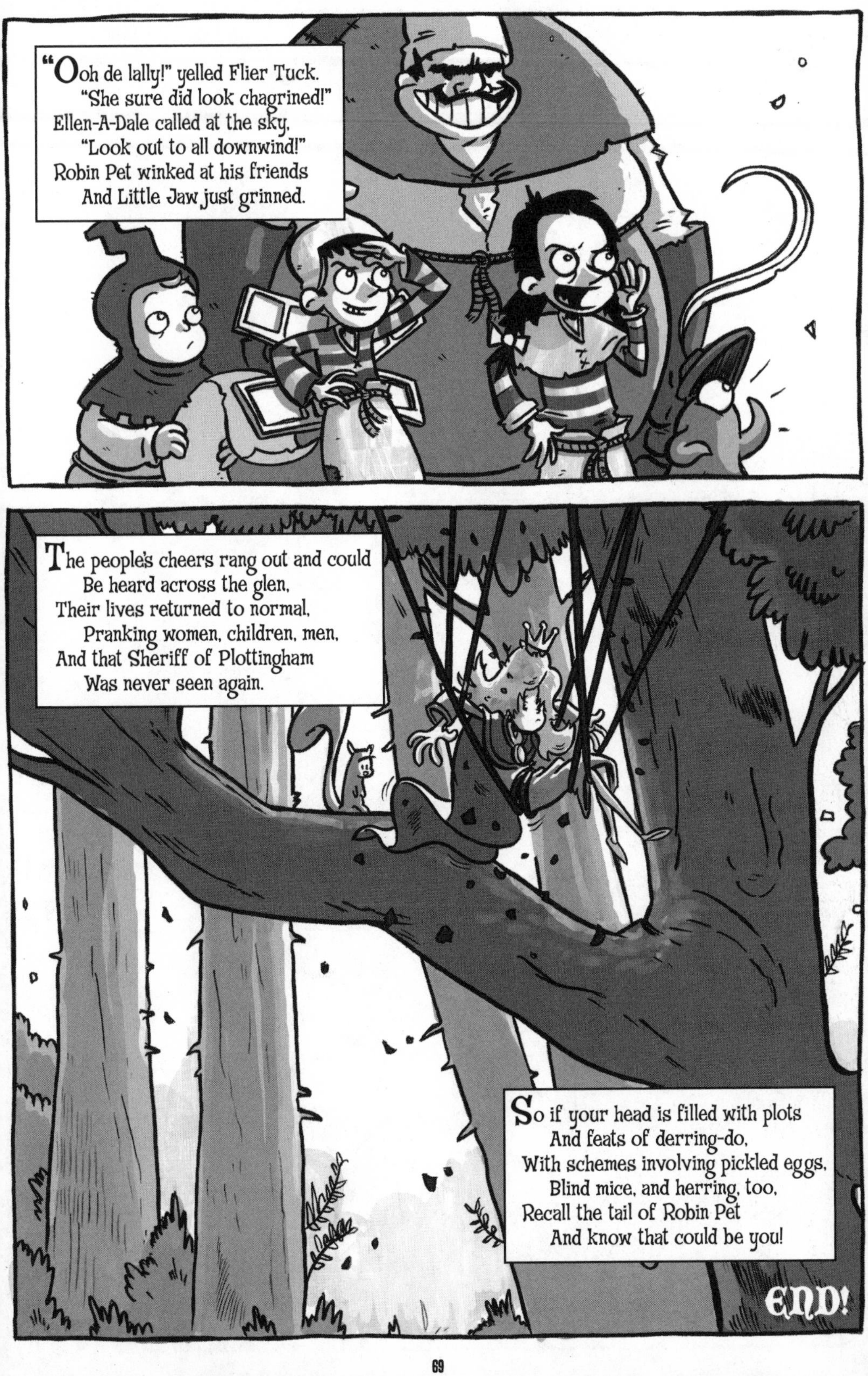
"Ooh de lally!" yelled Flier Tuck.
"She sure did look chagrined!"
Ellen-A-Dale called at the sky,
"Look out to all downwind!"
Robin Pet winked at his friends
And Little Jaw just grinned.
The people's cheers rang out and could
Be heard across the glen,
Their lives returned to normal,
Pranking women, children, men,
And that Sheriff of Plottingham
Was never seen again.
So if your head is filled with plots
And feats of derring-do,
With schemes involving pickled eggs,
Blind mice, and herring, too,
Recall the tail of Robin Pet
And know that could be you!
END!

HEIMERTZ vs. ~~the WOLFMAN!~~ MAIL

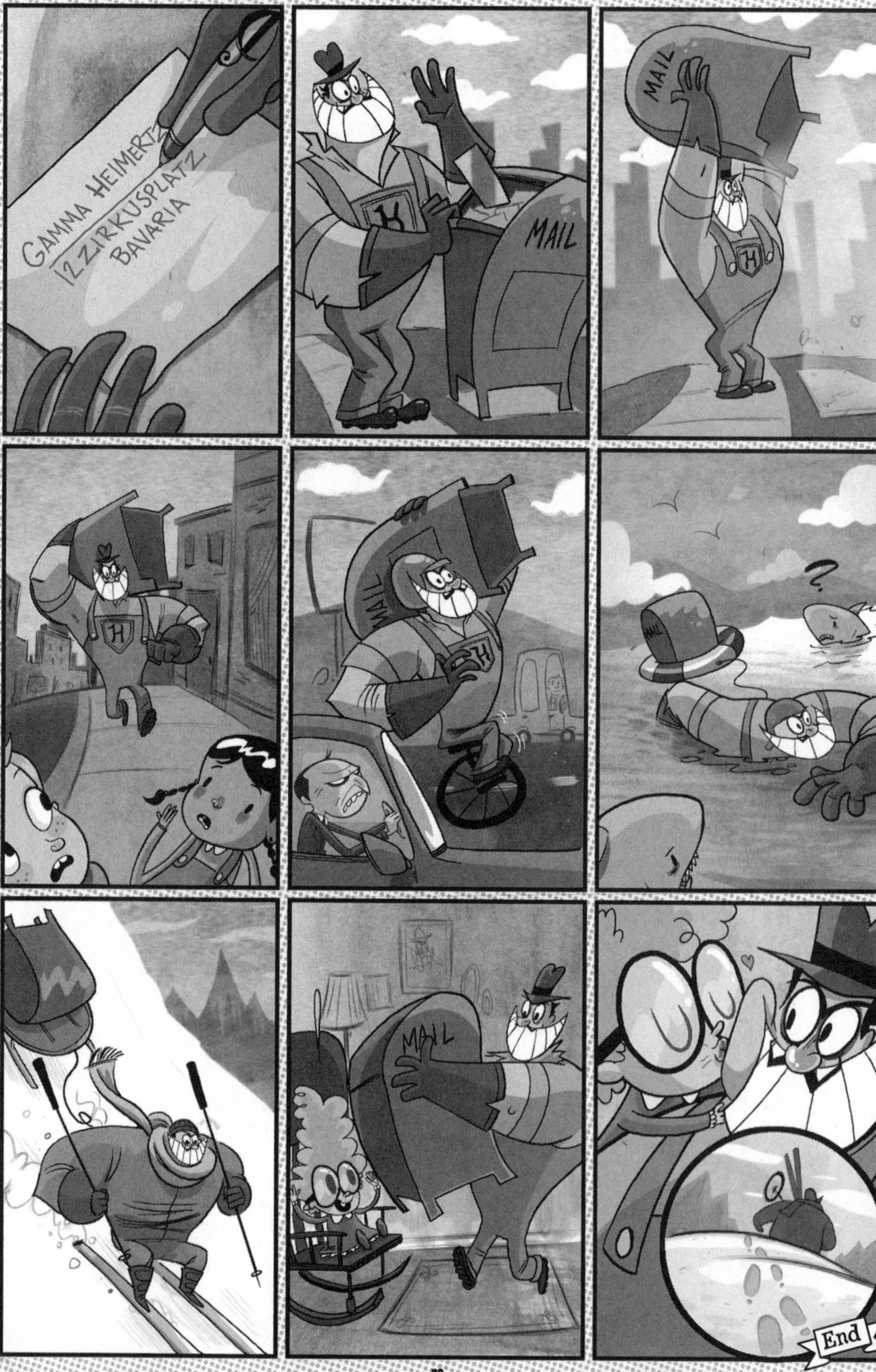
GAMMA HEIMERTZ
12 ZIRKUSPLATZ
BAVARIA
MAIL
MAIL
MAIL
?
MAIL
End

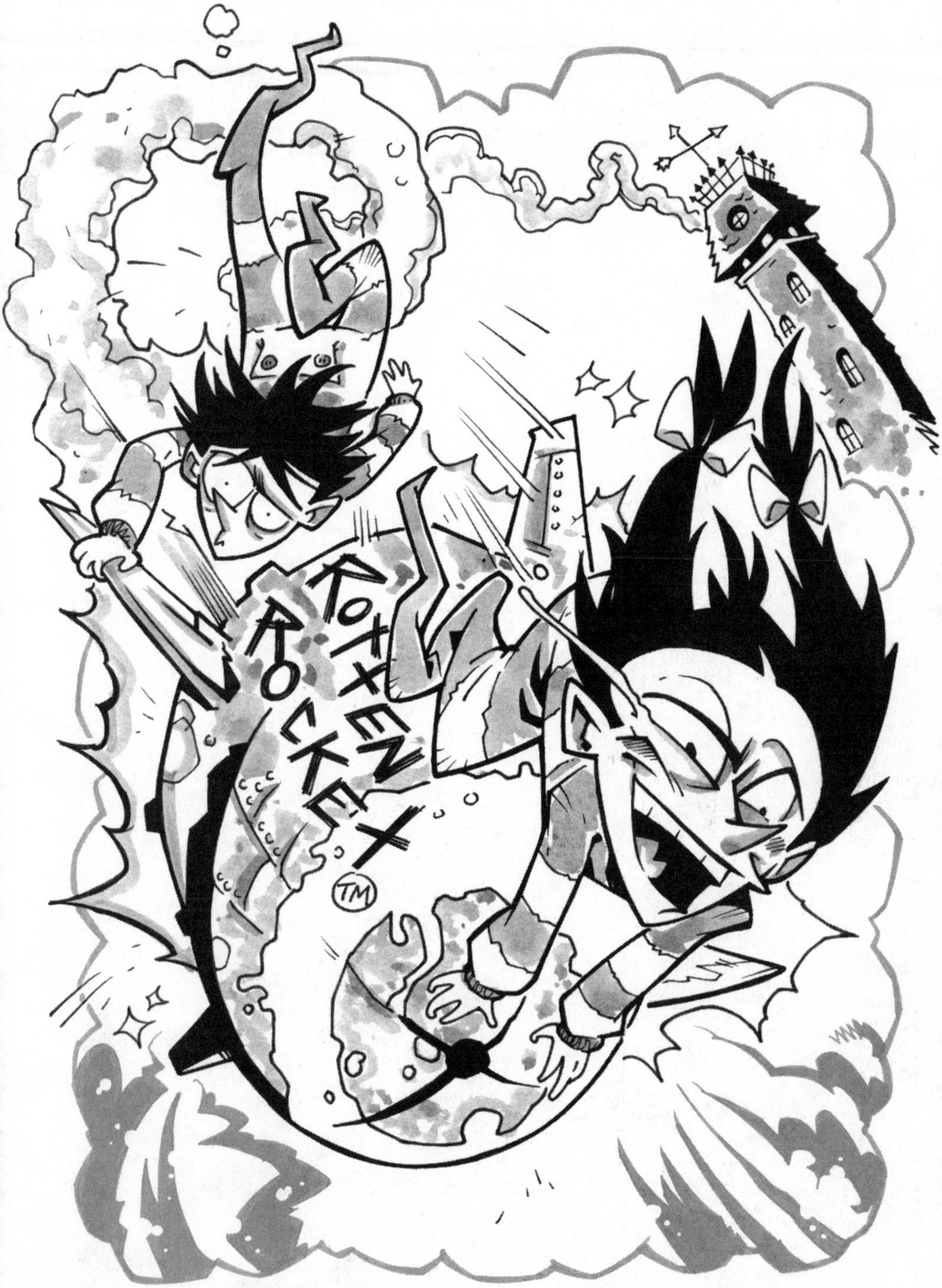
ROTTEN ROCKET
TM

PIN-UP by DAVE CROSLAND

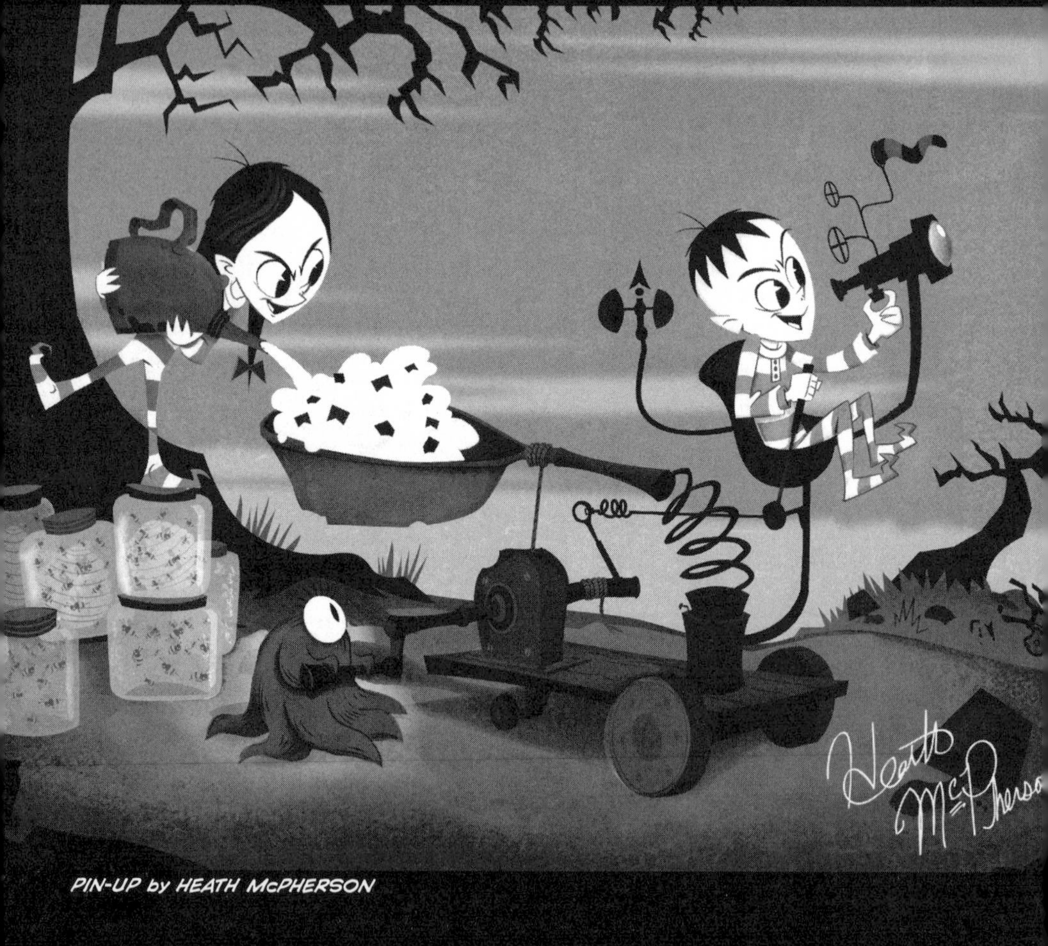
Heath McPherson

PIN-UP by HEATH McPHERSON

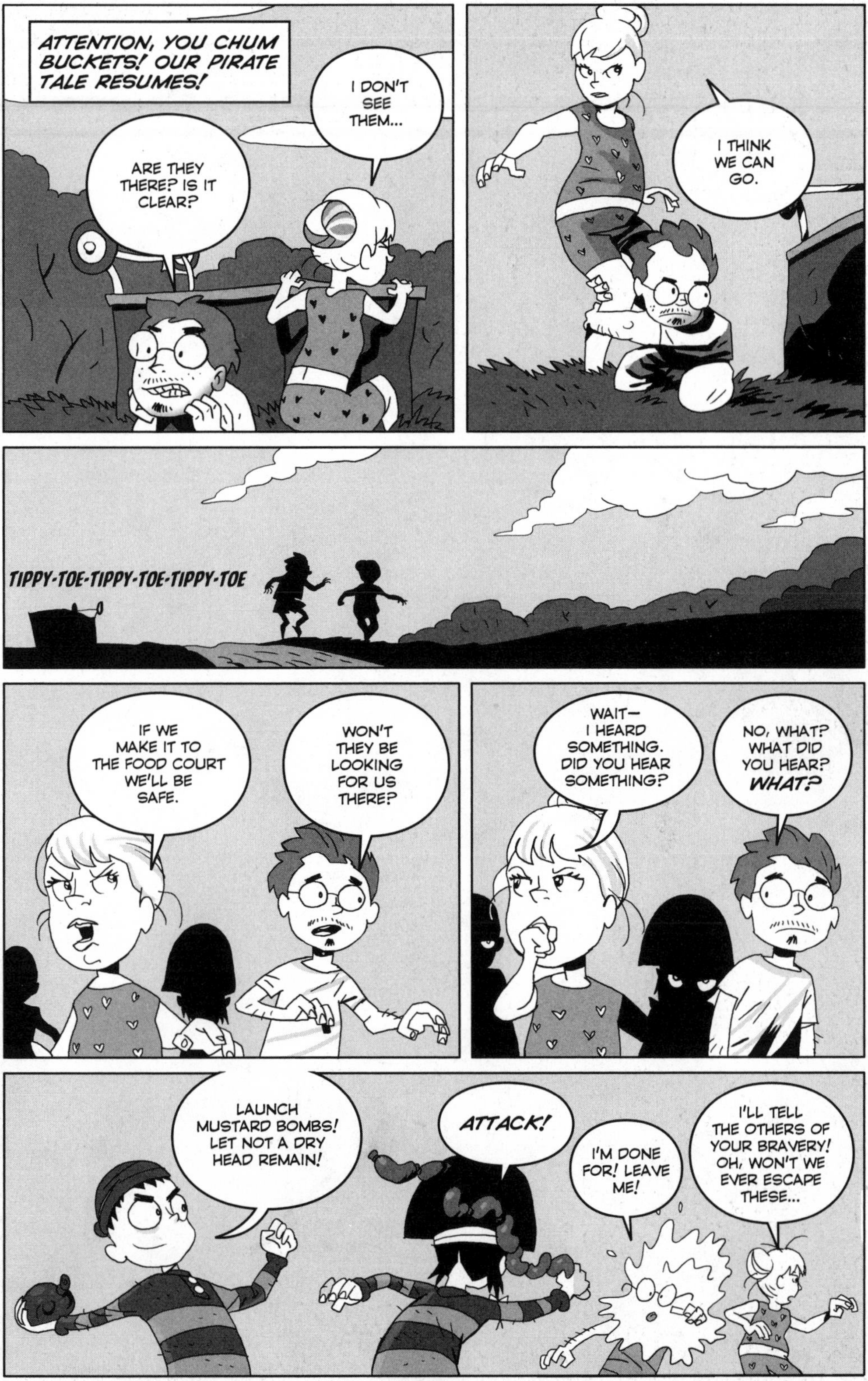
ATTENTION, YOU CHUM BUCKETS! OUR PIRATE TALE RESUMES!
ARE THEY THERE? IS IT CLEAR?
I DON'T SEE THEM...
I THINK WE CAN GO.
TIPPY-TOE-TIPPY-TOE-TIPPY-TOE
IF WE MAKE IT TO THE FOOD COURT WE'LL BE SAFE.
WON'T THEY BE LOOKING FOR US THERE?
WAIT— I HEARD SOMETHING. DID YOU HEAR SOMETHING?
NO, WHAT? WHAT DID YOU HEAR? WHAT?
LAUNCH MUSTARD BOMBS! LET NOT A DRY HEAD REMAIN!
ATTACK!
I'M DONE FOR! LEAVE ME!
I'LL TELL THE OTHERS OF YOUR BRAVERY! OH, WON'T WE EVER ESCAPE THESE...

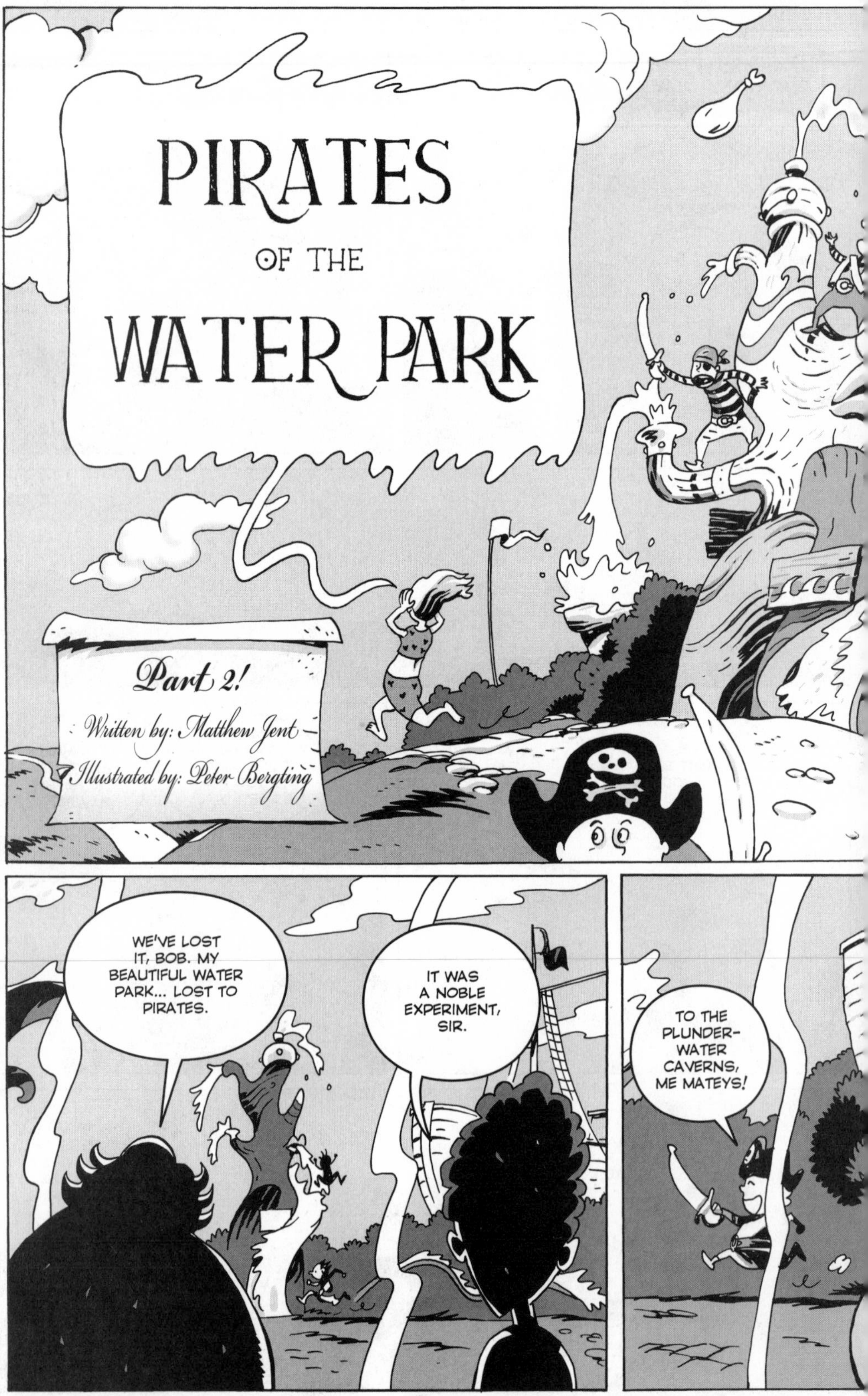
PIRATES OF THE WATER PARK
Part 2!
Written by: Matthew Jent
Illustrated by: Peter Bergting
WE'VE LOST IT, BOB. MY BEAUTIFUL WATER PARK... LOST TO PIRATES.
IT WAS A NOBLE EXPERIMENT, SIR.
TO THE PLUNDER-WATER CAVERNS, ME MATEYS!

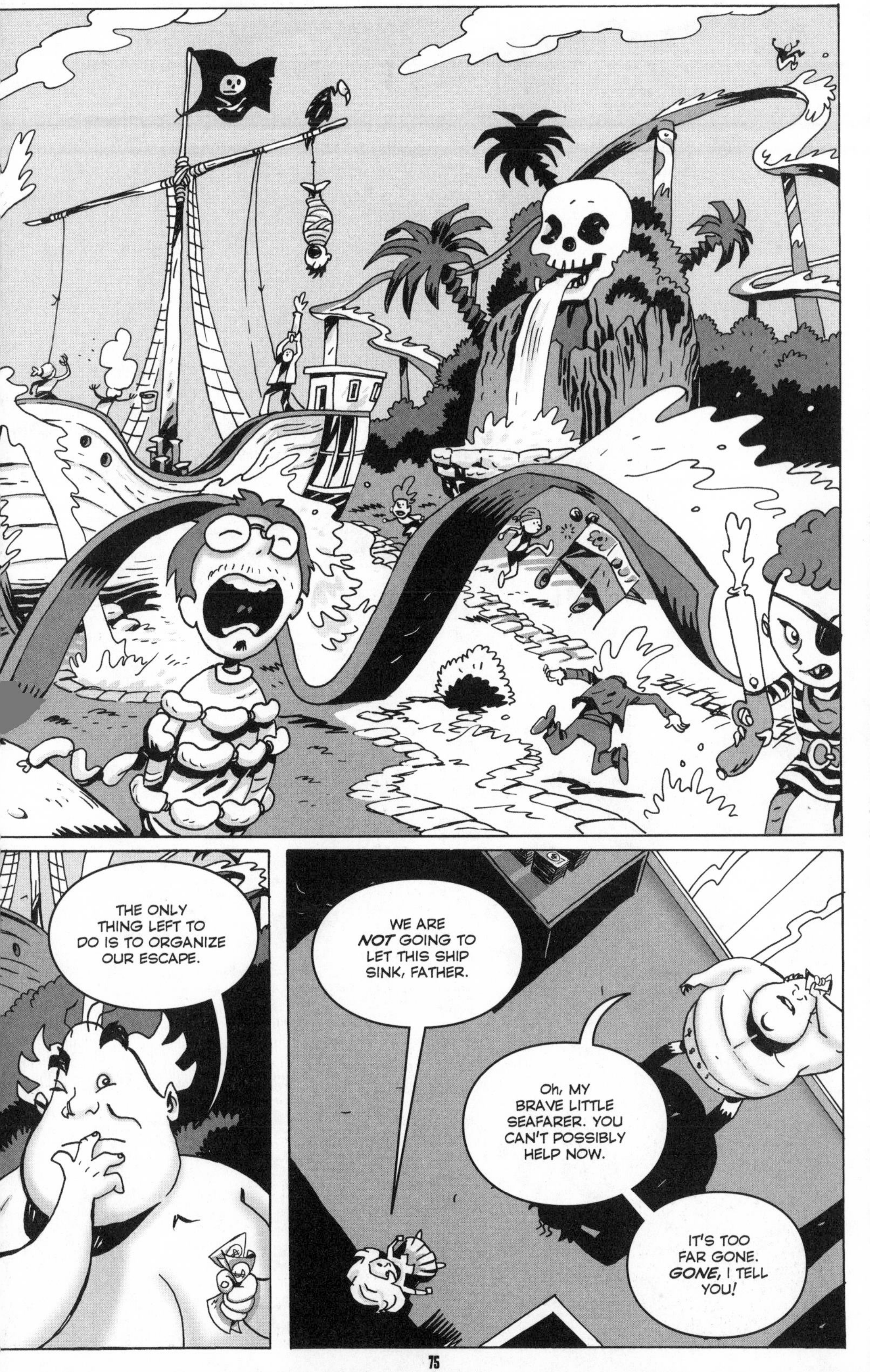

THE ONLY THING LEFT TO DO IS TO ORGANIZE OUR ESCAPE.
WE ARE *NOT* GOING TO LET THIS SHIP SINK, FATHER.
Oh, MY BRAVE LITTLE SEAFARER. YOU CAN'T POSSIBLY HELP NOW.
IT'S TOO FAR GONE. *GONE,* I TELL YOU!

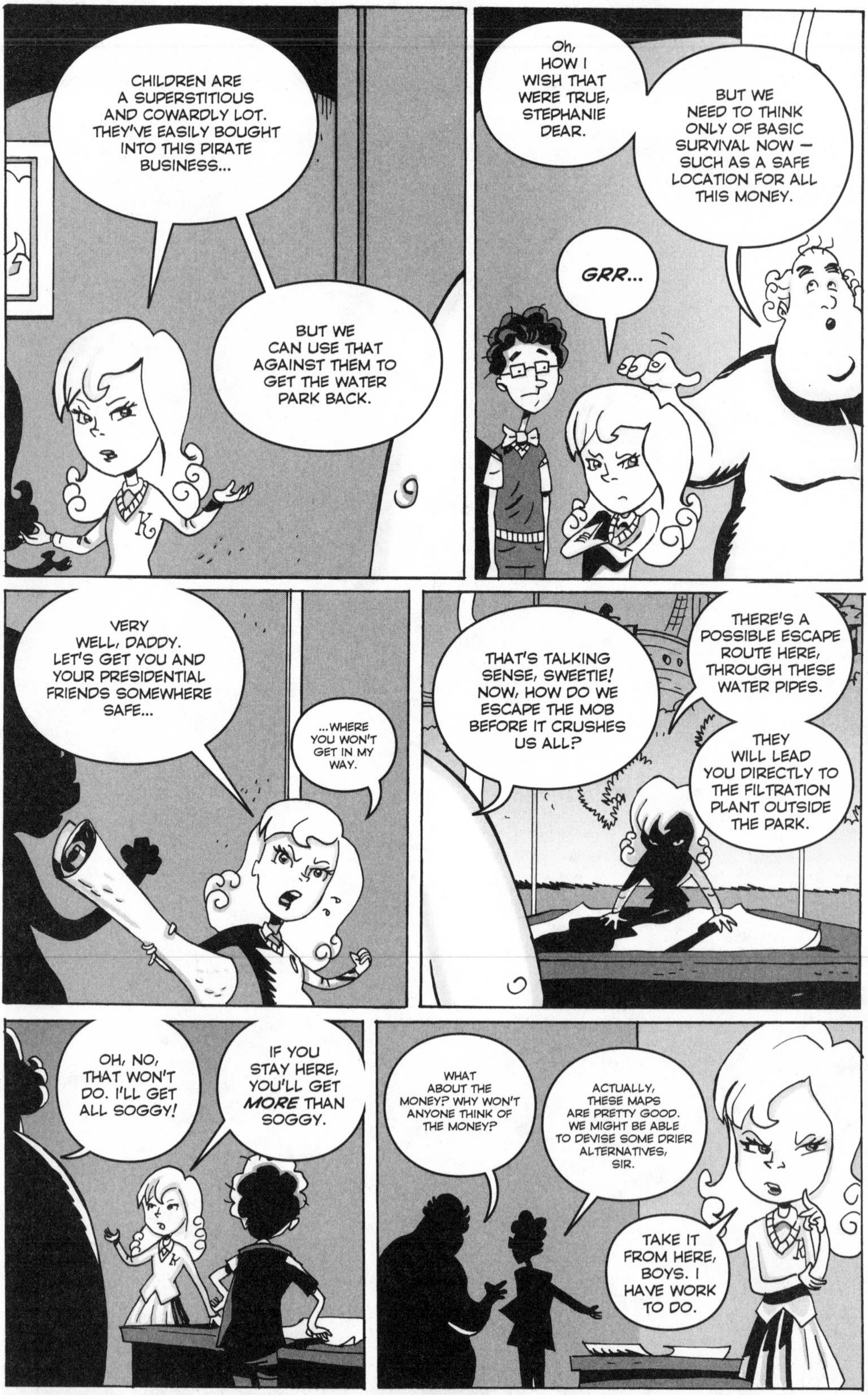
CHILDREN ARE A SUPERSTITIOUS AND COWARDLY LOT. THEY'VE EASILY BOUGHT INTO THIS PIRATE BUSINESS...
BUT WE CAN USE THAT AGAINST THEM TO GET THE WATER PARK BACK.
Oh, HOW I WISH THAT WERE TRUE, STEPHANIE DEAR.
BUT WE NEED TO THINK ONLY OF BASIC SURVIVAL NOW — SUCH AS A SAFE LOCATION FOR ALL THIS MONEY.
GRR...
VERY WELL, DADDY. LET'S GET YOU AND YOUR PRESIDENTIAL FRIENDS SOMEWHERE SAFE...
...WHERE YOU WON'T GET IN MY WAY.
THAT'S TALKING SENSE, SWEETIE! NOW, HOW DO WE ESCAPE THE MOB BEFORE IT CRUSHES US ALL?
THERE'S A POSSIBLE ESCAPE ROUTE HERE, THROUGH THESE WATER PIPES.
THEY WILL LEAD YOU DIRECTLY TO THE FILTRATION PLANT OUTSIDE THE PARK.
OH, NO, THAT WON'T DO. I'LL GET ALL SOGGY!
IF YOU STAY HERE, YOU'LL GET *MORE* THAN SOGGY.
WHAT ABOUT THE MONEY? WHY WON'T ANYONE THINK OF THE MONEY?
ACTUALLY, THESE MAPS ARE PRETTY GOOD. WE MIGHT BE ABLE TO DEVISE SOME DRIER ALTERNATIVES, SIR.
TAKE IT FROM HERE, BOYS. I HAVE WORK TO DO.

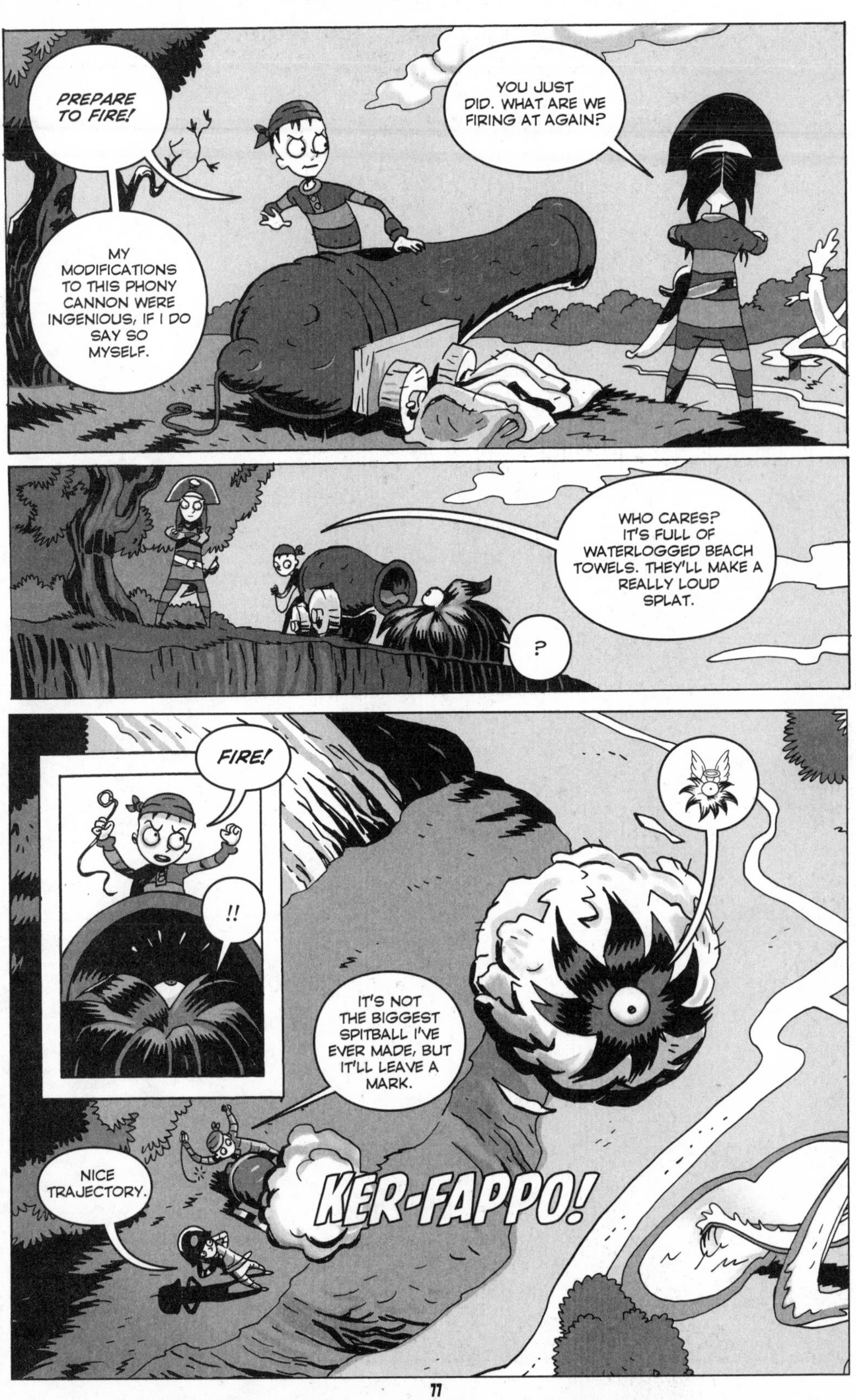
PREPARE TO FIRE!
MY MODIFICATIONS TO THIS PHONY CANNON WERE INGENIOUS, IF I DO SAY SO MYSELF.
YOU JUST DID. WHAT ARE WE FIRING AT AGAIN?
WHO CARES? IT'S FULL OF WATERLOGGED BEACH TOWELS. THEY'LL MAKE A REALLY LOUD SPLAT.
?
FIRE!
!!
IT'S NOT THE BIGGEST SPITBALL I'VE EVER MADE, BUT IT'LL LEAVE A MARK.
NICE TRAJECTORY.
KER-FAPPO!

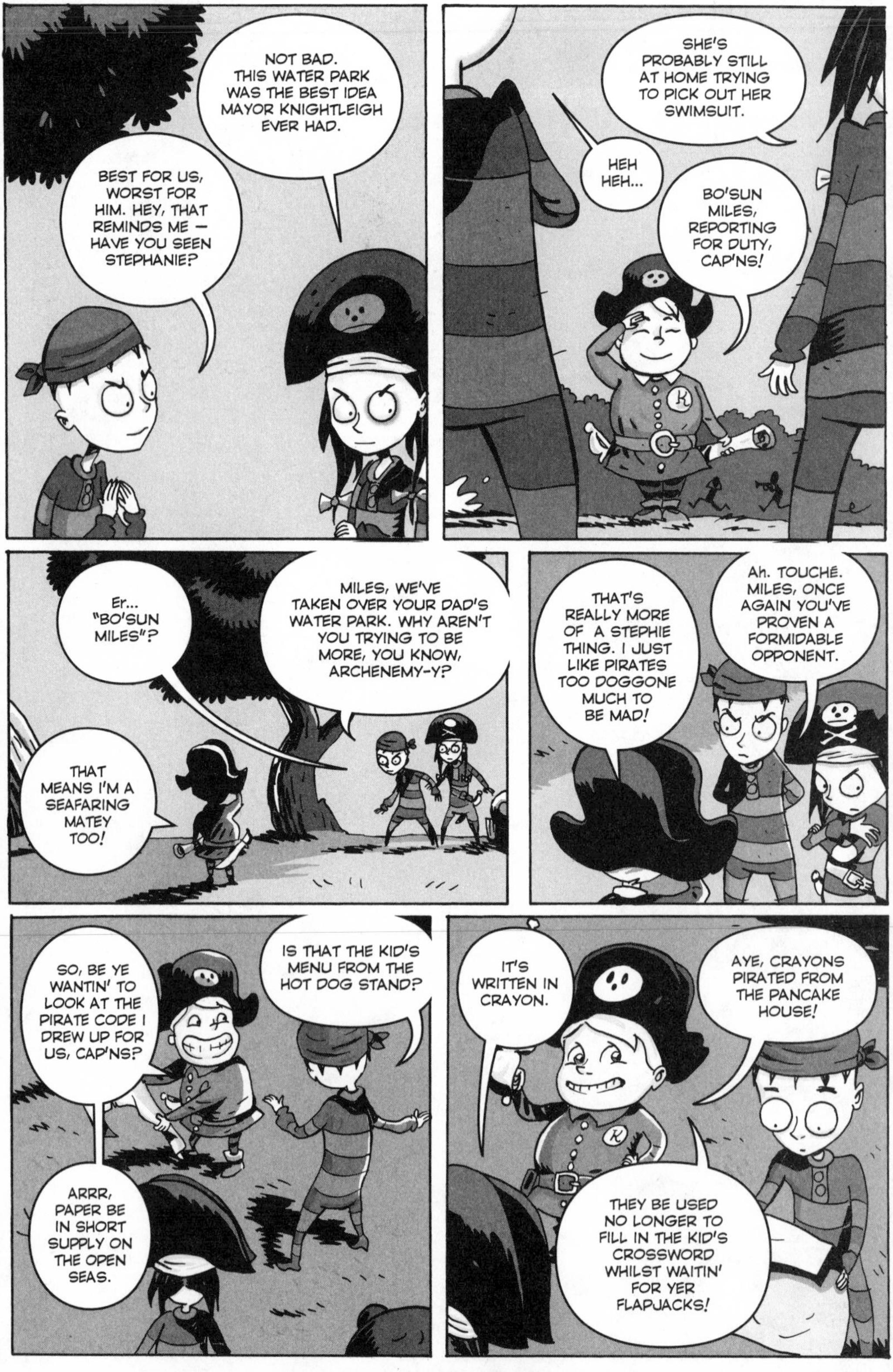
NOT BAD. THIS WATER PARK WAS THE BEST IDEA MAYOR KNIGHTLEIGH EVER HAD.
BEST FOR US, WORST FOR HIM. HEY, THAT REMINDS ME — HAVE YOU SEEN STEPHANIE?
SHE'S PROBABLY STILL AT HOME TRYING TO PICK OUT HER SWIMSUIT.
HEH HEH...
BO'SUN MILES, REPORTING FOR DUTY, CAP'NS!
Er... "BO'SUN MILES"?
THAT MEANS I'M A SEAFARING MATEY TOO!
MILES, WE'VE TAKEN OVER YOUR DAD'S WATER PARK. WHY AREN'T YOU TRYING TO BE MORE, YOU KNOW, ARCHENEMY-Y?
THAT'S REALLY MORE OF A STEPHIE THING. I JUST LIKE PIRATES TOO DOGGONE MUCH TO BE MAD!
Ah. TOUCHÉ. MILES, ONCE AGAIN YOU'VE PROVEN A FORMIDABLE OPPONENT.
SO, BE YE WANTIN' TO LOOK AT THE PIRATE CODE I DREW UP FOR US, CAP'NS?
IS THAT THE KID'S MENU FROM THE HOT DOG STAND?
ARRR, PAPER BE IN SHORT SUPPLY ON THE OPEN SEAS.
IT'S WRITTEN IN CRAYON.
AYE, CRAYONS PIRATED FROM THE PANCAKE HOUSE!
THEY BE USED NO LONGER TO FILL IN THE KID'S CROSSWORD WHILST WAITIN' FOR YER FLAPJACKS!

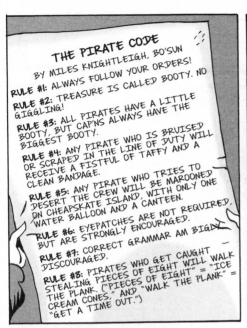

THE PIRATE CODE
BY MILES KNIGHTLEIGH, BO'SUN

RULE #1: ALWAYS FOLLOW YOUR ORDERS!

RULE #2: TREASURE IS CALLED BOOTY. NO GIGGLING!

RULE #3: ALL PIRATES HAVE A LITTLE BOOTY, BUT CAP'NS ALWAYS HAVE THE BIGGEST BOOTY.

RULE #4: ANY PIRATE WHO IS BRUISED OR SCRAPED IN THE LINE OF DUTY WILL RECEIVE A FISTFUL OF TAFFY AND A CLEAN BANDAGE.

RULE #5: ANY PIRATE WHO TRIES TO DESERT THE CREW WILL BE MAROONED ON CHEAPSKATE ISLAND, WITH ONLY ONE WATER BALLOON AND A CANTEEN.

RULE #6: EYEPATCHES ARE NOT REQUIRED, BUT ARE STRONGLY ENCOURAGED.

RULE #7: CORRECT GRAMMAR AM BIGLY DISCOURAGED.

RULE #8: PIRATES WHO GET CAUGHT STEALING PIECES OF EIGHT WILL WALK THE PLANK. ("PIECES OF EIGHT" = "ICE CREAM CONES," AND "WALK THE PLANK" = "GET A TIME OUT.")

"BOOTY?" WHERE'D YOU GET THIS STUFF?

IT WAS IN ME *HEARRRRRRT* ALL THIS TIME!

EYEPATCHES... TREASURE... INCORRECT GRAMMAR...

THIS WATER PARK IS SMALL TIME, ELLEN — WE COULD BE *REAL* PIRATES!

WE COULD SAIL DOWN THE RIVER AND TAKE NOD'S LIMBS!

DON'T TELL ME YOU'RE BUYING THIS STUFF?

YEAH, AND THEN WHAT?

JUST LIKE THE PIRATE CODE SAYS — TREASURE, BOOTY, PIRATING FOR ALL!

AND WE'RE THE CAPTAINS?

BETTER... WE'RE THE *CAP'NS!*

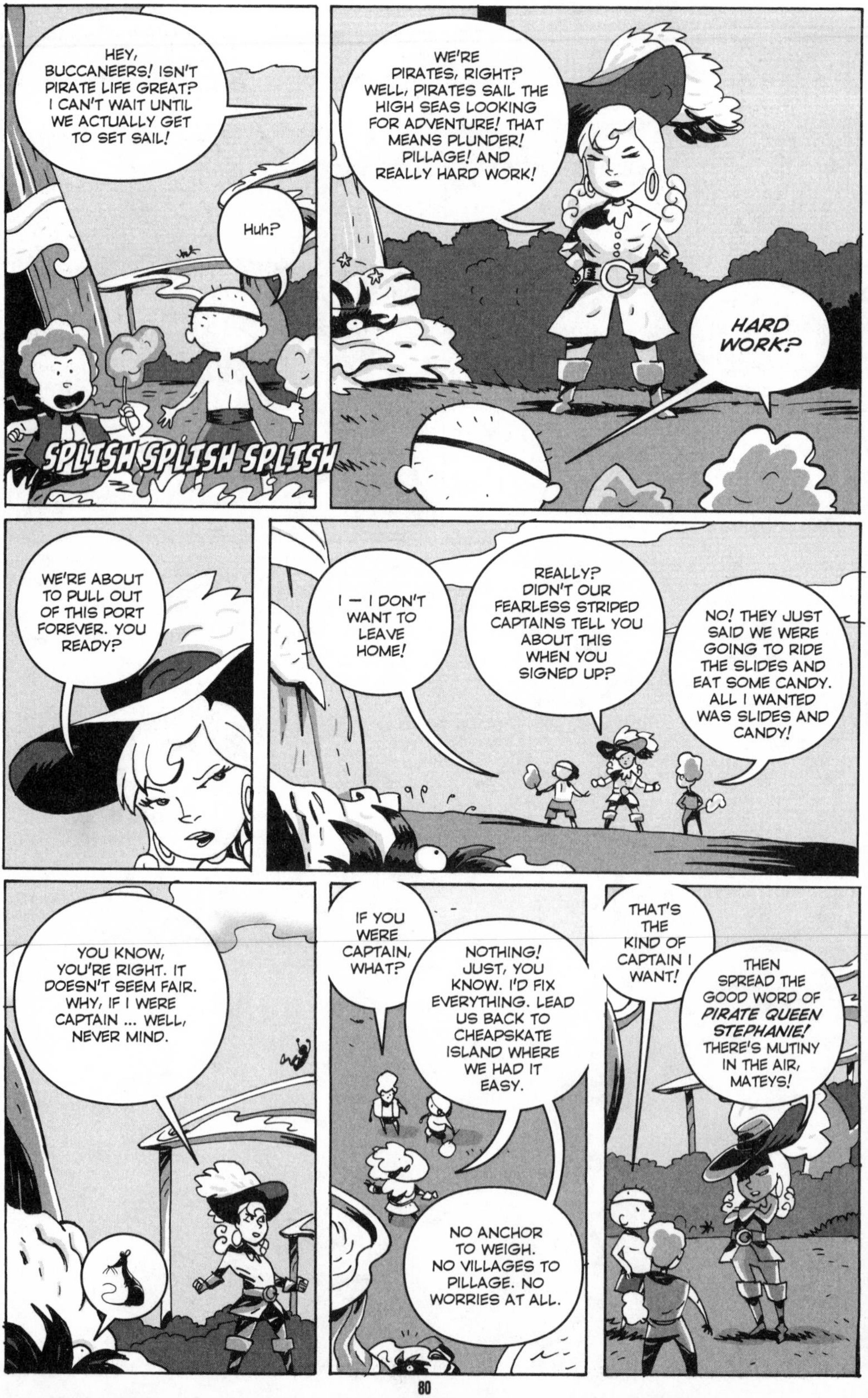
HEY, BUCCANEERS! ISN'T PIRATE LIFE GREAT? I CAN'T WAIT UNTIL WE ACTUALLY GET TO SET SAIL!
Huh?
SPLISH SPLISH SPLISH
WE'RE PIRATES, RIGHT? WELL, PIRATES SAIL THE HIGH SEAS LOOKING FOR ADVENTURE! THAT MEANS PLUNDER! PILLAGE! AND REALLY HARD WORK!
HARD WORK?
WE'RE ABOUT TO PULL OUT OF THIS PORT FOREVER. YOU READY?
I — I DON'T WANT TO LEAVE HOME!
REALLY? DIDN'T OUR FEARLESS STRIPED CAPTAINS TELL YOU ABOUT THIS WHEN YOU SIGNED UP?
NO! THEY JUST SAID WE WERE GOING TO RIDE THE SLIDES AND EAT SOME CANDY. ALL I WANTED WAS SLIDES AND CANDY!
YOU KNOW, YOU'RE RIGHT. IT DOESN'T SEEM FAIR. WHY, IF I WERE CAPTAIN ... WELL, NEVER MIND.
IF YOU WERE CAPTAIN, WHAT?
NOTHING! JUST, YOU KNOW. I'D FIX EVERYTHING. LEAD US BACK TO CHEAPSKATE ISLAND WHERE WE HAD IT EASY.
NO ANCHOR TO WEIGH. NO VILLAGES TO PILLAGE. NO WORRIES AT ALL.
THAT'S THE KIND OF CAPTAIN I WANT!
THEN SPREAD THE GOOD WORD OF PIRATE QUEEN STEPHANIE! THERE'S MUTINY IN THE AIR, MATEYS!

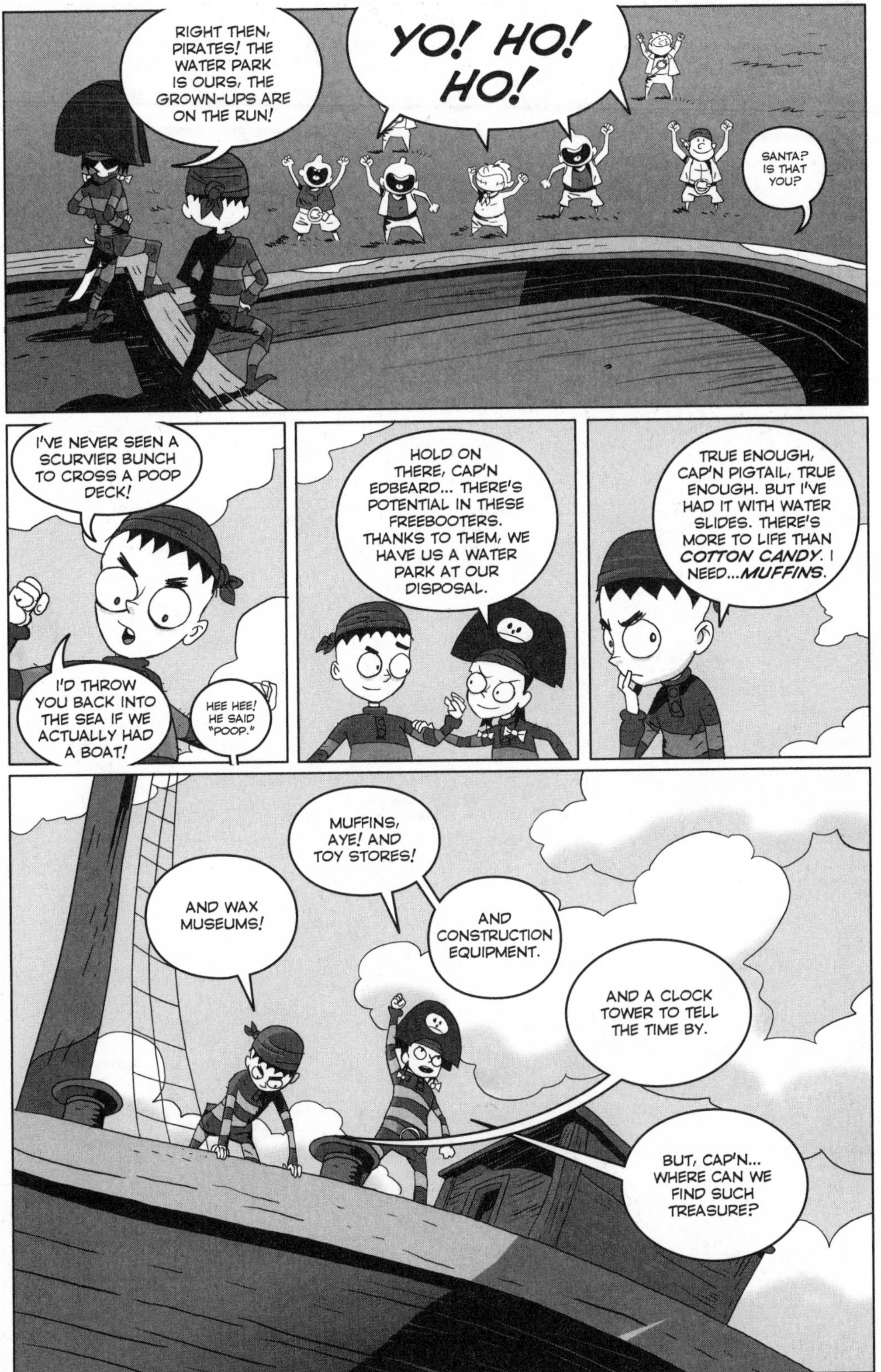
RIGHT THEN, PIRATES! THE WATER PARK IS OURS, THE GROWN-UPS ARE ON THE RUN!
YO! HO! HO!
SANTA? IS THAT YOU?
I'VE NEVER SEEN A SCURVIER BUNCH TO CROSS A POOP DECK!
I'D THROW YOU BACK INTO THE SEA IF WE ACTUALLY HAD A BOAT!
HEE HEE! HE SAID "POOP."
HOLD ON THERE, CAP'N EDBEARD... THERE'S POTENTIAL IN THESE FREEBOOTERS. THANKS TO THEM, WE HAVE US A WATER PARK AT OUR DISPOSAL.
TRUE ENOUGH, CAP'N PIGTAIL, TRUE ENOUGH. BUT I'VE HAD IT WITH WATER SLIDES. THERE'S MORE TO LIFE THAN COTTON CANDY. I NEED...MUFFINS.
MUFFINS, AYE! AND TOY STORES!
AND WAX MUSEUMS!
AND CONSTRUCTION EQUIPMENT.
AND A CLOCK TOWER TO TELL THE TIME BY.
BUT, CAP'N... WHERE CAN WE FIND SUCH TREASURE?

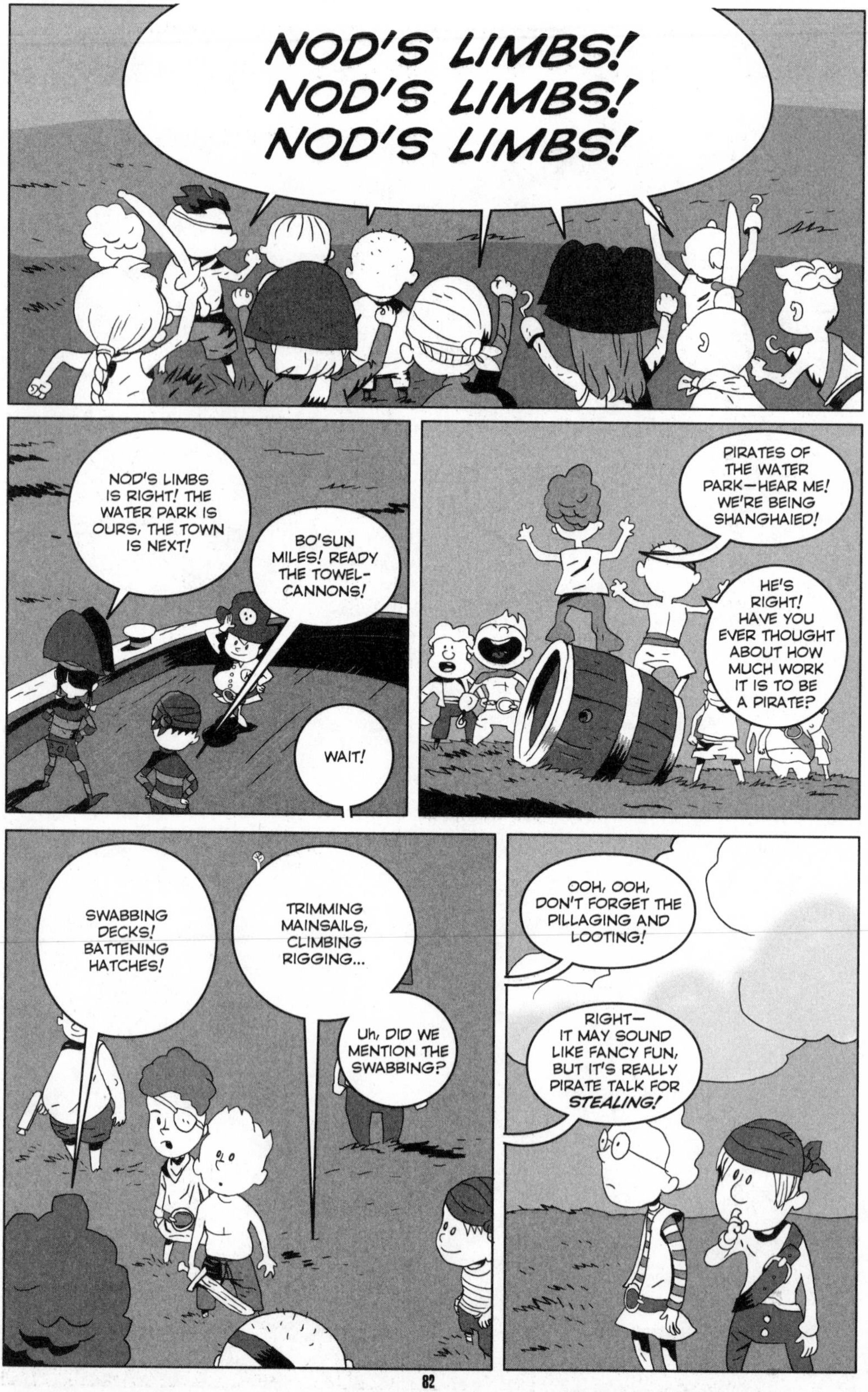
NOD'S LIMBS! NOD'S LIMBS! NOD'S LIMBS!
NOD'S LIMBS IS RIGHT! THE WATER PARK IS OURS, THE TOWN IS NEXT!
BO'SUN MILES! READY THE TOWEL-CANNONS!
WAIT!
PIRATES OF THE WATER PARK—HEAR ME! WE'RE BEING SHANGHAIED!
HE'S RIGHT! HAVE YOU EVER THOUGHT ABOUT HOW MUCH WORK IT IS TO BE A PIRATE?
SWABBING DECKS! BATTENING HATCHES!
TRIMMING MAINSAILS, CLIMBING RIGGING...
Uh, DID WE MENTION THE SWABBING?
OOH, OOH, DON'T FORGET THE PILLAGING AND LOOTING!
RIGHT— IT MAY SOUND LIKE FANCY FUN, BUT IT'S REALLY PIRATE TALK FOR *STEALING!*

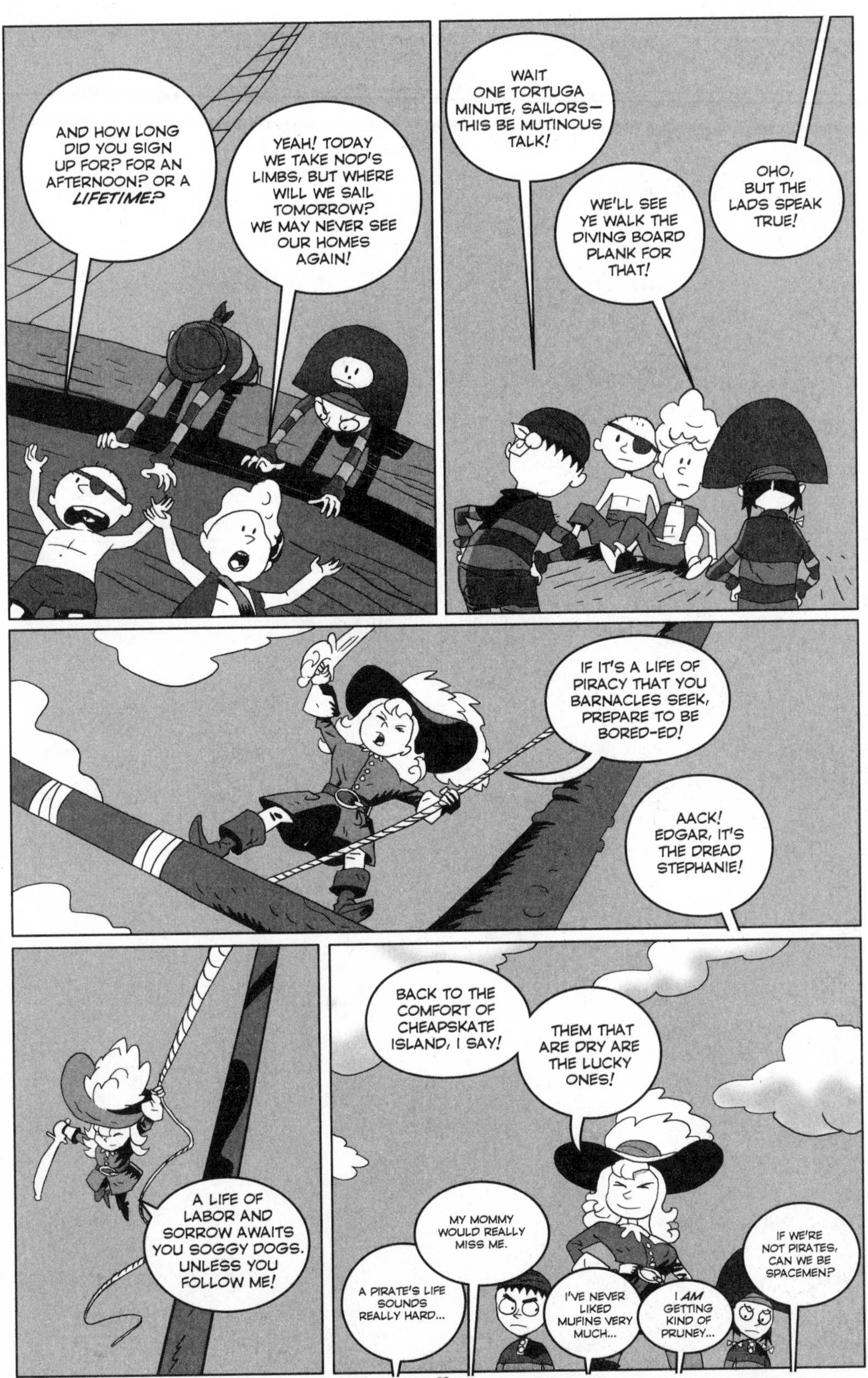
AND HOW LONG DID YOU SIGN UP FOR? FOR AN AFTERNOON? OR A *LIFETIME?*
YEAH! TODAY WE TAKE NOD'S LIMBS, BUT WHERE WILL WE SAIL TOMORROW? WE MAY NEVER SEE OUR HOMES AGAIN!
WAIT ONE TORTUGA MINUTE, SAILORS—THIS BE MUTINOUS TALK!
WE'LL SEE YE WALK THE DIVING BOARD PLANK FOR THAT!
OHO, BUT THE LADS SPEAK TRUE!
IF IT'S A LIFE OF PIRACY THAT YOU BARNACLES SEEK, PREPARE TO BE BORED-ED!
AACK! EDGAR, IT'S THE DREAD STEPHANIE!
A LIFE OF LABOR AND SORROW AWAITS YOU SOGGY DOGS. UNLESS YOU FOLLOW ME!
BACK TO THE COMFORT OF CHEAPSKATE ISLAND, I SAY!
THEM THAT ARE DRY ARE THE LUCKY ONES!
A PIRATE'S LIFE SOUNDS REALLY HARD...
MY MOMMY WOULD REALLY MISS ME.
I'VE NEVER LIKED MUFINS VERY MUCH...
I *AM* GETTING KIND OF PRUNEY...
IF WE'RE NOT PIRATES, CAN WE BE SPACEMEN?

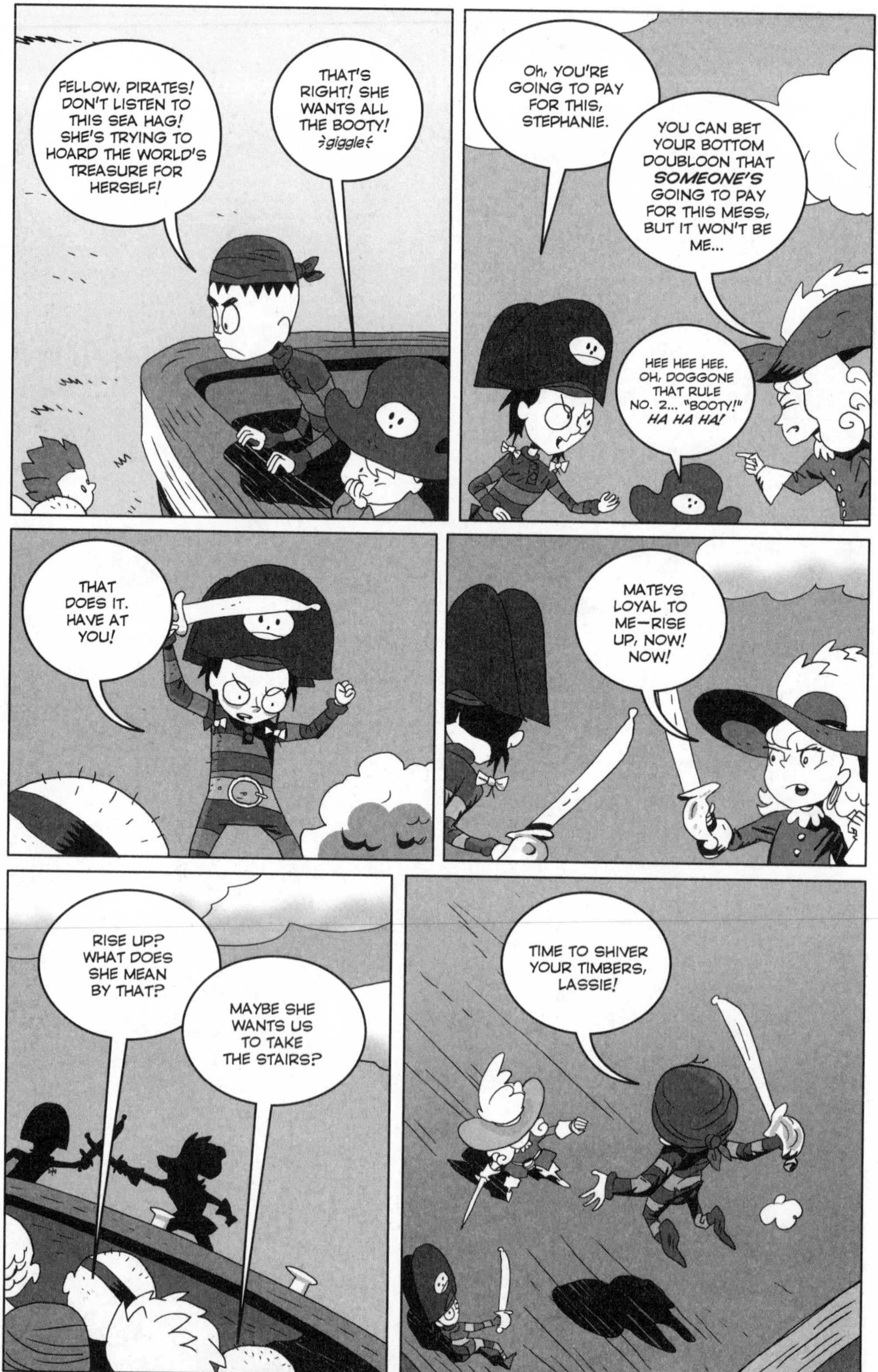
FELLOW, PIRATES! DON'T LISTEN TO THIS SEA HAG! SHE'S TRYING TO HOARD THE WORLD'S TREASURE FOR HERSELF!
THAT'S RIGHT! SHE WANTS ALL THE BOOTY! giggle
Oh, YOU'RE GOING TO PAY FOR THIS, STEPHANIE.
YOU CAN BET YOUR BOTTOM DOUBLOON THAT SOMEONE'S GOING TO PAY FOR THIS MESS, BUT IT WON'T BE ME...
HEE HEE HEE. OH, DOGGONE THAT RULE NO. 2... "BOOTY!" HA HA HA!
THAT DOES IT. HAVE AT YOU!
MATEYS LOYAL TO ME—RISE UP, NOW! NOW!
RISE UP? WHAT DOES SHE MEAN BY THAT?
MAYBE SHE WANTS US TO TAKE THE STAIRS?
TIME TO SHIVER YOUR TIMBERS, LASSIE!

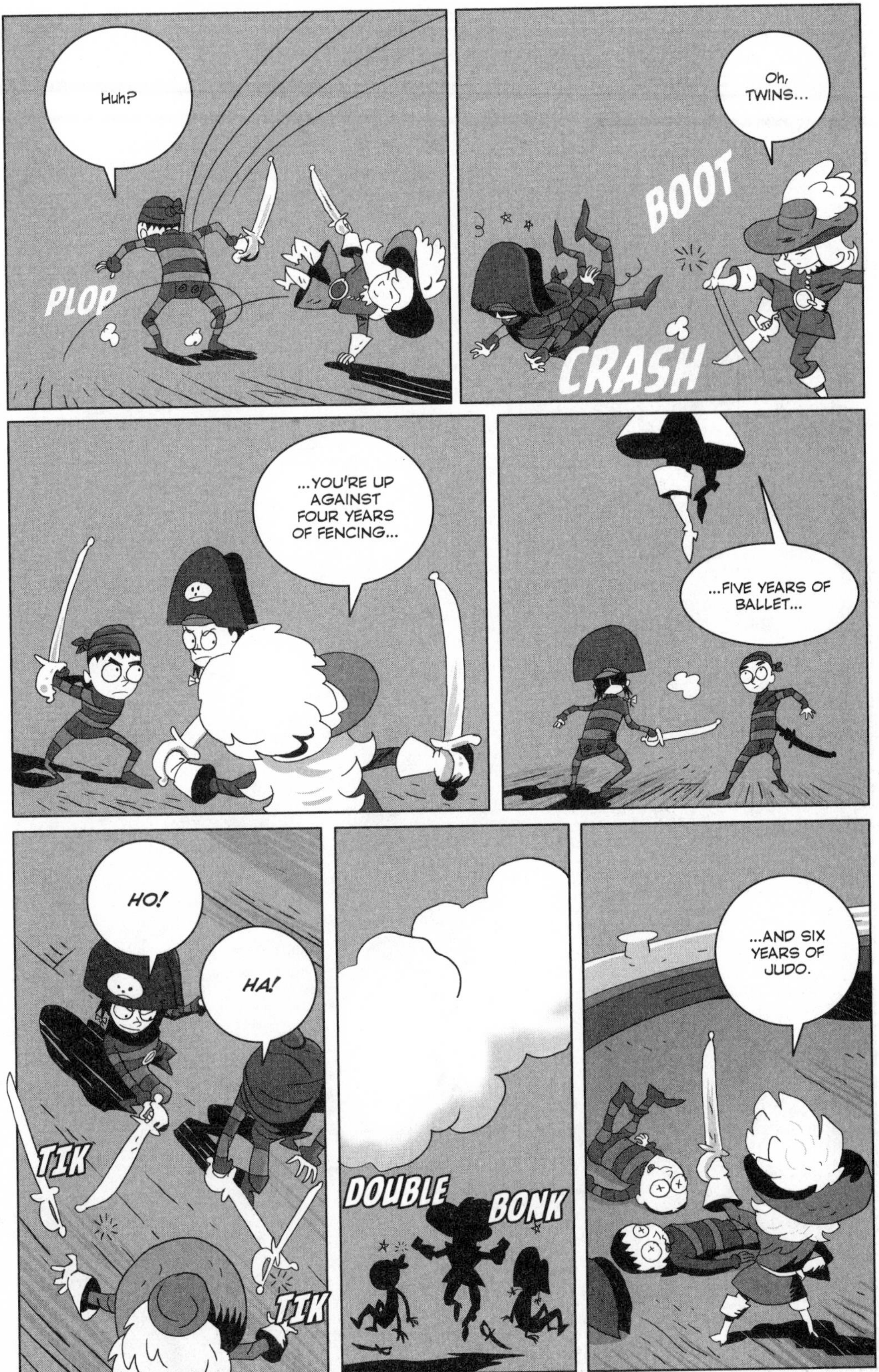
Huh?
PLOP
Oh, TWINS...
BOOT
CRASH
...YOU'RE UP AGAINST FOUR YEARS OF FENCING...
...FIVE YEARS OF BALLET...
HO!
HA!
TIK
TIK
DOUBLE
BONK
...AND SIX YEARS OF JUDO.

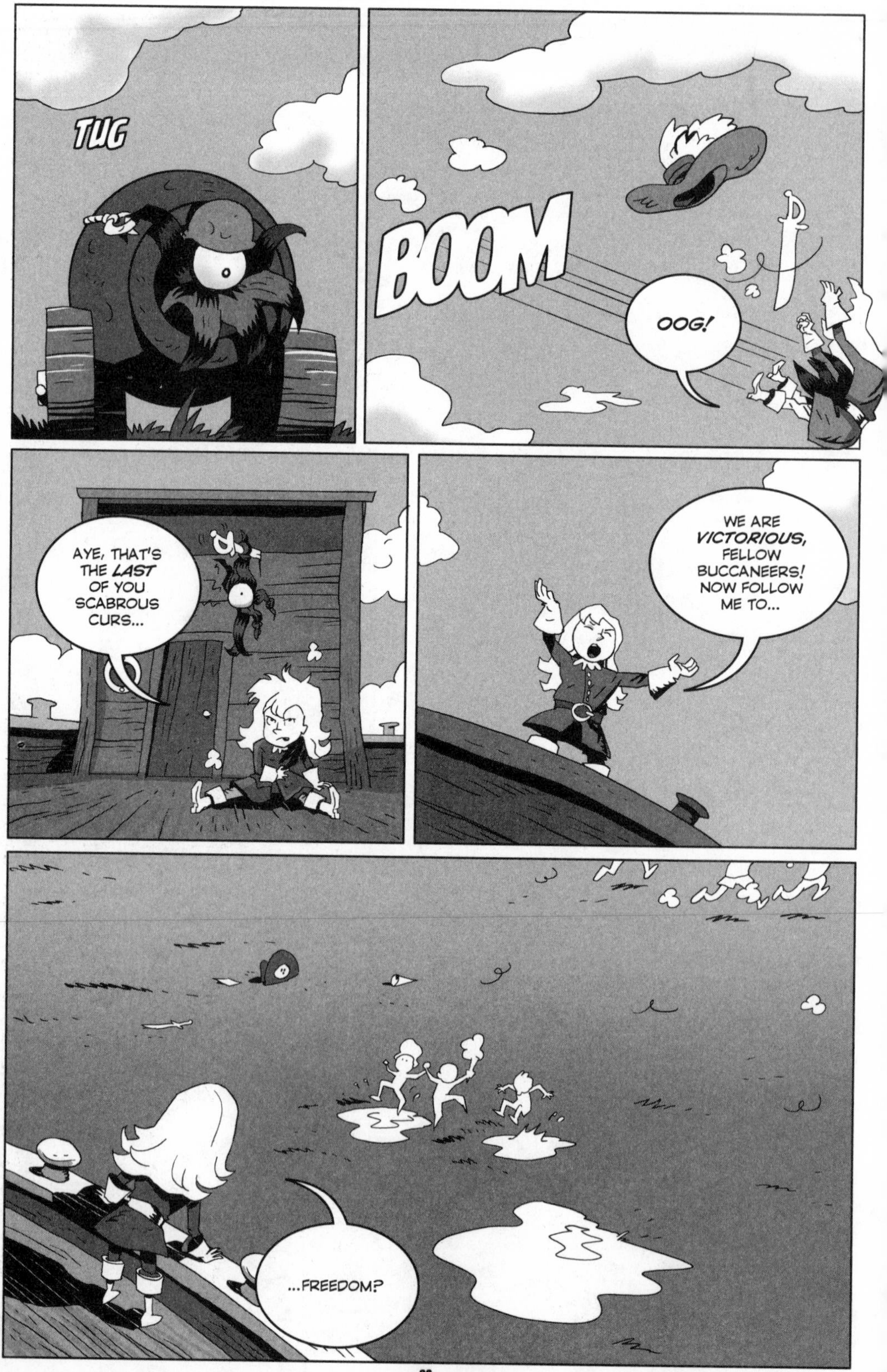
TUG
BOOM
OOG!
AYE, THAT'S THE LAST OF YOU SCABROUS CURS...
WE ARE VICTORIOUS, FELLOW BUCCANEERS! NOW FOLLOW ME TO...
...FREEDOM?

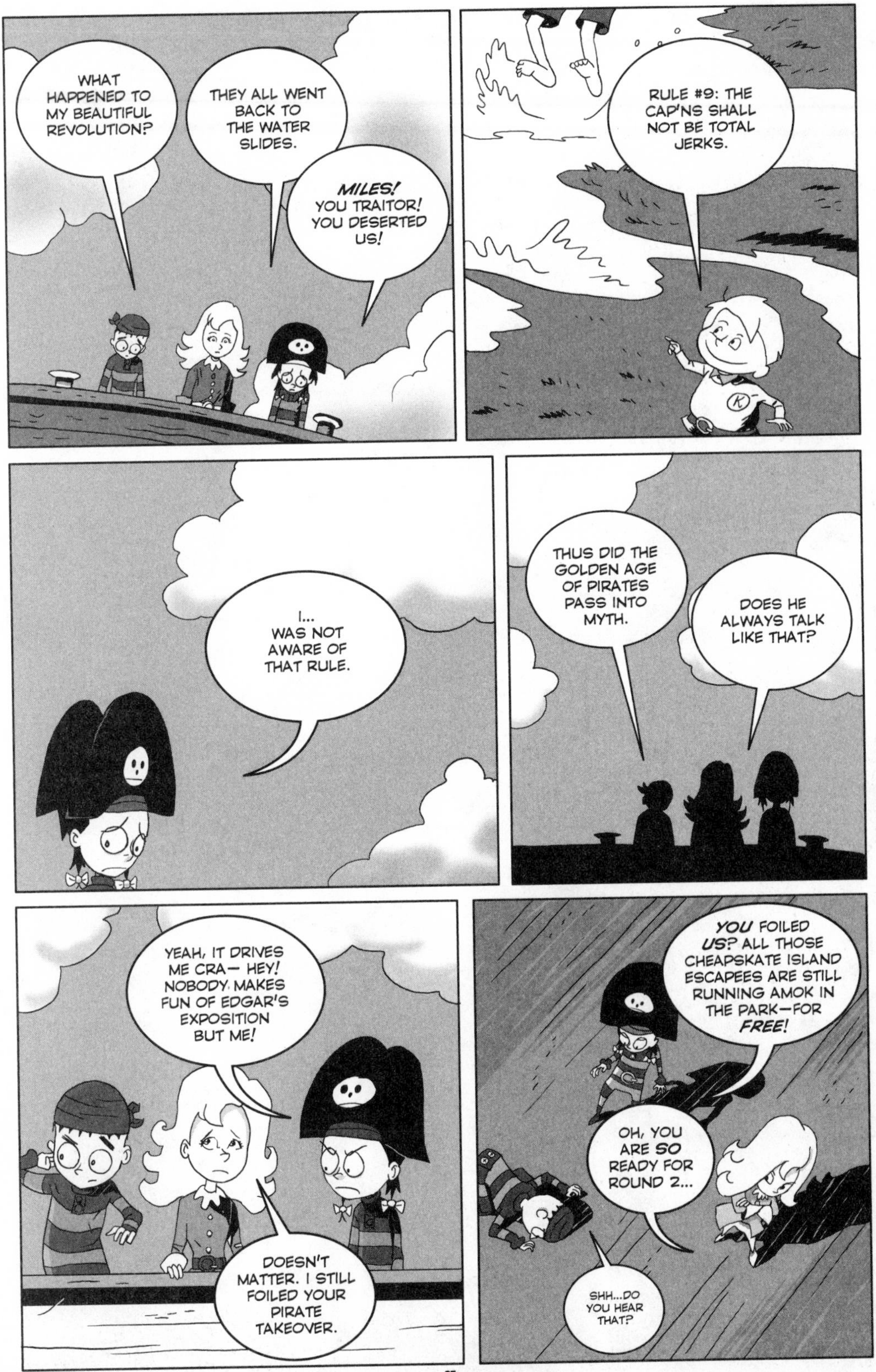
WHAT HAPPENED TO MY BEAUTIFUL REVOLUTION?
THEY ALL WENT BACK TO THE WATER SLIDES.
MILES! YOU TRAITOR! YOU DESERTED US!
RULE #9: THE CAP'NS SHALL NOT BE TOTAL JERKS.
I... WAS NOT AWARE OF THAT RULE.
THUS DID THE GOLDEN AGE OF PIRATES PASS INTO MYTH.
DOES HE ALWAYS TALK LIKE THAT?
YEAH, IT DRIVES ME CRA— HEY! NOBODY MAKES FUN OF EDGAR'S EXPOSITION BUT ME!
DOESN'T MATTER. I STILL FOILED YOUR PIRATE TAKEOVER.
YOU FOILED US? ALL THOSE CHEAPSKATE ISLAND ESCAPEES ARE STILL RUNNING AMOK IN THE PARK—FOR FREE!
OH, YOU ARE SO READY FOR ROUND 2...
SHH...DO YOU HEAR THAT?

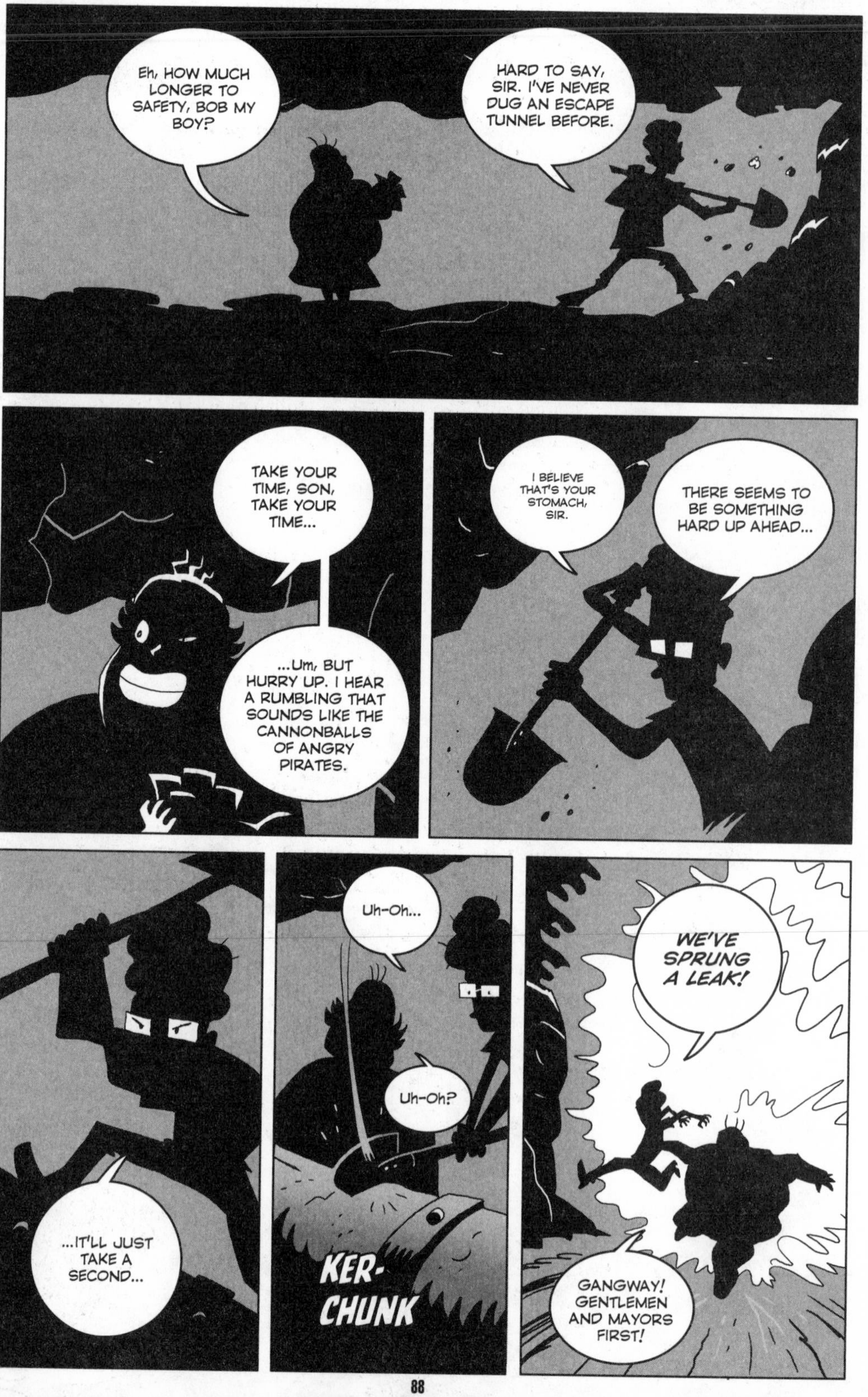

Eh, HOW MUCH LONGER TO SAFETY, BOB MY BOY?
HARD TO SAY, SIR. I'VE NEVER DUG AN ESCAPE TUNNEL BEFORE.
TAKE YOUR TIME, SON, TAKE YOUR TIME...
...Um, BUT HURRY UP. I HEAR A RUMBLING THAT SOUNDS LIKE THE CANNONBALLS OF ANGRY PIRATES.
I BELIEVE THAT'S YOUR STOMACH, SIR.
THERE SEEMS TO BE SOMETHING HARD UP AHEAD...
...IT'LL JUST TAKE A SECOND...
Uh-Oh...
Uh-Oh?
KER-CHUNK
WE'VE SPRUNG A LEAK!
GANGWAY! GENTLEMEN AND MAYORS FIRST!

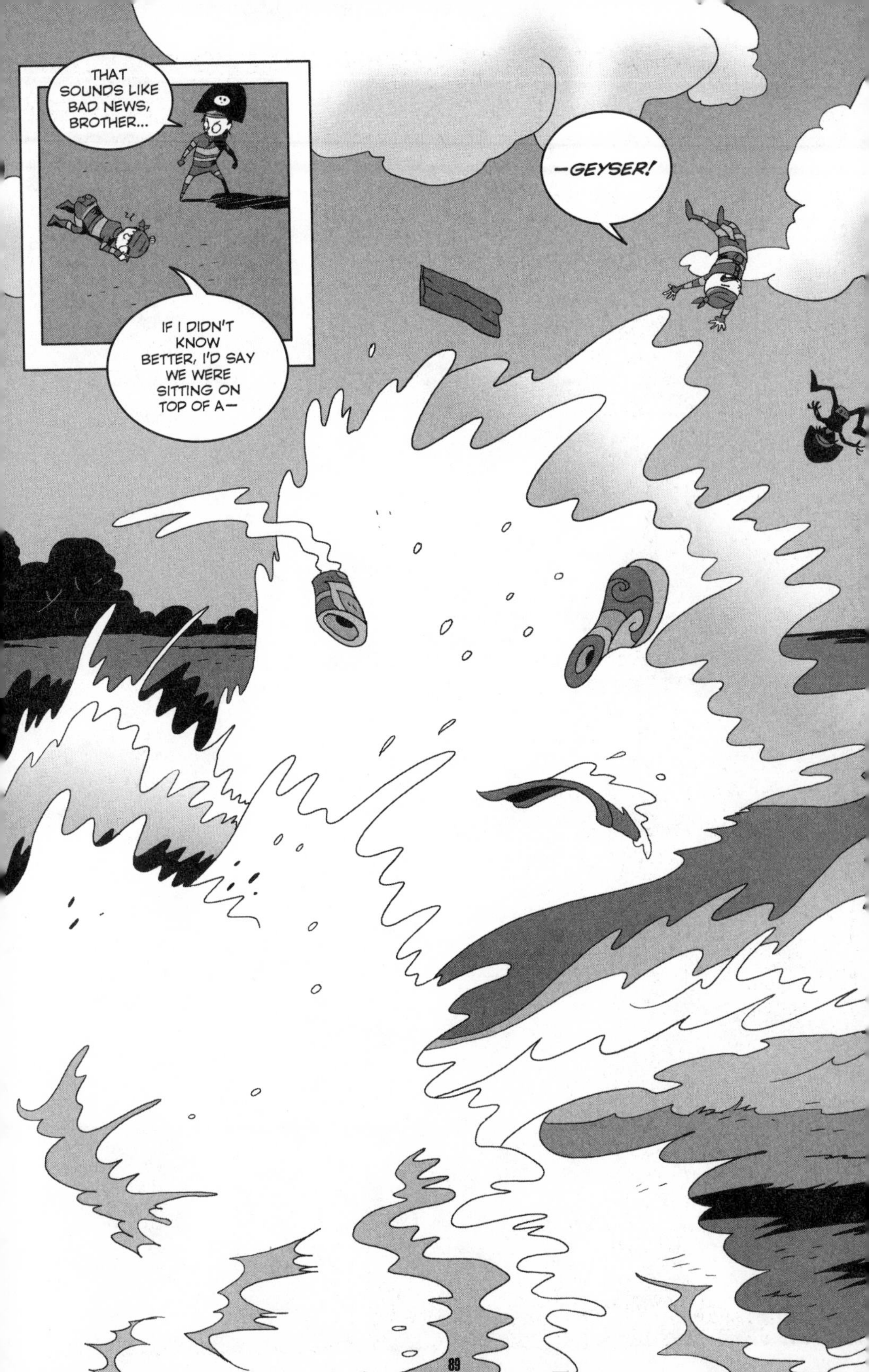
THAT SOUNDS LIKE BAD NEWS, BROTHER...
IF I DIDN'T KNOW BETTER, I'D SAY WE WERE SITTING ON TOP OF A—
—GEYSER!

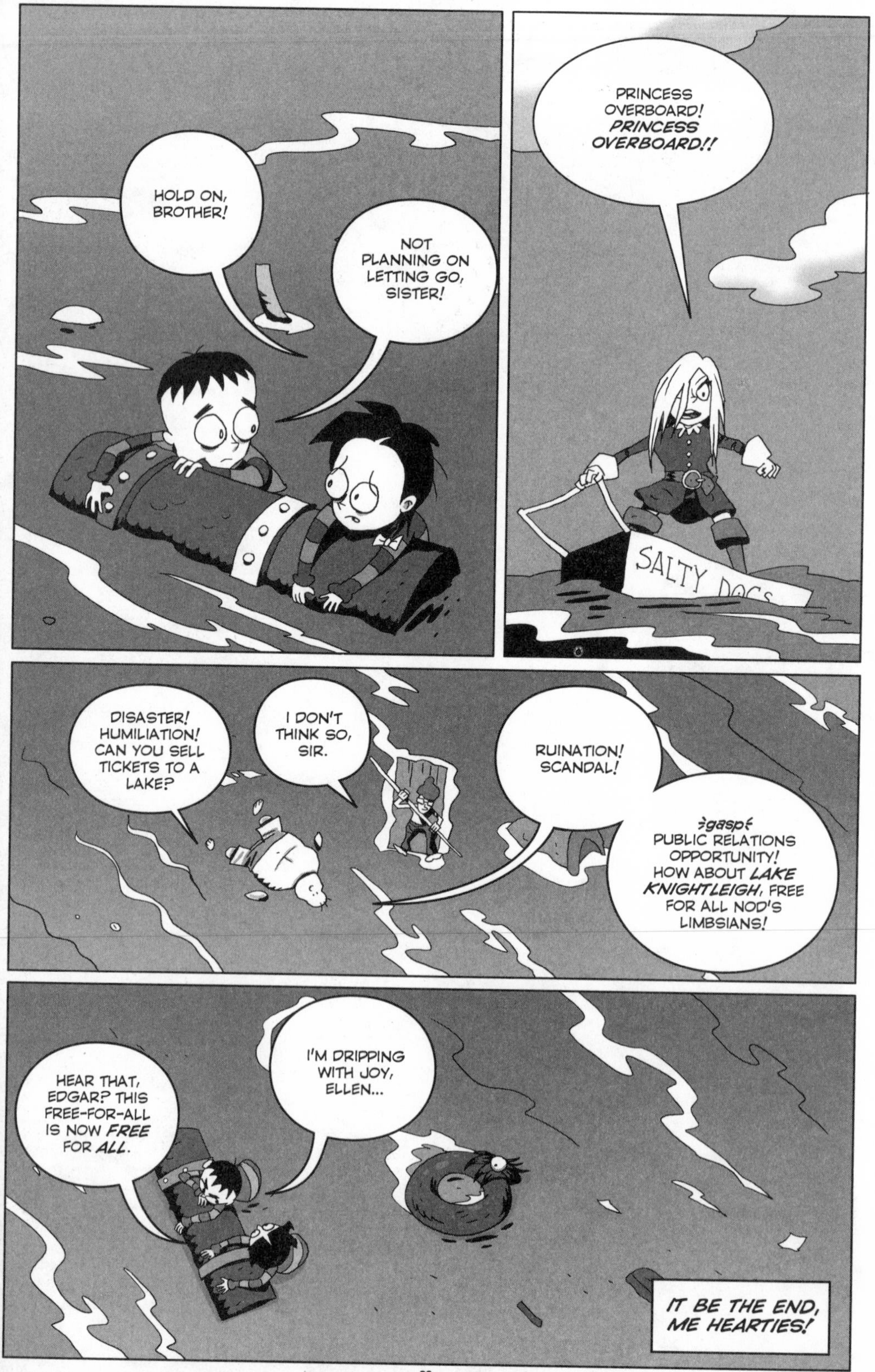
HOLD ON, BROTHER!
NOT PLANNING ON LETTING GO, SISTER!
PRINCESS OVERBOARD! PRINCESS OVERBOARD!!
SALTY DOGS
DISASTER! HUMILIATION! CAN YOU SELL TICKETS TO A LAKE?
I DON'T THINK SO, SIR.
RUINATION! SCANDAL!
gasp PUBLIC RELATIONS OPPORTUNITY! HOW ABOUT LAKE KNIGHTLEIGH, FREE FOR ALL NOD'S LIMBSIANS!
HEAR THAT, EDGAR? THIS FREE-FOR-ALL IS NOW FREE FOR ALL.
I'M DRIPPING WITH JOY, ELLEN...
IT BE THE END, ME HEARTIES!

THIS IS A FAKE ADVERTISEMENT.

HELTER SMELTER NOVELTY Co.

"Whoever Smelt It Dealt It!"

America's Third Favorite Novelty Fun Warehouse

NO MONEY BACK GUARANTEE *Since 1893* NOT LIABLE FOR INJURY

A wholly owned subsidiary of Smelterburg Industrial Conglomo-tainment Ltd.

INSTA-BLEMISH

Don't let your flawless complexion keep people from getting to know the REAL you! This top secret Insta-Blemish formula will end the anxiety and worry of freakishly clear skin—or your money back!

#63632 Zit Creme.............................. $3.29

REALISTIC CPA LICENSE

Impress your friends and terrify your enemies with this super-realistic Certified Public Accountant license. Captivate girls with promises of secure tax shelters, defeat bullies with threats of internal audits, and be the coolest kid on your block.

#1099A Accountancy Scam.............. $5.59

GIANT FISH

Need we say more?

#19057 Big Tuna................................ $7.49

NINJA DETECTOR

Right now, you might be surrounded by deadly ninjas. You'd know where they were hiding if you had a Ninja Detector. Buy one now, before it's too late.

#33225 Ninja Detector....................... $9.99

KILLER SMILE

Actual deadly smile will lay out an enemy at 50 feet. Must be 25 to order. (Check "I am 25" on order form.)

#82950 Killer Smile........................... $5.49

FAKE BEARD SPRAY

Need to look older? Want to catch a lady's eye? Instant beard clings to even the scrawniest jaw. Just shake, spray, and IMPRESS!

#37645 Weird Beard........................... $6.99

HAT OF SILENCE

Inconspicuous sombrero deadens all sound beneath its 3-foot brim. Perfect for infiltrating enemy headquarters, slinking past security guards, laughing obnoxiously in libraries, or skulking about shopping malls.

#88882 Silent Sombrero..................... $7.69

FAKE MILK

Looks like milk, smells like milk—tastes like a *Secret Flavor!* Hilarious!

#68682 Dairy Dupe Juice $3.99

NOVELTY BRIEFCASE

Look like a real businessman with this attaché-style briefcase made of supple, glove-soft Italian leather. Triple gusset interior with a center pocket for your laptop computer. Goldtone metal accents, sleek buckle closure, and a satin brass three-tumble-wheel lock. The whole neighborhood will wonder: Who's that handsome go-getter? Comes with mock investment portfolio and Real Ballpoint Pen.

#71835 Novelty Briefcase $699.99

SHOCK CLOCK

Switch out a sleeping sibling's alarm clock and he or she will awaken to a super-shocking surprise! "Good morning, Sleepy Head!" Also doubles as a hair curler.

#39855 Shock Clock.......................... $4.99

SHARK REPELLENT

Keep "nature's perfect predators" at bay at all times. Gives you peace of mind as you read, sleep, or mow the lawn. May not work on hammerheads or nurse sharks.

#X319845 Shark B Gone.................... $6.99

STINKY CARDS

Your friends won't know you're playing with a wonky deck, but they'll sure smell a rat...and other unflattering aromas!

#32196 Stinky Cards.......................... $3.49

CORNSTARCH GUN

Few firearms can adequately disperse even small quantities of cornstarch...not so our Cornstarch Gun! Just load the muzzle, tamp it down, adjust the flintlock, and BANG! Cornstarch right where you want it, when you want it.

#BB457 Cornstarch Dispenser........ $12.79

EXTRA HAND

You've got a water balloon in one hand and a sandwich in the other...and now you have to pick your nose! What to do? Look, problem solved!

#36211 Extra Hand............................ $3.95

GENUINE WHIZ-BANG-BOOM FIREWORK DISPLAY

The most spectacular display ever invented by man can be yours! Just light the fuse and step back to watch two hours of precision pyrotechnics set to a repeating loop of Tchaikovsky's *1812 Overture* (For safety purposes, the **Genuine Whiz-Bang-Boom Firework Display** does not include fuse, gunpowder, firework casings, or Tchaikovsky's *1812 Overture*. Do not light **Genuine Whiz-Bang-Boom Firework Display**. Do not remove from box.)

#34723 The G.W.B.B.F.D. $23.99

X.RAY SPECTACLES*

They really work! See things in a whole new way: The X.Ray Way!

#21342 X.Ray Spex............................ $6.99

**Clear glass lenses designed by noted optician Xavier Ray; not to be confused with X-ray technology or the ability to see through walls, doors, or clothing.*

FINGER STOCKS

Keep your prisoners snug with this classic containment device! If he can't take his fingers with him, he's not going anywhere!

#40736 Finger Stocks........................ $8.99

FAVERSHAM GASKET CUTTER

How many times have you cut a gasket only to realize the pipe fitting is a tad too wide or the hose nozzle is a tad too small? With this little beauty you always get the gasket you want, every time. "Always have 'er some Faversham!"

#18555 Gasket Cutter........................ $7.49

SUNSHINE!

Why do astronauts really go to space? Is it to study orbital strata and quasar nebulae and other cosmic hokum? No! It's to bottle sunshine, which they then bring back to Earth to warm the planet. Now you too can own your very own bottle of sunshine, and spread cheer to everyone around you.

#015699 Bottled Sunshine $3.92

ARMORED LONG JOHNS

Worried about your safety when you're dressed down to your britches? Fret no longer with our chain-mail long underwear (not responsible for chaffing or rusting)!

#29777 Armored Undergarment...... $12.99

CLEVELAND

Yes, you CAN rule Cleveland! Improve roads, build schools, make some speeches...visit the Rock and Roll Hall of Fame for free! And why not? YOU ARE THE MASTER OF CLEVELAND!

#80660 Cleveland............................ $11.99

RUDE NOISE CUSHION

Fits any chair. Choose from four noxious noises: please specify *Zbbbl, Pbbbt, Blooot,* or *Fpppbap*.

#00702 Rude Noise Cushion............ $2.49

CURSED TIKI IDOL

Are your siblings getting on your nerves? Are your teachers giving you too much homework? Strike back with your very own miniature taboo island god!

#12955 Cursed Tiki Idol.................... $4.49

PIRATE TIMBERS

Perfect for shivering. Comes with a buckle to be swashed!

#ARRR Pirate Timbers $3.49

SOUR NUTS

Turn your friends into sour-pussed squirrels! When someone dips into this attractive assortment of party nuts, no one will ever forget the distinctly *un-salty* surprise! Includes Lickity-lime cashews, Supra-lemon almonds, and Tart-attack-ack-orange peanuts. Do not combine will **Item #68682 Dairy Dupe Juice** under any circumstances.

#87366 Sour Nuts.............................. $3.79

CHESTER A. ARTHUR ACTION FIGURE

This heroic replica of the 21st U.S. president allows you to relive some of history's most exciting moments. Enact the Pendleton Civil Reform Act! Engage in polite debate with Rutherford B. Hayes! Establish bipartisan commissions! The power and glory of Chester Allan Arthur rests with you!

#05214 Chester A. Arthur Doll.......... $4.49

TRAINED BACTERIA

The World's Tiniest Pets—100,000 highly disciplined microorganisms come already trained to do fancy tricks: sit up, beg, roll over, shake hands, read a newspaper. Amaze your friends! Microscope not included.

#10964 Trained Bacteria.................... $2.99

SPRING-LOADED CHICKEN LEG

The perfect gift for your peg-legged friend who has everything!

#47811 Spring-Loaded Leg............... $9.99

FORTUNE-TELLER'S HAND

We all want to scare friends with horrible predictions for the future! What better to use than this authentic Fortune-Teller's Hand, plucked straight from an authentic fortune-teller!

#52849 All-Knowing Palm................ $5.49

"Pluto Is So a Planet" Fan Club

Fight the so-called "scientists" and join the crusade to end the lousy rumor that this beloved ninth planet is just another big rock floating around in space.

#99999 Pluto Club Membership Card..$.99

PEE SHOOTER

SOLD OUT!

#87125 The Wetster........................... $3.99

MINIATURE BUTLER

You'd be surprised at how efficient our 5" tall butler is! No Lord of the Manor ever had it so nice. Make room for him in your jacket pocket and he'll tidy up after you, tend to your hygiene, and mind your schedule. And he's oh so polite and well-spoken. Just add water. Some assembly required.

#36441 Miniature Butler.................... $9.99

MEANING OF LIFE

First discovered in an ancient garden and distilled over millenia down to it's pure essence, our patented *meaning of life* is all you've ever wanted...and then some! You'll never believe that something can be too good to be true again! Once sold to fabled kingdoms for great fortunes, the meaning of life can be yours FREE YES FREE with a purchase of SOUR NUTS (Item #87366).*

**Item #87366 currently out-of-stock.*

#98799 Meaning of Life.................... FREE*

ASSAULT TROMBONE!

"Step back, fool, or face my B-Flat Fortissimo!" With this brassy beauty, you'll always get the respect you deserve. Got an unwelcome invader in your personal space? Johnny Too-Tough think he can give you the business? Well, hit him with the old Bass Clef Glissando—guaranteed to buy you some room.

#51965 Assault Trombone............... $15.99

1 Million Novelties

Let there be no mistake than a Helter-Smelter product is a product of the highest quality. But what *is* quality? Philosopher Roger Pirsig argues that both rational and irrational notions of quality can co-exist; and so it is with the Helter-Smelter Novelty Co.—while it is possible that some of our products *may* exist, sometimes isn't better if they *don't*?

1 Billion Jokes

Imaginary items are the best kind!

HELTER SMELTER NOVELTY CO.

Dept.1313, Smelterburg Industrial Conglomo-tainment Ltd., Smelterburg, USA

1 Zillion Laughs

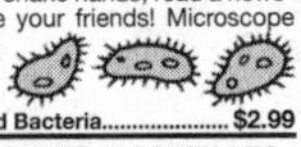

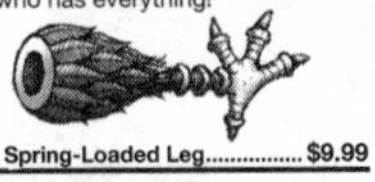

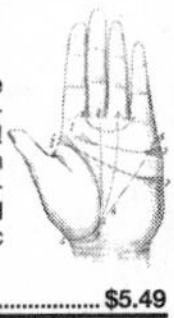

HEIMERTZ vs. ~~DRAGULA~~! FLOORING

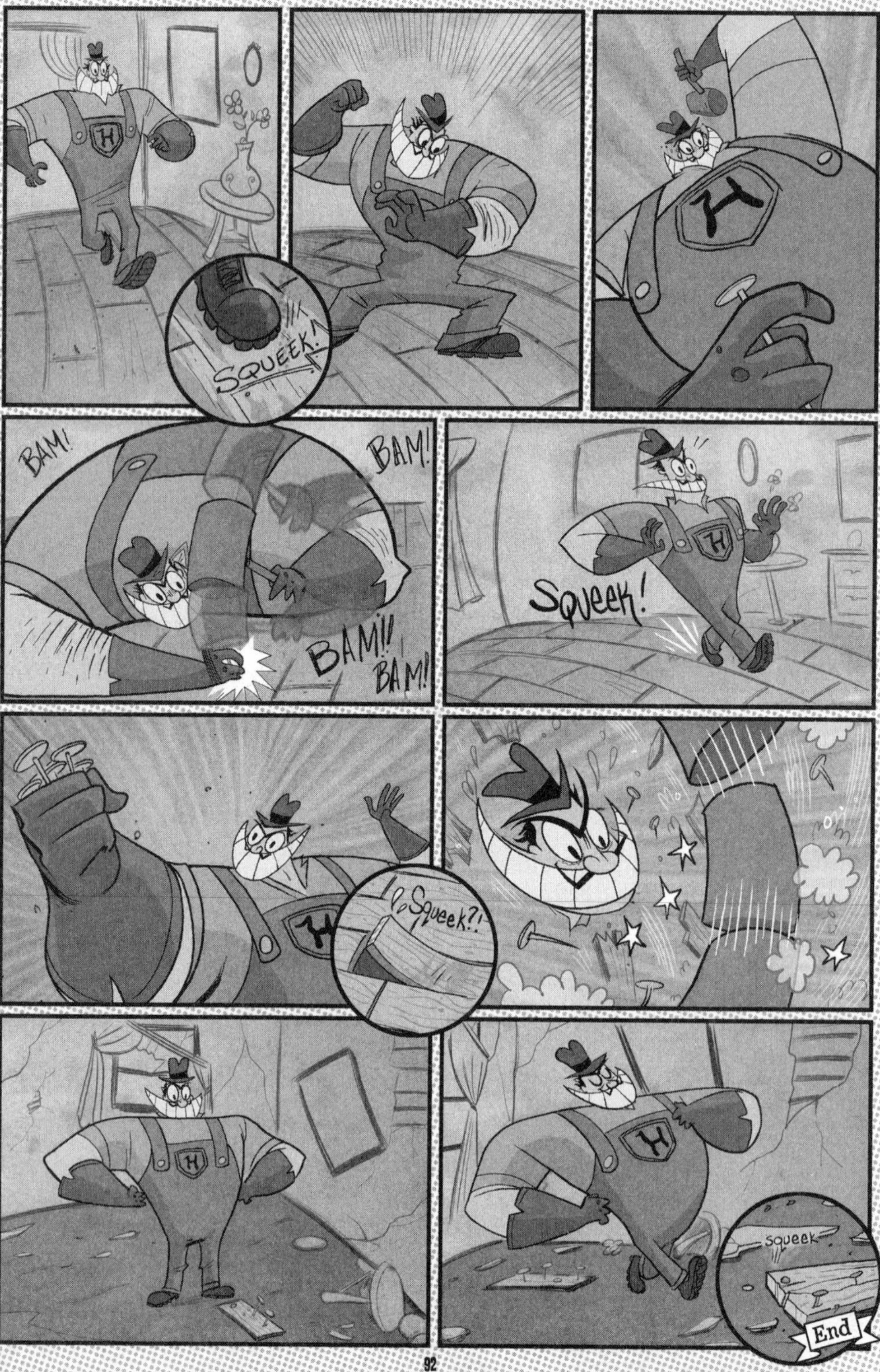
SQUEEK!
BAM!
BAM!
BAM!!
BAM!
Squeek!
Squeek?!
squeek
End

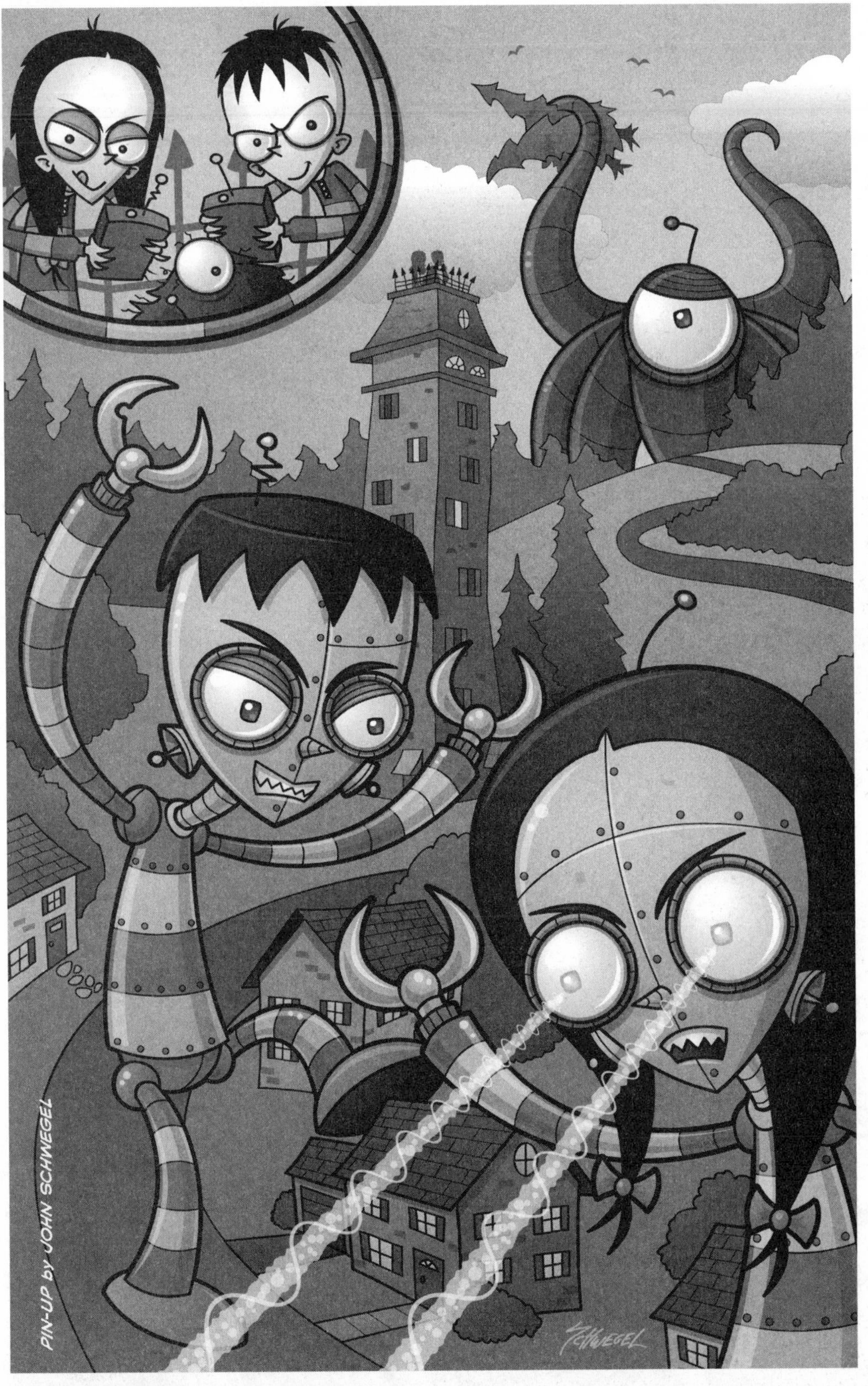
PIN-UP by JOHN SCHWEGEL
SCHWEGEL

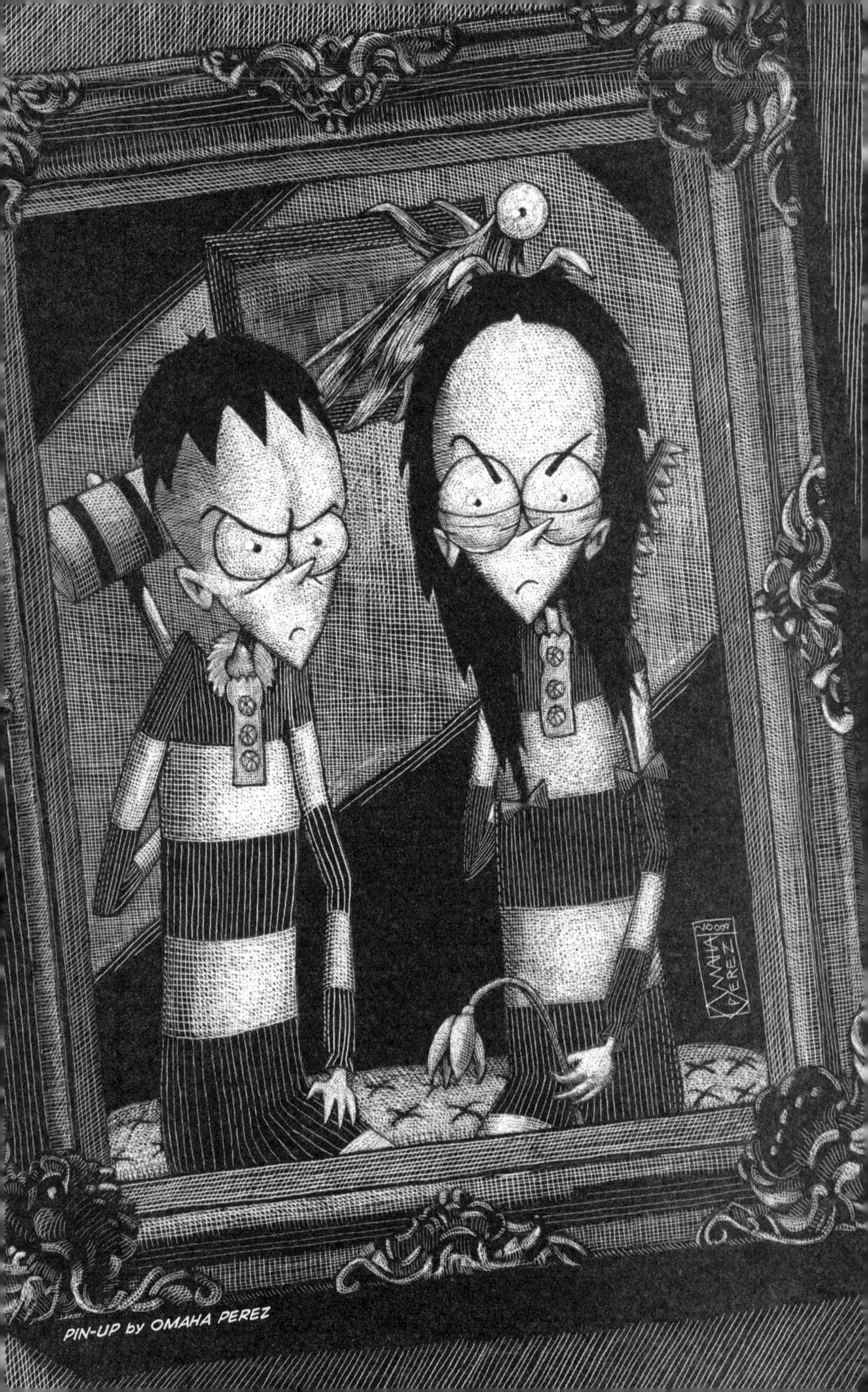

PIN-UP by OMAHA PEREZ

THE LOST CHAPTER

Charles Ogden had intended to open his book Pet's Revenge *with this vignette of the creature checking to see if it could watch TV in peace. Later, after heated conversations with his editors, astrologist, and illustrator, he gave the book a more active opening that showed Pet being chased, made miserable, and otherwise given good reason to seek revenge. Ogden remained partial to this passage, if only for the sound effect* **pock**.

MORE SLOWLY THAN THE MINUTE HAND OF a clock, a yellow eyeball inched through an opening in the wall. Only one eye— that was all the creature had to spy on the attic bedroom below.

Through the blackness, Pet could see the twins lying in their beds with their eyes closed, but this was by no means a guarantee that they were asleep. They wore matching striped footie pajamas— their chosen garb for daytime as well as night. On the floor between them sat a rusty bear trap with jaws wide open. Had Ellen laid it for Edgar, or Edgar for Ellen?

Edgar lay holding a croquet mallet. Ellen clutched a potted cactus; it sat in a slingshot aimed at Edgar's bed. An arsenal of mayhem lay within easy reach of the twins: a fireplace poker, an anchor, a stone urn, a coil of barbed wire, a sack- ful of doorknobs, the handle of a butter churn, and several spiky hood ornaments ripped from a fleet of limousines.

Pet observed this scene for five min- utes. Ten. Twenty. The twins made no movement or sound that would betray their intentions. Finally, Pet leaned far- ther out of its hiding place in the wall. Underneath its eye there flowed only an unkempt tuft of hair, and from inside that tangle appeared a tiny marble which Pet nudged out onto the floor. The marble hit with a *pock*.

Ellen's hands twitched, launching the cactus. The lob lacked real power, though, and it landed between the beds on the bear trap. The jaws clapped shut—CLACK!—and the pot shattered. Edgar's arm jerked, swinging the mal- let at his sister. It knocked the slingshot from her fingers and hit the wall over her pillow. Both twins smacked their lips and rolled over, breathing deeply.

Pet withdrew into the dumbwaiter where it hid and nudged a switch. A panel in the wall dropped, sealing the creature inside. The dumbwaiter shaft ran from the subbasement to the attic, but the dumbwaiter itself was too tiny for anyone but Pet, who used it as a taxi. Now the small elevator sank, sliding past the cluttered ninth-floor ballroom where Edgar's ill-fated motor-oil attack on Ellen had soaked into the floorboards. It descended past the eighth-floor library, where the twins had made a fort out of antique books. On the seventh floor, Pet pressed another switch. The dumbwaiter stopped and the panel slid open.

Pet crawled out past Edgar's pipe organ. It shambled through a thick layer of sawdust on the music room floor and into the den, where it slinked deftly around nooses, mousetraps, hidden cages, and spring-loaded buckets of burrs. Pet flipped on the television and bounced onto the tattered sofa.

At last it was safe to watch TV.

HEIMERTZ vs. ~~the DRAGON!~~ the MIME

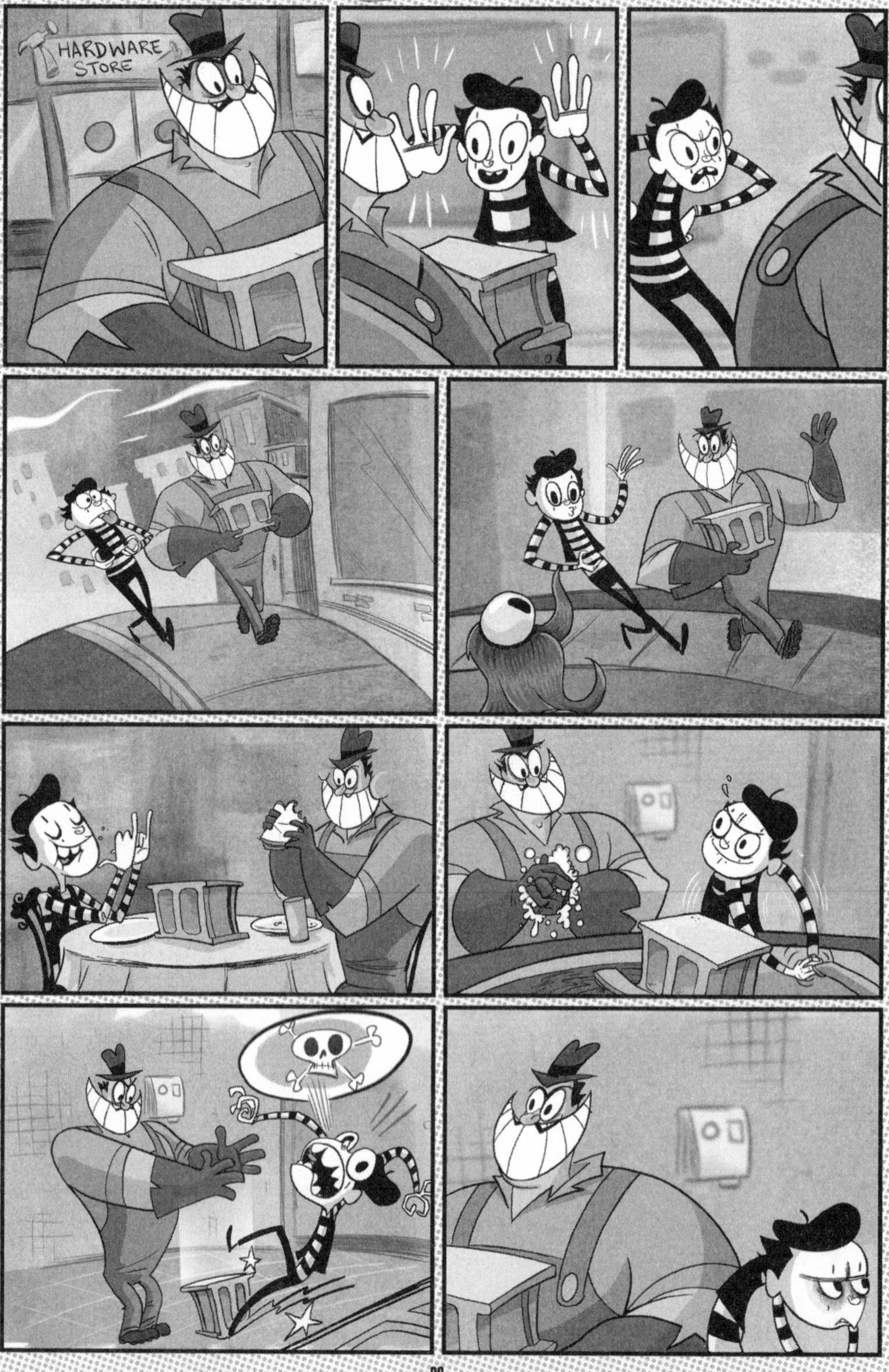
HARDWARE STORE

FAN ART GALLERY

Edgar & Ellen fans are fearlessly creative! Check out these great pieces of real, live, honest-to-goodness fan art. To see more great fan-created masterpieces—or to upload your own—visit edgarandellen.com.

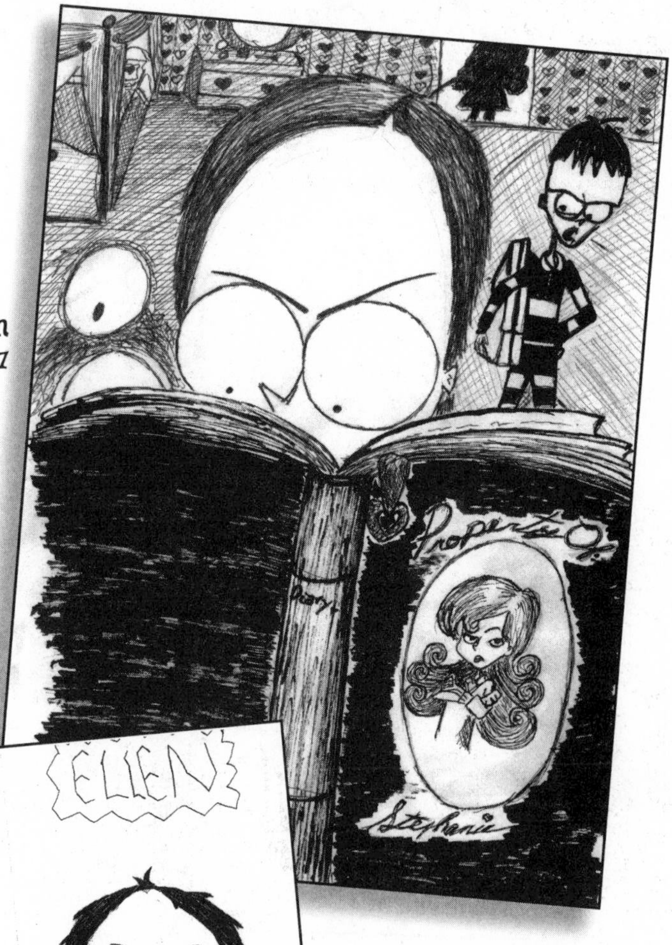
Property Of:
Stephanie

Abigail Green
Age 17

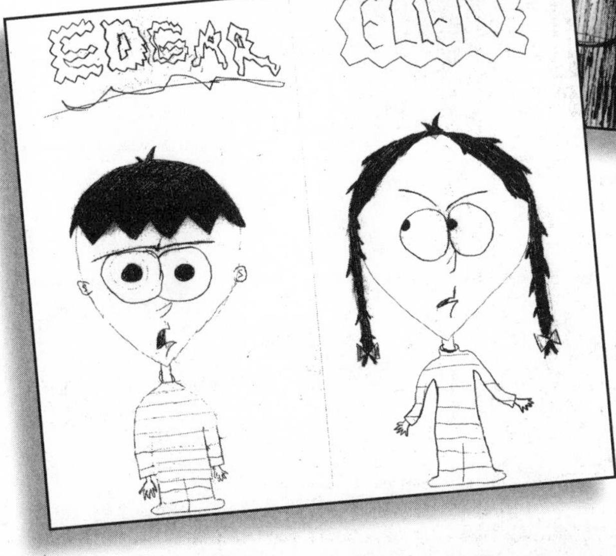
EDGAR
ELLEN

Abby Ramirez
Age 12

FAN ART GALLERY

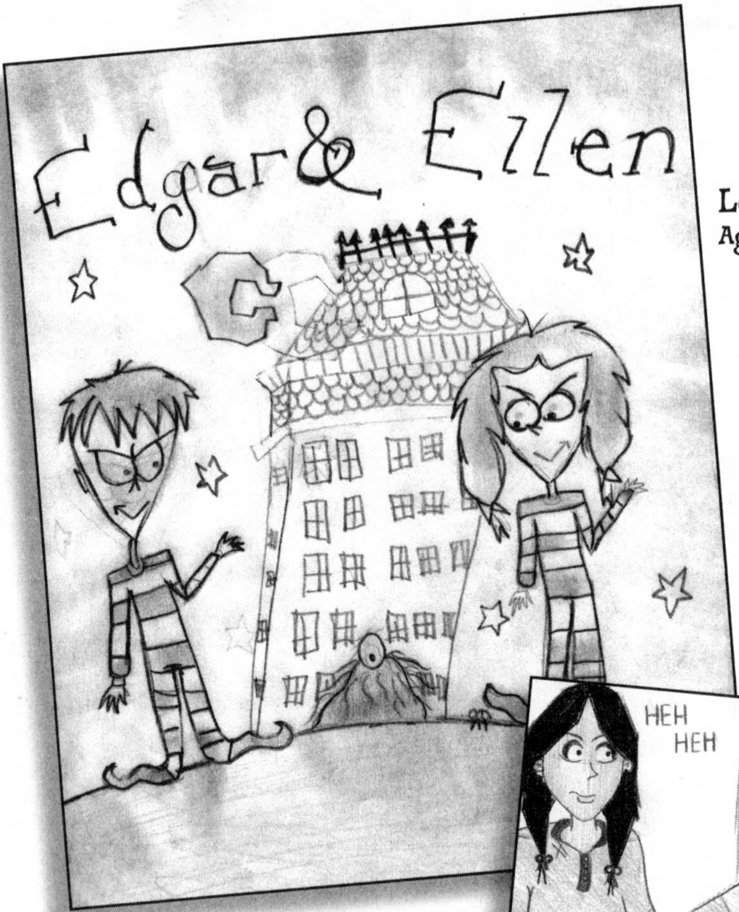
Edgar& Ellen

Leeann Leone
Age 13

Jameel Carpenter
Age 11

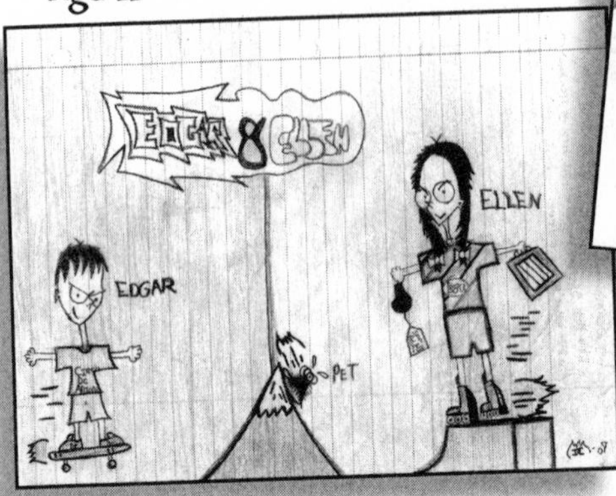
EDGAR 8 ELLEN
ELLEN
EDGAR
PET

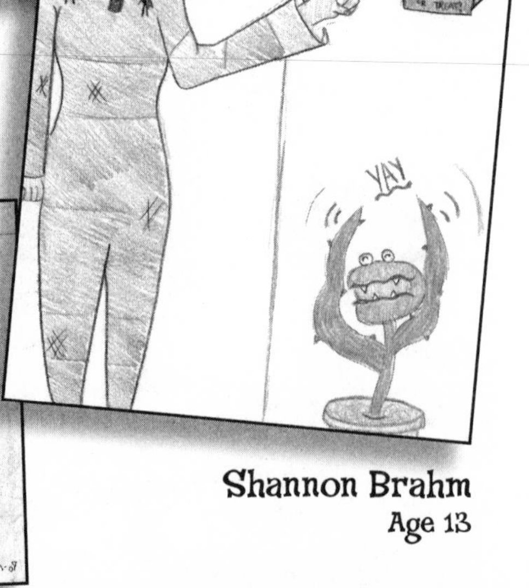
HEH
HEH
BIG
TRICK
YAY

Shannon Brahm
Age 13

FAN ART GALLERY

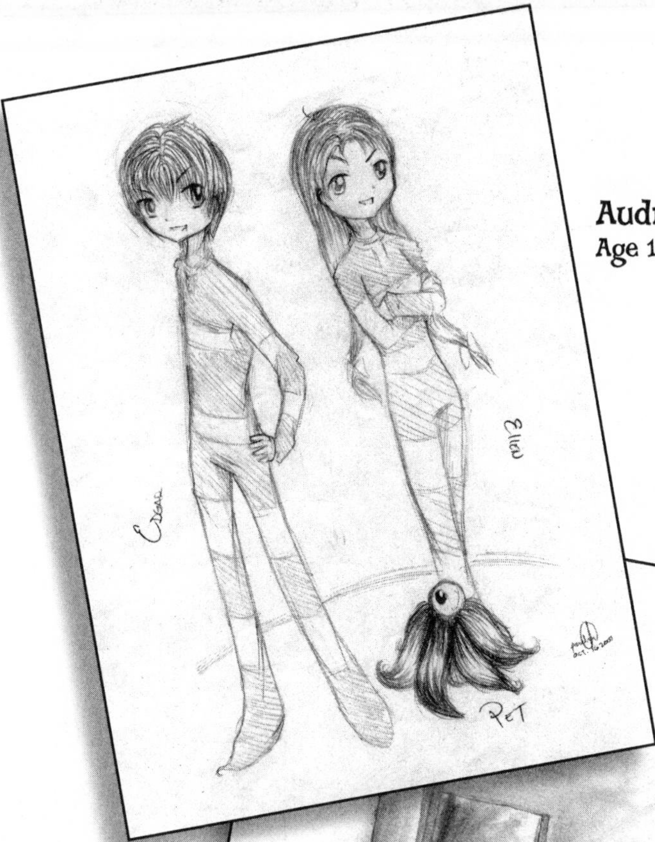
PeT

Audrey Sansona
Age 13

Tyler Schaeffer
Age 16

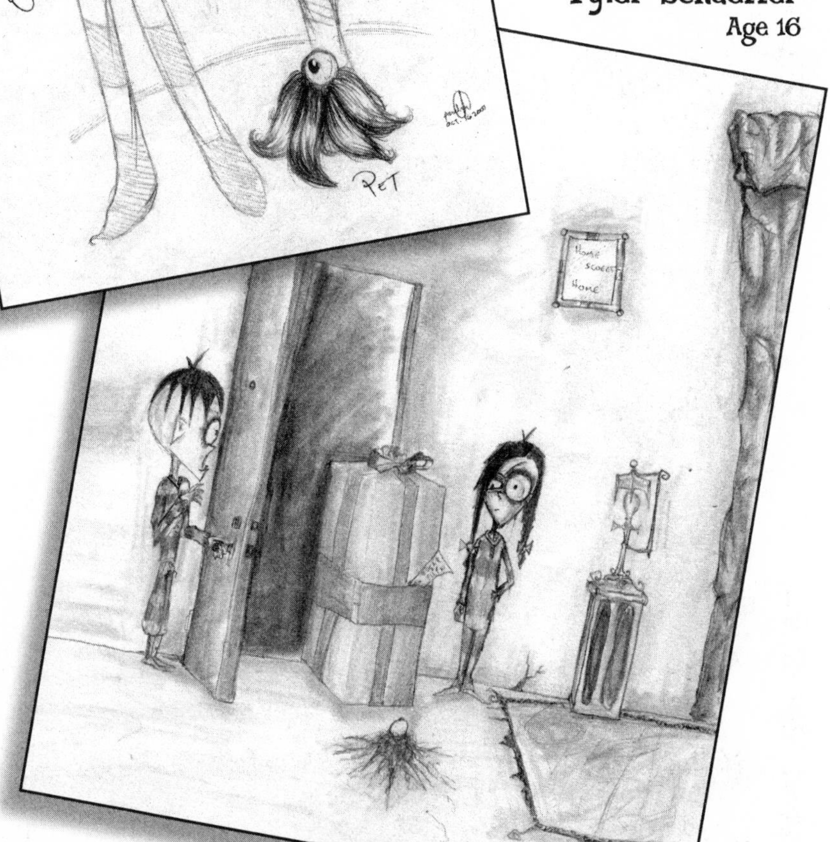

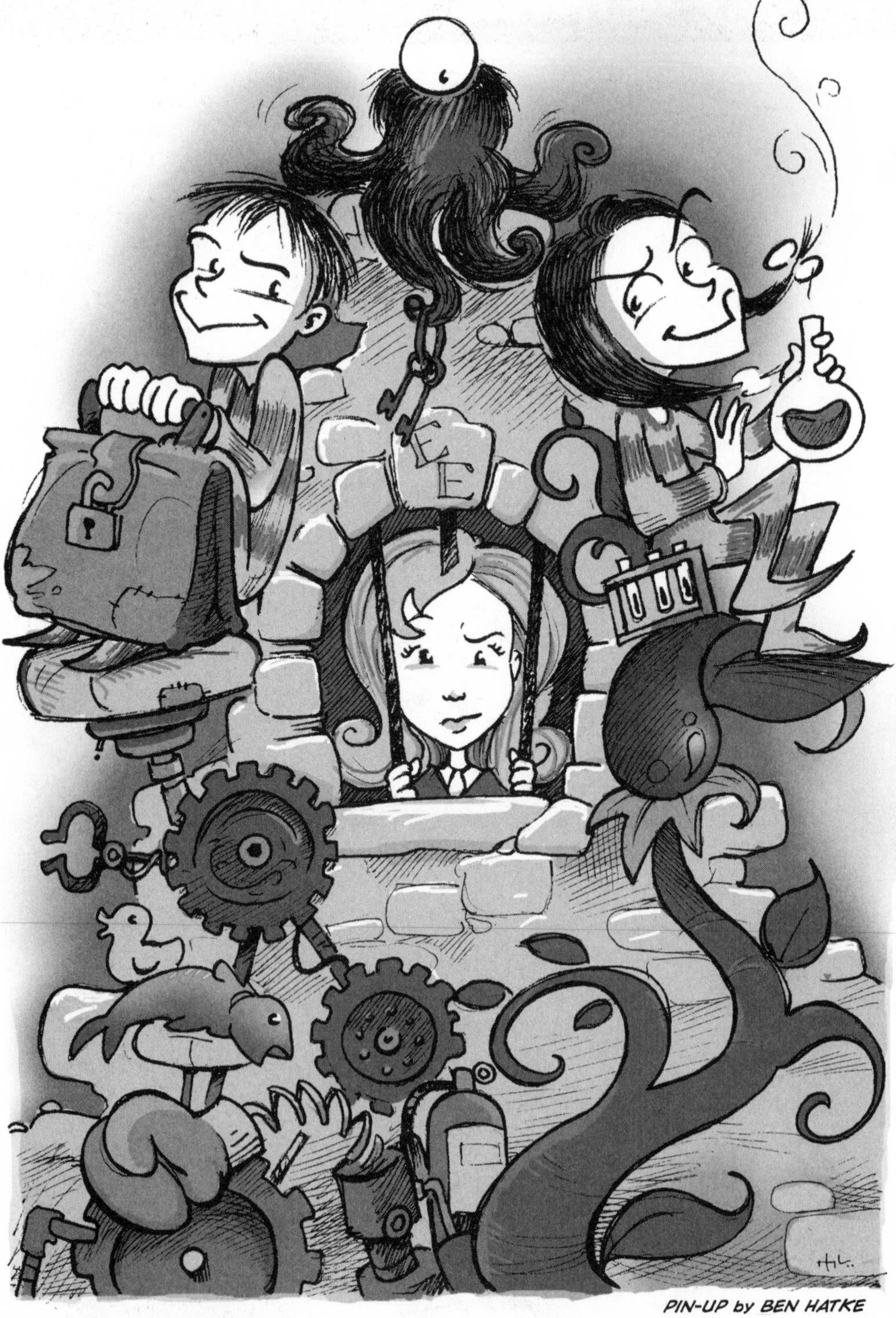

PIN-UP by BEN HATKE

ARTISTIC DEVELOPMENT

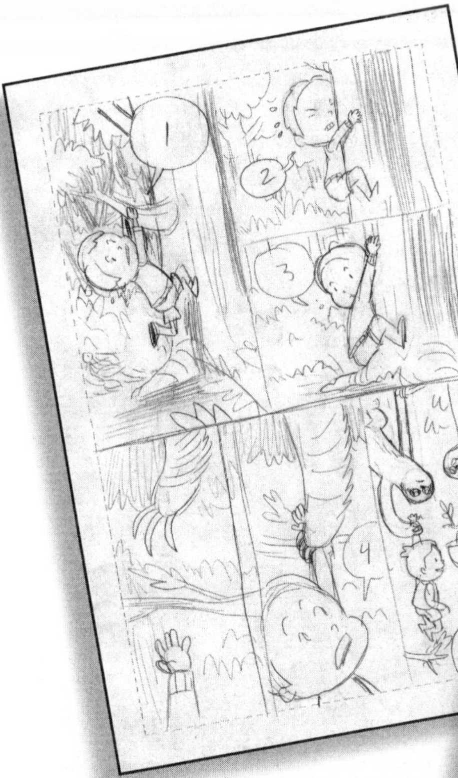
1
2
3
4

All of the pages in this volume start with a *thumbnail sketch*. Here we see Jacob Chabot's thumbnail for page 3 of "Miles Beyond." It gives everyone involved an idea as to what the artist is thinking. Layout, composition, and word balloon placement is settled at this stage. Notice the numbers inside the word ballons... they correspoind to the lines of dialog in the writer's script.

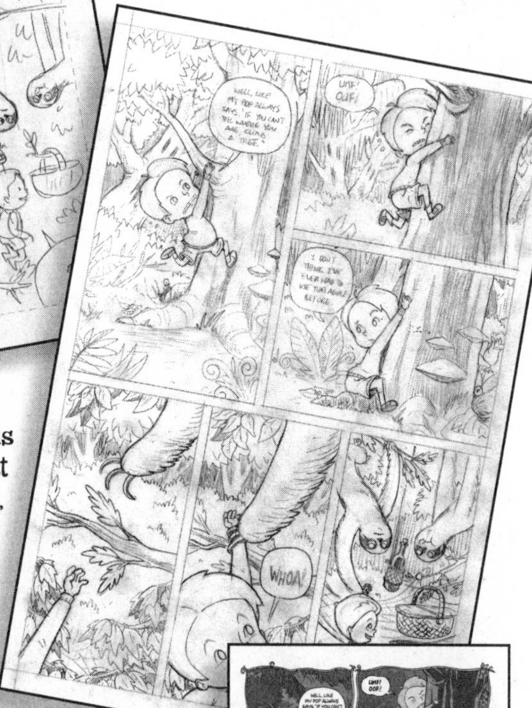
WHOA!

The next step is *final pencils*, where the artist tightens up his or her thumbnail, starts to indicate shadows, and generally adds a lot more detail. Here, Jacob has roughed in his hand-lettered dialog balloons.

The last step is *inking* (which makes things nice and black) and *shading* (which adds mood and depth). Voilà! Check out the full-size image on page 33!

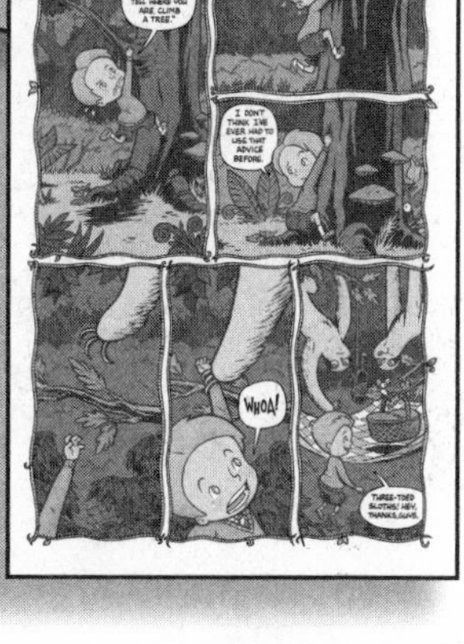
WELL, LIKE MY POP ALWAYS SAYS, "IF YOU CAN'T TELL WHERE YOU ARE, CLIMB A TREE."
UMF! OOF!
I DON'T THINK I'VE EVER HAD TO USE THAT ADVICE BEFORE.
WHOA!
THREE-TOED SLOTHS! HEY, THANKS, GUYS.

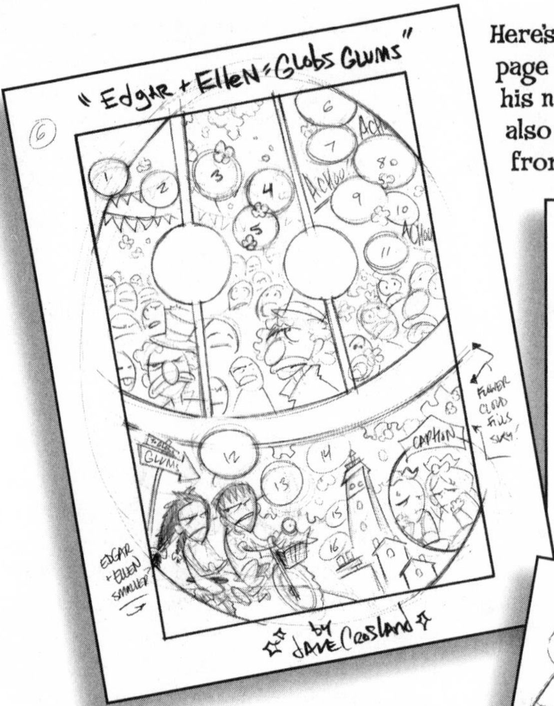
"Edgar + Ellen = Globs Glums"
6
ACHOO
FLOWER CLOUD FILLS SKY!
CAPTION
GLUMS
EDGAR + ELLEN SMALLER
by Dave Crosland

Here's Dave Crosland's thumbnail for page 6 of "Glob's Glums." Take note of his notes in the page margins! Dave also uses numbers to indicate dialog from the script.

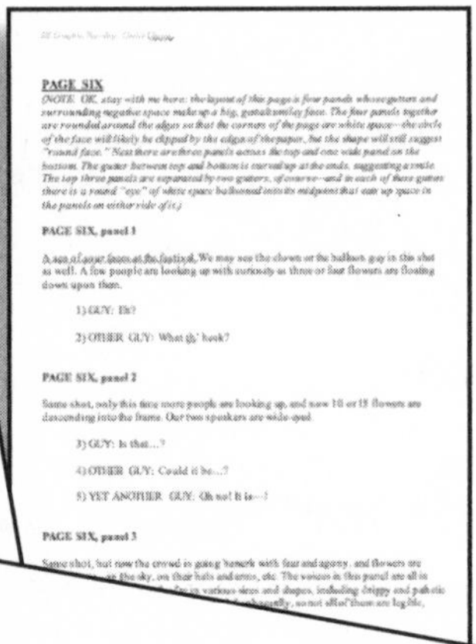

PAGE SIX

(NOTE: OK, stay with me here: the layout of this page is four panels whose gutters and surrounding negative space make up a big, goofy smiley face. The four panels together are rounded around the edges so that the corners of the page are white space—the circle of the face will likely be clipped by the edges of the paper, but the shape will still suggest "round face." Next there are three panels across the top and one wide panel on the bottom. The gutter between top and bottom is curved up at the ends, suggesting a smile. The top three panels are separated by two gutters, of course—and in each of these gutters there is a round "eye" of white space ballooned into its midpoint that eats up space in the panels on either side of it.)

PAGE SIX, panel 1

A sea of anxr faces at the festival. We may see the clown or the balloon guy in this shot as well. A few people are looking up with curiosity as three or four flowers are floating down upon them.

1) GUY: Eh?

2) OTHER GUY: What th' heck?

PAGE SIX, panel 2

Same shot, only this time more people are looking up, and now 10 or 15 flowers are descending into the frame. Our two speakers are wide-eyed.

3) GUY: Is that...?

4) OTHER GUY: Could it be...?

5) YET ANOTHER GUY: Oh no! It is—!

PAGE SIX, panel 3

Same shot, but now the crowd is going berserk with fear and agony, and flowers are ... in the sky, on their hats and arms, etc. The voices in this panel are all in ... in various sizes and shapes, including drippy and pathetic ... so not all of them are legible,

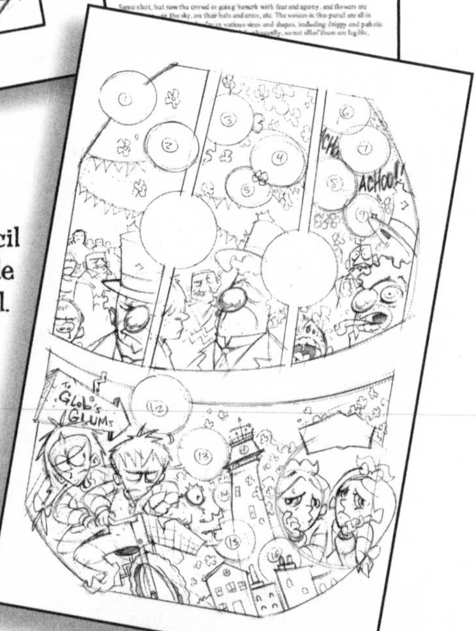
ACHOO!
To Glob's GLUMS

Next up is his final pencil drawing, which is just a little tighter than his thumbnail.

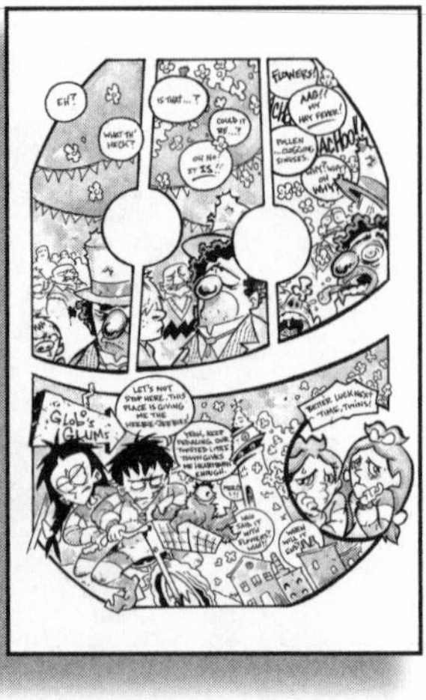
EH?
WHAT TH' HECK?
IS THAT...?
COULD IT BE...?
OH NO! IT IS...!
FLOWERS!
AAG! MY HAY FEVER!
ACHOO!
Glob's GLUMS

Check out the full-size image on page 56!

CREATOR BIOS

Kathryn Achenbach ("Robin Pet") rose to fame as *La Pluma Rojo,* the fiercest luchador to come out of Charlottesville, Virginia, since *El Pollo Loco* in 1906. Now based in Chicago, where she is known as "Platinum Hits" on the roller derby circuit, she spends as much time crafting poems, young adult books, cartoon scripts, and comics as she does jamming through packs of bloodthirsty roller-skating mercenaries using nothing but her wits, reflexes, and pointy, pointy elbows.

Peter Bergting ("Pirates of the Water Park") was born in Sweden but is happy anyway. He's reached the age of thirty-eight and is a bit confused that twenty years of working as an illustrator has managed to make him a comic book artist and not the rock star he thought he'd be when he bought his first electric guitar. His most recent claim to fame is his comic book *The Portent,* which is currently being developed into a motion picture (fingers crossed). Not that any success in Hollywood will bring him closer to being a rock star, but one must keep up hope, right?

If you've spent more than a few minutes in person with him, you'll know that he's a Mac fanatic and a devout skeptic. His hero is Carl Sagan. Peter plans on tattooing his face on the back of his head—that's the side of him his family mostly sees, since he's always working.

Rick Carton (Cover, "An Introduction") has been drawing longer than he's been walking. In his Chicago studio he has a cherished collection of every pencil ever worn down to a nub during his lengthy artistic career. He has never formally studied art; instead, the art community has diligently studied him. They have yet to release their findings.

Jacob Chabot ("Miles Beyond") grew up in the wild, wintery isolation of northern Maine, where they never showed the good cartoons on TV. Now, he lives in New York and gets the good cartoons, but can't see the stars at night. You can't have it all, I guess. Jacob draws the Eisner-nominated *Mighty Skullboy Army* when he gets around to it, as well as various comics for *Nickelodeon* and *Mad* magazines. Other comics and drawings and stuff can be found at beetlebugcomics. com.

Troy Cummings ("Slake," "Baby Way2-Real," "Card Battlers") was not born on March 24, 1874 in Budapest, Hungary. He also did not immigrate to the United States in 1878 aboard the SS *Fresia* with his mother and four brothers. Nor did he become a trapeze artist at the age of ten, dubbing himself "Ehrich, the Prince of the Air." He most certainly did not move on to perform card tricks at various circus sideshows, allowing him eventually to develop incredible escape acts that paved the way for him to become the most famous and wealthy illusionist in Vaudeville history. You're probably thinking of Harry Houdini.

Dave Crosland ("Glob's Glums") enjoys peanut butter, road trips, and samurai flicks. He dislikes yogurt and mosquitoes. Since graduating from the Columbus College of Art and Design in 2000, this delicious youngster's art has appeared in comic books such as *Everybody's DEAD, The Popgun Anthology,* and *Scarface: Scarred for Life.* He's also done a variety of work outside of comics, creating album covers for Gym Class Heroes and hip-hop guru Blueprint, a stage backdrop for Incubus, concert posters, tattoo flash, and designs for indie apparel. For more of his visual vitality, clickety-clack to hiredmeat.com.

CREATOR BIOS

Jose Garibaldi ("Heimertz vs.") has vanished, whereabouts currently unknown. If anyone has any knowledge of his location, please contact our shadow operatives in the usual fashion.

If **Doug Holgate** ("Robin Pet") wasn't spending all his time as an astronaut, Formula One driver, millionaire philanthropist, renowned adventurer and famous masked Mexican wrestler, El Tigre, Doug would most likely fill the hours as a freelance illustrator, comic artist, and toy designer based in Melbourne, Australia.

When he finds a moment to spare between searching for the lost city of El Dorado and fighting pirate hoardes, he likes to think he would spend it with his craft-obsessed girlfriend and two moth-eating cats.

Jade ("The Edgar & Ellen Revenge Squad") was born and raised in China under the name Weng Chen. From a very young age she was interested in drawing and manga, and at age fourteen had her first manga published. For the next ten years she would be published often in Chinese manga magazines, culminating with the release of three books of her own in 2002.

In 2006 she moved to the U.S., and now works as a freelance illustrator. Her work varies from original IP creation for video games to illustration for children's books and advertising materials.

Edgar and Ellen is her first opportunity to do manga for the U.S. market. In the future she hopes to publish her own original manga. For fun she has created "The Adventures of Messycow," a short manga about playing World of Warcraft, viewable at messycow.com. More of her personal work can be seen at wengchen.com.

Matthew Jent ("Pirates of the Water Park," "The Edgar & Ellen Revenge Squad") is bringing the mustache back. Last seen in San Francisco, California, he hears you are doing well and hopes to talk to you soon.

Charles Ogden ("An Introduction," "The Lost Chapter") is an avid camper and fisherman. He collects insects and has traveled in pursuit of various specimens to the North Pole, the South Pole, and Poland. Mr. Ogden and his insect collection make their home in a cool, dry, preservation-friendly environment, far removed from prying eyes.

Drew Scott ("Glob's Glums," "Card Battlers") is a writer, editor, and man-about-town in Evanston, Illinois. He has three children—Jack, Liam, and Katy—who wish he would stop frittering away his time on comics, and get a real job, like lion tamer.

Patrick van Slee ("Miles Beyond") is an amateur moondigger, and has to date built a modest collection of fossilized moonbees and exotic dirts, which he occasionally lends to local museums. When he isn't dreaming up bizarre creatures or looking for holes in this dimension, he likes to play ping-pong with aardvarks and horses, and sometimes he even wins. He lives in Chicago with his wife, Anna, and their two very fat cats, Francis P. McMuffin and Mr. Chillynose.

Read where the mischief begins . . .

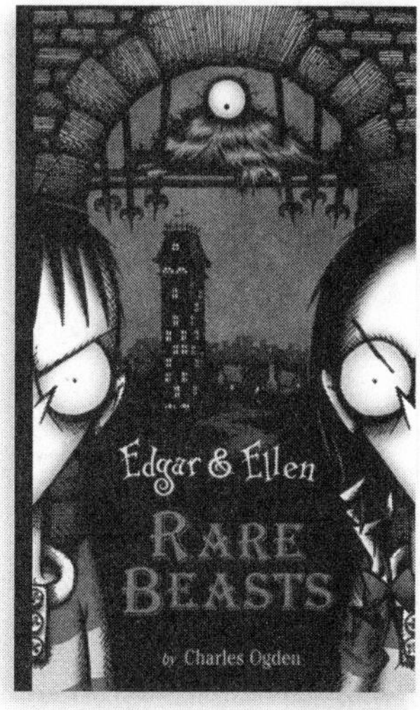
Edgar & Ellen
RARE BEASTS
by Charles Ogden

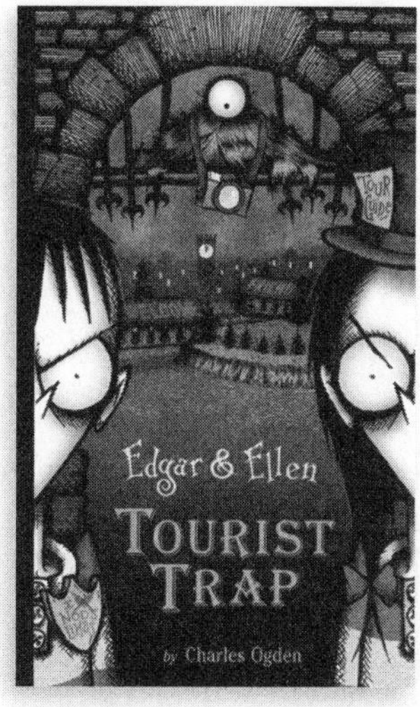
Edgar & Ellen
TOURIST TRAP
by Charles Ogden

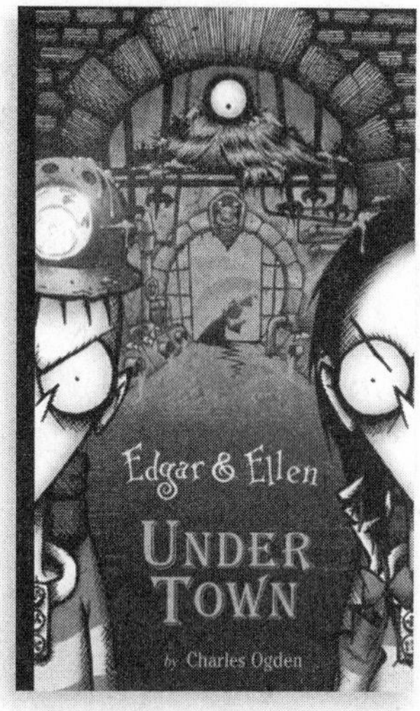
Edgar & Ellen
UNDER TOWN
by Charles Ogden

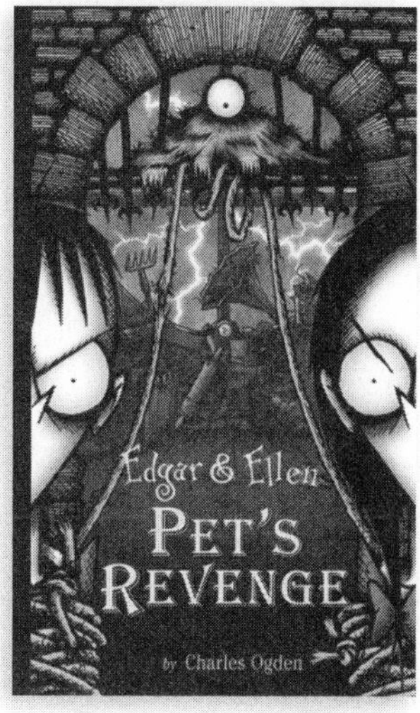
Edgar & Ellen
PET'S REVENGE
by Charles Ogden

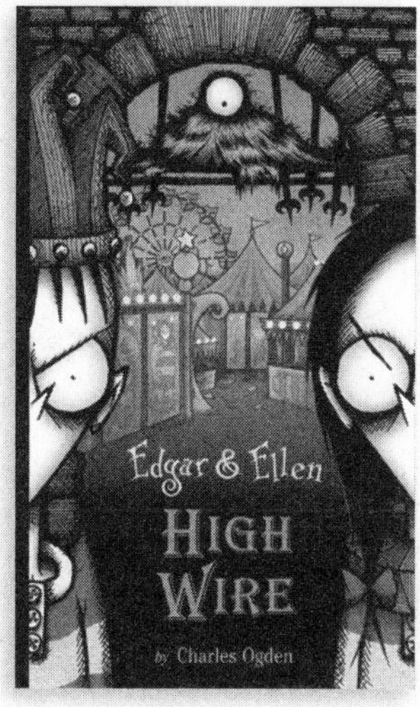
Edgar & Ellen
HIGH WIRE
by Charles Ogden

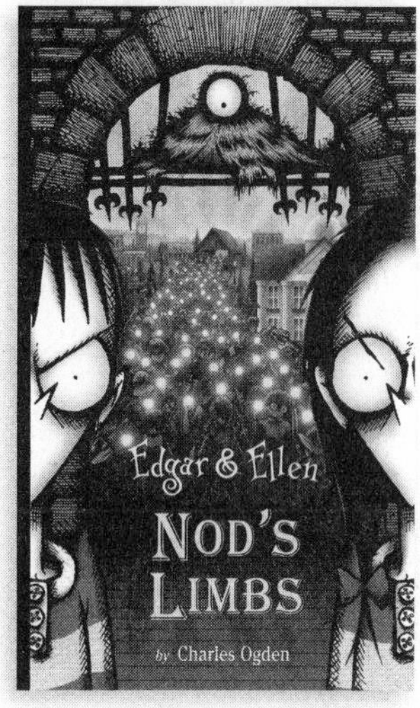
Edgar & Ellen
NOD'S LIMBS
by Charles Ogden

Available Now at Your Favorite Bookseller

EDGARANDELLEN.COM

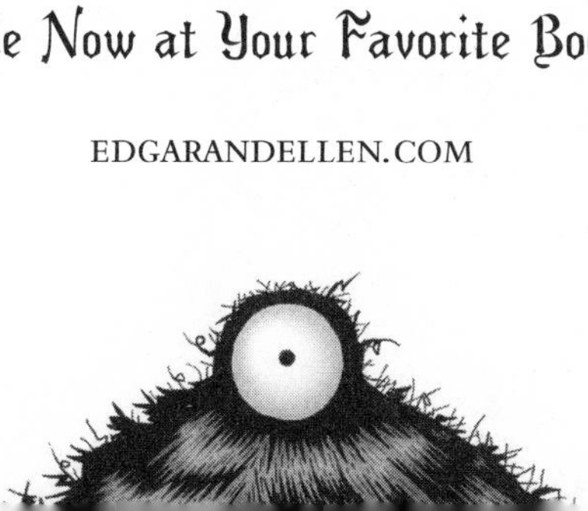

The mischief continues. . . .

Edgar & Ellen
NODYSSEY #1
HOT
AIR
— *by* Charles Ogden —

Edgar & Ellen
NODYSSEY #2
FROST
BITES
— *by* Charles Ogden —

Edgar & Ellen
NODYSSEY #3
SPLIT
ENDS
— *by* Charles Ogden —

Available Now at Your Favorite Bookseller

EDGARANDELLEN.COM